CW01394890

EARTHCHILD

DANIELLE LAUREN

OACHOA

ALSO BY DANIELLE LAUREN

Spiritchild

EARTHCHILD

DANIELLE LAUREN

OACHOA

First published in Great Britain in 2022 by Oachoa Publishing

Copyright © Danielle Lauren, 2022

Danielle Lauren asserts the moral right to be identified as the author of this work in accordance with the Copyright, Designs and Patents Act 1988.

A CIP catalogue record for this book is available from the British Library.

Jacket, map, and internal illustrations by Lena Yang.

Hardback ISBN: 978-1-7397410-2-0

eBook ISBN: 978-1-7397410-3-7

Printed and bound in Great Britain by Clays Ltd, Elcograf S.p.A.

For those who have known the darkness inside.
There is light in you too.
Let your light shine.

PREFACE

YNESHIA

DRAGONTAIL PENINSULA

ASHFALL BAY

THE GREAT FALL

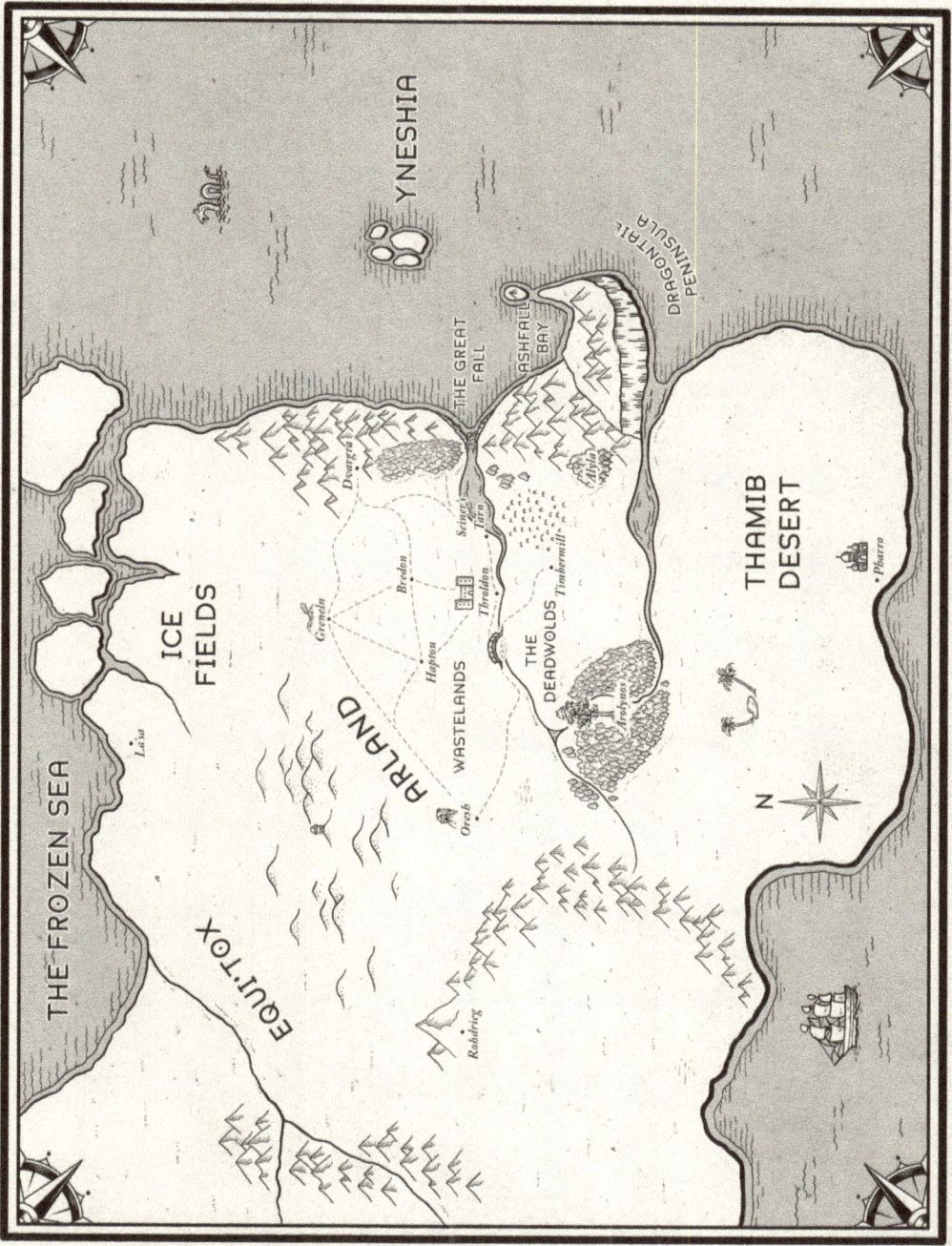

THE FROZEN SEA

ICE FIELDS

EQUITOX

ARLAND

Laisa

Dangrad

Sriner

Jorn

Bredon

Gervein

Thraldon

Hapton

WASTELANDS

Orch

THE DEADWOLDS

Timbermill

Atvia

Arabynos

THAMIB DESERT

Pharre

Robulrory

N

PART I

1

A KIND OF COMFORT

The stars winked out one by one as a new day chased them from the sky, and Fae wished — not for the first time — that she could join them.

The sun peeked over the rugged horizon of the Edge Mountains, far away to the east. Dawn's light reached down to dance upon the surface of the Amedi river as it flowed past, glittering and oblivious to its beauty. Frosted dewdrops sparkled in the grasses along the banks. Atop the new University walls, the view over it all was spectacular. But Fae wasn't here to take in the view. No, Fae's mind was far, far away.

The crisp, spring mornings that so many were relieved to see after gruelling winter months transported her somewhere else entirely — the same place her nightmares kept taking her.

It had been a year. To the day. And while she had tried so hard to get back to normal, to bury herself in rebuilding a world united after Anson, she couldn't seem to shake the echoes of that nightmare. The one that always seemed to have its claws in her chest these days.

The one that was real. That had happened.

The one where she died.

The ground shuddered beneath her feet. That seemed to happen a lot these days. As if it too understood what haunted her.

Fae took a deep, cleansing breath, and watched the frigid air fog as she exhaled long and slow. Spring it may be, but warm weather was still a way off for Throldon.

She sighed, tucking a strand of ash-blonde hair behind her ear, and huffed a low laugh. She'd once kept her hair draped *over* her ears, to hide the absence of their tapered, upswept arches — the trait that marked her as different among her elven brethren. But now that she knew her true heritage, knew that she was and always had been human... Well, it had taken some getting used to in the beginning.

She missed Arolynos. The elven tree-city had been her home for fifteen years. It was warm, and lovely, and it nestled within the Great Tree in Il'arys with such grace. It was where she had learned to dance, where she had learned to heal.

Where the Aethyr had put her, to keep her safe.

Fae turned to face the city that she called home as often as not these days.

Below, Throldon slowly stretched awake, small flurries of activity marking a few early risers.

The human capital was still in the midst of rebuilding. Stone houses patched with timber boards stood between others covered in scaffold skeletons. Some places had had to be vacated entirely while they were repaired. Some were still yet to be touched, and sat crumbling and brooding among the progress, waiting their turns.

Putting a city back together again after decades of anarchy and ruination took time, it turned out.

Building the University had been one of the first projects to break ground, a symbol of the races coming together to benefit Arland as a whole. Builders and craftspeople had come from as far away as Dvargra, the mountain stronghold of the highly innovative dwarves, and her own precious Arolynos, the forest haven of the elves. Even Kagos stopped by from time to time, although the dragons of Hearthstone didn't exactly *help*. Merely presented themselves. Which was still more than they'd ever done before.

The high stone walls of the University sprawled a short way from the northern bank of the Amedi River, shielding a hum of activity behind them. A breathtaking amalgam of crafts, trades, and skills were being lavished on the complex. And yet despite all of that, it remained a work in progress, likely would for years yet, the rebuilding of the city in general happening at whatever pace the workers could manage.

Fae ran a hand through her hair, mussing it all over again. It was getting ridiculously long, growing past her waist now. She clicked her tongue and wove it into a quick braid to stop the ends from flying across her face in the morning breeze. Tossing the braid over one shoulder, she massaged her closed eyelids, as if she could rub away the weight of fatigue that made her want to curl up in the nearest corner and sleep for a week.

But, as an old friend had once said to her, *Even the moons cannot stop the sun crossing the sky.*

Fae sighed, a flavour of sadness tainting it this time. Turning from the view, she climbed down the stone stairs that led from the University walls, and strode out into the city.

The River Quarter had been the worst affected by the years of the Unity and the Survivors' rule; both groups had been hell-bent on destroying any social structure in the capital. North of the University walls, Throldon's slums extended from what used to be the city limits, on into the city centre. Fae stepped carefully around boggy gaps in roads not yet filled in, ducking under the scaffolds that had made it this far into the impoverished district.

It was still a high sight better than it had been when Fae first stepped foot in the human city.

Her city.

She eyed a group of children playing outside one house that had seen better days, yet was still far from the worst of them. Two boys chased each other around the small yard while the girls sat on the doorstep, wrapped up against the morning chill with shawls and blankets as they gossiped. Fae smiled. A year ago, those children would have stared hollow-eyed at her as if she was the ghost, not them. Now, she could see the merry crackle of a fire through the windows, the frames lovingly repainted a bright green. The tempting smells of breakfast wafted out to greet her, followed by an aproned woman with a lovely face, her hair tied back in a pale ribbon. The woman chided the boys sternly for getting their clothes dirty before the day had even begun, but her eyes twinkled as she sent them to wash up for breakfast.

Then her eyes lifted, and met Fae's across the yard.

"My Lady." She sketched a half-curtsy, like she didn't quite know what was appropriate. Behind her, small faces lined the windows, peered around the doorframe, craning to see what had diverted their mother long enough to miss them snatching a slice of fresh bread from the table before they'd washed the dirt from their hands.

Fae felt the heat rise in her cheeks. This is why she avoided venturing out in the city.

From the open doorway, she heard a small voice gasp. "Bitchbreaker!"

Fae's lips twitched. It was one of the more imaginative names she'd heard people make up for her. She smothered a chuckle as the woman in the door whirled to deliver a hissed rebuke to whoever had uttered the name, her own face flushing.

With a nod to the family, Fae tugged the hood of her cloak up over her head, and continued on her way.

Weaving through the labyrinthine lanes of the River Quarter, Fae made her way towards the Trade District on the western side of the city. After the city centre, this quarter had fared the best over the last few decades, providing essential services and trades to keep any regime running, whether it was organised or otherwise.

The Rebel Unity had certainly laid claim to the latter, the leaders — if that's what they could even be called — ruling by one simple law: every man for himself. Tired of always having to answer to the next person up in the food chain, they demolished the chain, and destroyed most of Arland in the process. The Survivors hadn't been any better. Lady Black had been organised, but had wrought even more misery than her predecessors on people like the family in the yard.

Fae passed Ironmonger Street, the heat of the forges drawing sweat from her pores even from here. Crossing Old Gallows Square, she smiled at the market stalls being erected around the edges, much preferring their cheerful canvases and bright wares to the emptiness of her first experience here. A quick glance at the rooftops along one edge of the square had her cringing. The chimney stacks still hadn't been rebuilt here, their crumbled ruins a conspicuous dent in the roofline. She really ought to find someone to fix that. Kagos sure as hell wouldn't.

Ducking down a lane just off the square, she trudged a familiar path to the stable courtyard at the far end, her footsteps getting heavier with every stride.

She wasn't surprised to find the person she was looking for standing in the courtyard, out under the open sky. Surrounded by unusually low buildings, the courtyard offered a rare unencumbered view upward, which today was turning a stunning cerulean blue.

A lump stuck in Fae's throat. Fanrell was so like his brother in many ways. His near-black hair hung down the length of his bare back, his eyes the same burning amber as Immrith's had been. But while Immrith had had a kind of wild joy hidden within his gruffness, Fanrell was all tightly coiled anger.

Sure enough, as he turned, his hooves scuffing across the cobbles, his eyes held fire within them.

The centaurs of Equi'tox were not an emotional race, not outwardly. But Fae had known Immrith well — or at least, a part of her had — and he had been different. He had felt joy, and fear, and compassion, and courage.

Watching his brother now, Fae wondered if Fanrell had ever seen the war within his brother, to be as stony as the rest of his race, when his heart had wished for more.

Fanrell turned his gaze back to the sky again, as Immrith had often done. The black, tribal tattoos down his bare ribs shifted with the motion, and his near-black tail, a match for his hair, swished impatiently. Even the muscles beneath the dark chestnut colouring of his lower body — the same as that of a horse — seemed tense.

"I leave tonight," he said by way of a greeting, glaring at the sky. Fae nodded. He probably would have left at dawn, begun his long pilgrimage home for the anniversary of his brother's funeral, had Kagos not called a Council meeting. Six months early.

"Can I do anything for you?" she breathed, trying in vain not to see the flames of Immrith's funeral pyre like she did in the worst of her dreams, as if her mind wouldn't let her forget his sacrifice.

Fanrell shook his head, his hair brushing over the curve of his spine where it segued from human torso to horse's back.

"You honour him with your memories," he said, and Fae wondered if his ever-present scowl softened just a fraction. "That is what my people will do when I return. That is what you do every day." He turned to fix her with his burning amber gaze. "Do not think I don't see it." He looked her up and down, and frowned again. "You should eat more."

Fae breathed out a surprised laugh. The centaur's lips twitched. Practically a roaring laugh from him. He was right though. She'd seen herself in the mirror this morning. She looked half-starved, her eyes hollowed-out shadows, her cheekbones cutting across her face in brutal lines. She'd always been on the small side. She'd once believed that putting on some weight might encourage her elf ears to come in. Until she learned she would never grow elf ears.

But she was a ghost of herself these days.

"I am finding this time of year... difficult," she admitted. And her nightmares had been worsening, as if they knew it too.

Fanrell nodded his understanding, and turned back to his skyward vigil.

"I wonder what the dragon wants," he said. He'd heard enough stories about Immrith's final hours to know that his brother had died fighting at Kagos's side, and had granted the dragon a grudging respect from that alone.

Fae cast her eyes skyward along with him. She found a kind of comfort in the sky and its occupants these days: the sun, the twin moons, the stars. No matter how dark her thoughts, there was always light above. "I guess we'll find out later." The meeting wasn't until the afternoon. "How long will you be? In Equi'tox?" She'd come to enjoy the centaur's company on the occasions that they crossed paths in the city. He was a being of few measured words, and she found him much easier to deal with than some humans, who seemed to believe flowery words and lengthy discussions were necessary to agree on often simple matters. These days she had little energy for it. She would miss him.

Fanrell let out a breath. "The *Ateth Memori'i* will be three days," he said. "But I will stay for some weeks this time, I think." He didn't need to remind her how long he had been in the city since his last visit home. He had offered more than enough. Especially since the last time a centaur had come to Throldon, he'd lost his life. And Fanrell had lost a brother.

"Ipgar and Remi will stay," he added, referring to the two juvenile centaurs that had accompanied him to Throldon, both eager to see the wider world. Many of the younger ones were. It was their elders that kept the rest away.

"They won't miss you?" Fae knew the centaurs didn't "miss" each other in the way that the other races did, but Fanrell caught her meaning.

"They have been instructed how to conduct themselves." Another twitch of his lips. Fae didn't doubt it. The two younger members of his race idolised him. She'd be very surprised if they put a single hoof out of line while he was away.

"I am sure they will do you proud," she said, stomping her feet on the cobbles to chase the cold from her toes.

Fanrell turned to watch her again. "Go. Eat. Sleep." He raised a pointed brow when she opened her mouth to protest, the words dying on her lips at the look in his eyes. "I will see you at Council before I leave."

She met his gaze, trying to read any emotion behind his stony expression, but whatever he felt about his upcoming journey home, he kept it buried deep inside. Maybe he himself didn't even know how he felt about it.

Fae nodded, drawing her cloak tight around herself. "I will see you later then." She turned to leave, and paused. "Fanrell."

"Hmm."

"If it is appropriate, please carry my heartfelt condolences to your family."

"We do not offer 'heartfelt condolences' in Equi'tox."

"I know." She hesitated. "Then, just know that mine are with you."

Fanrell stared at her a moment, and nodded. He turned back to his vigil of the sky; conversation over.

As Fae stepped back into the square, she almost collided with someone extremely tall and broad-chested coming the other way.

"Oh! Sorry—" She went to tug her hood lower over her face. She wasn't in the mood for being recognised again this morning.

"Fae?"

She paused. She would recognise that voice anywhere, even if her heart didn't quite skip at the sound of it the way it used to. She'd changed too much since she'd first laced her fingers with his, exchanged gazes full of promise.

She looked up.

Ty smiled down at her. "I should have known you'd be here." He glanced at the lane behind her. "How is he?"

Fae shrugged and pulled a small smile onto her face. "As you'd expect. Taciturn and blunt." The centaur always was. She sighed and ran a hand over her weary face. "I think he's alright. It is the return home that troubles him more than his grief."

Ty nodded his understanding, golden hair sliding across his forehead. It needed cutting, something he often neglected in favour of his work rebuilding this city. "The centaurs certainly deal with death differently to the rest of us."

Fae hummed her agreement. They fell into silence. Not an awkward silence, for they had never been that, but not as comfortable as it had once been either. It was a silence that whistled through the space where once they had been close enough for his heart to whisper softly to hers.

A year ago, he had held her hand as they watched the funeral pyres stain the sky orange.

A year ago, they had made plans to rebuild this world together.

A year ago, she had thought she could wish for nothing more.

But she wasn't the sunny, light person that had left the canopy of Arolynos all that time ago. Something in her had fundamentally changed when she'd fought Anson, perhaps irreparably broken. She no longer recognised herself.

She'd hauled a cloak of apathy around the shadows within, thrown herself into the work of rebuilding to avoid examining them too closely. Work that was so important she couldn't begrudge it. Work that had slowly pulled Ty from her, and had in turn given her an escape from facing the darkening storm clouds inside herself. Work that left no time to nourish the fledgling embers that had once glowed between them. Fae didn't have anything left in her to feed them in any case.

The space between them grew more every day. Until people no longer asked where one was of the other. Until they no longer came as a pair. Until Fae walked alone with a hollow ache inside her that had nothing to do with the absence of him and everything to do with the dreams that shoved her awake in the darkest hours of the night.

She cleared her throat and stepped around him. "Are you hoping to offer some well wishes before he travels? He leaves after the meeting." There had never been a dearth of things to talk about with Ty — they shared responsibilities in plenty of projects — but none of it ever felt like the right thing to say these days. Once, she'd have teased him for his work ethic, or volunteered to help him manage a class of his students. But the exhaustion that chased Fae day after day was too entrenched in her bones

8

for her to spend energy on anything that didn't absolutely require her attention. And rescuing this relationship would take more than she had to give. He'd be better off without her now anyway.

Ty watched her as he shook his head. "No," he said. "The tremors last night brought down a wall in the city. I'm on my way to have a look."

Fae nodded. Of course. There was nothing Throldon could ask of Ty that he would refuse. He'd never been able to ignore someone that needed help. And Throldon had plenty of those. He was supposed to be an Eldra of Arolynos, one of the governing council of elves. Still was, in fact. But he'd taken his role of ambassador to heart, and now rarely left the human city in the heart of Arland. Fae suspected he would never consider his work here finished. Or at least, not until Throldon equalled Arolynos in his eyes.

Perhaps it was the clouds that shadowed her thoughts, but she couldn't see that ever happening.

A crease appeared in Ty's brow, and he tipped his head towards her as though he would say something. But he seemed to think better of it. His lips pressed together, holding whatever it was inside. Just like she did. His storm-grey eyes swam with words unsaid, with the ghost of what they once were. There was affection there too, she didn't think there would ever *not* be feelings between them. But the rest of it was too much for her to think on. For her to unwrap the layers of reasons why she wasn't the person she used to be.

The very idea of it made her feel heavy.

"Well—" She turned to leave. "I'll see you at the meeting then."

Something like hurt flickered in his gaze. But she could see the call of his duties pulling at him.

In the end, he turned away too. "Yes," he said. "I'll see you there."

2

REBUILDING

Fae's next stop was just south of the castle complex, where Sheha had taken rooms for her visits in the capital. She arrived to find her adopted sister already poring over endless documents spilling over the desk at the far end of the living area. So many sketches and building plans and lists lay one atop the other in a mess of paper Fae hadn't believed her sister was capable of making until this last year.

Sheha waved that she'd be a minute, her golden hair a shining curtain in the sunlight pouring into the room, the tips of her tapered ears just peeking out between the strands. Fae dumped a paper bag of fresh pastries on the dining table — purchased from the bakery down the street after Fanrell's suggestion that she eat something — and walked over to the wall of glass looking south over some of Throldon's finest rooftops. Sheha's apartment was beautiful; a rare gem in an otherwise dilapidated city. The great room was big enough for two large settees, the desk, and a dining table for six, with a yawning fireplace adorning the western wall. There were two lovely bedrooms beyond, and it even had access to its own bathing room, a sure sign that it had once been owned by someone of considerable wealth.

Now, places like this sat empty all over the city, and were made available for visitors to the castle. Fae didn't like to dwell on what had happened to their previous tenants.

With a sigh that bordered on dramatic, Sheha finally put down her pen and looked up from her work, her grey eyes sparkling.

"So, are you burning the midnight oil or is this an early start?" Fae asked, one eyebrow raised.

Sheha batted the question away and glared down at her paperwork, as if it were to blame for everything. "There's just so much work to do!" she said, dodging the question.

"There is always so much work to do," Fae said, coming to look over her sister's shoulder. She made a face and stepped away again. "There has been since before we came, and likely will be for years yet. You still need to sleep in between."

Sheha glanced up, her eyes missing nothing. "Uhuh, and when was the last time *you* slept, *Niha*?" She looked Fae up and down, and rose to move to the dining table. Forgoing the luxury of plates, she dropped into a chair and tore open the paper bag, pointedly patting the seat beside her. "Sit." She pushed one pastry across the polished surface. "Eat."

Fae did as she was told, and hummed with pleasure at the first bite.

"The tremors woke me this morning," she confessed. Although it could hardly have been called morning — the world was still black and cold when the earth tremors had pulled her from her nightmares.

Sheha paused before biting off another piece of her breakfast, her gaze full of worry.

"Dreams again?"

Fae nodded. The same dreams that had plagued her all year. That had gotten worse as the strange rumblings beneath the earth started shaking the very ground they stood upon.

The dreams where she relived, again and again, the day of the Survivors' trials. Where she heard again, the snap of two boys' necks. Saw the emptiness in their killers' eyes. Saw the hole in Hal's chest as it emptied his life's blood onto the cracked tiled floor.

Saw the flames of Immrith's funeral pyre.

And always that call to the north. The call that had tugged her from Arolynos and on to her destiny. It still pulled at her, even now, in her dreams. Pulled her to a place of ice and cold...

Fae squeezed her eyes shut against the flood of memories but nothing she could do would banish the echo of that crackling voice, of the broken god hellbent on killing her.

That was when she clawed herself awake, to the tremors that always took her back to that day.

So like the way the ground had shaken when she'd given the last of herself to end Anson.

Sheha's hand closed around hers, and Fae willed her fist to unclench. She looked down at the crescent shapes her nails had pressed into her palm, and breathed a shaky breath.

"It's been a year," Sheha said gently, clasping both hands around Fae's. "You survived. He's gone. Black is still in her cell." Because the leader of the Survivors had proved that even without the influence of a broken god, she was still no saint.

Fae forced a ghost of a smile onto her face, the pastry turning leaden in her stomach.

"A child called me 'Bitchbreaker' this morning," she said.

Sheha blinked. Then roared a laugh.

"Oh I like that one!" She grinned. "Much better than 'Stormbreaker'." She made a face. "That one's always felt too heavy for my liking." Another chuckle escaped her. "These humans have such colourful ways of saying things. I can't imagine I'll ever be bored here." The city's "colourful" dialect had worked its way into all of their vocabularies; these days Fae often found herself invoking gods without a second thought, in spite of her elven upbringing.

Sheha's eyes flickered across the room as a loose sheet of paper floated free of the stack on her desk. She'd taken to her new work with the Council of the Races — and the University in particular — with such zeal that even Ty had been surprised by it. "They are such a messy people. So much done in the name of fear. But they have so much potential." She waved a hand at the wide expanse of windows, and the view beyond. "Look at this city. They've come back so much stronger *because* of those mistakes. They could very well change the world." Taking another bite of her pastry, she concluded, "I like them."

Fae waved to the overflowing desk. "They do seem to be keeping you busy."

Sheha hummed, shooting another accusatory glare at the piles of work scattered across the surface.

Fae worried at a fingernail and tried to sound casual as she asked, "Have you spoken to Ty lately?"

The kind of relationship Fae had with Ty had always been different to the bond she shared with Sheha, the twins occupying different spaces in her life. Ty had always been a close friend, grown into something more as they traveled across Arland together, fought together, and saved Eah'lara together. Sheha was her family. The sister who raised her.

But Sheha's silence held more than Fae was willing to get into over breakfast. The first time Fae had tried to use Shae as a go-between, her sister had very firmly reminded her that if she wanted to speak to Ty, she could very well do it herself. They'd been through enough together. Something as simple as holding a conversation shouldn't be so hard.

The look she fixed Fae with now carried the same words without her having to even open her mouth.

Fae sighed. "Do you miss Arolynos sometimes?" she asked instead, twining her fingers together. Both siblings had intended to split their days equally between the human capital and their home in the forests of Il'arys, as ambassadors. But rebuilding Throldon was crucial to the recovery of Arland, and demanded much from them. These days they spent most of their time here.

Her sister allowed her the change of direction, and leaned back in her chair.

"Of course. But what we do here is *so* important." Her gaze drifted to the view outside her expansive windows. "The Aethyr benefit from the work we do here. Even us non-Whisperers can feel it." She shot Fae a wink. Sheha and Ty had always been better at Listening to spiritkind than most elves, even if they hadn't chosen to follow that path. "And when we return to Arolynos, the improvement is all the sweeter."

Fae could well imagine it. When the spirits of the world were being suffocated in their own realm, the life in the forest of Il'arys had suffered along with them. The Great Tree itself, in which almost the entirety of Arolynos rested, had started to show signs of decay, even breaking in places, something that had never been seen before. But since Fae had banished Anson and his dark influence, the Spirit Realm had begun to heal, and the forest had come back from its winter sleep even stronger as a result.

For a few minutes, Fae and Sheha simply watched the sunlight glint off the rooftops of the city in companionable silence.

Eventually, Sheha cleared her throat. "What do you think Kagos wants?"

Fae shrugged. "Fanrell asked the same. I don't think anyone knows. You know how he likes to make an entrance."

"You went to see Fanrell?" There was that concern in her eyes again. Fae's sister didn't miss the importance of that visit.

Fae nodded. "He leaves after Council. It's a long journey back to Equi'tox, even if he gallops the whole way." And even then, he would still need to rest.

Sheha's gaze drifted back over the rooftops. "How is he?"

"You know how the centaurs are." And that said enough about how much they let on about their feelings. If they let themselves have any. "Ipgar and Remi are staying though."

Sheha nodded. "That's good." But her attention wandered. Finally she said, "I wish I'd met Immrith. The scouts always speak well of him."

Fae blinked back the sudden burn of tears.

"You would've liked him," she said.

Fae spent another hour with Sheha, shamelessly using the time to chase her shadows away before she left for her final destination: the castle itself.

Sheha's apartment wasn't far from the bailey gatehouse, but Fae still endured hushed whispers of "Stormbreaker," "Lightbringer," and her most hated, "Saviour."

Pulling her hood forward over her face, she trudged through the streets as quickly as she could without breaking into a run, crossed the square that faced the gate, and ducked inside.

Walking across the bailey courtyard was better in some ways, and worse in others.

On the one hand, most of the soldiers here already knew her. They had either been here a year ago, seen that chaos with their own eyes, or they'd seen her passing in and out enough times since then that her appearance was less of an event than it was for the general populous she tried so hard to avoid.

On the other hand, that also meant that most of them were familiar with exactly what had happened last year. Exactly how much power she'd wielded, destroying a fragment of a god and most of the Great

Hall in the process. The looks she got here weren't the awestruck wonder of the civilians, who only knew her as the one who brought about the end of the Survivors' brutal rule and ushered in the new council.

No, the looks she got from these men and women were a mix of respect, and fear.

Shoving down the wave of nausea at the reminder, she strode unfalteringly to the steps of the castle complex, and disappeared inside.

She found her mother in the Great Hall, the first room in the castle to have been refurbished. Huge glass windows covered the wall that looked out onto the central quadrangle, currently budding with the encouraging signs of spring. Any sign of the Survivors' trials had been erased; broken floor tiles had been replaced, shattered window panes had been restored to their former stained-glass glory, the violence and blood-drenched horrors permeating the room scrubbed away by the very woman who now paced restlessly across the view of the quad.

"Anxious?" Fae said as she stepped into the hall. The tables had been set up in a circle in the middle of the room, as they usually were for the Council of the Races. If it were a city council meeting, they would be set out in a rectangle, with Laina at the head. But when consulting with the races of the world, everyone came to the table as equals.

Fae's mother would have preferred it to be that way for running the city as well, but Hal had insisted the people of Throldon needed a leader to turn to after the decades of anarchy they had endured.

Laina looked up, her brown eyes shining in the sunlight streaming through the windows. Fae's own ocean-green eyes had been her father's, the amber ring that circled them a muted reminder of the power the Aethyr had gifted her.

Loaned her, really.

"We only just had our first Council six months ago!" Laina said, worrying at a nail with her teeth. "What couldn't wait until the next one?"

Fae came up to her mother and gently pulled the hand from her mouth. Laina had fretted over her first Council meeting as well, but once everyone had assembled, she had conducted herself with the grace and authority of a queen.

Even if she did insist on being called "Councilwoman".

"I'm sure he has his reasons," Fae soothed with a smile. "You know what he's like." From the first time she'd met the dragon, he'd always loved a dramatic reveal.

"You don't think it's about the quakes, do you?" Laina resumed her pacing. "Last night's collapsed a new section of the University walls. The builders are talking about having to recalculate all their drawings if the structures are going to have to withstand this kind of movement on a regular basis. And they're getting worse." She blew out a sigh and ran a hand through her strawberry-blonde hair, pulling strands from the braid she'd tied there. "I haven't had any reports from the suburbs yet. I don't know if there were any homes affected." Her hand returned to her lips, as if she might start chewing it again.

She turned to face Fae, her face brimming with worry. "I've never heard of so many quakes before. And they only started after you defeated Anson." She hesitated a beat. "Is there anything in the Spirit Realm? Anything that might explain why this is happening?"

Fae pressed her lips together as she shook her head. She looked in on Eah'lara every day, and every time the tremors woke her, hoping to glean some hint as to why the earth had begun to shake. Especially since she had nearly died to save it.

"No," she said. "Eah'lara looks as it should. It's almost back to how I would expect it to look." A year ago, this section of Eah'lara had been a black hole where shimmering connections and starry nebulae should have filled the Spiritual Plane. Only after she'd banished the dark shroud of Anson had the Aethyr been able to trickle back into the void.

Laina ran a frustrated hand through her hair again, growling as it tangled in the braid a second time. She pulled the ribbon out and started yanking her fingers angrily through the strands.

"Here," Fae reached out a hand to take the ribbon from her mother, and motioned for her to turn around. Laina obliged, and Fae began combing sections back with her fingers, deftly weaving them together the way Sheha had taught her so many years ago.

"Whether it's the earth trembling beneath our feet, or an army of raiders storming through the streets, we'll face it together. Even Kagos will help, for all that he likes to play at being aloof." Fae knew the dragon had a soft side to him, even if he never let it show. She tied the ribbon in a bow at the end of Laina's hair, and turned her by the shoulders. Looking her mother in the eyes, she said, "Fanrell is here, as are Sheha and Ty, the dwarves are coming..." She paused. "Whatever it is, we'll face it together." She waited for Laina to nod. Having spent the fifteen years before her appointment to Throldon as a traveling healer, Fae's mother still found the responsibilities of an entire city rather daunting.

"Lord Graem wasn't able to make it this time," Laina said, referring to the dwarves' usual seat at the table. Before Fae could voice her surprise, she went on. "He sent someone in his stead." There was twinkle in her eye as she said it, but before she could tell Fae who had come from Dvargra, an earth-sundering roar rumbled through the castle.

3

PIECES ON THE BOARD

Fae and Laina reached the main castle gates just as a shadow blotted out the clear blue of the sky.

Clouds of dust stirred from the packed earth underfoot, and great gusts of wind whipped at their skirts, tugged the hair from their braids. The downdraft caused by wings the size of a tall-ship's sails sent soldiers and craftsmen alike scurrying for shelter under the sloped roofs of the armouries, forges, and saddleries hugging the bailey wall.

An enormous black dragon descended into the castle complex, his green-gold dorsal ridge gleaming in the sunlight as his clawed, chimney-crushing feet finally touched ground.

Fae grinned when she saw that Aiya was not the only one perched between the fins running the length of Kagos's back. A smaller figure slid to the ground before the dragon even had a chance to fully lower his head, and sprinted across the bailey towards them.

"Max!" Fae opened her arms to the girl, whose grin was wide as she flung an arm around Fae's waist. "It is good to see you!"

"You have no idea!" Max said. "I nagged Aiya for days to let me come!"

Fae laughed. Across the courtyard, Aiya lifted a hand in greeting.

Then Kagos transformed.

And as his body changed, the accompanying, deafening sound of boulders tumbling into a ravine echoed across the city.

It was like watching giant invisible hands practice the ancient art of paper-folding in high speed. First his leathery wings collapsed, appearing to thin until they looked no thicker than a mayfly's, then his neck and body followed. As the din rumbled on, Kagos's entire, colossal form folded in on itself over and over until finally, all that was left was a figure no bigger than a tall man. He was covered in the black scales of his dragon form, but for his ebony-skinned feet, hands, and head. His face changed from long and pointed to flat and oval, his nostrils narrowed to slits in his face. Fan-shaped ears held the green-gold hue of his dorsal fins, but his eyes remained their liquid obsidian black.

Fae waved as Kagos accepted the thick, silk robe Aiya held for him.

"Show off," Max muttered beside her.

A smile tugged at Fae's lips. "He *is*, isn't he?" She took a step back to look at her properly. When they had first met, Max had been a street urchin scraping a living from the streets of Throldon, so thin that at first glance she could have passed for either a boy or a girl.

But now, the girl was showing the benefits of three square meals a day, and the freedom to be a child for what few years she had left to do so. Her hair shone a golden-brown and her flushed cheeks bore a smattering of freckles across the bridge of her nose. She filled out her riding leathers, similar to those Aiya appeared to live in, and in her arms...

"Is this the infamous Pig?" Fae's eyes sparkled as she beheld the rusty-red snout that poked from the edge of Max's leathers. The hatchling even deigned to utter an inelegant snort in answer.

Max's eyes creased in delight as the baby dragon nuzzled up to snuffle at her neck.

"Yes," she said, and her voice was filled with utter adoration for the creature. "Say hello, Pig." The hatchling snorted happily again. "She wanted to come too." She tapped the dragon on the end of her little nose. "Didn't you Pig?" Big copper eyes turned toward Fae, and that slender, tapered head cocked to one side.

Max laughed, and Fae realised the tiny dragon must have said something in the unique mind-to-mind connection that belonged to dragons and their riders. Not that Max would be riding Pig for a long while yet.

"Pig says you smell funny," Max explained. She turned her attention to the hatchling. "Hush now, that's not polite."

"*Hera*," Aiya corrected as she approached to stand behind her charge, "picks up on all sorts of scents. I hardly think she will have been referring to your personal hygiene." She inclined her head in greeting, her waist-length black braid swinging over her shoulder as she turned to Laina as well. "It is good to see you, Fae, Councilwoman." Aiya was beautiful, the grey eyes of her people stark in contrast to the creamy brown of her skin. The funnel collar of her thigh-length riding coat covered the lower half of her face, muffling her words slightly, and she lifted a graceful hand to undo the toggles that fastened it.

Kagos stepped up behind her, eyeing Fae with eyes of deepest black. "Spiritchild."

"Kagos." She met his eyes, not intimidated by his glower. "It's good of you to grace us with your presence." She let her lips quirk.

The answering gleam in his eyes was the only sign of his amusement. "I come when it is necessary to do so." He turned to Laina without further word. "Councilwoman Woods."

"Kagos," Laina replied somewhat stiffly. "The Great Hall is ready for us. I imagine the rest will join us shortly. Not many will have missed your arrival." Indeed, his roar would have been heard across the city.

The dragon smirked. "Isn't that the point?"

Aiya rolled her eyes at his back as he strode into the castle, his hands folded into the sleeves of his robe. "He doesn't actually like to be the centre of attention," she said by way of apology, as if that explained his arrogance.

But Fae just shook her head. "You know, I have yet to see any evidence of that claim." The elf had said something similar the previous year, and Kagos had been just as prone to bouts of showmanship then as now.

"I know," Aiya replied, her eyes crinkling at the corners, even as her cheeks flushed. "He hides it so well."

A laugh bubbled from Fae, a feeling so rare these days it made her giddy. She threw an arm around the rider's shoulders. "Ah, it is good to see you, Aiya. Even if your partner can be an insufferably obstinate mule."

"I resent that." Kagos's dry voice echoed down the hall beyond the doors.

Fae slapped a hand to her mouth, and Aiya's face reddened even more, but Max burst into howls of laughter.

Laina grimaced, clearly finding this visit taxing before it had even begun. "Shall we?" She indicated they follow behind Kagos with a wave of her hand.

Fae nodded, her eyes dancing as she lowered her hand to her side, working to keep her face schooled into a picture of professionalism.

"Of course, Mother," she said, struggling to completely smother the laughter in her voice. "Come on Max." She steered the still-howling girl through the castle doors. "Let's go and find some rooms for you and Pig."

"*Hera*," Aiya muttered behind them.

After showing Max her rooms, and where she could request food for her voraciously hungry hatchling, Fae rejoined the others in the Great Hall.

"Where's the girl?" Kagos said by way of a greeting.

"Max is exploring what the kitchens have to offer her and Pi— Hera." Fae corrected herself at the flash in his eyes. "She'll be along as soon as she's done."

His acknowledging nod was barely a jerk of his head, and Aiya offered another look of apology.

Fae gave a tiny shake of her head. The rider needn't have worried; she was all too aware of Kagos's quirks.

Just like with Immrith, a part of her knew the dragon very well.

But she'd never quite understood the depths of Aiya's feelings for Kagos. True, he was a good man — well, dragon — underneath all of his swagger and arrogance, but still... And then there was the matter that, regardless of feelings, dragons simply did not have relationships outside of their own kind. The ability to alter their forms to more closely mirror those of the other races of the world was one that took centuries of practice. Hera wouldn't gain that skill within Max's human lifetime.

"So, when will we find out what was so important it required another Council meeting only six months after the last one?" Laina said, her face revealing nothing of the nail-biting worry Fae knew was tucked tightly beneath her regal facade.

"Oh I think we'll wait for the others to arrive first, don't you?" Kagos replied, taking a seat at the circle of tables. "Wouldn't want them to miss out on the excitement."

Laina tapped her foot on the tiles, and seemed about to demand an answer from him, but checked herself. "I'll go and tell the kitchen staff to have refreshments sent up," she said instead, and swept from the room.

Aiya sighed her exasperation but Fae was the one to round on Kagos.

"Why must you be so aggravating? Do you find it entertaining?" She didn't go into how much pressure Laina was under already, what with the quakes and rebuilding a city full of people, some of whom had, until not *that* long ago, caused grievous harm to the rest.

No, Laina was doing an admirable job of keeping her own worries buried beneath the face of a respected and competent leader, and Fae wouldn't undermine that. But that didn't mean Kagos could play games with her feelings.

Kagos let out a long breath and leaned back in his chair. "Spiritchild, when you have lived as long as I, you learn to find amusement in any situation."

"You forget, Kagos, that parts of me *have* lived almost as long as you," Fae reminded him, the amber around her eyes flashing almost pointedly. "And *I* do not enjoy the distress of others."

Kagos waved a lazy hand, dismissing her concerns. "You think too much on it, Spiritchild. It is just a game. And we are all but pieces on the board."

"Kagos!" Aiya gasped a warning.

"Is that how you think of us?" Fae's voice lowered dangerously. She may not have her Aethyrial powers anymore, but in this form, Kagos was just like a man, and she was quite happy to slap him across the face, history or no.

But the look Kagos shot her held no more dry humour. "You will soon see how I regard you, Spiritchild, and the members of this Council. Have patience, and stop assuming the worst. Baev'ill knew me better."

Fae clamped her lips shut against the retort she wanted to scream at him. He was right, the part of her that had once belonged to a being known as Baev'ill *did* know the dragon better than the heartless mask he put on for the world beyond Hearthstone.

But it had been so long since she'd accessed those memories, it was as if they belonged to a different lifetime altogether. And now that she turned to inspect them, she found them somewhat faded, like a painting left out in the sun too long.

Huffing her grievance, she dropped into a seat further around the table, and glared out into the courtyard instead. Out of the corner of her eye, she saw Aiya shoot her partner a cutting glare, but any further thoughts on the matter were interrupted by the sound of racing footsteps beyond the huge double doors of the hall.

"Aiya!" Max called as she skidded to a halt in the entranceway. "Look who I found!" Stepping into view with a little more decorum, were two of the elven scouts who had played a part in reclaiming Throldon the previous year.

Fae leapt up, her surprise at seeing them a joy. "Aren! Stef!" She rushed over to embrace them both as they towered over her slight frame. At over six feet tall each, they were of average height for elves. Aren had cut his hair in the last year, and they now both wore their sun-kissed ebony short, but it had always been their eyes that made the brothers stand out: Stef's were a molten steel-grey, while Aren's were pure silver.

"What brings you to Throldon?" Fae asked, stepping back to look at them. They'd returned to Arolynos after taking news of Immrith's death to his people in Equi'tox, and aside from the odd visit to the University, they'd remained in their forest home within the trees of Il'arys.

Aren shrugged. "Well, we heard that some familiar faces might be getting together," he said, sliding his hands into his pockets with a lop-sided smile. "So we might have rearranged our teaching stint at the University to tie the two together."

"He missed you," Stef added dryly.

Aren gaped. "I did not! Well, maybe a little. After traipsing across Arland to find Laina, and then fighting together to save humanity from Anson, Arolynos has become a bit..."

"Tame?" Stef supplied, a glint in his eye.

Fae felt a smile pull at her lips. "Well, I'm glad you're here. Maybe you can add a bit of cheer..." She glanced pointedly behind her to where Kagos remained seated, imperious as a monarch on his throne.

Aren followed her gaze and mouthed a silent "Ah."

"Mhm," Fae muttered. "Laina is worried about these tremors in the earth, and Ty is so absorbed in his work, I barely see him except to discuss more work. Sheha's not much better..." But at least she knew how to talk to her sister.

Aren's eyes narrowed. Fae shook her head. She didn't want to get into it right now. Stef patted her arm without a word, and she smiled gratefully up at him.

A small snuffle sounded behind Aren, and Pig's tiny snout appeared at his ankle.

All together, Pig was only around three feet long, her tail accounting for more than a third of that. Her little legs shuffled her ponderously around Aren and Stef's feet, like a tiny barrel rocking from side to side.

Stef crouched down and held out a hand to the hatchling. "Who's this little one?" Although the twinkle in his eye suggested that he already had an idea.

Fae cast about for Pig's partner, and found her already perusing the food the kitchen staff were trying to arrange on a far table. "Max!"

The girl startled, dropping a bread roll on the floor. Pig quickly abandoned Stef's attentions to waddle across the room and snatch at the food before it could be cleaned up.

At Fae's call, Aiya spotted her charge and marched across the room, her eyes dark as she hissed, "Pick her up!" She scooped up Pig and deposited her in Max's arms, forcing the girl to relinquish her plate back to the table. "We are not in Hearthstone, where everyone knows a hatchling when they see one!" She folded her arms and glared down at the girl. "Hera must be in your sight *at all times*. No exceptions. Are we clear?" Max swallowed, but nodded, uncharacteristically quiet.

When Aiya turned back towards the others, her expression softened enough for Fae to see that doling out discipline wasn't something that came naturally to her. But, when she glanced at Kagos, it looked as though the rider would much rather she be the one to deliver Max's lessons than him.

Aren whistled quietly. Max slumped over to them, Pig nestled safely in her arms again. The hatchling snuffled happily, as if utterly oblivious to the girl's misery.

Before Fae could offer her sympathies, more voices echoed through the gallery beyond the doors, and Laina reappeared with Hal by her side, where he had been ever since convincing her to take a broken Throldon as her next patient.

The ex-ranger-turned-councilman's beard had clearly seen a barber recently, its usually wild tendencies tamed into a neat, trim shape, and his sandy hair was combed back from his face. He wore fitted trousers and a smart, white shirt which, while informal by castle standards, was worlds apart from his previously travel-limited wardrobe. But despite his improvement in style, his piercing blue eyes still twinkled just the same, the smile lines decorating his deeply tanned face creasing at the sight of who awaited them.

"'Tis right good to see you all," he said, his thick accent not having altered one bit in his time in the capital. "I look forward to catchin' up plenty after." He smiled to each of them, shaking hands with Aren and Stef, and embracing Fae and Max fiercely.

Behind Hal was a man called David, whom Fae had met only twice before, and a smaller figure who all but stomped her way into the hall.

"Jesse!" Fae practically squealed.

"Ah yes," Laina smiled. "I didn't get around to telling you who Lord Graem sent."

The dwarf, whose scowl cast its own shadows, stood nearly two feet shorter than the scouts, and a good six inches below Fae's meagre height, but she somehow managed to glare at them as if they were on a level nonetheless.

"I haven't seen you in an age!" Fae continued, ignoring the glower. "How goes it? How is Dvargra?"

"Fine," Jesse grumbled, her dark eyes narrowing. "Or it was fine until Graem pulled me from sentry duty to trek down here." The journey from the mountain stronghold of the dwarves would have taken a good few days, and those miles of foothills would still be biting cold.

Fae winced in sympathy, and she saw the scouts do likewise. "Why *did* Lord Graem send you? You didn't come alone, surely?"

"No, no, I came with a group of our scouts. Got a few runners in there too with messages to distribute, news to collect, you know how it is. As for why our esteemed lord chose *me*—" Jesse cast her a dark look. "Payback for running off across the continent with a certain teenage boy last year." She rolled her eyes and shoved her hands under her arms, giving her the look of a chastised teenager herself. "I didn't bother reminding him that said teenager was in fact an eons-old spirit with a quest to save the world." An eons-old spirit that now lived within Fae. Jesse let out a long breath, and some of the tension defused from her. "Not worth the hassle. I'd rather jog up and down the Gatekeepers in silk slippers than argue with that man. In any case, he has his hands full reintegrating displaced villagers back where they belong, and then deciding what to do with the settlements. I don't envy him." Her eyes took in the hall. "So here I am." She released her hands to her hips, and indicated the others filling the room. "Looks like most of the old gang is too."

Fae nodded as Fanrell, and finally Sheha and Ty entered to take their seats at the table.

Ty's dark grey eyes scanned the room, snagged and caught on hers. A small smile crossed his lips as he nodded his greeting, Fae returning the gesture. She turned back to the group to find Stef watching her.

"What?"

The scout shook his head. "Nothing." But a quiet understanding flickered across his features, and he gave her shoulder a brief squeeze when they broke apart to take their places around the table. Fanrell remained standing. Sitting just wasn't in a centaur's repertoire.

With everyone finally present, Kagos glanced towards Laina.

She waved a hand for him to begin, and while the gesture might have been intended to look casual, Fae saw the tension in her mother's wrist that spoke an added undertone: Kagos called this meeting, he could damn well explain it himself. There had been talk of gathering this council more often than once a year, but there was just so much rebuilding to do all around. After much discussion, they'd decided on once-yearly meetings until the races had stabilised a bit more. Throldon in particular had a lot of work to do.

Which Kagos knew.

Nodding his thanks, Kagos stood, somehow managing to make his position look like the head of the table, for all that its surface was round for a reason.

He stuffed his ebony hands into his sleeves, and pulled himself up to his not insignificant height, drawing their gazes up with him.

"Welcome all," he began magnanimously, and Laina bristled ever so slightly in her seat. "I called the Council of the Races before its time to ask of you first, a question." He paused. "And then, I hope, a solution." He turned to Laina, and fixed her with his obsidian gaze.

"Are you aware," he asked, "that as we speak, there is an army marching on Throldon?"

4

SILVER AND STEEL

The room erupted.

Fae watched as reactions flared across the Great Hall. Everyone had questions.

And while Kagos gave the outward impression of being cooly amused, a quiet worry shimmered behind his eyes.

Laina's face drained of all colour, her lips a bloodless line.

Pig dived back into Max's jacket at the uproar. The girl retreated to the food table to soothe the hatchling with morsels of cheese and figs.

Kagos waited for the panic to subside before continuing.

"I'll take that to mean you were *not* aware," he said.

"You know damn well we weren't," Hal growled at him, going from easy-going ranger to disciplined soldier in a heartbeat. "Otherwise we might be tryin' to put together a defence, rather than just tryin' to put together our city!"

"We don't *have* any defences," Laina whispered, her eyes distant, and Fae could well imagine what was going through her head. Her childhood home had been sacked by the Unity.

"Where are they coming from?" David spoke up, leaning forward over the table.

"They march from the south," Kagos replied smoothly. "Around fifty-thousand of them, if my estimates are correct."

"Fifty-thousand..." Hal swore softly. "We'll be lucky if we can raise a tenth of that."

"How long?" Laina asked.

"Three weeks, at the most," Kagos answered, and this time his voice held a gentleness that reminded them why he was here.

In a strange way, he counted most of the people here friends. And from the time Fae had spent with him last year, she didn't think there were many others he would name as such.

"Where have they even come from?" Aren asked, confusion furrowing his brow. Everyone in Arland was represented at this table.

"Anneal!" Hal called, his voice thundering through the room and out to the gallery beyond. A head appeared around the door.

"Yes, Councilman?" the young pageboy answered.

"Find me a map," he said. "There'll be some in my study." The boy disappeared, and Hal rubbed a hand across his beard.

Fae raised an eyebrow. "Your study?" She recalled Hal's bunker, in which she had once sheltered from a brutal storm. Dug from the cold, hard ground of the Wastelands, it was no more than a well-cared-for burrow. But at that, it was still a haven from the harsh conditions of its surroundings. Life had changed so much for him since they'd defeated Anson.

She looked around. It had changed a lot for most of them.

Hal gave her a wry smile, as if he knew exactly the direction of her thoughts. "Aye. Got more rooms than I know what to do with now. And somehow I keep needin' more."

"What nations would even want to attack Throldon?" Sheha asked the room.

Jesse snorted. "After the last thirty years? Take your pick." Indeed, the previous few decades had not been Arland's proudest.

"And while the city is returning to a semblance of normality, we still don't have a full garrison. It's ripe for the taking," David added.

Hal grunted a nod. Laina blanched impossibly further.

"Alright." Jesse straightened. "What would someone stand to gain from taking the city? We've just said it doesn't have much in the way of forces. It has no walls to defend. It's barely recovering from a string of incompetent regimes..." She ticked points off on her fingers. "What's the benefit?"

The pageboy chose that moment to dash full-tilt into the hall, his arms overflowing with scrolls and papers.

"Woah, easy there Anneal," Hal said as the boy came to a stop beside the table. "Thank you, drop 'em here." Maps safely deposited, Anneal retreated back to the safety of the gallery beyond the doors, out of earshot, but within range if needed.

"Ah, this is the one." Hal drew out a scroll as long as his arm, and spread it across the table, drawing a dagger from his boot to anchor one side.

Without comment, Jesse pulled one of the curved daggers from her belt and laid it over the opposite end, then moved to stand beside him.

"Pharro," she said.

"Hmm," Hal muttered to himself, his piercing blue eyes scanning the entirety of the map. "Most like."

Ty came around to stand over his shoulder. "It's the only nation to the south of here on this continent."

"But it's no more than a port town." David craned over to inspect the tiny dot on the far southern coast.

"On *this* map," Jesse pointed out. "This is going to be at least thirty years out of date, if not older."

Fanrell pointed to another mark on the paper. "This one would need to sail around the mountains if they wanted to attack. They would also approach from the south."

Kagos shook his head. "We'd have seen an armada that big from Dragontail."

Fae leaned over for a better look, and saw a world expanded far beyond her knowledge of it.

Despite the six Aethyr that had lent her their powers — and memories — to defeat Anson, her knowledge of the mortal world was limited to what she herself had lived through. The spirits didn't care whether the beings they inhabited lived in Arland or — Fae peered over the map at a smattering of islands in the ocean pinned under Hal's dagger — Yneshia. The only thing they were concerned about was the nature of the lifeform itself.

The map was a work of art, coloured pen strokes beautifully outlining the peaks of the Edge Mountains, the silvery line of the Amedi River, and the verdant forests of Arolynos. The towns and cities that had once decorated the plains of Arland were depicted in miniature renditions of themselves. Even sleepy Greneln was represented by a tiny illustration of their unique underground dwellings.

Fae found herself drawn to the expanse far to the north, further even than she'd travelled the previous year. The area, marked only as "Ice Fields" was hypnotising in its beauty; huge, bare islands separated by nothing but huge cracks of ocean picked out in blue and white inks. Not a single trace of civilisation marred the landscape.

She cocked her head. Something about that empty space captivated her. Caught her and held her fast.

A chill crept over her skin, as if blown straight from that icy expanse.

She shivered, and rubbed a hand over her arm. No one else seemed to have noticed. No one else mentioned the sudden cold in the room. In fact, David was dabbing beads of sweat from his brow.

Fae glanced back at the map. At that unmarked section of the continent. Equi'tox squatted across the north-western corner, with annotations and illustrations for their villages. The Ice Fields were not that much further north — why were they so bare?

But the army wasn't coming from the north. Fae dragged her eyes back to the swathe of land south of Throldon. To the west of it lay her beloved Arolynos — the forest of Il'arys marked by its human name of Acreage — to the east lay the other elven settlement of Alyla, abutting the Hearthstone mountains, and the Dragontail peninsula. But leagues of nothingness stretched on further still, over an empty region marked as "Thamib", until the map finally revealed a coast line, and a smattering of markings of a distant civilisation.

"What *is* 'Pharro'?" she asked, reading the name written alongside one such marking, nestled into a small bay on the coast itself.

At the answering silence, she looked around. No one seemed to know.

"Well that's just great," Jesse muttered.

"There are histories of a desert nation to the south," Kagos spoke up, his hand delving even deeper into his sleeves. "But the War of the Races did not end well for any nation. I do not believe they have been heard of this far north since The Rains." He cocked his head contemplatively. "In all honesty I think we'd rather forgotten about them."

"Well if this is them, it don't look like they forgot us," Hal said, stabbing the map with his finger. "Especially if they've bin keepin' a close enough eye on us to know when to march!"

"Indeed." Kagos sat back in his chair and fell silent. Aiya stared at him as his gaze glazed over the map, as if he might find some hidden solution concealed among the pen strokes.

"We might've had records of these other cities before the Unity," Laina said, pointing to the illustrations of places Fae had never heard of. "But a lot has been lost or destroyed by the raiders over the years." She indicated the map itself. "We've salvaged what little we've found, but it's barely a fraction of what should be here." Lines bracketed her mouth, and Fae remembered what they had found instead of books in the library last year.

"Neither the Unity, nor the Survivors cared about record-keeping," she said, recalling the shelves of children awaiting the chance to fight for their lives.

"No," Laina agreed. She turned back to Kagos. "Do you think they could be reasoned with?"

Kagos's face pinched. "An army of fifty-thousand doesn't seem particularly indicative of a willingness to talk."

The table fell silent.

"Well, shit," Jesse muttered.

After hours of deliberation, Sheha called to adjourn the Council. After going around in circles, they all agreed that a night of sleep *could* help them to see something they *might* have missed, although no one sounded particularly hopeful. The only one who knew what he was doing, was Fanrell.

"I must leave," he said before they went their separate ways. "But I will take word of this army to my Elders. Perhaps Equi'tox can help."

Laina clasped his hand. "Thank you Fanrell," she said earnestly, though they all knew how long it would take him to reach his homeland. Any help that returned would likely return to a smouldering ruin, if this army was as ill-intentioned as it appeared.

Fanrell nodded, a new rage simmering in his eyes before he turned and cantered away into the city.

David slumped from the castle with a muttered goodbye, his eyes shuttered. Jesse, Kagos, Aiya, and Max filed away to their rooms in the south wing. Laina looked as if she might keel over at any moment, but she stood straight-backed and held her head high as she bid farewell to the council delegates. Finally, only Sheha and Ty remained.

Fae hugged Sheha goodnight. And then she stood before Ty.

He looked down at her with his eyes of dark, storm-grey, and his mouth quirked up at the corner.

"To the ends of the earth, remember?" he said, and they were words from eons ago, when they had been more to each other than they were now. But the meaning remained, and Fae found herself smiling back despite herself.

"To the ends of the earth," she agreed, and hugged him as she would have done before everything changed. His arms were solid and warm around her, but his embrace no longer made her heart skip, as it once had.

Pulling away, Ty nodded his farewell, and followed Sheha down the steps into the night, leaving Fae behind with her mother once more.

Laina blew out a breath, sending an errant strand of strawberry-blonde hair dancing.

Once, Fae could have skated across Eah'lara to see this army for herself. She could have carried her friends with her, so they'd have a better idea of what they faced. Could have drawn power from Eah'lara to defend Arland, to defend her family.

But that was a different time. And she'd only just started learning to live with her new... normality.

Kagos's news had put a harpoon through that, and ripped out the heart of what she'd been trying to rebuild inside herself. An acceptance of herself as she was.

Fae looped an arm through Laina's, and together they walked back inside and up the sweeping staircase to the private quarters. Words didn't seem adequate to convey the maelstrom going through either of their minds. Fortunately, no words were needed. Just the reassuring comfort of each other's company.

They stopped at the door to Laina's rooms. Fae hugged her mother tightly.

"I'll see you in the morning," she said, and hoped her tone added the words she wanted her to hear. *I'm here for you.*

Laina's nod was heavy, her brown eyes dulled. But as she went to reach for the doorknob, the sound of soft steps from the other end of the hallway made her pause.

Fae looked up to see Hal stop before his own rooms, further along. He raised a hand to wave but hesitated, his gaze resting on Laina, eyes tightening.

He looked as though he wanted to say something, looked as though he was straining at the seams.

Then he smiled, and tapped two fingers to his temple in salute. "Ladies," he said, and ducked into his rooms, closing the door behind him with a quiet *snick*.

Fae watched Laina stare at the spot where he'd been, as if she'd imagined it.

"Goodnight, Fae," she said distantly. She opened her own door and slipped inside, the sound of its closing echoing Hal's.

Fae drew in a deep breath, and blew it out long and slow, running a hand over her hair and down the length of her braid to pull the ribbon out at the end. Combing her fingers through the strands of ash-blonde so pale it was almost silver, she turned to the room opposite her mother's.

They were the same guest quarters she always used, but she'd never tried to make them her own. The furniture sat exactly where it had when she'd first set foot in here, the bed made up with linen chosen by the few staff that had found their way back to the work they'd had before the city was turned upside-down.

It wasn't home. It was just somewhere to stay.

But Arolynos hadn't felt like home in a long while either. On the occasions she'd traveled across Arland to visit, her old rooms had felt too cramped, the forest too open, the tree-city *too* joyous and free. There was nothing to work on there, no toil, no sense of achievement for a job well done. No purpose.

In Throldon, there was so much to do, so many parts of the city that needed fixing, so many people that still needed help. And yet...

It was like she didn't fit anymore. Anywhere. Her very skin was too tight, her body too big to fit what was left behind after Anson.

She just existed. Present to do what needed doing. Day after day.

And now an army was coming for them...

Weeks, months of not enough sleep pressed down on her, and Fae felt her eyes droop heavily. She groaned, and rubbed at her face. Soon she would have no choice but to give in to the call of sleep. Even if she was doomed to wake in a few short hours.

She shucked her skirt and blouse, kicking her simple shoes off with them. Moving over to the matching ewer and basin on the side — she couldn't face the walk down the hall to the bathing rooms — she splashed water over her face, scraping her hair back with wet fingers. Using a towel to pat herself dry, she dug out a nightdress from the bottom drawer of the dresser. She preferred flannel trousers and sleep shirt but it was easier to wear whatever the staff left for her.

Finally collapsing into bed, she barely had enough presence of mind left to turn the lamp down low, before her eyes dropped shut.

She dreamed.

The dreams never left her. They've stayed with her all this time.

Haunting her.

They call to her, the way the Aethyr called her to her destiny, pulling her along until she stands on that monument, six spiritual guides waiting to join with her.

She dreams of the pain of that becoming, of folding the lives of seven beings, thousands of years of existence, into her one mind.

She dreams of floating, a single dust mote lost in eons of existence.

And in the dream, she becomes power.

But even in the dream, she knows what's to come. Thrashes against it.

She faces Anson, the dark shroud of a broken god hovering over her, glaring at her with his single, baleful red eye.

Hal lies on the ground, the hole in his chest pouring his life's blood onto the floor, spreading until the cracked tiles are slick with it.

The glazed eyes of two boys stare up at her in a circle of white rope.

The hollow gazes of their killers mock her.

Immrith's funeral pyre burns hot and damning behind her.

And she feels her powers evaporate.

She fights — she dances, her blades singing through the air.

And she falls.

Her body lies broken on the ground. And she knows she is dying.

The pain — the pain — grates through her bones. Every breath is fire.

Footsteps prowl towards her.

And a god purrs above.

Just as she draws her last breath, a seed of her power spears out to anchor her to Eah'lara — to anchor her to life.

She rises again, hurling her power at the god, driving him back, ripping him from his anchor.

Storms of lightning and wind surround her, locking her into a battle that cannot be stopped.

No, *she begs of her dream.* No.

The god descends, smothers her, drowns her in his darkness, but she thrusts her power up like a spear, and throws all of it — every last drop — into him.

And then, that moment when her power runs out.

The god hovers above her still, pulsating with her power, but there is nothing left within her to give.

That feeling of hopelessness. Of defeat.

It is the end.

And then the god explodes, the cataclysm enough to shatter windows, to make the very earth buck beneath her feet.

The earth rolls, and heaves, and moves.

And something else awakens.

A great, slumbering awareness roars in pain, rumbling through her blood.

As the ground shudders and shakes, the castle crumbles around her.

And she watches.

She rises through the wreckage of the castle, until she floats far above it, the world laid out as a map inked in pen strokes and drawings.

Across the map, she sees the weave of the Aethyr, the web of Eah'lara, where all living things are connected to each other.

One thread glows brighter than the rest. It arrows away to the north. Far, far, to the north. Further than even the map can go. Up here, the map is blank, barren, penned only in ice and light.

And it calls to her.

She has heard the call of the Aethyr before. This is older, it draws from deep within her, it echoes through her bones, sings in her blood.

She follows the bright thread. The one that sings to her. The one that hums to her bones and drinks from her soul.

Over the city, over the plains, over the Northern Tundra where she found her destiny before.

Over the ice.

The dream takes her down to the frozen fields where the light shines bright and the thread leads her on.

It takes her through the cold to where the wind dances.

It takes her across the blue and white.

And stops.

She shivers.

She wakes.

Fae opened her eyes to stinging cold and cruel winds that cut straight through the nightdress to her skin.

Blinking to clear them, she wrapped her arms around herself and clamped her legs together in a vain attempt to retain some heat in her body. She shivered.

She tried screwing her eyes shut, then flinging them wide open again.

But the view was the same.

She stood ankle-deep in snow, hard, slick ice beneath. Yet more snow flew around her with seemingly little aim. A watery light covered the sky in such a way that she couldn't tell if it was dawn or dusk, or if it was just always this grey.

Her whole body shuddered, the cold working its way perilously deep into her.

Behind her lay leagues upon leagues of powdered white.

Before her, a mountain that looked to be made of solid ice reared up to meet the sky, and set within it, huge gates of frosted silver and steel, at least ten feet tall. Their surfaces were moulded to match the temper of the snow: all swirls and flakes and whimsy.

Fae started as a figure peeled away from the gateposts.

The man was dressed for the weather, unlike her, with hair the colour of the rich, Oreshian *kahveh* that Hal loved to hate, or the darkest, bitterest chocolate, and eyes the colour of deepest indigo.

And behind those eyes, something *other* prowled. Something that had Fae's instincts screaming, *Danger!*

He smiled, and Fae's heart stuttered a warning.

"Took you long enough," he drawled.

5

CAGED

The knock at Jade's door didn't startle her.

Whoever was on the other side was clearly in a hurry, the rap of knuckles loud and staccato against the iron threshold.

She waited for the sound of the lock sliding back before opening the door herself, her expression set into a cool indifference perfected over six years of brutal practice.

A Brotherhood acolyte stood outlined against the grey stone hall, his blood-red robes appearing even more sinister in the dim light.

"Sorcerer Supreme wants you."

She nodded, and stepped from her room, letting the heavy door close behind her. She didn't bother with the locks — there was a reason they were only operable from the outside.

Jade followed the acolyte through the maze of stone corridors, almost offering to lead the way when he seemed to lose his bearings.

She suppressed a smirk. *Must be new.*

Finally, they stepped into the harsh light of the Sorcerer Supreme's Atrium.

"Jade Xid, Supremacy," the acolyte announced, his voice tinged with the acrid tang of fear.

Good, Jade thought, watching him back from the chamber, closing the hulking doors of gilded gold behind him. *Fear is good.*

Left standing alone on the sunken floor in the middle of the atrium — designed, she knew, to make his visitors feel small — Jade looked up at the man who'd summoned her.

The Sorcerer Supreme stood on the opposite balcony with his back to her, his profile framed by the wide pillars that held up the domed ceiling. Outside the walls of the Sanctum, the city of Pharro sprawled into the distance. Beyond that, the desert shimmered a dusty orange.

Had this been Jade's first occasion to stand before the Sorcerer Supreme, she might have fidgeted. She might even have sweated in the relentless dry heat that pulsed through the open sides of the atrium, a stark contrast to the cool, dark stone of the Brotherhood's Sanctum beneath.

But she had long ago mastered those instincts. She was the embodiment of stillness now.

Finally, the Sorcerer Supreme spoke.

"The supply beasts have outgrown their cages," he said, and while he didn't raise his voice, his words slithered against her skin, scraped through her blood. "They are being moved to new enclosures, and I want you there to avoid any... incidents." He turned, and she faced the full impact of his gaze. His eyes were utterly black — not a fleck of colour graced them, nothing to lessen the chill that crept along her spine every time he turned them to her.

Those eyes regarded her now, sweeping over the white of her clothes, looking for any trace of her *precious* blood. She squashed the shudder that threatened to give her away.

Seemingly satisfied, the Sorcerer Supreme turned back to his view, the silver-edged white of his own robes rippling in the breeze.

"Do not disappoint me."

Jade nodded, even though he no longer looked at her. "Supremacy," she replied, knowing a dismissal when she heard it. She turned to the door, had her hand on the gilded handle.

"Oh, and Xid?" She swallowed at the reminder of what she was now: Xid — prisoner, bought and paid for. In her case, the price had been paid in blood.

Dropping her hand from the door, she turned, cool mask in place.

"Yes, Supremacy." She willed her eyes to stay blank.

"Report for vialling beforehand."

She hesitated. Just a fraction of a second, but it was enough.

"Xid." His head turned, fixing her with his black gaze.

"Of course, Supremacy," she recovered, her voice flat and monotonous.

The Sorcerer Supreme's mouth curled up at the corner, but Jade endured it. Better a smile than the other thing.

Finally he turned from her once more. "Go."

Keeping her steps even, she pulled the doors open, and escaped to the cool dark of the passageways beyond.

She didn't acknowledge the shadows that trailed her. Aside from their relentless presence whenever she left her rooms, they didn't acknowledge her either. They ignored each other, and it was an arrangement that suited both parties well.

Treading a well-known path through the stone maze, Jade barely heard the shuffling footsteps of the Brotherhood acolytes wandering the halls. But echoing mournfully through the walls, the familiar anguished cries of the other creatures held down here coiled around her.

Reaching her rooms, she stepped inside, letting one of her shadows close and lock the door behind her. She dropped to the bed, and ran a hand through her short, black hair, unseating the white headband she wore across her forehead.

A white headband to go with her white tunic, white trousers, and her white slippers, all to ensure that no one made any attempts to bleed her without authorisation.

Jade had learnt early on, that a mark on her whites was worth a mark on her body.

And she had the scars to prove it.

6

LA'SA

The man with danger in his eyes looked over Fae like he was contemplating a new set of clothes.

"Tiny little thing aren't you?" he said, coming to stand before her. A shaft of sunlight escaped the cloud cover to spear the ground between them, catching on the deep caramel of his skin. The brightness reflecting off the snow made his eyes look as though there was another world hiding behind them, the depths of them as unfathomable as the night sky, while the sun picked out shades of dark in his hair that didn't even have names.

He folded his arms, and his coat pulled tight across his biceps. He cocked his head to the side, and she was reminded acutely of a predator sizing up its prey. "How do you hold all that power in such a small body?"

Fae blinked. "I don't have any power." Her jaw clenched, teeth rattling together.

The man continued to look at her. "Uhuh," he said blandly. Something in his voice made her skin prickle.

Fae shivered again. She couldn't feel her feet, and her fingers were screaming in protest even tucked under her arms. If she didn't get somewhere warm, or at least find some more clothes, she would die of exposure in no time. She looked around, her eyes settling on the gates of silver and steel. "Where am I? How did I get here?" But she knew how. She'd followed the thread.

She hadn't skated across Eah'lara in over a year. That was part of the power she'd lost.

The man's lips twisted into a knowing smile that didn't quite reach his eyes.

Another shiver shook Fae's body so hard she almost lost her footing, her feet now completely numb in the snow.

The man's smile faltered, and he straightened, arms dropping to his sides. He looked her over as if only now realising that she stood ankle-deep in snow, wearing nothing but a nightdress. Turning from her, he ploughed back to the gates, his thick boots more than fit for purpose. Glancing over his shoulder, he called, "Keep up. The bears aren't the only ones out here who appreciate a free meal."

Reaching the wrought expanse of metal that didn't seem as simple as either silver *or* steel up close, he curled his gloved fingers around a swirl in the patterned surface, and hauled.

The gate swung outward, its groan of protest echoing through the mountain like a fog horn. Shuffling stiffly towards it, Fae peered into the gloom. Behind the gates, a high, broad tunnel disappeared into the ice and rock, the light reflecting off the snow illuminating only a short distance inside.

She hesitated. Follow the strange man with danger his eyes into the dark cave in the mountains? Or stay out here and die in the snow?

It wasn't much of a choice.

She stopped shivering.

Something flashed across the man's face. "After you," he said, and his voice held a new edge to it.

She glanced up at him, and stepped into the gloom.

He hauled the gate shut behind them, and Fae expected to be plunged into darkness. But the tunnel was bathed in a cool, blue glow, odd, refracted rays of sunlight making their way through the ice in the mountain to catch on mineral deposits in the rocks. The path ahead... sparkled.

It reminded her a little of Eah'lara, and she paused in her observations to look in on the Spirit Realm.

The nebulae of star-like spirit dust sparkled here too, the connections between all living things cast about like so many glittering threads of spider-silk. Glowing orbs floated contentedly in the ether, a handful of smaller ones drifting instinctively towards Fae. It had always been thus, even when her powers were spent; she was part-Aethyr — they were as drawn to her as she was to them.

Fae closed her eyes, feeling the warmth of the orbs brush against her skin. The voices of the Aethyr singing their peaceful symphony lulled her. She could easily fall asleep right here... It was so soothing... and warm...

"Hey!" Her strange guide snapped her from her thoughts, and she opened her eyes back to the mortal realm. His brows knitted together as he shrugged off his coat and threw it over her shoulders. It was still warm from his body, and the fur-lined collar tickled her nose. "Come on, keep moving," he said tightly, and strode off down the passageway.

Fae forced herself into a stiff jog to keep up, her blood warming just enough to remind her that it was *freezing* here. But her legs felt like lead, and she was so *tired*. Her frozen feet scraped against a jagged piece of ice, and she cried out as pain radiated up her leg.

The man glanced down and cursed under his breath.

"Why aren't you even wearing any shoes?" he demanded.

"I was *asleep*," Fae snapped back, hopping a little on one foot while she waited for the pain to dissipate from the other.

His eyebrows arched high enough to almost disappear into his hair, but he refrained from commenting further on the subject. "Come on," he said instead, and Fae heard a tone of urgency in his voice. "We're nearly there."

True to his word, a minute later they emerged from the tunnel.

Fae's mouth dropped open as she beheld what lay beyond.

The mountain was hollowed out into a vast crater of ice and rock, the far side too distant for her to see properly. Around its edges, more vaulted tunnels led away from the central core, disappearing deeper into the mountain. Natural light poured in from above, the mountain's peak forgone entirely in favour of the open sky. And all down the walls, crystals and minerals reflected pure sunlight like diamonds embedded on every surface.

In the centre of the crater, an entire town sat sheltered within the cocoon of the mountain's embrace. Small cabins hunkered down beside huge, open-sided chalets with roaring fires at their hearts. The smell of roasting food and steaming drinks made Fae's toes curl in anticipation, her mouth watering instantly.

Children dashed along cobbled streets, while parents looked on with long-suffering amusement.

But it wasn't long before some of those gazes turned to Fae as she followed her guide through the streets. She realised she must look a state, barefoot and wearing nothing but a nightdress and an oversized coat, where even the children were bundled up with gloves and thick boots. She hunched her shoulders and tried in vain to make herself as invisible as possible.

But something in the eyes of everyone they passed had Fae looking again.

"Where *are* we?" she asked again, finding herself staring into the eyes of a tiny child whose gaze twinkled with ancient wisdom.

Her companion grunted before answering.

"You are standing in the heart of La'sa," he answered. Then added a grumbled, "Finally."

Fae whipped around, her numb feet tripping on the cobbles. She couldn't have heard him right.

"La'sa?" she gaped. She'd heard of it only in stories told to her as a child. "As in the Lost Place? The legendary city of lost elves? The *Aly'sa*?"

The man tapped his ears. They were round — a human's ears.

"Not all elves," he said.

She stared at him. "La'sa," she repeated, her voice flat with disbelief.

He growled, gripping her arm to pull her along. "Yes, now keep moving or you're going to end up losing your toes."

She looked down to see that her feet had indeed turned an unhealthy grey. Biting down a retort, she let him lead her to a large chalet perched on the edge of a wide, circular plaza. He steered her inside, to a huge living space clearly designed to host a crowd, and pushed her into a plump, leather armchair set beside a crackling fire.

"Stay there," he said, before stomping from the room.

He needn't have bothered — she wasn't going anywhere. Fae pulled over a pouffe upholstered in heavily-patched corduroy, and propped her feet up in front of the fire. She was careful not to get too close to the flames, but even warming her feet gently was agony to her frozen flesh. She gritted her teeth and watched as the grey colour receded, slowly revealing a much healthier shade of pink as her circulation returned.

She wriggled her toes, glad to see that all ten responded.

Leaning forward, still with the stranger's coat around her shoulders, she pulled one foot up to rest on the opposite knee, and twisted to inspect her soles.

"Let me do that for you," a kindly voice said from the door.

Fae looked up to find a small, full-figured woman tapping the snow from her boots on the porch. She tugged the wooly hat from her head and shook a mane of silver hair loose until it settled about her shoulders. Sparkling blue eyes regarded Fae over cheeks rosy from the cold as she peeled the coat from her shoulders.

"I see Sheree wasn't telling tales," she said, nodding to the coat still draped around Fae, and dropping her own over the back of another chair. "She said she saw Luca walking through town with a new visitor." She winked, and dropped her voice to a stage-whisper. "We don't get many of those around here."

Fae smiled. A mask, to cover the maelstrom of emotions running through her mind, but until she knew what exactly she was doing here, and who these people were, she would at least maintain basic courtesy. Besides, first impressions of this woman were good. And she looked as though she might be even shorter than Fae, which didn't happen very often.

The woman pulled another pouffe over. "May I?" She indicated the foot Fae still had rested on her knee, ready to inspect. Nodding, Fae wordlessly extended her leg into her waiting hands.

"My name's Madja," the woman said as she poked and prodded the sole of Fae's foot with firm yet gentle hands. Healer's hands.

Fae would know, she had them too. Not that she'd had much occasion to use them in recent months.

"Fae," she replied when it seemed that Madja was waiting for a response. "Not that I'm not grateful for your help" — because Eah knew, she'd be an ice block by now without it — "but I need to get back..." She stumbled to a halt. *How* was she going to get back? She hadn't skated across Eah'lara since before her fight against Anson. Hadn't had the power to do so...

Just then, the door banged open, and her guide reappeared, bearing armfuls of what looked like blankets and bed linen.

"Ah, just the man," Madja said dryly, releasing Fae's foot back to the pouffe before picking up the other. Without turning her attention from the task at hand, she added, "I'd put money on Luca not having introduced himself yet." Her voice held a stern edge to it, but when she glanced up to meet Fae's eye, there was a twinkle in the blue of hers.

"I was a bit busy trying to make sure she didn't lose a toe or ten," came the terse response as Luca dumped his bundle onto a large leather settee. Digging something from the pile, he stomped over. "I was about to come and get you," he said to Madja, thrusting a pair of thick, wooly socks towards her. She made a noise in the back of her throat that sounded as though she doubted that, but she took the socks from him regardless.

"You were lucky with these," she said to Fae, rolling the socks onto her feet one at a time. "You could have sliced them open on the ice and not even known it. As it is" — she finally let go of Fae's feet and looked up — "only a couple of grazes. They'll be fine once you warm up a bit."

She stood and turned to Luca, whose eyes were dark as night now that he was in out of the bright snow. "I take it you didn't get around to explaining why Fae's here?"

Fae started. *What?*

But before she could ask the question aloud, Luca squared his shoulders and crossed his arms.

"Actually, she wisped herself here," he drawled, his voice holding an edge that had Fae's senses standing to attention. "In her sleep."

Majda's eyes widened, and she turned back to Fae.

"Well," she said, astonishment clear across her face. "Then we have even more to talk about."

Fae looked between them — at Madja's expression of amazed disbelief, and Luca's smirk of cool amusement.

She wriggled her toes in her fluffy socks. Shrugged deeper into her borrowed coat.

Something Luca had said before caught her attention, and she glanced up at Madja again. No tapered elf-ears poked out from beneath her mane of silver hair either.

So, not elves.

Then, "Who *are* you people?"

7

JUST AN ODDITY

Madja and Luca exchanged a glance.

"I told her we're in La'sa," Luca said, his posture not altering in the slightest: feet set slightly apart, shoulders squared, arms folded.

"But La'sa is the lost city of *elves*. It is a story told by elven parents, to elven children tucked up in bed at night." Fae cast a pointed look at their ears. "You're not elves."

"Exactly," Luca countered. "So it's not the lost city of elves, then, is it?"

"Or we're not in La'sa at all and you're just spinning me stories," Fae argued. Luca's intractable scowl made her want to bare her teeth and snarl at him. Regardless that it was his coat she wore.

Madja held her hands up, palms out between them.

"There is clearly a lot to talk about." She shot Luca a glare. "And we are not the only ones with a right to the conversation." She turned back to Fae. "Why don't we find you some clothes, and then we can sit down and explain everything." Her eyes flicked towards Luca, who still hadn't uncrossed his arms. "Properly."

Fae considered her bare legs sticking out from beneath Luca's coat, and decided that clothes probably weren't such a bad idea.

She glanced back up at Madja. "Alright. Thank you."

Madja jerked a brisk nod, and held out her hand.

"Good," she said, helping Fae to her feet. "You and I will go and find you some clothes." She raised an eyebrow at Fae's fluffy socks, which were at least offering some relief from the worst of the lingering tenderness. "And some boots. Luca, you fetch the others. We won't be long."

Luca's answering grunt was the only indication that he'd heard, and then Madja was whisking Fae out and into the streets again.

They passed more chalets serving hot food, the mouthwatering aromas of spiced apples and roasting sausages curling through the air to meet them at they strode through the town. A carpenter whittled on a stool in front of his workshop. A clothier hung her wares from the eaves of her timber-framed shopfront. And everywhere they went, the townsfolk waved cheerily to Madja, calling her name out across a square, exchanging a few words of greeting.

She turned to Fae. "Don't mind them," she said, although there was a quiet pride in her eyes. She returned the wave of a particularly enthusiastic child. "As I said, we don't get many visitors."

Fae retreated into the collar of Luca's coat, trying to hide away from the sea of gazes latching onto her.

Just like they did in Throldon.

At least here she wasn't famous. Just an oddity to be gawked at.

She felt the apathy — the numbness — that had been her armour for the past year tighten around her again. A palimpsest of normalcy that she'd drawn over herself to hide the shadows beneath — from herself and from the world. Apathy was far safer than what threatened to pull her under most days.

That same veil dropped over her now. It was that or breaking. And she didn't feel safe enough here to risk the latter.

Wherever *here* really was.

Mercifully, Madja steered Fae out of the bustling town centre and into another of the tunnels bored into the mountainside. Like the one she'd entered through, this one was lit by the blue glow of ice-filtered daylight, and dusted with glittering mineral rocks. Unlike the entrance tunnel, its vaulted ceiling was covered in sweeping patterns etched into the ice, rivalling some of Throldon's oldest churches. Around the periphery, smaller passageways speared from the main hall, some disappearing off on winding paths of their own, others leading to small caverns in various states of use.

"It is beautiful here," Fae said, craning her neck, trying to look everywhere at once. What looked like a class in session filled one communal space, the floor covered in rugs and cushions and fat candles in tall glass jars, while another held an enormous table surrounded by a hodgepodge assortment of chairs and stools. The walls were decorated with yet more etchings and carvings of all styles. She even spotted a swan shaped in the ice of one corridor.

Madja hummed ahead of her. "Yes, we are blessed to call such a sanctuary our home."

Fae cast a glance at the woman. The elves spoke of Arolynos as their sanctuary too. Their haven.

She wondered at the comparison, and then Madja led her down a side corridor, and stopped at one door. Knocking on the worn pine, she called out as she entered.

It was a bedroom, outfitted with simple furniture, all built of the same pine as the door. There was a bed big enough for two to sleep comfortably, draped with about a dozen different blankets, a heavy wardrobe pushed against one wall, and a small desk and chair at another. There were no windows, but the soft glow of candles set within blocks of pink salt lit the room enough that she didn't immediately notice.

A face appeared from a second doorway tucked behind the wardrobe, and a woman who could have been Madja's twin emerged.

"Ah! Sheree!" Madja reached out to the newcomer, and waved Fae in from where she hovered by the door. "Fae, this is Sheree, domestic goddess extraordinaire, and my sister."

Sheree blushed at the attention, batting away the compliment. "I just like to make sure everything and everyone is looked after, is all."

"Well, Fae needs some looking after," Madja said, giving Fae a little push forward. "Do you think we have some spare clothes she can wear while she's visiting?" She gave Fae a look that spoke volumes about the extraordinary nature of that "visit". "She's arrived rather... unprepared for the weather."

Whatever Sheree thought of Fae's state of dress, she didn't make any mention of it. She simply clicked her tongue, as if having strangers turn up in nightclothes was perfectly normal, and she had only to locate the nearest set of spares put aside for just such a thing.

"I'm sure we have something that will fit you — you look about Irya's size," she said finally. "I'll go and see what I can find." And she bustled from the room.

Fae turned back to Madja. This was all beginning to make her dizzy. Who were these people? And why had she come here? She'd followed the Aethyr's threads through Eah'lara before, but that had been back when she was in full possession of her powers — and awake. When she fought Anson, she gave up everything she'd been gifted by the Aethyr in order to defeat him, in order to tear his corrupt influence from the world. For the past year, she'd been Spiritchild in no more than name.

But this...

...was all too much. Too many questions. She didn't know where to even begin. She was leagues from home, powerless, and alone. These people... she didn't know them. Didn't know if their smiles were laced with poison. If their clothes hid daggers for her back. Panic swelled. Her head filled with thunderclouds, pressure building. She felt like she ought to feel tears burning in her eyes but her armour was working too well. And she couldn't break here. She shoved it all down. She blinked and brought her focus back to the room tucked within a mountain of rock and ice. Madja was watching her, a look of puzzlement on her face.

"You really don't know why you're here do you?" she said.

Fae shook her head. "No, I really don't understand..." she turned about, arms extended, taking in the room, the mountain, the town within it. "Well, any of this." She sighed, casting her mind back to the monument that had been the beginning of everything for her. She supposed that travelling to new places and finding herself faced with people she wasn't expecting wasn't *entirely* unfamiliar territory.

"And I can't stay. I have people who need me..." She faltered. *Did* they need her?

Madja's blue eyes were needle-sharp as they watched her. Fae suspected there wasn't much that escaped the woman's notice.

Sheree returned in a flurry, dropping a pile of clothes on the bed. "Right, I've got a few spares from around the place." She pulled a tunic woven of some material Fae didn't recognise, and held it up to her. "I think I've got your sizing right." She grabbed a couple more items from the stack. "Go and try these on, and we'll start from there." Thrusting an armful of clothes at her, she took Fae by the shoulders and guided her to the second door in the room.

It turned out to be a small bathing chamber. A wash basin sat upon a small cabinet, and a deep copper tub with two huge faucets hanging over the side took pride of place in the middle of the room. Through yet another door was the privy.

The stone floor was warm underfoot, and Fae lifted one foot, as if expecting to find something different underneath.

"Heated from the hot springs under the mountain," Sheree explained when she saw Fae's expression. She pointed to the clothes in her arms. "Try those on and let me know what you think." And she pulled the door closed behind her.

When she emerged, Fae looked as though she belonged in this strange place.

Sheree had discarded the first tunic she'd given her, replacing it instead with a jumper of impossibly soft wool, knitted in seemingly every colour on offer. Shades of blue and red and purple and green cocooned her. Fae didn't think she'd ever want to take it off. Sheree laughed when she said so, her eyes twinkling with delight, and said she was sure she could find another. She'd also found Fae a pair of long, thick leggings, and brown leather boots that came up to her knees. Lastly, she passed her a shearling-lined coat that came halfway down her thighs, and a fluffy scarf that matched her socks.

"There." Sheree stood back to admire her work. Folding her arms, she glanced at Madja, who'd commandeered the chair.

"That's more like it," she agreed with a nod.

Fae plucked at her sleeve. "You didn't have to, really..." she said feebly, secretly very glad that they had.

"Oh, psh," Sheree said, dismissing the comment with a wave.

Madja chuckled, and the sound was warm and bright. "Oh yes we did." Her eyes danced with mischief. "Or we'd've had more than one juvenile tripping over themselves gawking at those matchstick legs of yours. And I'm not just talking about the young ones." She threw Fae a wink that had her blushing. "We'll have to feed you up while you're here, girl."

"But" — Fae's mind snagged on the implication — "I can't stay here." she repeated. She looked between the sisters. Surely they knew that?

Madja's smile dimmed. Sheree suddenly became very interested in the floor.

"Yes." Madja cleared her throat. "Thank you, Sheree." She stood, and gestured to the door. "Shall we?"

Uncomfortably aware of the tension that had seeped into the room at those four little words, Fae followed Madja out into the corridor, and back through the ice tunnels.

"Madja," she said after a minute of walking in silence. "Am I a prisoner?"

Madja stopped dead in the middle of the corridor, and spun around to face her.

"Dear child, no!" she hissed, and Fae immediately regretted the look of horror on the woman's face. In this strange place, her instinct was to err on the side of wariness. Nothing had set off any alarm bells, but that didn't mean there wasn't something sinister going on. But despite all that, Fae couldn't help but feel like Madja and Sheree were good people. And while her brief experience of Luca hadn't exactly been warming, she didn't think he meant her harm.

Madja spent a long moment scanning her face, although what she was looking for, Fae couldn't fathom. Eventually, she let out a long breath, and ran a trembling hand through her silver hair.

"I'm sorry," Fae said, alarmed at the waves of distress pouring from her. "I didn't mean to... I just..." She stumbled for words. "I just don't understand why I'm here. And you all seem to know. And I need to get back. And—"

Madja reached out to place a hand on her arm. "It's alright, child." She patted her absently. "There are a few more who will want to meet you, and then we can explain everything we know." She offered Fae a strained smile, patted her on the arm once more, then turned back to leading the way through the tunnels.

It quickly became clear that they were climbing through the mountain, the light peering through the ice brightening the further they went. The bustle of the living quarters and communal areas faded away behind them, and soon they were surrounded by nothing but ice and silence.

Finally, Madja brought Fae to a room at the end of a corridor of light. It looked just like all the other spaces given over to communal use that she'd seen below, but instead of being lit by candles and salt lamps, this room was bathed in sunlight.

It was as if the entire far wall of the room was a solid sheet of glass, the ice so clear that she could see through it and out over the snowy plains beyond.

Aside from the breathtaking view, the room held only an assortment of armchairs, arranged in a circle around a huge hunk of some type of raw crystal, its surface alternating between rough, white edges and smooth, glassy facets that reflected the sunlight to cast rainbows on the walls.

There were thirteen seats. Four were occupied.

"Fae," Madja walked over to stand behind an empty chair. "Let me introduce you to the High Magi of La'sa."

8

MAGI

Fae gawped. The High *what*?

"The High Magi of La'sa," a familiar voice repeated, as if reading her thoughts. Fae looked up to see Luca sitting forward in a wide bucket of a chair, the deep-padded back as low as the broad arms. His eyes were alert, watching her, and she had that same distinct feeling that something *other* prowled behind them.

"It's a long, involved story," Madja winced, almost apologetically.

"Please, Madja, don't undersell it." A tall, powerfully-built man with blue-black hair rose from his seat — little more than a high kitchen stool with a short, wooden back — and stalked across the circle with languid strides to stand before them. "It's a tale centuries in the telling, and *unimaginably* dull for the last five." He inclined his head, a smile of pure arrogance gracing his lips. "Kallis," he purred, lifting a hand to his chest even as his eyes of burning copper scanned Fae lazily from head to toe, and back up again to meet her eyes. His smile widened. "And what a *pleasure* it is to meet you, Fae."

"Behave, Kallis," a voice that chimed like the tinkle of small bells came from behind him. "At least let the poor girl sit down before you try to invite her to your bed." Madja levelled a remonstrative look at Kallis, who merely shrugged innocently, hands upheld, and shot Fae a roguish wink before returning to his stool.

Madja guided Fae into one of the free seats, and sat beside her.

The one who'd called Kallis off was a willowy woman whose pale, sea-foam-green eyes stood out in stark contrast to the rich sable of her skin.

"We must apologise for Kallis," she said dryly, toying with one of the hundreds of ebony braids cascading over her shoulders. "We'd have thrown him out to the bears centuries ago, except that he's actually rather useful." Kallis gave a half-bow from his seat.

Madja cleared her throat. "Fae," she said. "I'd like you to meet Demilda" — the woman waved delicately from her high-backed chair — "and Terrence." The final figure at the circle, a short, stocky-looking, bearded man with brown eyes the same colour as his hair, nodded his greeting.

"Luca you've met." He glared at them. Fae was beginning to think he didn't have any other expressions.

Then Madja spoke again, and Fae's thoughts on the people in the chairs evaporated.

"Now that you're here, I don't know where to start," she said. "We've been trying to get your attention for so long, I hadn't considered that you might not know why."

Luca saved her the trouble of finding the right words.

"Last year, there was a massive outburst of power in the world," he said, cutting straight to the point. The rest of them went suddenly very still. "Big enough to destroy a god." He fixed Fae with a flat stare. "Sound familiar?"

Fae swallowed, remembering all too well the events that replayed in her nightmares.

"It was only a piece of a god," she said, not sure whether to defend herself or not. It felt a lot like she was on trial for saving the world.

Luca gave a curt nod. "Well that victory had a cost," he continued, and his voice was lethally quiet. "Have you noticed anything unusual since then? Anything that wasn't happening before?"

Fae frowned, casting her mind back over the last year. The shimmering beauty of Eah'lara had recovered in the wake of her battle with Anson, the spiritual connections returning to fill the void that had spread around Throldon under the god's influence. The races of the world had begun rebuilding together, creating a united Arland for the first time in centuries. Even the reclusive dragons were getting involved.

And then an echo of her mother's words came back to her, hitting her like a thunder strike.

I've never heard of so many quakes before. And they only started after you defeated Anson.

"The earthquakes?" she whispered, horror uncurling in her gut. The earth had first bucked beneath her feet in her final defeat of the god, as if it, too, rejected the scourge above.

But what if it had been the opposite?

"*I* did that?" The quakes had started as no more than rumblings underfoot. Easily dismissed. But now...

The most recent quake in Throldon had brought down newly-built walls. What would the next one do?

"Wait—" A thought occurred to her. "How did you know that was me?"

Madja reached over and gripped her hand. "Your power comes from the same well as ours — they are drawn to each other." She smiled. "We did not call to you, we called to your power. And your power answered." Seeing the horror creep over Fae's face, Madja squeezed her hand. "It is not your fault. The god needed to go. You were just the conduit to achieving that. The vessel for the required power. But the release of that power you held — enough to prise him from the world — has left a rent, deep in the very fabric of the earth. You've seen the quakes. There are other signs occurring elsewhere — tidal waves flooding island nations out to sea, and mountains of fire waking after centuries of sleep." Madja's eyes met Fae's, and hope blossomed there.

"We need your help to repair the damage."

Fae blinked at her. "But, I don't have any power left." She looked over at Luca. He'd mentioned her power before too. "I used all of it. It's gone." She stared down at her empty hands, and clenched them into fists. "I have nothing left."

Kallis snorted loudly. "My dear, one does not simply run out of Source Magic. As Madja said, you are a conduit, not a finite reservoir. A Magi's power comes straight from the source of all energies, from the earth itself." He spread his arms, taking in the room and everything else beyond it. "And it is very much still here."

Fae's brow wrinkled in confusion. "But my powers came from the Aethyr, not the earth. I'm not a Magi."

"The Aethyr might have given you Eah'lara, Spiritchild — yes, we know who you are." Demilda smiled knowingly when Fae started at the use of her unique designation. "But you are also Magi."

"It's possible you have a distant ancestor who was Magi," Madja said gently to her side. "Or perhaps you were always meant to tap into the earth's power — it goes that way sometimes." She sighed, and the sound was almost forlorn. "Maybe the Aethyr, in imbuing you with their power, unwittingly granted you access to the Source as well."

"However it happened," Luca cut in, straightening in his seat, "you are undoubtedly wielding Source Magic. We have felt the ripples even here."

"But—" Fae cast about for something, anything, that made sense. "I've never even used 'Source Magic' before."

"Haven't you?" Luca leaned forward, bracing his arms on his knees. "Haven't you ever noticed the elements responding to you? The wind, or rain? Or fire? Those are manifestations of the Source." The indigo of his eyes flashed, as if he already knew the answer. "Think back, and then tell me you've never used Source Magic."

Fae opened her mouth to argue, and then a flash of memory interrupted her.

You burned. The wind blew around you. Like a tornado. But just around you. Ty's voice filled her head from so long ago, the words uttered in the wake of an uncontrolled release of her power. Power she'd thought belonged to the Aethyr.

But... the Aethyr had always said their power lived in connections, in tethering living things to one another.

And, if she dug through her faded memories, through the muddied eons of knowledge gifted by her Aethyrial guides, they'd never once laid claim to the fire, the wind, or the storms.

The storm of her becoming. Or the one of her undoing.

As if summoned by the thought, her nightmares rose up again, and her memories were thrown back to that day.

To the rage of wind and lightning that had whipped around her and Lady Black as they fought. The storm that had torn through the Great Hall to cut her off from everyone else, left her alone to fight for her life, and the lives of everyone in that city.

Those terrible events played out in her mind's eye again, only this time she was awake to feel the trembling in the mountain as she remembered the feel of her body breaking. Of the air stopping dead in her chest.

She felt the ground beneath her feet shudder — another quake — and she remembered what it felt like to know she was dying.

Fae fought the crushing fear of her nightmares to remember where she was. She'd survived Anson. She had not died.

But these people, these... *Magi*... were asking her to wield that power again.

The power that had almost gotten her killed.

A wave of panic surged through her, and she couldn't breathe again, couldn't move. Her heart thrashed in her chest as if it wanted to escape. And she was again frozen in that helpless moment where she had nothing left to give but death.

A crashing roar filled her ears, and part of her mind was distantly aware of the cries of the Magi as the room shook around her. Shards of ice tumbled from the ceiling to shatter on the floor, their breaking a delicate counterpoint to the deep rumble as the mountain itself groaned in protest. It sounded like Anson's roar, and the shattering of the windows in the Great Hall.

And then Luca was in front of her, gripping her shoulders so hard it hurt.

"This power moves through you, whether you want it or not." His eyes blazed, and it was like she could see the universe inside them. "If you cannot learn to control it, it will destroy you, and everything around you." The ground quaked again, and he shook her roughly, his voice rising above the din. "You will bring down cities, with everyone you love inside."

The words were a slap in the face, and they wrenched Fae from the nightmares that plagued her.

Forcing herself to breathe — to remember that she *could* breathe — Fae redirected her attention to the feel of the chair beneath her fingertips, to the ground beneath her feet, to the bone-crushing grip of Luca's hands on her shoulders.

And as the room came back into focus, she saw that the Magi had all leapt from their chairs, their arms outstretched to the walls, as if expecting to hold the very mountain itself upright. And the walls were... shimmering... curtained in light of different colours. White and blue and earthy brown and vibrant green rippled across the surface of the ice like gently lapping waves on a shallow shore. And every now and then, shadows skittered over them all, like a web holding the colours together.

Fae breathed again, just as the tremors subsided, both in the mountain, and in her, until nothing but stillness remained.

The Magi relaxed their stances, and the shimmering curtains flickered out, leaving the glassy blue sheen of the ice, and the endless white of the snow visible beyond. Luca released her, and straightened.

"What was that?" Fae pointed to where the colours had been.

Demilda brushed at her skirts, flicking a braid back over her shoulder before returning to her seat. "Just a little of our magic to offset a little of yours."

"If that's only a little, I'd hate to think what she could do with full control," Terrence grumbled, dropping into his chair of worn, patched leather. Kallis grabbed his stool and spun it to straddle the back. Luca retreated to his.

Fae gaped at them. And then something about what they'd said caught at the corner of her mind. She brought her gaze back to Luca, still watching her.

"You think *I'm* doing that? That I'm *still* doing it?" She looked at Madja, hoping to see something else in her eyes. "Even if I summoned wind and storms before, I've never moved the ground. I thought you said that it was the power released fighting Anson that caused the earthquakes?"

"It did." Madja dipped her head, and came to stand beside her seat. "And normally, outbursts of untrained power like yours would just be absorbed, unnoticed. But with the damage, there's... a tear, a rift in the fabric of the earth, and the capacity to absorb rogue power surges seems to have weakened with it."

"So you think I'm making it worse." Fae's voice was barely more than a whisper.

Madja crouched down before her. "But we can help you." Her lips quirked into an ironic smile. "We sought you out to help us, but it looks like we will need to help you first. We've all had to learn to control our powers at some point. You can too. We'll teach you."

Fae shook her head. They weren't getting it: she had nothing left to control. But she said, "How can you want to help me when all I've done is break what I tried to fix?"

"We don't have much of a choice here, darling," Kallis drawled lazily from across the circle.

Madja shot him a scowl. Kallis threw placating hands up and beat a hasty retreat.

Madja turned back to Fae. "Let's teach you to control Source Magic at least, so you're not releasing untempered bursts of power anymore." She smiled, warm and comforting. "We can talk about mending rifts afterwards."

Terrence cleared his throat. "One could argue that the fractures in the earth need fixing either way, Madja," he rumbled. His voice was deep and gravelly; the kind of voice Fae instantly wanted to listen to.

"I might remind you, Terrence, that no good ever came of forcing a Magi to wield magics against their will." Madja fixed him with a glare so cold, even Kallis looked content to stay out of the line of fire. "Especially an untrained one." For a second, it looked as though Terrence might argue his point, the golden brown of his cheeks reddening. But something in Madja's gaze checked him, and he swallowed his words.

Madja continued, "We have plenty of other Magi here. We have other options. We just..." She let out a small laugh, admonishing herself. "Well, we thought you knew what you were doing already."

"Sorry," Fae whispered to her feet. Sorry for not having the power they needed to fix what she'd broken. Sorry for not being the person she used to be. Sorry for all of it.

Madja smiled softly. "Don't worry on it for now. Let's start at the beginning and get control over the Source Magics. The rest can come after." She stood and offered a hand to Fae. "For now, let's get you settled and show you around. I'm sure you have plenty of other questions."

Fae nodded dumbly, her mind whirring as she allowed Madja to help her to her feet. She understood now why the woman had been cagey about her returning to Throldon.

Pushing the crushing weight of her thoughts to the side, Fae embraced the numbness that had kept her afloat until now. There was too much for her to deal with all at once. Too much to worry about. She needed to focus on the one thing she needed most: getting home. But how?

She'd have to stay long enough to prove to them that she didn't have anything left, no matter how much that hurt. Maybe then they'd help her return to Throldon. And hopefully it wouldn't be too late.

It should be easy enough. She would know if she had powers. She would feel... something. Wouldn't she?

As for the rest of it... she wasn't sure what she would do about the rest of it. She didn't even know if there was anything she *could* do, although these people seemed convinced that there was.

Her head throbbed. This was too much.

"I'll walk you back to your rooms." Fae looked up to find Luca standing beside her again, his expression unreadable.

"Thank you Luca," Madja said, and it seemed that in the last few minutes, an immense weariness had come over her too. She looked at Fae with a tired smile, and said, "I'll stop by later, if that's alright with you?"

Fae nodded again. "Sure." She didn't quite trust herself with more words right now. And when Luca extended his arm to the door, she let him lead the way from the room.

They walked in silence all the way to the rooms where Sheree had brought her clothes, Fae lost in her own thoughts, Luca apparently lost in his.

He stopped on the threshold as she entered and dropped to sit on the bed.

"Madja is right," he said, arms folded as he leant against the doorframe. "Magi are conduits through which the earth's magics flow. We are vessels. Valves, even. And unstable or unwilling Magi make dangerously unpredictable conduits." He pushed himself off the door to stand upright. "But she's lying to you too."

Fae turned to look at him. Madja didn't seem the type to lie. But then, she'd only known her a few hours, if that.

"She's trying to protect you." Luca's eyes flickered, and Fae could see there was more to it than he was saying. But when his gaze fixed on her again, it was hard, and unwavering.

"You're powerful. You might not believe it yet, but you are." He paused, as if debating whether or not to go on.

Coming to a decision, he continued. "We've already tried to shore up the damage in the earth. With everything we've got." He turned and began walking down the corridor, leaving Fae scrabbling to the doorway to hear the rest.

"You work it out."

9

BLOOD AND WINGS

The beasts were to be moved in one day. And Jade's presence was non-negotiable.

She submitted herself for vialling as ordered, sitting straight-backed in the steel-framed chair as another acolyte pierced her skin to draw five vials of her life's blood, her shadows hovering by the door.

As she watched dark red pool in the vials, the screams of the other creatures imprisoned down here echoed through the maze, as if they could smell her submission. Her betrayal.

Finally, the acolyte stoppered the last vial, and placed it on a tray with the others, their glass sides clinking softly together. He swabbed her arm, putting pressure on the pinprick until it stopped bleeding. Then he sprayed it with a clear coating of sealant, to ensure she would not bleed any more than had been collected.

She'd often wondered what would happen to the men responsible for drawing her blood if traces of it were found on her clothes after these sessions. Would they be punished? Would she?

Needless to say, she'd never needed to find out. They were nothing if not meticulous in their work.

Whatever that was.

The acolyte dismissed her, and finally, she returned to her rooms.

When she reached the door, one of her shadows stepped forward. He was tall, about six feet, with dark eyes, deeply bronzed skin, and near-black hair. She might once have thought him attractive. But she didn't think such things anymore.

Jade stepped over her threshold, and her shadow closed the door behind her. The scrape of the iron bolt sliding home on the other side was the only sound, and then silence.

She'd picked the lock on the door in her early days — a skill she'd honed before her life was confined by stone walls. The next day, the bolt had been fitted across the outside, and she'd earned her first lashes.

And learned that it wasn't just doors and locks that held her here.

Thoughts buzzed like a thousand bees inside her head, keeping sleep at arm's length. She lay back on the narrow bed, and contemplated the bond that really kept her here.

Different from the other bonds she held, this one was forced upon her. It pulled at her blood, clung to her very cells like oil, black and sticky, the tether taut and strong.

Without it, she could probably leave here whenever she wanted. Walk right out the front door.

She toyed with the familiar tension in her mind of that ever-present restraint. Tugged at it ever so slightly. Worked a little slack into it, and let go.

With that bond, she could never leave.

Not for the first time, she wondered if that was such a bad thing.

Her accommodations with the Brotherhood were better than Ixio had ever given her. Ixio, who'd had her scrabbling through tight caves searching for the valuable gem deposits that grew in the dark and damp.

She fingered the bond in her mind again. Tugged at it. Let it go.

Once, Pharro had been one of many humble ports dotted along the desert's edge. But after the War of the Races, humanity had scattered to the four corners, and it had since grown into a city of as many colours as there were fish in the sea; people could trace their lineage to the far north as easily as to the next town over. It was crowded and loud. Stone buildings better suited to the cooler north crammed in beside the low, sand-coloured homes of the south. Graceful minarets shared space with stocky towers. New styles sprang up throughout the centuries, hybrids squatting awkwardly between the originals, all of them stitched together by winding alleys and the calls of hawkers selling their wares.

Life in Pharro had always been down to the luck of the draw. A rare few were born to riches. Most weren't.

Some of the children she'd known before were fortunate enough to work in the homes of wealthy families, with rooms to themselves. But sometimes those were the employers who thought their money gave them the right to treat their workers like property: bodies to do with however they pleased.

Others worked for the poorest traders, with little more than a dirt floor to sleep on and a palm roof overhead, but those were the ones that were treated like family. Being a worker in Pharro was a hard life; sometimes that was the only family they had.

Ixio hadn't been poor, but he'd hoarded his wealth like a drake squatting over its treasure, and treated his workers like dirt. But he'd treated everyone like dirt equally, unless they were paying him. And he'd never hurt anyone, unless they weren't.

He'd slept on a pallet in his office while the workers slept on the floor of his warehouse. They'd all eaten from the same pot, and looked out for each other. No one had kept vials of her blood for whatever dark purposes they deemed fit.

They'd been a kind of family.

She'd been free.

She tugged at her bond. Released it.

It didn't matter now anyway.

Ixio was still dead, and there was no escaping the Brotherhood.

The scrape of the lock woke her early the next morning.

She was upright and alert by the time the door swung open.

This time, instead of another nameless acolyte, Brother Gerard appeared on the threshold. With pale skin and cruel eyes, he was one of her least favourite of the Brotherhood.

"Come," was all the warning she got before he swept away again, leaving the door open behind him.

Jade surged forward. For one of the Brothers to come himself was unusual in extreme, and couldn't mean anything good. Pushing her instant trepidation aside, she hastened from her room, ignoring her shadows as they fell into step behind, and jogged to catch up with Brother Gerard.

Her eyes traced his back as he strode ahead. There was a stiffness to his broad shoulders, his footsteps clipped and hurried.

Something was definitely wrong.

Then Jade heard the shrieks of the other creatures down here. And her heart sank.

Schooling her features into her habitual mask of cool indifference, she followed calmly behind Brother Gerard as he led the way to the cages.

As soon as they entered the wing of cells set aside for the creatures held here, she saw why she'd been summoned.

And it took all of her will power not to back from the chamber and run.

As she had submitted to having her blood taken the previous night, so the Brotherhood had also apparently decided to replenish their stocks from each of the six dragons imprisoned here before moving them.

The creatures were hysterical.

The large red one thrashed about his cage, the bars biting into his ruined wings as he flapped them wildly in the too-small space. The green was curled into the back corner of his enclosure, hissing viciously at anyone who came near. The delicate silver female was shaking as she paced the floor of her cage, one of her flanks worn almost raw by constantly scraping against the bars, her scales dull and flaking.

Each of the six displayed their distress openly and in their own way. An acolyte leaned against the far wall, one arm clutched tightly with the other, the sleeve of his blood-red robes dark and wet. It was enough to tell Jade why the Brother had come for her.

She fought against her instinct to balk at the horrors here, and approached the wall of cages.

Halfway across the room, six pairs of reptilian eyes swivelled to her.

The room went deadly still. Except Jade. She stepped up to the caged red, wrapped her hands around the iron bars imprisoning him.

He watched her, the bronze eyes he shared with his siblings unblinking.

Jade willed her face to be dispassionate, to not reveal what went on beneath.

Inside, she stroked one of the other bonds held within her.

The red, just as practiced as she was at this, did not alter his expression.

Brother Gerard gripped her roughly by the arm and hauled her away from the cages.

"You submit," he snarled at the dragons, his cold, cruel eyes narrowing dangerously as he pinned each of them with a venomous glare.

The red hissed at him, and twin tendrils of dread and pride unfurled inside Jade.

She held the eyes of the green while Brother Gerard stared down the red.

Don't be afraid, she willed the dragon. *Don't be afraid.*

Brother Gerard dragged Jade closer again, and shoved her up against the cages, the bars digging into her cheek as he held her there with one hand.

"You submit," he hissed again.

With his other hand, he gripped her little finger and wrenched it back. Until it snapped.

Pain radiated through her hand and travelled up her arm. Jade breathed, and swallowed it.

Sank below the part of her that felt, and let the pain out with her breath.

The silver cried out this time, but the dragon didn't move.

"You *submit!*" Brother Gerard roared, and broke the next finger along.

Jade grunted, and found another bond within her.

Don't be afraid, she begged as she stroked it, screwing her eyes shut to hide the pain she knew must surely be showing there.

The dragons went motionless. Not a sound came from one of them.

Jade cracked her eyes open. Six gazes of pure, molten hatred were turned on Brother Gerard.

Her pride bloomed bright and beautiful in this place of horrors.

Inside, she gathered up and held close the six bonds that she wouldn't be without. The six bonds that were woven into her very soul. The bonds that held her heart.

Brother Gerard hauled her from the cages again and threw her from him. One of her shadows caught her before she could fall to the ground. Probably because he knew what would befall him and his partner if Jade were to shed a drop of blood onto her white tunic.

She was the only one in the whole Sanctum dressed in white. Besides the Sorcerer Supreme himself.

She was the only one whose blood was deemed valuable enough to warrant it.

Jade cradled her hand to her chest, fighting the nausea that rose with every movement.

Brother Gerard barked orders, and her shadows flanked her as each cage was opened, and a red-robed acolyte admitted to gather the required vials of blood. The red dragon shook with promises of retribution, but he stood his ground as his sample was taken. His eyes held hers, and between them passed a different sort of promise.

One that Jade fully intended to fulfil.

Half an hour later, Jade's fingers were splinted — the breaks all closed and bloodless, as was the Brotherhood's way — and she was back in her room.

She lay back upon the bed and closed her eyes.

In her mind, she visualised the bonds within her.

The six that were woven into the fibres of her being. That held her heart in the circle of their wings.

And the one of oil and blood.

She ran mental fingers down the bonds of wings and talons, caressing them as she went.

I'm okay, she promised.

And then she picked up the bond that had been forced upon them. The one that held all of them here.

Toying with that tether of blood and oil, she tugged at it gently, working a little more slack into the restraint. And let it drop.

10

NOTHING SPECIAL

Fae was lost.

After a restless night trying to silence the thoughts circling through her head, she abandoned all hopes of sleep and ran herself a deep bath in the copper tub adjacent to her room.

Hot water gushed from one faucet, and she added a little cold until the temperature was just right for her to sink into, the surface coming up over her shoulders. She stayed until her skin was wrinkled and papery, but even the soothing warmth of the waters couldn't calm her mind.

On top of the fact that these Magi seemed to think she'd somehow been unwittingly wielding their Source Magic for over a year — despite having no power left in her to wield — there was still the small matter of a nameless army supposedly marching on Throldon that her friends were dealing with.

Not that she knew what to do about that either.

She needed to go home.

Fae rose from the bath and dried herself with a thick, fluffy towel wide enough to skim the floor. She shimmied into some more of the leggings Sheree had found her, and dragged another oversized jumper over her head — this one in so many shades of green it reminded her of Arolynos — pulling her hair free to hang loose down her back. Stuffing her feet into the boots and looping her scarf around her neck, she left to track down Madja in search of more answers, hoping that it was at least morning; the soft blue glow of the mountain gave little away to guess the time of day.

It turned out she did not remember the way as well as she'd thought.

She'd been sure she remembered the route through the passageways from the day before — down the main thoroughfare, past the communal space on the left, then there was the swan carved into the ice, down the hall to the right...

She turned in a circle. Nothing stood out as familiar. Frustration welled, but it was safely behind a familiar curtain of apathy. If she let it out, there was no telling what other emotions would follow.

Fae growled at a pointedly blank section of wall.

"Oof, what did it do? Insult your mother?" She flushed with embarrassment as a man she hadn't met yet approached from further along the corridor. Tall and broad-shouldered, he moved with the confidence of a warrior. His dark hair was shorn the same length from the crown of his head to the stubble shading his jaw, and his eyes were a blend of every colour: vivid blues and greens swirled like paints dropped into water, a starburst of earthy brown radiating out from the centre.

"So?" He grinned, and the white of his teeth contrasted sharply with the deep olive hue of his skin. "What did this cur of a wall do to make you snarl so? Tell me, I am known for defending a young lady's honour."

"Please, stop," Fae choked out a laugh, cheeks heating. She coughed to clear her throat. The man's eyes twinkled with amusement while she attempted to collect her wits, but he politely did as asked and refrained from saying more, crossing arms of thickly corded muscle across his sleeveless leather jerkin as he waited.

"I'm lost," she admitted finally, and the words hit deeper than he knew. "The wall had the misfortune of being closest when I realised, that's all."

"Ah," he said sympathetically. "Well then, let me help you get to where you need to go, and we can leave the wall to be about its business." He offered her his arm, and a lop-sided smile when she hesitated. "There is not a person in La'sa you cannot trust," he said, then tipped his head in thought. "Perhaps Kallis, but I think he would say the same, which in itself tells you a lot."

Fae rolled her eyes, remembering the High Magi from the day before. "Yes, I think I might agree with you there." She eyed the warrior with the easy smile, his arm outstretched, and decided he rather reminded her of Aren when he turned on his charm. "Thank you...?"

"Alexi," the man supplied with a little half-bow. "At your service."

Fae smiled. "Thank you, Alexi. I'm Fae."

"I thought you were lost?" He threw her a puzzled look, his brows knitting together before his face broke into another dazzling smile. "I know who you are, Fae. It is not often we see a new face around here."

"So I keep hearing."

"Just don't let it go to your head." He winked at her. "So, where to?"

"Town, I think," Fae replied. "I need to speak to Madja."

"Then let us go and find Madja." Alexi stepped to the side, indicating the way to the town — she'd been going in completely the wrong direction.

"It's so easy to get turned around here," Fae said as they walked through the tunnelled hallways. The soft blue glow was supplemented occasionally with tridents of candles set into the wall, the stands thrust deep into the ice. "What time is it? Is it even daylight?"

Alexi chuckled, and the sound rumbled deep in his chest. "You'll find that we've all rather given up worrying about time here." He cast a sideways glance down at her. "Whether it's light or dark, there's always someone about."

They emerged onto the main thoroughfare that opened out to the centre of the mountain, and finally stepped into the dawn.

Over one side of the mountain ridge, the watery blue of the sky was washed with pale yellow, not a hint of cloud in sight. And in the hollow of the mountain, the town was indeed awake, and humming with activity.

"We should check in the Meeting House," Alexi said, pointing towards a familiar plaza in the centre, and the large chalet Luca had brought her to before. "If anyone knows where Madja is, they will be there."

Fae turned to look up at him. "Thank you for your help, I know where I am now. Please, don't let me keep you any longer."

Alexi's lips twitched into an amused smile. "Not at all, fair Fae. Should you ever need rescuing from the Warrens again, I am at your service." He sketched another bow, deeper this time, and flashed her a grin. "I hope I will see you again soon." Then he strode off through the cobbled streets, leaving her standing at the edge of the town.

The air was biting, and she immediately regretted not bringing the shearling coat Sheree had given her, but there was no way she'd make it back to her room now without a guide. Hugging her arms around herself, she made a beeline for the Meeting House, her boots clomping over the ground as she went. A fine dusting of snow coated everything, the cobbles slick underfoot, and she narrowly avoided breaking her neck when she lost her footing, throwing her arms out wildly to catch her balance.

Despite that, she made it to the chalet in one piece, hands cupped in front of her face to chase the chill from her fingertips.

She stomped up the steps onto the wrap-around porch, kicking the snow from her boots even as she continued to try breathing life back into her fingers.

"You know, most people would choose a coat in this weather." She looked up to see Luca leaning against the frame of the Meeting House, just as he'd been when she first opened her eyes on the snowy plains.

Choosing to ignore his jibe — and the way his gaze made every hair stand on end — Fae went to walk past him. "I'm looking for Madja. Do you know where she is?"

Luca straightened to let her pass, and trailed her inside. "She's not here," he said.

She turned from the empty lounge area to face him. "Do you know where I can find her? I have some more questions."

He crossed his arms. "She's resting. Madja tends to prefer the twilight hours. She'll probably appear around noon."

"Oh." Fae fought the instinct to tuck her hands under her arms again. The warmth of the room was slow to revive her fingers, and the tips tingled as sensation crept back in. "Um, alright." She really did not want to talk to him, but she needed to say something. "I need to... get word back to Throldon. They'll be wondering where I've gone." She looked at his intractable stare, his folded arms, and thought he looked about as likely to help her as a snow bear.

"I'd say you need to train," he said flatly. "We don't know when another of your power surges will hit, seeing as you don't seem to have any control over them, and I don't fancy having a mountain fall on top of us."

Fae glared at him. There he was again, telling her she was wielding power she just plain didn't have. "Look, if you won't help me, I can always skate back myself, and you can figure out your Source Magic problem yourselves." She felt bad for saying it, but damn it if his face didn't just make her want to dig her heels in.

His lips curved up in a smile that didn't reach his eyes, and the hairs on the back of her neck prickled. "We call it wisping here. And it's quite a rare skill. But tell me—" He stalked closer to her until they were almost toe-to-toe. "When was the last time you did that conscious? You said you were asleep yesterday."

Fae went quiet.

She hadn't done anything more than *look* at Eah'lara since Anson. Since the day she danced with death.

"I haven't been able to summon any power since that day," she admitted in a whisper. The day she'd thrown all of her powers into a god and hoped it was enough.

It very nearly hadn't been.

"Well we know that's not true." His voice dropped to little more than hers. "If we've been feeling your power surges from here."

"But I haven't *done* anything," she insisted. She'd tried. Repeatedly. At least once a day, she reached for the place where her power had once been. She hadn't told anyone, not even Sheha. Because every day, she came up empty-handed.

And the shadows inside her took a step closer to pulling her under.

Luca arched one eyebrow. "Like you didn't do anything yesterday?" He gave her a look that reminded her of how Sheha looked at students she suspected of being intentionally dense. "You're doing things unconsciously, which is even more dangerous. You may have lost your handle on the power, but like we said before, you are a conduit. The magic will come through you either way. You need to learn how to control the flow."

He sighed, and ran a hand through the dark strands of his hair, unseating her impression of him as the intractable predator. "Look, we can get a message to your friends. You can write it yourself. But you'd be a fool to try and go yourself in this state. If you even can."

Fae felt her temper flare at how casually he talked about the fracture inside her. The hole that made her feel so much less than inadequate. Once, she had saved people with her powers. But now, she was nothing. A symbol. Nothing special. Not even useful.

And now, these Magi kept telling her she was using power she *didn't have*.

That she was worse than useless — she was dangerous.

After everything she'd gone through, that hurt more than anything.

"I don't know what you think you want from me," she snarled at him, a wounded animal, "but I'm telling you, I *don't have it*." And as the words came out, the idea that she might be capable of hurting people burned like acid in her gut. "I'm not some earth-shattering Magi." And then she was shouting. "I am *powerless!*"

The silence left in the wake of her declaration was deafening. Her ragged breathing the only sound. Luca's eyes widened enough that he was no longer glaring at her. He looked almost shocked. And something softer...

Unable to face the pity she caught as it flitted across his face, Fae turned on her heel and stormed from the chalet.

11

WHEN IT'S SAFE

The frigid mountain air hit Fae the second she stepped outside, and she immediately regretted leaving the warmth of the Meeting House.

But there was no way she was going back inside now. Not when Luca had almost looked as though he felt sorry for her...

Shaking her head free of that thought, she stalked through the snow in search of something warm.

Two streets down from the Meeting House, she found a food cart serving steaming mugs of liquid chocolate and ordered one, just to have something warm to wrap her hands around. When the woman manning the cart held out her drink, Fae realised she had nothing with which to pay for it.

"Oh," she said, realising her error.

The vendor smiled. "It's on the house." She pushed the steaming cup into Fae's hands.

Fae stuttered an awkward, "Thank you," and hurriedly stepped away to let the next customer past.

She spent the next hour wandering along cobbled streets, peering in shop windows and admiring the beautifully quaint town of La'sa, tucked away all snug in its mountain fortress of ice. But as she walked, she noticed a somber undercurrent.

Sure, the townspeople smiled, exchanged pleasantries and went about their business normally enough, but there was a stagnant feel to it all, as if they were simply going through the motions.

A bit like how she felt walking through Throldon.

Once she noticed it, she saw it more and more. In the way shoppers purchased wares from the timber-framed stores along the street, in the way a group of teenagers hurried from the warren of tunnels in the mountainside to duck into the shelter of a welcoming cafe.

And in the way a small child watched them with longing in her eyes.

Her hot drink long since gone, the cold chased Fae back to the Meeting House, where she sorely hoped Luca had found something else to do.

She was relieved to find it empty, and dropped into a squashy armchair by the fire already roaring in the hearth.

"There you are!" Fae turned to see Sheree standing in the doorway. "I came looking for you this morning but you'd already left. Have you had breakfast?" Fae shook her head. "Come come! Let me show you the kitchen."

Sheree ushered Fae deeper into the Meeting House, which, it turned out, was far bigger than it first looked. From the living space, they walked down a corridor with multiple doors leading from it.

"That's the common room," Sheree said gesturing at the room they'd just left as she bustled ahead. "We've got store rooms, meeting rooms, studios..." She waved at different doors as she went, and Fae caught glimpses of smaller spaces set with shelves, racks, desks, chairs, or left bare for some other use. Sheree stopped at the end of the corridor. "This is the kitchen." She pushed the door open, and waved Fae through.

The kitchen was easily five times the size of the common room. Set along one wall were ovens of all shapes and sizes and uses. Pots and pans dangled from the ceiling, vast hoods hung over huge burners, and the sounds and smells of cooking filled the room, adding to the din of chatter. A length of open countertop divided the kitchen itself from lines of long tables bracketed by benches and chairs, and beyond that, a wall of glass looked out onto a sweeping, frost-kissed garden.

Before Fae had the opportunity to do more than gasp at the noise, Sheree steered her over to the counter. Dishes of hot and cold meats, cheese, fried potatoes, bread, and fruit covered the surface. Sheree grabbed a plate from the stack.

"You need to get some flesh on your bones girl," she muttered as she heaped fried potatoes and beans onto the plate. "You're not much more than a frost-covered stick out there. Sausages?" She hovered over a dish of sausages and crispy bacon, the smell of salt and fat mouthwatering.

Fae shook her head. "No, thank you." Even after a year of living in Throldon, she'd never gotten used to eating meat. Elves very rarely did, and she'd grown up in a city of elves.

Sheree cocked her head and continued working her way down the counter, avoiding the meat as she went.

By the time she was done, the plate was piled high with more food than Fae could ever hope to eat in one sitting, but Sheree wasn't finished yet. At the end of the counter, ranks of mismatched cups and mugs waited in neat rows, flanked by two huge copper kettles.

"Tea, or *kahveh*?" She asked, selecting one upturned mug from the front, and deftly spinning it the right way up.

"Tea, please." Fae answered, and Sheree hefted the appropriate kettle while still balancing the plate in the other hand. "Can I help...?" Fae stepped forward to take over one of the tasks, but Sheree clicked her tongue in warning and set the kettle back down, not a drop spilled. Turning to the tables, Sheree's eyes swept the room.

"Ah, here we go," she said, marching between the benches to a table near the back wall, Fae jogging to keep up.

"Room for one more?" Sheree asked cheerily, sliding the loaded plate onto the table. "Fae, this is Arissa, Taniq, and Rylan." A young woman and two teenage boys nodded their greeting. "Are you free today? I have it on good authority that training was cancelled." Her eyes twinkled as she regarded each of them.

"Aw c'mon, Sheree." The boy who spoke looked no older than around sixteen, with bright green, uptilted eyes, skin the colour of fine sand, and coppery hair. "Don't tell us you've found something else for us to do? We were going to enjoy the day off!"

"Hush, Rylan!" The young woman said, her sky-blue eyes flashing. She flicked a river of blonde hair over her shoulder and leaned forward. "What do you need us for, Sheree?"

Sheree smiled and turned back to Fae. "These three will be able to show you around and answer any questions I'm sure you have about La'sa." She added softly, "If you want to send word back home, let me know. I'll see that it goes with the next messenger." Fae wasn't sure how to respond to the offer. She'd needed something to say to Luca and that had been the first thing to come to mind. She had no idea what she would even say if she *was* to send word back to Throldon: *Sorry, I've magicked myself to the legendary city of lost elves only it's more of a town and they're not elves, they're Magi and they say I'm one of them and I need to use magic to stitch the earth back together because apparently I broke it and anyway I don't know how I got myself here or how to get back to you. Good luck in the war!*

Sheree patted Fae on the arm and pressed the mug of tea into her hands. "I'm afraid I can't stay, but if you need anything, I'm normally around here somewhere. If not, one if these three will probably know where to find me."

"Don't worry Sheree," the other boy spoke up, his elven-grey eyes warm and sincere against caramel skin. "She's in safe hands."

"Hm," Sheree muttered, eyeing them all with a shrewd gaze, but she pushed Fae gently onto the bench and squeezed her shoulder. "I'll see you later." And then she was gone.

Three pairs of eyes watched Fae from across the table.

"So you're the new girl, huh?" The boy with the bright green eyes looked her up and down. He propped his elbow on the table, leaning his head on his fist.

"I thought everyone knew," Fae replied flatly.

The woman whipped out a hand to knock Rylan's arm from under his head, nearly dropping his face into the cold remains of his breakfast. The other boy howled with laughter as he flailed to keep himself from face-planting the table, narrowly missing his mug in his efforts. He chuckled again when his friend turned a withering glare on the blonde.

"Rylan seems to have forgotten how to behave after five hundred years of having the same faces put up with his nonsense." The woman scowled at him, and then turned her blue eyes on Fae. "I'm Arissa." She indicated herself with a delicate hand. Then gestured to the other boy at their table. "That one's Taniq."

"Pleasure," Taniq said with a half-wave.

"There was no need to dump me into my plate!" Rylan growled.

"There was when you were acting like an animal with no manners," Arissa replied sweetly.

"Animals don't have manners."

"A rabbit has more manners than you."

"I was just *asking!*" he spluttered.

"Calm down, you're making a scene." Indeed, half-a-dozen others were throwing amused glances their way. Those glances skittered away when they fell on Fae.

She groaned.

Arissa looked up. "Show's over!" she called. "I'll aim for his *kahveh* next time!" A few chortled replies, and people went back to their meals.

"Honestly," she tutted, shaking her head.

"It's alright," Fae said, stabbing her fork into a slice of potato. "I get it back home too."

"Ooh, do tell," Rylan, recovered from his humiliation, leaned forward. "What d'ya do?"

"*Rylan,*" Taniq rumbled a warning this time.

Rylan spread his hands out to either side. "What?"

Arissa came to the rescue. "So, Fae" — she pushed her empty plate to the side — "what brings you to La'sa?"

Fae shrugged, and decided a piece of the truth wouldn't hurt. They'd probably hear it from someone else anyway. "Your, uh... High Magi think I can help with the earthquakes."

"Uhuh," Arissa's eyes narrowed. She already knew Fae was hedging.

"What can you do?" Taniq asked innocently. "All the Magi are already here. What's your thing?"

Fae cleared her throat. "They think I'm a Magi too." They exchanged a glance. "What?"

"What do you know about Magi?" Arissa asked carefully.

Fae shrugged. "Nothing, until I came here. Why?"

Rylan clapped his hands and rubbed them together with a grin. "Ooh, we're going to have fun with you!"

"*Rylan!*" Arissa hissed.

"What?" Rylan scowled at her, his almond-shaped eyes narrowing to slits. "Look, Sheree brought her to us to answer questions, right?" He waited for any arguments, and when none were forthcoming, he turned back to Fae.

"Right, Magi" — he gestured to the three of them — "wield Source Magic. You've probably been told that much already. There are six elements, and six main types of wielder: Auroras wield air, Incendi wield fire." He indicated himself. "Mizulae wield water" — he waved one hand to Arissa — "Therasae wield earth" — the other, he waved at Taniq. "Luxos wield light, and Umbrae wield dark. Those two are less common. Sometimes you get a dual wielder, like yours truly." He gave a tip of his head. "Very rarely, you get Powers, who wield three or more. I've only heard of a handful of those ever existing."

Fae swallowed, trying not to think of the elements she'd commanded before her powers had vanished. "What happened to the Magi then, if I've never heard of you before?"

"We came here," Rylan said simply. Fae frowned in confusion.

Arissa sighed. "Magi haven't had the best luck historically," she said. "We've been abused and exploited for our gifts by anyone wanting an advantage over their enemies. When the War of the Races broke out, Magi were drafted by the hundreds, and we fell in droves. So we gathered together as many as would come — as many as were left — and hid ourselves away to protect our knowledge and our legacy." Her face became somber. "We lost a lot of people back then."

Even Rylan had gone quiet. Taniq's hand twitched as if he wanted to reach out to Arissa. To take her hand in his own.

Something Arissa said earlier whispered in Fae's ear.

"Wait..." She looked between them. It couldn't be possible. Elves lived for hundreds of years, but even they aged. If these Magi had been here that long, they should be wrinkled and ancient by now.

Taniq was the one to nod, an errant strand of wavy black hair falling into his eyes. He brushed it back. "Every single person you see in La'sa has been here since the War of the Races. Which is why your sudden appearance is rather... unprecedented."

Fae was struck dumb. She gaped at them, her food forgotten.

Eventually, she managed, "*How?*"

"That's part of the magic of La'sa," Rylan answered, plucking the bread from her plate. "The shield around it protects us from discovery, but it also holds time in a kind of stasis. So none of us age." He took a bite from the crust. "You'd think I'd be glad to be this old and still look this good," he garbled around his mouthful.

Arissa rolled her eyes in disgust.

"Well," Taniq added, "*most* of us didn't age."

Fae turned to him. "What do you mean?" Rylan eyed her plate

greedily, and she pushed it towards him. She didn't feel like eating anymore.

"The time magic affected some of us differently," Taniq continued. "Most of us got stuck with whatever age we were when the barrier first went up. But it didn't work on some — they aged and died the same as before."

"Some of the children aged and then froze when they reached adulthood." Rylan supplied around another mouthful of food.

"And some of them are stuck as children until the barrier comes down."

"When will the barrier come down?" Fae asked.

Arissa shrugged. "When it's safe."

Fae snorted. "So never then." The Magi stared at her. "For the last thirty years, Arland has been under the influence of a broken god. And now there's an army marching on Throldon from a nation I hadn't even heard of until two days ago." She blew out a frustrated breath, and thrust her fingers into her hair. So much was spinning out of control, and where once she might've been able to do something about it, now all she could do was watch as the world unraveled around her. The weight of it threatened to punch through her shield of apathy and drown her.

Rylan made a noise in the back of his throat. "Alright, Misery Jane," he grumbled, mopping up the last of her breakfast. "What do you wield anyway?" Stuffing the last forkful in his mouth, he pushed the plate away and clasped his hands together, waiting for her answer.

"I wasn't even aware I was doing it until your High Magi told me I was," she said truthfully.

Taniq nodded sagely. "It can be a bit like that the first few times," he said. "Tell us what happened and we'll work it out." He gestured to the three of them. "Between us, we cover the main elements. I'm sure we'll recognise what you're using."

Fae wavered. "I don't really like to talk about it."

Rylan cast her a bemused look. "Why not?"

All three of them watched her, the same expression on their faces.

She took a breath. "The last time I used Source Magic..." *Breathe*, she reminded herself. *Breathe.* She let the air out long and slow. "The last time I used it, I nearly died." There, she'd said it.

The shadows whispered in her ear. The echoes of a broken god.

She shoved them behind her curtain and straightened her shoulders.

Rylan nodded, his green eyes losing their cocky glint. "Ah," he said. "Well that's happened to most of us too. The first time I wielded Source Magic, I nearly burnt down my parent's house in a tantrum." His lips twitched in the ghost of a smile, his gaze gone distant. "Fire and air together can make quite the inferno, I learned."

"Once, early on in my training years, I nearly drowned myself," Arissa said with a shudder. "That's not something I'll ever forget."

"I opened a sinkhole in my grandparents' vegetable garden," Taniq added. "I was only trying to help them dig up the carrots."

Rylan barked a laugh. "Only you would have a near-death experience doing something so domestic, Taniq Shalla!"

Taniq flashed him a self-conscious grin, his caramel skin flushing, and the atmosphere at the table lightened again.

"So you see, Fae" — Rylan leaned across the table, brandishing a discarded fork — "we've all nearly killed ourselves with Source Magic. So spill. What did you do?"

Arissa looked half inclined to rebuke him again, but her eyes gleamed with curiosity.

Fae supposed if it'd been five hundred years since she'd met anyone new, she'd be incurably curious too.

Clinging to how easily her new friends told their stories like it was a life raft, she dredged up those least favoured of her memories.

"I've been told that I burned a couple of times."

"Clearly fire," Rylan volunteered.

"Genius," Arissa muttered.

Fae smiled. "I've had the wind respond to me too."

"Ooh, dual wielder," Rylan's eyebrows arched. "Very interesting. Welcome to the club."

Fae studied her hands. "And I've summoned storms," she finished, shoving the worst of her nightmares aside and slamming the door on them. She looked up quickly. "And that's it."

The three of them stared at her in stunned silence.

"That's water," Arissa whispered.

"Wait," Taniq held out a hand before she could comment further on that, his eyes wide. "Didn't you say the High Magi want your help with the earthquakes?" He glanced to either side, as if checking that no one overheard them, and dropped his voice low. "Can you wield earth too?"

Fae shook her head. "They seem to think I can, but I've never done it before." She left out the High Magi's theories on where the earthquakes were actually coming from.

Taniq let out a breath. Arissa's eyes were still wide, her already fair skin paled.

Rylan shook his head.

"Even without earth, that repertoire still makes you a Power."

Fae shook her head again. "Maybe it would," she said with a sigh, getting tired of the same line. "But I don't have any power anymore. I lost it all... before."

"That's not possible," Arissa breathed.

"I know, I know," Fae held her hands up before they could explain it again. "The power comes from the earth, I am just a conduit, it doesn't just disappear."

"Exactly," Taniq said. "You can't lose your ability to channel the Source. It's inbuilt — a part of you." He stroked his jaw with a strong hand, his grey eyes narrowed in thought. "I suppose you might lose your ability to *control* it though..."

"Interesting theory, Shalla," a familiar drawl interrupted from behind her. "I shall be sure to test it in our training."

Fae suppressed the shiver that ran through her, and turned to face the man who stood there.

12

BUTTERFLIES TO NECTAR

Luca stood behind Fae with a half-smile that made him look like a panther toying with a cornered mouse. Fae returned his gaze flatly.

"High Magi Fialli," Arissa addressed him. "You're taking on Fae's training personally?"

Luca's eyes flicked to her, one eyebrow lifting a fraction. "We will be working together initially, yes."

"Of course the High Magi would work with Fae," Rylan whispered, not very quietly. "A Power to train a Power."

Luca's other eyebrow slid up to meet the first. "Indeed?"

Fae glowered at Rylan. "I said I don't like talking about it."

Arissa leaned forward to grip her arm. "And we told you: everyone here has a near-death story. You need to own yours." She released Fae to gesture at Luca. "Besides, I'll wager High Magi Fialli has one that trounces all over ours."

"Oh, there are more than one," Luca said with a playful smile, and it changed his whole face. His gaze darted to Fae, and something like understanding flitted across it. "But none that would be deemed appropriate for the breakfast table." As her companions groaned over his demurral, Fae saw the shadow that passed behind his eyes.

But this... camaraderie he seemed to have with the other Magi was so different to the predatory watchfulness she'd seen of him so far.

"Do you really think Fae can help with the rift in the earth, High Magi?" Taniq said suddenly. The others went quiet, listening intently for the answer.

Luca glanced down at her, his indigo gaze boring into hers. "Well, I suppose that remains to be seen," he said, his expression unreadable. A moment passed, a minute, then Luca shot the other three a look. "Do you mind if I borrow Fae for a bit?"

A chorus of, "Of course," "Not at all," and, "See you later, Fae," followed, and the younger Magi cleared the plates and vacated the table. Luca slid onto their bench opposite her.

"So," he said, resting his chin upon his clasped hands. "A Power, huh?"

Fae snorted. "Not really, seeing as I don't have any."

Luca stared at her like he was trying to solve a particularly tricky puzzle.

"Come with me," he said finally. Standing again, he held out a hand for her.

Ignoring it, Fae rose. Luca slid his hands into his pockets with a shrug, and led the way from the kitchen.

They stepped out into the chill mountain air again, and Fae gave an involuntary shudder.

Luca eyed her. "First, we'll get you a coat," he said dryly. He himself wore only a shirt in thick, white linen, tucked into black trousers. The heavy-duty boots on his feet were like many others she'd seen around the town: hardy and well-worn. Army boots.

"There's one in my room," she said. "I just miscalculated the weather this morning." More like she'd completely forgotten she was somewhere a coat was required in all seasons, regardless of weather.

"Perfect." Luca altered course for the cavernous tunnels into the mountain. "Then that's where we'll go."

Fae paid close attention to the route this time, making note of how many lefts and rights he took before stopping outside the room she'd been given. She ducked inside to grab her coat, stuffing a pair of gloves in the pocket as an afterthought.

Luca nodded his approval as she pulled the door closed behind her, and set off deeper into the tunnel complex.

"I thought we were going that way?" Fae pointed back the way they'd come.

Luca's lips twitched. "There's a reason we call these tunnels the Warrens," he said. "They run throughout the mountain complex. You don't have to walk across the Core to get to the other side of La'sa."

"The Core?"

Luca waved behind him. "The town centre."

Fae nodded. "So we're going to the other side of the mountain?"

His lips twitched again. "You'll see."

Fae fought the urge to slap his arm, and grasped at a change of topic instead.

"How much do you tell the people here? About the earthquakes? About what caused them?"

He shot her a look. "Everything. Everyone here is over five hundred years old — well over any of our natural life spans. They deserve to be kept in the loop with regards to anything that might threaten that life."

"Why is that?" Fae asked. "Why stop time progressing? And... how?"

"It was a collective decision. We knew the gods left something behind after the Rains. We didn't want to forget what we came here for. History has a habit of repeating itself, with each generation thinking it can do better than the last. We didn't want to risk future generations underestimating the remaining threat to our people. So we chose to stay, in order to protect that future."

Luca sighed. "As for how — that's complicated. It involves wielding light and dark magic together so that time is unaffected by their passing."

Fae nodded, although she didn't have a hope of understanding what he was talking about.

So she ploughed on with her next question. "So now that Anson's gone, when do you take the barrier down?"

Luca's glance was back to his customary watchfulness. "That's for the Magi to decide."

"I thought you said I was Magi." Fae arched an eyebrow at him.

"I thought you said you weren't."

He came to a halt and considered her through narrowed eyes.

She was about to snap something back at him when he said, "We're here."

Fae turned.

Beside them, a wide archway led into an arena of sorts. It was open to the sky, as the Core was, but the walls were unbroken all the way around, the only entrance being where they stood. Deep steps carved up the sides provided ample seating for an audience. Like a small amphitheatre. But it was empty now.

"This is our training arena," Luca said, stepping past her to walk onto the field of fine, loose shale. "Someone thought we might put on plays here, but it never took off. So we repurposed it."

Fae entered behind him. Along the same wall as the entrance, wooden lean-tos sheltered straw training dummies, painted targets, and an array of weapons.

Her eyes caught on two slender swords at the end of the store. "Alright," she said, tearing her gaze away to turn back to Luca. "So what am I here for?"

Luca reached into one weapons rack and pulled out two unadorned lengths of some kind of hardwood.

"Like I said before," he threw one to her. "Training."

Fae fumbled the catch, and the staff fell to the ground. How long had it been since she'd practiced with her swords? She bent to pick up the staff. Too long, apparently.

"I thought you wanted me to train in Source Magic." She planted the staff on the ground. "I didn't realise you wanted to spar." Her eyes drifted to the swords again.

Luca's eyes followed her gaze. "Yes." He spun his staff, and planted it likewise. "But you said you didn't want to talk about that. So I thought you might prefer this option."

Fae fought the urge to growl. She didn't have time for this. She needed to prove to him that she didn't have this power he seemed so convinced of, so that she could return home to...

To what? she scoffed inwardly. *What can I do to help?*

"Look, just ask what you have to ask," she snapped, eager to get this over with.

Luca leaned on his staff. "Alright," he said. "What elements have you wielded before? At least three, if Rylan is correct."

Fae rolled her eyes. "They think I've commanded fire, air, and water before." She held a hand up. "But I was barely aware I was doing any of that. And—"

"I know I know." Luca straightened and took a step back, sweeping the staff around his body in lazy circles. "You don't have any powers anymore. Let me ask you this instead." He swung the staff up to rest across his shoulders. "How did you sense the power you had before? How did it feel?"

Fae blinked. "Um..."

He prowled forward, his eyes fixed on her. "Where did it live in you? How did you grasp it?" He stopped a single stride from her, his gaze searing hers.

"It..." She'd never really grabbed hold of her power. Not until that final moment... "It came from Eah'lara," she said finally. "I saw it, and I held it in the Spirit Realm."

Luca gave her a look, but bobbed his head. "Alright then." He tossed the staff to one side and eased back, folding his arms across his chest. "Can you still see Eah'lara?"

Fae nodded. "Can you?"

He shook his head. "That's not my specialty. But I'll find you an Echo who can."

"An Echo?" Fae cocked her head to one side.

"Yes." Luca frowned. "Like you. Someone who can see the Spirit Realm." He shot her a confused glance. "What do you call it?"

Fae shifted her weight. "Well, all elves have a sense of Eah'lara. But the Whisperers are the strongest."

"You're not an elf," Luca pointed out.

"I'm different."

"Ah yes." Luca smiled. "The Spiritchild."

"Yes." Fae narrowed her eyes. "No one ever explained how you know so much about me."

Luca batted her implied question away. "I'll let someone better versed in the workings of our intelligence network fill you in on those details. For now though" — he held both arms out to her, ceding the floor — "I want you to look to where you found your power before. I'm going to draw air. See if you can feel it." He dropped his arms, and a light breeze ruffled her hair.

With a final scowl, Fae closed her eyes, and found Eah'lara.

It was beautiful here. The shimmering nebulae that made up the fabric of the Spirit Realm were formed of crystalline whites and purest blues. The silvery threads woven across it glittered enchantingly, and the choral voices of the Aethyr soothed her, as they always did. The glowing orbs of

Aethyr-in-waiting bobbed placidly about, tiny sparkling spirit particles hovering like dust motes in the air.

Fae breathed deep and cast her senses toward Luca. Standing near him like this, she could see his aura outlined against the backdrop of Eah'lara, like a silhouette against a curtain of shimmering white. The spirit dust gravitated towards him, like butterflies to nectar, giving him a glittering shadow.

Yet more particles sank into her own skin, recognising her as one of their ilk.

She was distantly aware of the wind picking up around her in the physical world, as if through a doorway behind her. She watched Luca's outline, trying to sense any changes in Eah'lara that heralded the power she had known for so brief a time.

But all she saw was the gentle eddies of spirit dust, swirling around him.

Behind her, she felt the wind picking up, until it whipped at her hair.

And then, something changed.

The threads of Aethyr moved as if brushed by a breath of wind.

And the glittering spirit dust erupted.

A vortex of energies spun furiously around Luca's aura. It tunnelled through the fabric of Eah'lara, anchoring him to... something else.

Fae opened her eyes, and her heart stopped.

Within the walls of the arena, a tornado bellowed around her and Luca. It picked up snow and shale and sand until she could see nothing beyond the eye in which they stood.

And in her mind's eye, it was cracked tiles beneath her feet, and the shadow of a broken god looming before her.

The numbness she'd relied on for so long to hold her afloat was swept away in an instant. Her breath caught in her chest, her blood pounded in her ears, and she was trapped and helpless all over again. Her breathing came in gasps, and panic swept over her.

Luca's eyes flared in alarm, and the wind dropped like a stone, the snow drifting down to join it.

But he didn't rush to her side. Instead, he watched her from where he stood.

"Breathe," he instructed. But Fae's vision was darkening around the edges. She couldn't gulp enough air, her heart racing a thundering tattoo in her chest. Her knees buckled beneath her.

"Breathe, Fae." His voice sounded so far away, whipped away by the wind still battering at her mind.

The world narrowed to a pinprick, coloured spots dancing before her eyes.

And then he was there, hauling her up by the shoulders.

"*Breathe*, Fae," he commanded. His voice held that same edge. The one that had her every nerve standing on end. The one that tasted of danger. He grasped her chin until she was looking into his eyes, their depths so fathomless she could lose herself in them, and she saw his power billow across them, like seeing the reflection of snow drift across the midnight darkness of his gaze.

The sight was enough to startle Fae from her panic spiral.

She drew in a ragged breath, and let it out slowly. And another.

And the world crept back into view.

"Much better." Luca's drawl brought her fully back to herself, and she snatched herself from him. He shot her a predatory smirk that didn't quite reach his eyes.

"That was fun. Shall we try it again?"

13

THE ARCHIVES

Fae couldn't decide if Luca was mad or just sadistic.

The ease with which he controlled power she'd only ever called blindly was breathtaking.

"We'll use fire this time." He held out a hand, and flames danced across his fingertips.

She gaped at him, and his eyes flashed her a challenge.

Slamming her lips shut, she squared her shoulders and shot him a glare of her own.

She couldn't decide what she wanted more. To prove him wrong, so she could get the hell away from this place; or to find her power again, so she could knock him on his ass.

His answering grin was lupine, and the fire coalesced into a ball the size of his fist.

Fae closed her eyes again, and opened her senses to Eah'lara.

Once again, the nebulae of the Spirit Realm shimmered blue and white, the voices of the Aethyr singing harmoniously through the ether. But when Fae cast her eye towards Luca's aura, it was different.

The spirit particles still clung to his outline, as they did around everyone, but this time they glittered with sparks of orange and red, as if catching the reflection of the fire he wielded.

Fae watched again, the heat of the flames at her back as the threads swayed in response to Luca's crescendo of power.

When the spirit dust erupted around him again, the power tunnelling through Eah'lara, the flickering orange-red made it look as though his aura was on fire.

Fae almost opened her eyes. Then she remembered why she was here.

Reaching out with her senses, she felt for the energy around him. Tried to see where he drew it from.

But whatever he was doing, it felt alien to her. It didn't have the same feel as the power gifted to her by the Aethyr. It was raw, untempered, and it tore at her senses like sand against her skin.

Gritting her teeth, Fae reached again.

She needed to prove to him that she didn't have this power.

And yet she yearned to reclaim what had once been hers.

She felt it burn against her skin.

Felt tears prick her eyes.

But there was nothing here to grasp at.

Fae choked back a sob, and withdrew.

The heat died down. And she opened her eyes.

Luca snuffed out the last of his fire with a clench of his fist, his expression as inscrutable as always.

"So?"

Fae shook her head, and dashed the tears from her eyes.

"I told you," she said, breathing deep. "I don't have it anymore." She picked up her staff where it had fallen to the ground, just for something to do with her hands. "I can't see where your power comes from. And I can't get a feel for it."

"Well no," Luca replied, retrieving his own staff to stow back in the weapons store. "You're looking at it from the Spirit Realm. We've already told you Source Magic comes from the earth itself. You won't see it from Eah'lara."

Fae scowled at him. "Then why bother with this? How are you still so convinced that I can wield it?"

Luca cocked his head, his expression blank. "Because you already have."

Fae let out a snarl of frustration, and hurled her staff at him. He caught it deftly in one hand, which only stoked her anger.

"We're done here." And for the second time that day, she turned her back on him and stormed from the arena.

It took her a few wrong turns before she found corridors that looked familiar, but Fae eventually found her way back to her room.

She threw herself onto the bed, coat, boots and all.

"Damn it," she breathed at the ceiling.

She didn't have the power Luca had. And the blatant control he had over his elements grated hard when she couldn't so much as summon a puff of air.

But he'd made her *want* to. He'd made her want to try.

She didn't want to prove him wrong anymore.

She wanted to prove him *right*.

If she could wield Source Magic the way he and the other High Magi seemed to think she could, she'd be able to return to Throldon — she'd be able to help.

A soft knock interrupted her thoughts, and Sheree's silver mane appeared around the door.

"Ah!" The woman stepped inside. "Arissa said you'd gone off with Luca. I didn't suspect it would last long." Her sparkling blue eyes looked her over, angled slightly in concern. "Did he help you?"

Fae sat up on the bed. "No," she said. "Well..." She thought about her change of heart, then shook her head. "No." She couldn't afford to feed anyone's hopes of what she might manage. Least of all her own.

Sheree couldn't quite keep the disappointment from her face. "Never mind, dear. These things can take time." She shot her a smile. "Heavens know, Madja spent years getting to grips with her magic."

Fae returned the smile. "What about you?"

"Oh!" Sheree shook her head. "I'm not a Magi, dear. No, Madja was the only one in our family. You'll find that sometimes." A flicker of sadness passed across her face. "There are a few others like that here. Never had any other Magi in the family. So we became their family."

"Sheree," Fae said, a thought occurring to her. "What *are* Magi?" At Sheree's puzzled frown, she explained, "You're clearly not elves, but I wouldn't say you're human either, and I haven't seen any dwarves among you. Luca mentioned that you have people who can see Eah'lara, which is an elven trait. And then there's this Source Magic, which doesn't belong to any race that I've ever heard of." She spread her hands, her riddle laid out before her.

Sheree sighed, and came to sit beside Fae on the bed. "Actually, Source Magic belongs to all the races. The Magi have always been more comfortable intermingling than non-Magi. Almost everyone here has a... complicated heritage." A small laugh escaped her. "I think you'd be hard pressed to find many here who could tell you exactly which races they've come from." She shrugged. "We're just Magi."

"But you said you're not."

"No." Sheree tipped her head to the side. "There are always a few that don't inherit the gift. Or whose abilities are small enough that they don't practice. But we all belong together." She gave Fae a small smile, and patted her leg. "Sometimes it's easier to be the ones who don't have to shoulder the burden." She seemed lost to her thoughts for a moment, then she cleared her throat and stood, brushing her trousers free of invisible creases.

"Anyway, I must be off. I just wanted to check in, see if you needed anything?" Fae was about to shake her head no, when she paused.

"Actually..." She stood. "I want to learn more about La'sa. I feel like I've opened a book in the middle and I've missed all the introductions." Sheree laughed, and Fae cast her a sheepish glance. "Is there anywhere I can find out a bit more about La'sa, about Magi history?" She added hopefully, "Maybe it'll help me work out my own Source Magic."

Sheree regarded her shrewdly. "You know, the High Magi will answer any questions you have. And I know they want to help you."

Fae examined her feet. "I don't want to bother them..." But when she looked back up at Sheree, she had a feeling that nothing much passed the blue-eyed gaze of Madja's sister unnoticed either.

"Mhm," she hummed, looking decidedly unconvinced. "You're welcome to the Archives if you feel up to the task. Half the reason we came here was to protect all the knowledge and lore the Magi warded. We are custodians of histories long forgotten, and learning long abandoned." She said the last with a tinge of pride to her voice. "But if you really want to try your hand at navigating it, the Archives are in the northern quadrant."

Fae nodded her thanks. "I'll find it."

Sheree gave her a long look. "I hope you find what you're looking for." And then she was gone.

It was as Fae trudged her way across the snow-dusted Core, Sheree's words playing through her head, that she stopped in her tracks to consider it.

What *was* she looking for? The history of La'sa, clearly not home to the *Aly'sa* as she'd been taught? The origins of the Magi? Answers to solving her own powerlessness?

She shied away from the last; it had far too many facets for her to examine in detail just yet.

She puffed out a breath, and watched it cloud in the air before drifting away with the curls of steam and chimney smoke from the cabins lining the street. Tugging her coat close around her, she strode on.

Maybe she'd know what she was looking for when she saw it.

When she finally reached the vaulted hall of the northern tunnel, her ears were so cold they hurt, and she made a silent vow to find a hat somewhere after her excursion to the Archives.

Three arches led from the hall. To either side, wide corridors branched away into seminar halls and private study rooms. But ahead, the entrance to the Archives themselves was something entirely different.

The third archway was formed into countless sheets of paper; scrolls of it, reams of it, books bursting at the seams with it. Each sheet was painstakingly carved from the ice and rock, the patterns continuing seamlessly from one material to the other and back again, a work of art and devotion that must have taken years to complete.

Fae gaped openly at the detailing as she passed, in awe of the craftsmanship required to achieve it.

Below the arch, a circular desk perched across the entrance, with two Magi stationed in the centre. One helped a visitor on the far side of the circle. The other approached Fae.

"Can I help you?" she said with smiling, downturned eyes. But Fae's awe had moved from the archway above her, to what lay beyond it.

Behind the desk, rows upon rows of smaller tables lined the near side of the chamber, all equipped with comfortable chairs and some form of lamplight. But along the far wall, shelves and shelves of books and scrolls and drawers of records stretched as far as she could see in either direction, and disappeared into the depths of the mountain. She thought the library at Throldon had been impressive. But that was nothing compared to this. The shelves here were three times the height of a normal room, with ladders to allow access to the upper levels. Every now and then, Fae caught sight of small lights flashing down the dark aisles.

She pointed to one, as it emerged alongside a young-looking Magi from one such aisle. "What are the lights?"

The helper's smile broadened. "They're Luxo Lamps," she explained — probably something she hadn't had to do for five hundred years. "Our Magi found a way to combine light and fire magic to create lamps that don't burn, but provide a clear, unwavering light to see by. Here—" She tucked a loose strand of cherry-red hair behind her ear and reached beneath her counter. The oversized teacup she produced contained what looked like one of the glowing orbs that bobbed through Eah'lara. It emitted a steady, pure white light.

"I believe it was an Echo who originally came up with the idea," the helper added as an afterthought. She held the lamp out to Fae. "For you to use while you browse?" There was a knowing twinkle in her eye.

Fae bobbed her head as she took a hold of the lamp. "Thank you," she said.

"Any time. I'm Annie, by the way." Her red hair gleamed in the lamplight as Fae passed the cup from one hand to the other.

"Fae."

Annie smiled. "I know," she said. "Nice to meet you, Fae. Please let me know if you need anything."

"Thank you." Fae bobbed her head again, and stepped past the desk into the Archives.

Having no idea of where to start, she arrowed down the nearest aisle, the Luxo Lamp piercing the gloom that immediately enveloped her.

Over her left shoulder, books lined the shelves from top to bottom, and as far as her small light extended. To her right, scrolls and drawers jostled for space. There were scrolls wedged into baskets at floor level, while others were stuffed in bundles into pigeonholes. The drawers were all sizes, and occurred at odd intervals, opening out to reveal a wild assortment of papers and documents, maps and drawings and diagrams that Fae had trouble deciphering.

Unsure of what to make of the scrolls and papers, she turned to the books, and pulled the first one from the shelf. Opening it to the first page, she found a language she didn't recognise. Returning it to its place, she selected another. This one appeared to be written in some form of pictograms. The third one was in the common tongue, but covered theories and interpretations of star patterns. The fourth was a collection of detailed renditions of plants and herbs.

I could be here forever and never find a single book on Source Magic. Her eyes rolled at the irony, roaming the endless expanse of books in this aisle alone.

She sighed, gathering up her lamp, and trudged back to the front desk.

Annie smiled at her return. "Did you find what you were looking for?" Again, that gleam in her eyes.

Fae narrowed her eyes back at her, lips twitching. "You knew I wouldn't, didn't you?"

Annie's laugh was as bright and clear as bells. "I don't think anyone really knows where everything is in here, but you might find a *few* people who know where *some* of it is. I'd have been surprised if you found what you were looking for on day one."

Fae laughed. "Alright then, could you point me in the direction of histories? More specifically about Magi, Source Magic, or La'sa? Please."

Annie led her down a different aisle, to a section that smelled of age and dust, selecting books as she went. Once they'd amassed more than the two of them could safely carry without risking damage to the ancient texts, Annie set Fae up at one of the reading tables, her stack of books spread out around her, the trusty Luxo Lamp lighting the pages from its teacup holder.

Fae was still bent over those same books hours later when Luca managed to track her down again.

The prickling feeling on the back of her neck was the only warning she got before he dropped into the seat opposite.

He said nothing, merely leaned back in his chair, hands clasped over his waist as his eyes scanned the titles sprawled across the table.

Fae ignored him, ignored the way her very cells seemed to stand to attention when he was near, and continued with her reading.

She had found a very interesting account of the War of Races written by a Magi, covering details about the war that she'd never been taught.

But then, she'd been taught by the Aethyr. Their memories of the war, it would appear, were not complete.

Luca's presence opposite her kept drawing her attention from the page. She read the same paragraph for a fourth time before she finally closed the book and looked up.

"You know, anyone would think you're following me, the way you keep turning up wherever I am."

Luca examined a fingernail. "La'sa is not so big a place." He plucked at non-existent lint on his shirt. Then jerked his chin towards the books. "What are you looking for?"

Fae narrowed her eyes at him. If he thought he was going to hound her into summoning Source Magic, he had another thing coming.

She sighed. Sheree was right though. He did want her to find her power. And she supposed she did too, even if their motives differed.

Shoving her desire to scowl at him aside, she pointed to the book she'd been reading when he arrived.

"I was reading about the War of the Races, but your version has far more in it than the one the rest of the world knows. It's like everyone forgot about you all. Or we were never meant to know." Luca's face shuttered, his body going preternaturally still, and Fae's senses blared a warning: *Danger!*

But if this man — this *Power* — had wanted to hurt her, he could have simply left her out in the snow.

She ploughed on, refusing to acknowledge the bead of sweat rolling down her spine. "Why doesn't anyone know about Magi? Or La'sa?" And then, the question every part of her screamed at her not to ask: "Why are you hiding?"

14

ECLECTIC HERITAGE

At first, Fae thought Luca wasn't going to answer. He sat statue-still, his eyes staring at something that wasn't there, the light of the Luxo Lamp swallowed by their darkness.

When he spoke, his voice was so low she almost couldn't hear him.

"You want to know why we've kept ourselves from the world — why we *hide.*" The last was a sneer, his face contorting into a mask of such pure self-loathing that Fae flinched. Then she blinked, and it was gone, his expression back to a blank canvas, reminiscing on the past.

His eyes flicked up to meet hers, and while his features where schooled into flat disinterest, she saw the pain in those eyes. He let out a long breath, and settled back into his chair again.

"I was alive a hundred years before the war broke out," he began. "And even then, we lived apart from non-Magi. We were hunted for our power. We live longer, and channel magics they can't understand. They were scared of us, or jealous. Or wanted to use us to advance their own interests. Children with access to the Source came to our communities to escape the attention they drew just being who they were. And to be with others like them. Sometimes their families came with them. Sometimes they didn't." He sighed, and ran a hand through the short strands of his dark hair. "You've probably seen that we have an... eclectic heritage among Magi.

Our communities have always been a mix of humans, elves, and dwarves; so too are our offspring."

"What about centaurs?" Fae asked, thinking of Immrith and Fanrell.

Luca shook his head. "No, the centaurs have never shown any signs of Source Magic. But they have always had open communications with the spirits."

"So have the elves."

Luca shot her a look. "Remind me to introduce you Irya while you are here. Then we'll talk about the elves and their spirits."

Fae bristled at his tone, but she wasn't here to discuss elves and the Aethyr.

Luca continued. "When tensions started rising across Arland, kings and their generals began drafting Magi to fight. They promised protections in exchange for service, and sent soldiers to enforce their summons. Some of us ran, and were hunted down like animals. Some of us signed up to fight. To protect those who couldn't protect themselves, and to draw attention away from our vulnerable." He blew out a breath, and the pages of one of Fae's open books fluttered in answer. "When the war finally broke, we knew it was more than just humans against elves and dwarves. Our Echoes felt the greater beings above, pulling the strings, pushing the races to war. So even more of our numbers joined the fight. Because we were the only ones with half a chance of fighting something like that. We tried to turn the tide, tried to protect innocent lives from the ruins of a war that had spiralled out of control — from forces wielded by higher beings than us."

Luca's jaw clenched as he relived memories older than history itself. "But we were impossibly outmatched against the powers of gods. Because that's what we were up against. Gods. We had no hope. We were on the brink of being wiped out." His eyes glazed over, and he suddenly looked as if he hadn't slept for a week. "We had a decision to make. Stand beside our people, the same people who'd hunted us and exploited us for our powers, but who were themselves powerless against the war raging around them. Or protect our legacy. Protect all the knowledge of Source Magic and the history that we'd collected over centuries, history we knew was being burned in cities all over Arland.

"A select group gathered together our records, our young, all traces of Source Magic, and went into hiding, to weather the storm and emerge with our legacy intact on the other side. A few fighters went to protect them. But most of the strongest stayed to fight. We knew where to go when the fighting was over. Where to find the rest of our people when the dust settled." A storm cloud passed over Luca's face. "None of them came back." The silence that followed his words was deafening, laden with the weight of souls lost.

When he spoke again, his voice had a hoarseness to it, as if he held his emotions in check by the barest of threads. "And now, between the destruction those gods rained down on the earth then, and the power needed to rid the last of them from it five hundred years later, we stand on a new brink, only it's not just the Magi who will lose this time."

He leaned forward, bracing his elbows on the table to run both hands through his hair — the most emotion Fae had seen him display yet.

Then he met her eyes, and the pain in his gaze took her breath away.

"There aren't enough of us left to mend this rift. We need you. We need you to help us fix it."

Fae opened her mouth to say... something, anything that might chase the haunted look from his eyes.

When the earth trembled.

In an instant, Luca was on his feet, all trace of those emotions wiped from his face.

He glanced across at Fae, eyes wide, as the rumbling beneath their feet rolled on.

Fae held her arms to the sides. "I'm not doing it."

Luca looked her up and down, and grunted, apparently satisfied. "Come on then," was the only warning she got before he strode from the Archives, the walls roaring like some great beast awakening.

Jogging to keep up, Fae followed behind as he stalked from the northern quadrant and into the Core. Windows rattled in their panes, voices raised in alarm as people stopped to stare wide-eyed at the mountain shuddering around them.

As they reached the central plaza, Fae saw the other High Magi angling in towards the Meeting House. Terrence stopped when he caught sight of her standing beside Luca, and she could have sworn she heard him mutter, "Interesting."

They all filed into the common room just as the rumbling abated, and the mountain stilled.

Kallis dropped into a chair, eyeing Fae from beneath blue-black lashes. "Well this makes things more exciting," he drawled.

Demilda batted him on the shoulder, but perched on the arm of his chair. "Yes, what was that?"

"An earth tremor," Fae supplied flatly. "The same as all the others we've been experiencing this past year." She looked around at them like they'd all lost their minds.

"No." Terrence stepped forward. After Luca's history lesson, Fae could see the dwarven ancestry in his stocky frame. "That was not like the ones we've felt this year." He shot her a pointed look, and levelled a finger in her direction. "Your outbursts have directly correlated with all of the quakes over the last twelve months, including the first one." He folded his arms across his chest. "But this time, there was no power surge." He looked to his fellow High Magi. "Any volunteers for why that might be?"

There was a pause, and then Kallis swore a blue streak. But it was Madja who spoke.

"The damage has reached a critical point," she said, and her face drained of all colour, her voice tremulous. "We're running out of time."

Luca's lips pressed together, the muscles of his jaw clenched. Demilda looked like she might be sick, the sable of her skin greying. Terrence's face was thunderous.

"What happens next?" Fae asked into the room.

Five faces turned to her.

"If we cannot stop it," Terrence answered, "the earth will split itself apart. The quakes will open great chasms in the ground, swallowing towns and cities whole. Worse still, they could put the earth under such pressure that mountains will emerge from the flats, or from the sea. Rivers of fire from the heart of the earth will spill over the land, and ash will fall from the sky. The movement of the earth will cause insurmountable swells in the ocean, drowning thousands. There will be no escape. Everyone and everything on this earth will be affected."

Fae's blood ran cold. What he was describing was the end of the world as they knew it — worse by far than the Rains. And her family lay in its path.

"What can we do?" she said, in barely more than a whisper.

"Well, Fae dearest," Kallis volunteered. "It'd be mighty useful if you could work out how to tap into your Source Magic, seeing as that's the only thing we haven't tried yet."

Fae flushed with guilt. She didn't have the answer they so desperately needed.

"*Kallis*," Luca warned, but it was half-hearted. He'd already told Fae they needed her, and one look at his face revealed the twist of pain she had so wanted to chase away in the Archives.

"What?" Kallis threw his hands to either side in question. "Isn't that why we had the Dreamweaver draw her here? Isn't that why you're trying to train her? Isn't that the whole point of this?" He surged to his feet, his copper eyes blazing with barely concealed anger, and something else... "If she's not the answer, why aren't we looking for other solutions?"

"Because we've tried everything else," Madja remonstrated gently.

"My ass have we tried everything!" he yelled suddenly, throwing an arm out towards the northern quadrant, and the Archives. "We have *centuries* of knowledge sitting there. What was the *point* in losing almost all of our people saving it, if it's of no use when it matters! If it's just going to be destroyed along with everything else in this worthless world anyway!" Demilda laid a hand on his arm, trying to calm him. But he shrugged her off, and hurled himself from the building.

In the silence that followed, Fae knew her decision.

"I'll try," she breathed.

Luca's eyes darted to hers, and in them, she saw a spark of hope coaxed to life.

She nodded to him. "I'll try," she said.

Demilda smiled tightly. "We know you will, Fae." She looked to the door Kallis had stalked through. "He's just worried. We all are." She stood, resting a hand on Fae's shoulder as she passed, and left the same way.

Terrence muttered something about the Archives, and followed Demilda out.

Madja stared at Fae with something that looked almost like pride. She dashed a tear from her eye, and Fae thought there was a bittersweetness to her gaze as well.

"Madja." Luca drew the woman's attention from Fae. "We can't wait any longer."

Madja nodded, and pulled in a deep breath. "I know," she said, giving herself a little shake. "Alright, I'll tell her to meet you in the Crystal Chamber."

Fae looked between them. "Who? What's the Crystal Chamber?"

Luca glanced back at her, the spark in his eyes a bright flame.

"It's time you met Irya."

15

TEN SECONDS

Hal tried to swallow but his mouth was dry as paper. For what felt like the hundredth time, he glanced over to check on their progress.

A strong hand pulled him back as the view sent his vision swimming again.

Ty smiled thinly over his shoulder. "You should probably avoid looking down so much."

Hal nodded, fixing his gaze on Aiya's back instead.

When Kagos had first mentioned the impending army, Hal's first instinct had been to set his eyes on it. He'd always been a practical man, coping with situations he could see before him far better than planning and hypotheticals.

At first, he'd fully intended to come out on foot. Aren and Stef had even volunteered to come with him. And then Aiya had suggested they fly.

And that was how Hal came uncomfortably close to the realisation that he was, in actual fact, rather terrified of heights. Not battlement heights. Soaring through the sky with nothing but wind and miles of open air in any direction heights.

It was worse when they banked, the plate-sized scales of Kagos's true form shifting under his legs as the ground tipped up towards them. He was most glad of Ty's reassuring presence at his back in those moments;

the elf was far better balanced than he was, and somehow felt more solid than the huge dragon on which they rode.

But Hal had brought Ty along for another reason. He'd noticed the quiet insanity brewing behind the other man's eyes. The same insanity that plagued them all since Fae had disappeared. It had been all they could do just to stop Ty charging off into the world to find her. Throwing himself into preparations for this battle would give him something productive to do with all that fretful energy humming through him.

That's what Laina had done.

Hal closed his eyes. He wished he could take some of the pain that Laina carried. He saw it every day, though she hid it well for the good of her city. It had split itself into shards, different every time he looked at her. There was the pain of losing her daughter again. It came up when anyone wondered out loud where Fae had gone, and it showed around her eyes. Whenever some new need arose in the city, she rubbed at her temples, her responsibility to Throldon ever-present. That was the second pain: that Fae couldn't be her priority. Then there was the pain of wondering if she had gotten used to not having a daughter. That one was the worst. Those were the moments when Laina went quiet, when her gaze went distant. She'd spent so many years learning to accept that she would never see her daughter again, she worried that she'd already gotten over her loss again.

Hal's brow knitted so hard it made his head ache. It had broken him to lose his children. If they were to come back to him after all his years alone, only to be lost again... he didn't think he'd survive it.

"There it is!" Aiya called from her perch higher up on Kagos's neck. Hal dashed the tears from his cheeks — he hadn't even noticed he was crying — and glanced down, thankful for Ty's hand braced on his shoulder.

His stomach plummeted. And it was nothing to do with the height.

Kagos had been right. The army was vast.

It wasn't clear at first, how far that sea of canvas stretched; the tan-coloured tents blended right into the desert. Then a wind blew across the dunes, and the full extent of it became apparent in the endless flap of fabric against the sand.

"I've never seen an army," Ty whispered behind him, his eyes wide as he scanned the ground. "It just keeps going."

Hal glanced over his shoulder at the elf. "Aye, and Kagos was right.

There must be about fifty thousand here." He swallowed. "They must be serious." He allowed himself ten seconds of abject dread before wrenching his focus back to the reason he was hanging in the sky when he'd much, *much* rather have his feet on the ground.

"See those?" Hal pointed to wooden towers interspersed among the tents. "It'll slow them down to be haulin' those along." He squinted, as if it would make the purpose of the towers become clearer. "They don't look like trebuchets..." And not knowing made them even more dangerous. They'd likely only discover the machines' true purpose when they were being leveraged against them.

As he scanned the army looking for weaknesses, his soldier's intuition filled him with foreboding.

"We don't have the numbers to stand against that," Ty said behind him, his voice as heavy as Hal felt.

But he hadn't survived this long by giving up when the odds looked thin.

"Alright, I think we've seen enough," he called up to Aiya. "Let's turn this bird around."

Kagos's rumble of disapproval shook through Hal's thighs, and he let out a bark of hysteria. Aiya shot an incredulous glance over her shoulder.

"No use moping," he said, hauling himself up by the bootstraps. "There's work to be done." He turned his gaze northward again.

"Let's go home."

16

CONNECTIONS

When Luca brought Fae back to the room made of ice so clear she could see the world outside, there was no one waiting for them. His face remained expressionless but for the tiniest furrow in the centre of his brow.

"Stay here," he grunted. "I'll go and see what's kept her." And he left Fae with no one for company but the hunk of crystal inside the circle of chairs.

The view of the Ice Fields beyond La'sa beckoned. She went to step towards the window, when she heard something.

She stopped, and turned just as the sound erupted into barely suppressed laughter.

A tiny woman with hair the colour of autumn crouched behind the crystal, her hand pressed to her mouth, eyes screwed shut as she shook with mirth.

"Um..." Fae looked about for any other hidden Magi, but found none. "Hello?"

The woman held a finger to her lips. "Shh." She took a few steadying breaths, and finally opened her eyes.

They were pure white. She was blind.

She eased to her feet, a wicked grin across her face. "Tell me, did he scowl?" Fae blinked. "He sounded like he was scowling." The woman ran a finger along the back of Kallis's stool. "I told Madja we'd be a while, so she's gone to sort through the stores with her sister for the thousandth time. He won't find them." She approached Fae, navigating the assorted chairs as if she could see them perfectly.

"I'm Irya," she said, holding out a hand as honey-brown as her face. It was a traditional human greeting, and it occurred to Fae that no one else here had done so until now. She took the woman's hand.

Irya's grasp was firm and sure; she squeezed her hand once, and let go, retreating to the plushest chair in the circle and flopping down into it. She was petite, like Fae, perhaps an inch shorter, but curvier. Her hips swayed when she walked, and she stood straight-backed and confident. So different from the blind people Fae had met in Throldon that she wondered if she'd interpreted her white eyes correctly.

Realising she'd neither moved nor said anything yet, Fae stepped forward to drop into the chair next to her. "I'm Fae."

"Oh, I know." Irya flapped an elegant hand dismissively. "Everyone knows who you are — you'll have to get used to that." She leaned forward in her seat, her face unerringly pointed in Fae's direction. "So tell me, did Luca the Implacable scowl?"

Fae thought on it. "Um, a little bit, I guess."

"Ha!" Irya slapped her thigh and threw herself back into her seat. "He's such a stick-in-the-mud. Serves him right to have to go on a snowflake chase while we talk."

Fae's brow wrinkled. "Do you not like him?"

"Hm?" Irya steepled her fingers, playing them about one another. "Oh he's fine. I just like to get a rise out of him when I can." She smirked. "Helps while away the centuries."

Fae's lips kicked up at the corner. She liked this Magi. A lot.

Irya's brow lifted. "Okay, a couple things we'll have to get straight: first off, I can't *see* your face, strictly speaking. I'll explain that later. So if you think something, say it. I'm better at picking up vocal queues than anyone here, but there's a lot that comes from what people can see, that I can't. Second, don't bother lying. I can smell it a mile away, and it's just plain rude to lie to a blind girl. So" — she paddled her hand in the air — "speak up."

"You're not what I expected," Fae said truthfully.

Irya sighed mournfully. "I never am." She played a strand of auburn hair around her fingers. "What *did* you expect?"

"I don't know," Fae cast about for an answer. She hadn't heard anything about Irya aside from her name. But the way the others had talked about her... "Someone more serious?"

"Ha!" Irya barked again. "There's no fun in being serious. When you've been alive five hundred years longer than you expected, you've got to find ways to keep life a bit interesting." She waggled her eyebrows at Fae suggestively.

Fae laughed. "You are definitely not what I expected."

"Good!" Irya clapped her hands together, and sat forward. "I'd hate to be boring. Now" — she pointed straight at Fae — "what's this I hear about you claiming you 'ran out' of power." She made air quotes with her fingers, and then arched one eyebrow severely. "I assume they've already tried to tell you, you can't?"

Fae nodded, and then remembered the other woman couldn't see it. "Yes, it's all I've heard since getting here. But it doesn't change the fact that I haven't had any power since... for over a year."

"Uhuh." Irya sat back, bringing her steepled fingers to her chin. "Sounds like some classic avoidance going on there." Her white eyes regarded Fae as if they *could* see her sitting there. "Might that have anything to do with the impressive outburst that finally prised that awful god from this earth?"

"Well... yes." Fae didn't know what else to say. "I'm sorry but, how do you all know all this?" She waved an arm around the circle, referring to the High Magi not present. "You all seem to know who I am, what I've done, and everyone has an opinion on what I should still be able to do. How?"

Irya drummed her fingers together. "That's my fault I'm afraid."

"I'm sorry?"

She kicked her feet over one arm of her chair, leaning her back against the other. "I've been keeping an eye on things from up here for centuries. Well, me and the other Echoes. But I'm the best." Not a hint of arrogance in that statement, simply pure fact.

"Luca told me about Echoes." Fae searched back through the mountain of information she'd taken in over the past couple of days. "You're like the elf Whisperers."

Irya tipped her head back and roared with laughter. She wiped a tear from her eye and levelled her strange gaze back at Fae.

"The Whisperers *wish* they were like me," she cried. "No, Fae. Echoes are much, *much* better."

"What do you mean?"

Irya cast her eyes to the icy ceiling. "Where to begin?" She tapped her fingertips against her chin. Then threw her hands up as if there was nothing else for it. "I guess at the beginning."

Fae rolled her eyes. "I've heard that before."

Irya ticktocked her finger in the air. "No, you've heard the Aethyr's version of events. Which does *not* start at the beginning." She interlaced her fingers behind her head. "Don't worry, I'll leave out the boring stuff.

"I'm guessing you know about the Aethyreomma and the Rains and how the Aethyr came into our world?" Fae nodded. "Speak up, girl."

"Oh. Yes," Fae said. "And about the gods, obviously."

Irya tipped her head. "Obviously. But we'll skip over them and their childish spat that nearly ended us all and focus on the Aethyr. One character flaw of the Aethyr is that they're rather self-involved. Aethyreomma was indeed a celestial being who took a shine to our little world and meddled where she ought not to have meddled. And everything that followed is true. But what the Aethyr never paid much attention to is that they inhabit Eah'lara — our Spirit Realm. And Eah'lara was already here when they fell to earth in the Rains."

Fae nodded along, following so far.

Irya glanced towards her, as if she should be understanding more. "Eah'lara was already here because we *already had* spirits. The Aethyr are not spirits. They are the offshoots of a celestial being that never should have gotten involved in our world. Nonetheless, they inhabit Eah'lara alongside our native spirits, crowding up the Spirit Realm with their chatter."

Fae frowned. "Right..."

"So the elves — and your Whisperers — who were gifted with affinity for all living things or whatever, were actually given an affinity for sensing the Aethyr. They don't see Eah'lara like you and I do. They don't understand the intricacies of *actual* spirit life because they don't have a sense for it. Unless they're Echoes too, in which case, fair enough. Eah'lara is *our* playground."

"But…" Fae scrambled to catch up. "So what do the spirits do?"

"They're like the life-force in everything. The movement in the air. The growth in the grass. The flicker of life in your chest." She lifted a hand to her heart. "They've always been here, or life wouldn't exist."

"So the Aethyr…"

"The Aethyr like connections. That's their thing. They've all come from one being so they're obsessed with how everything connects together. They're part of the reason it's so easy for me to keep an eye on things from up here. Spirits though, they don't care really. They just are. They exist. That might be why the Aethyr still haven't really noticed them, even after cohabitating for so long."

Fae's head spun. "So when the Aethyr told me that all life was at risk because of the strain being put on their web…" She couldn't finish the thought. Was everything that had happened last year a lie?

Irya swung her legs down off the chair and sat forward, her arms braced on her knees. "Well, they weren't entirely wrong were they? You saw Eah'lara. And the effect that had on everything else. That was all true. There was no avoiding it. Anson was poisoning the world. The Aethyr *and* the spirits. He had to go." She reached out and gripped Fae's hand. "And you did what you had to do. What you were chosen to do, to save us all."

Swallowing thickly, Fae nodded, not trusting her words. Irya patted her hand, and sat back, finally falling silent.

Fae cleared her throat. "That still leaves the problem of me and Source Magic."

"Ah yes!" Irya clapped her hands and jumped to her feet. "I have a theory on that, but you're going to have to work with me on this one. Stand up." Fae stood. "Right. So my theory is this: the Aethyr planted a seed in your mother so that when you were born, you possessed their power, correct?"

"So I understand it," Fae murmured.

"And their strength is in connecting things. I think that in combining you, as a mortal being, and the Aethyr, as inhabitants of Eah'lara, that they've managed to *connect* you to a power source that you wouldn't otherwise have possessed. Namely, *the* Source."

Fae was reminded of the conversation she'd had with Bek, just before she'd taken the Aethyr's powers into herself. About how they had wanted to connect her to their power. Had they meant to connect her to this Source as well? Given that their memories had become hers — however distant they felt now — and she hadn't heard of it before, she somehow doubted it. Which meant that this had all been a colossal mistake.

"I can feel your doubt in the air like a bad smell," Irya said, her nose crinkling. "Alright then, riddle me this: Aethyr don't normally inhabit the sentient races do they?"

"No," Fae confirmed. "They think that a person's soul makes it impossible for them to do so. Like it takes up too much space."

Irya snorted. "Okay, but what if it's because the sentient races have this... potential for Source Magic, and *that's* what's taking up the space."

A thought niggled at Fae. "But centaurs and dragons don't—"

Irya batted her words aside. "Dragons have their own magic. They're *dragons.* They're the only beings that predate Eah'lara. And centaurs are more connected to Eah'lara than the Source. That's why they have their spirit quests. And yes, before you ask, they were doing that before the Aethyr came along." She dropped her hands. "My point is, there is potential in all of us to channel Source Magic to varying degrees. Even you, as a human. It's just that in creating you — the Spiritchild — the Aethyr blew the connection wide open. So you're a being of both Eah'lara *and* the Source of Magic itself."

"Alright." Fae rubbed at her temples. "Say that you're right. How does that explain my complete *lack* of any powers now — either from the Spirit Realm *or* the earth?"

"Fear." Irya said simply, with a shrug. "You're afraid of them. Sure, you'd have been tapped out after fighting a *god* — we all would have been. But that connection inside you is still there, it's still open." She held out her hands. "Close your eyes, and look at Eah'lara with me."

And just because she had the unsettling feeling that Irya *could* see if she didn't, Fae closed her eyes, and looked into Eah'lara.

And stumbled back at what she saw.

Irya whipped a hand out and grabbed Fae's wrist before she could fall over her chair.

"Easy," Irya soothed. "There you are. Now you know what *you* look like in the Spirit Realm." Because unlike with anyone else Fae had ever seen through the fabric of Eah'lara, Irya stood before her as clearly as in the real world. Not an outline, not a silhouette behind a white canvas. The woman, the Echo herself stood before her. Her auburn hair floated behind her as if underwater, and a slow, impish grin spread across her face. And her eyes... her eyes contained the shimmering nebulae of Eah'lara itself.

"We're called Echoes for a reason," she said, letting Fae's hand drop. "While our attention is directed into the Spirit Realm, our forms are literally echoed here. If your focus is elsewhere, well, everyone else is just a shape, right?" She waited for Fae to nod, before allowing her eyes to drift out over the glittering, star-like pastels of the Spirit Realm, mirrored in her eyes. "I spend a lot of my time here," she said, passing a hand through a cloud of spirit dust. "It's how I navigate the world."

Fae gasped her understanding. "You use the outlines to see where everything is."

Irya nodded. "It's not perfect. I can't really interact with people across the veil." She shrugged. "But it's better than the nothingness I was born with." She gestured to her eyes, and dropped her hand, turning her attention back to Fae.

"Now, where do you — *did* you — draw your power from? Before."

Fae held her arms out to the pearlescent clouds of Eah'lara. "Here."

Irya shook her head. "Uh uh. We've already told you it doesn't come from here. Whenever you drew Source Magic — when you wielded the elements — where did that come from?"

Fae pondered the question. "The first time was in a vision." When she'd decided to fight back against the horrors being inflicted on innocent human villagers.

"Okay, and...?"

Fae played a finger over a glistening thread, and tried to imagine Eah'lara before it was strung with these connections. "Then it was when I was fighting Anson." Her voice dropped to barely a whisper. Irya said nothing. Waiting for her to work it out.

She thought back to how her powers had cowered inside her when faced with the black shroud of Anson, until she'd wrenched them into the fight. She'd pulled them from—

"Inside myself," she breathed. She'd pulled her powers from inside herself. Whenever she'd wielded them — Aethyrial or elemental — the power had come from within her.

Irya nodded, her smile approving. "Exactly."

"But I still don't know *how*," Fae protested, the same frustration rising to the surface.

"And in that way, you're no different to any other Magi newly come to their powers."

"How does that help?"

Irya smiled knowingly. "It's easily fixed by training."

Fae's eyes narrowed. "You mean with Luca."

Irya laughed. "Luca's very good. He trained young Magi before the war. But he's no Echo; he's wise enough to leave that stuff to those of us" — she gestured to herself — "who are."

Fae groaned, and opened her eyes to the mortal plane.

Irya opened her eyes in the same moment, and took a seamless step towards her.

"The power to fight — and to heal — is inside you." She stabbed an elegant finger against Fae's chest. "The Aethyr couldn't access it without literally becoming a part of you. Because it is *inside*. It doesn't come from anywhere else." Her lips kicked up into a wicked grin.

"Have fun training." And she sashayed from the chamber, weaving between the chairs like it was a dance she practiced twenty times a day.

17

THE DREAMWEAVER

Fae fell into bed, exhausted.

Luca still hadn't returned after her meeting with Irya, so she'd wandered down from the Crystal Chamber unescorted, her mind reeling with information.

She had no idea what time it was, but she couldn't face anything else La'sa had to throw at her. She found her room, kicked off her boots, peeled the coat from her shoulders, and let sleep drag her under.

The dream was waiting for her.

Anson's dark shroud hovers above, his red eye glaring down, filled with black malice.

And she knows she is going to die.

The powers of the Aethyr arrow in, anchoring her to Eah'lara, and she rises to fight again.

She throws her power in bolts of lightning-fire at the darkness looming above, throwing everything she has at the broken god bent on destroying her. She thrusts a spear of her power into him, pushing everything through it. The end of her power reels through her hands like the end of a rope, and she stands, empty-handed and helpless beneath the dark smog of a god. She has nothing left.

And then Anson explodes, his essence evaporating in the fire of her power.

And in the earth beneath her, something rips apart.

A roar of pain shakes the world.

The walls of her dream crumble around her. The ground heaves and bucks underfoot.

A wave of panic crests inside Fae, her fear about to drown her.

The dark shroud that haunted her is ended, but her own shadows chase her now, tumbling down into a pit she can't escape, as the darkness shakes around her.

Out of nowhere, a light shines through the dark, chasing away her shadows. It wraps around her, warm and bright, and she no longer feels alone.

Fae woke with a start to see her room bathed in light — far more than the little salt lamps gave off. Then she felt the hand on her arm, and turned to find Luca sitting on the edge of her bed.

Her room gave a shudder, and stilled.

Luca's face was blank but for a tension in his jaw, indigo eyes unreadable. The light in the room faded. He removed his hand from her arm, and rose from the bed. The place where his hand had been felt cold in his absence. Her heart lurched.

Fae hadn't realised how long she'd been alone. How long she'd walked among friends and still drowned in her own shadows.

She whipped out and gripped his wrist.

"Please," she whispered, hating herself for saying it, but unable not to. "Stay."

Luca's eyes flared at the corners, and for a moment, it looked as though he would refuse.

Then he sat down again, and she released his wrist. He kept his back to her as he pulled off his boots, the broad shape of his shoulders rigid under his shirt. Then he was leaning back against the headboard, propping his feet up on the bed. Fae settled her head back onto the pillows.

She wanted to apologise. For her nightmares. For taking on a god in the first place. For everything.

"Sleep," his voice rumbled when she opened her mouth to speak. "I'll be here." He folded his arms behind his head, and closed his eyes.

Something inside her gentled at his words, and her eyes slid closed, the sound of his breathing lulling her back to sleep.

The next morning, Fae woke to find her room empty but for a note left on the desk.

Haven't gone far. See you at breakfast.

She cringed, and rubbed her hands over her eyes. Had she really begged him to stay last night?

Groaning, she slunk into the bathing room, and ran the bath as hot as she could bear it. Catching sight of herself in the mirror, she snatched up a comb and began pulling it through the snarls in her hair. She must have tossed and turned in her sleep before Luca had woken her. Because once she'd fallen back to sleep with him beside her... well, she hadn't slept that peacefully since Anson.

She emerged from the tub when the fog of sleep finally dissipated, towelled off, and dressed in clean clothes. Brushing her silvery hair until it lay smooth down her back, she caught sight of Luca's note again. She grabbed her coat and scarf and headed for the kitchen.

Only a few stragglers were left when she arrived for breakfast. Fae helped herself to a much smaller portion than the one Sheree had served her the day before, and dropped into a seat that looked out over the gardens.

Luca found her just as she was finishing her tea.

"Morning." His greeting was gruff, just like most interactions she'd had with him so far.

"Morning," she replied quietly. What did he think about spending the night in her room to fend off her nightmares? She wished the ground would open up and swallow her whole every time she thought about it. Which, she supposed, it might well do if they couldn't figure out how to mend the earth.

Luca jerked his chin to her empty plate. "Are you done?" Fae nodded. "Come with me, there's someone I think you should meet."

Curiosity piqued, Fae followed him out into the gardens. The frosty grass crunched under her boots, the air so cold it hurt to breathe. She pulled her scarf up over her mouth and shoved her hands deep into her pockets, wondering how on earth Luca walked through the open Core in just his shirt.

"Do you dream about it a lot?" he asked quietly, without breaking his stride.

"What?"

He cast her a look over his shoulder. "The fight that nearly killed you."

Fae stumbled to a halt, the colour draining from her face in an instant.

"How did you...?" Had he done something last night that let him see into her nightmares?

Luca came to a stop and turned to face her. The two of them stood alone on the lawn, the borders lined with box hedges and vegetable beds wrapped against the chill.

Fae's heart thundered in her chest at the idea that someone might know how broken she was inside. But Luca met her gaze with the same unreadable expression he always wore, his eyes intense as he considered her.

"I've had my fair share of nightmares chase me from sleep. I know what it is to be haunted by your past."

Fae stilled. The way he'd talked about the war in the Archives... She had no doubt he'd lived through plenty of horrors.

"How bad?"

He shook his head. "You don't want mine added to your own." He turned his body, and motioned for her to follow. "But I'm hoping Athanasius can help with that."

"Who's Athanasius?" Fae jogged to draw level with him.

Luca's face tightened as he led her from the garden and out into the streets of La'sa.

"He's known as the Dreamweaver. He called you here, inserting La'sa into your dreams."

Fae gaped. She'd never heard of anything like it. "How?"

Luca shrugged. "No one really understands how he does it. He's technically an Echo, like Irya, but he's not like any of the others. All I know is that he traced your power surges back to you. And then..." He shrugged again. "He did what he does."

"Huh." Fae thought back to how her dreams had often ended in a call — a pull — to the north, to the ice and the cold. She'd likened it to the call that had tugged her to the monument in the Northern Tundra where she'd met her Aethyrial guides, had taken them into herself to become... more. But while the Northern Tundra had been cold, it hadn't been made of ice. Hadn't had the same light to it that she'd sensed in her dreams. No, now that she knew what it had been, there was no doubt her dreams had been calling her here.

She followed Luca out of the Core, and into the eastern quadrant, on the opposite side of La'sa from her room.

"The Dreamweaver doesn't leave his chambers very often," Luca said as they climbed a wide spiral walkway with walls the same glassy clarity of the Crystal Chamber. "Being close to everyone else can be difficult for him." He approached a wooden door at the end of a corridor that looked out onto the snow. "No one else lives in this quadrant. It's mostly store rooms."

Fae stopped him when he went to knock. "Does he know we're coming?" She couldn't imagine a surprise visit going down particularly well with a recluse the likes of which he'd just described.

Luca's lips twitched, and he rapped his knuckles lightly on the wood.

A heartbeat passed, and the door opened to reveal a man who appeared to be in his sixties, with short, white hair, and striking hazel eyes. His leathery cheeks creased into a smile when he saw them, and he stepped back to let them in.

"Luca! Fae! I've been expecting you. Come in! Come in!" He waved them through, and Fae found herself staring at this bright spark of a man as he bustled about. He took their coats, and showed them through to a light and airy sitting room, with the same glassy walls overlooking the wintery landscape outside La'sa. Four china cups were arranged on a low table, curls of steam escaping the spout of a portly teapot set between them. Luca eyed the fourth cup, but said nothing as he was ushered into a deep-seated armchair by the crackling fire.

The Dreamweaver gestured Fae towards a matching chair, before perching on the couch to serve the tea.

"I'm glad you got my messages," he chatted as he poured. "I was beginning to think I'd lost my touch." He looked up at her, eyes twinkling. "But you're here now." He passed the tea out with a smile, before sitting back with a cup of his own. "What can I do for you?" Again, that twinkle in his eye.

Fae smiled. "What do *you* think we're here for?" She had a feeling he already knew, even if she herself wasn't clear on the details.

The Dreamweaver's smile widened, his eyes creasing at the corners. He glanced at Luca over his teacup. "Astute, this one, isn't she?" Luca inclined his head in agreement.

The Dreamweaver nodded to himself, turning his attention back to Fae. "But I'm forgetting myself!" He put his cup back on the table with a clatter. "I must apologise, my dear. I have become accustomed to everyone knowing my name already." He placed a hand to his chest. "I am Athanasius, but please call me Ath. Everyone here will have you address me as the Dreamweaver, but I will beg you to ignore them." He fixed her with a look that brooked no argument until she nodded.

He leaned forward to reclaim his cup. "I must warn you, Luca, that my daughter is likely to join us. Just as she is unlikely to be happy about what you have come to ask me."

Luca seemed unsurprised by the revelation, only nodding where he sat. "Does it count, if I have not had to ask you?"

The Dreamweaver's eyes crinkled. "You know as well as I that she will not see it that way."

Fae looked between the two of them. What were they talking about?

Just then, she heard footsteps pounding along the corridor outside, and the door burst open.

Irya exploded into the room, her glare somehow conveying a rage Fae would not have thought possible from the easy-going, playful person she'd met the day before.

Irya's sightless eyes moved from the tea set on the table, to Fae, to the serene smile on the Dreamweaver's face, before landing on Luca. Her frown deepened. "Luca Fialli, what are you doing here?"

18

ONE CHANCE

"Now now, Irya." The Dreamweaver sat forward to pour the final cup of tea. "Sit down and let us talk like civilised people." He patted the couch beside him.

But Irya remained standing, her gaze fixed on Luca.

Fae's eyes darted between them, feeling out of her depth twice over. What was going on? And why was Irya radiating such rage?

"Irya," the Dreamweaver pressed firmly, his voice soft but unyielding.

The Echo huffed and stomped over to the couch. Without taking her eyes from Luca, she dropped into her seat, ignoring the cup of tea on the table. "Say what you came to say, and then leave."

"He will do no such thing, Irya," the Dreamweaver rebuked her. "Where are the manners I taught you?"

"Father, Luca does not consider the price demanded of you when he asks for your help." Irya placed a hand on the Dreamweaver's arm. "The war is over, he has no need of your abilities."

He arched an eyebrow at her. "Then perhaps he has come to enjoy a cup of tea, like old friends."

A guilty twinge flashed across Luca's face, and in the silence that followed, Irya's eyes narrowed.

The Dreamweaver sighed. "Your poker face needs work, High Magi." He rubbed a hand through his hair. "Irya, Luca has not asked anything of me yet. And it is my choice whether to weave threads or no."

Catching the look of utter confusion on Fae's face, Athanasius turned from the stand-off happening across his living room, and addressed her instead.

"Luca has come to ask me to help with your dreams, my dear. To dampen the darkness that haunts you, and to help moderate the power surges that escape you." His expression then changed to one of such utter exasperation, Fae almost wanted to laugh. "Irya is trying to stick her nose into my business because she cares about her old man." He held a hand up when Irya went to interject. "My abilities demand a price. In doing this, I would likely have to take your nightmares into my own dreams." He smiled. "But, I have had centuries more practice at commanding dreams, and I am not going to bring the mountain down around us even if I can't get a handle on yours." He turned back to Irya. "I am no fool to need a chaperone to make decisions for me." Irya reddened, but still looked as though she wanted to say more. Athanasius held his hand up again, his voice softening. "Luca would not ask this of me if it was not important. The quakes are getting worse. And I can feel the violence of Fae's dreams even from here. If I can remove them, I can likely slow the progression of the quakes. I am not so selfish as to shy from that."

The fire in Irya's eyes finally quieted. Her lips pressed together as she swallowed whatever words she had wanted to wield in his defence.

Fae, though, had made her own decision.

"Thank you, Dreamweav—" she caught the look on his face "—Ath. I wish Luca had explained fully before we'd come. Because I can't let you do that." Three sets of eyes widened in surprise.

"Fae—" Luca began, sitting forward in his seat.

She shook her head resolutely. "I have already said I will train with you. I will do what I need to do to learn to control this Source Magic. But I will not let someone else take on my nightmares for me." She met his eyes, and let him see how unmovable she was on this. "They are horrible, yes, but they are mine." She felt her hands trembling, and took a breath to steady herself. "And I will deal with them on my own." She was not ready to admit defeat. Not yet.

"My dear," the Dreamweaver spoke softly. "Your dreams are for you to conquer, of course. But in them, your power flows unchecked out into the world. My strength is in Eah'lara — I do not work with Source Magic — but even the Echoes sense the disturbance when your power surges."

Fae glanced to Irya, but the Echo had gone quiet, waiting to see who would emerge victorious from this debate.

"Then I will train," Fae repeated. She looked to both Irya and Luca. "I will take any help I can get, but *I* will learn to control it."

The Dreamweaver watched her for a long minute, finally acquiescing with a nod.

"Alright," he said. "But I add one condition, because this decision is not to be taken lightly." He sat forward, leaning his elbows on his knees as he fixed her with a gaze of such intensity she didn't dare look away from it. "If you cannot gain mastery over your nightmares, and they rip away your control again, I will take them from you, until you are strong enough to take them back." He let her see the sincerity in his hazel eyes. "Agreed?"

Irya blanched, and Fae wished she had not been the one to put her father in such a position.

She would just have to learn control quickly then.

She nodded her agreement, and the Dreamweaver returned the gesture. Luca let out the breath it seemed as though he'd been holding the entire time. Irya visibly sagged in her seat.

Athanasius stood. "Now if you'll excuse me, I'd like a word with my daughter."

He ushered them out, as polite as when he'd welcomed them in, and they descended the quiet, sloping corridor back to the empty passageways of the eastern quadrant.

"Why is Irya so mad at you?" Fae asked. The Echo had seemed unreasonably hostile when she'd arrived, beyond what Luca had come to ask.

Lines bracketed Luca's mouth. "The Dreamweaver and I worked together for a time during the war. He wasn't the same for a long time afterwards."

"He seemed fine to me." Indeed, the man Fae had just met appeared better than most people she knew, Magi or no.

"He took years to recover, and it aged him plenty. Even now he is not the man he was, although he covers it well." He fell silent, the air around him thick with tension.

"How did he know we were coming?" Fae asked.

This time, she just caught the twitch in Luca's lips. "As he said, he is no fool. Despite the distance he keeps, he has a finger on the pulse of most of what goes on around here. He already knew about your dreams. He knew I'd bring you."

She nodded, just as they emerged from the tunnels and out into the Core. She turned to him.

"So, when do we start?"

Luca surprised Fae by seeking out Madja first.

"Madja is a Mizula-Theras dual wielder," he explained on the way to Meeting House. "She can practice water with you as well as introduce you to earth." Thereby covering both a familiar element, and the one she really needed to master.

"What about you?" Fae asked. He had wielded air and fire when they'd last attempted training — surely she would need to learn them too?

"Oh we'll train as well," he assured her. "You'll train with all the High Magi."

Fae frowned. "But, if I learn water and earth with Madja, and air and fire with you, surely that's it?" Those were the four she needed.

Luca shot her a sidelong glance. "We all wield our elements differently, so it'll benefit you to train with all of us. The way Madja wields water might not resonate with you, while Demilda's methods could click straight away. Plus, Powers test all elements. With you wielding four of the six, *and* walking Eah'lara like an Echo, it would be remiss of me to skip the others. So you'll train with all of us."

They found Madja in the stores with Sheree, cataloguing what appeared to be an already obsessively tidy system.

"Madja." Luca knocked on the door, jerking his head in summons.

"Hi Fae," Sheree trilled from where she worked.

Fae waved from the threshold, before Luca steered her out again, Madja in tow.

They went back to the arena, Luca peeling away to sit halfway up the stepped sides. Fae frowned up at him.

"Don't mind him, dear," Madja said. "He's just as curious as the rest of us about you."

Fae grumbled, "Doesn't he have anything better to do?"

Madja shot her a look. "No, dear." And it was clear from her tone what she meant by that — there was nothing more important than getting a handle on Fae's magic.

Fae swallowed. "Alright then." She squared her shoulders, and opened her hands out before her. "What do I need to do?"

Madja's method of teaching couldn't have been more different from Luca's: more of a show-and-tell. Unstoppering a flask at her belt, she manipulated water from within into the air between them, talking about the element's properties as she did. She described how water could be made into either ice or steam depending on how much she allowed the molecules within it to move. How the tension created by those molecules formed a kind of membrane on the surface that she could manipulate as well. And how the presence of the element in all living things made almost anything vulnerable to malicious water-wielding.

"Oh yes," she said when Fae blanched at the implications of that. "Don't be fooled into thinking this is all about playing in the rain and watching flowers grow." She halted the droplets she'd been twirling through the air so that they hovered between them. "Water is the most malleable of the elements. It can hide in the air, flow through small spaces, soak into the ground, or form a wall solid enough to stop an opponent. It can carry other substances — liquid or solid — and it can wash away impurities and contaminants. And in the wrong hands, it can be deadly." The droplets changed shape before Fae's eyes, and hardened into needles of ice. Without so much as raising a finger, Madja drove the needles into the ground to quiver at Fae's feet.

Something flickered behind Madja's eyes. "Never forget how dangerous the elements can be, Fae. To others, and to yourself."

Halfway up the arena seating, Luca coughed.

Madja shook herself, and the ice needles flowed into water drops to rise from the ground again.

"It takes strength to hold onto the elements. Like a reservoir within you." The droplets played along her fingers before flowing up her arm. "Hold on too much, and the magic will take a toll. It will change you. Most Magi are altered in some way by their element. The trick is to control how much. Remember, you are a conduit: let it flow *through* you." She lifted a hand and watched as the water circled her shoulders.

"Cast your mind towards me, and feel for the water," she said. "It can be slippery, and quick. Even if you can't grasp it yet, try and get a taste for how it feels. How it moves."

Fae tried to do as she was asking, casting her senses out from herself as she had the first time she found Eah'lara, in the forests of Il'arys.

But no matter how many ways she tried to go about it — no matter how many times she directed her senses *away* from Eah'lara — she kept coming back to the Spirit Realm beyond the veil.

"You're relying too much on your connection to Eah'lara," Madja said at one point. "The Source Magic doesn't come from there."

"I know!" Fae growled in frustration. "I'm trying to feel on *this* side of the veil" — she threw her hands up — "but there's nothing here!"

Madja looked at her pointedly, her water droplets spinning through the air around her.

"I know, I know." Fae dropped to a cross-legged seat on the ground, staring hard at those drops, willing them to speak to her, to tell her their secrets.

Nothing.

"I think that's enough for today in any case," Madja said, letting the water fall to the ground, where two clods of earth rolled from the shale covering the arena floor. "Just on the off-chance—" Madja gestured to the mud-balls. "See if you can feel that."

Fae squinted at the earth, and tried projecting her senses towards it.

After a couple of minutes, she shook her head. Madja sighed, and the balls rolled back into their divots, the shale sliding into place until there was no sign of her experiment.

"Never mind, dear," she said with a tired smile. "Perhaps you will have more luck with the others." She cast a glance up at Luca, who stood and began making his way down the steps. "It is unfortunate that you don't have the time you should have to learn your elements. We wouldn't normally push the process like this."

"But, as you said," Luca said as he rejoined them, "we don't have the time not to." He held out a hand and pulled Fae from the ground. "Especially if you want to control them before the Dreamweaver intervenes."

"You went to the Dreamweaver?" Madja arched an eyebrow at Luca.

He nodded. "But Fae here wants to control her elements without his help." Madja's eyes darted to Fae with a flash of approval. "Athanasius has given her one chance. If her powers slip her leash again, he'll take the nightmares that are causing the surges."

"But I'm going to figure this out before then," Fae said, determined to manage her demons herself.

"And I'm going to help you." Luca's gaze met hers and held it.

"Thank you Madja," he said, his eyes still fixed on Fae. "We're going to work on fire." His lips curled into a smirk. "I think it will suit your mood."

19

CRUEL KNOTS

After the fiasco of vialling the dragons, Jade had been kept under even more intense watch than usual.

The door to her room was kept open, and she now had four shadows, instead of her usual two. They watched her eat. They watched her sleep. Although what they thought she was going to do, she couldn't fathom. She was kept in a windowless room, at the end of a blind corridor, in a stone maze underground.

Not to mention they had a constant supply of her blood.

And her dragons.

After being reminded what Brother Gerard was prepared to do to her if they failed to cooperate, the dragons had submitted sullenly to the barked orders of the acolytes as they were harried from their former cells to bigger units further along in the wing.

She was glad they'd been moved to bigger cages. If there was one thing the Brotherhood did well, it was keeping their "supplies" well-fed, and they had indeed outgrown their original cells.

In the six years since she'd found them while clambering through caves for Ixio, they'd gone from lizards no longer than her forearm to great beasts that could probably just about carry her on their backs, if they ever got the chance to try. Between hatching in a cave to a worker girl not even into puberty, and being hauled straight into captivity, they'd never had the chance to stretch their wings and soar the skies.

A lump formed in her throat at the thought. If she hadn't been in that cave, searching for gems, it would never have collapsed, would never have revealed their abandoned clutch, hidden in a concealed alcove in the rock. They would have remained undisturbed, and been spared this loathsome fate.

And she would have gone back to Ixio's warehouse, to sleep on the floor with the other workers.

Her lips twisted into an ugly grimace. What cruel knots, the threads of fate had woven for her.

One of her shadows approached the open door.

"You're needed at the cages."

Jade started. "Again?" She clamped a hand over her mouth. It wasn't wise to question orders.

But the shadow simply nodded, and stepped aside to let her pass. It was the tall one with the dark eyes, eyes that softened as she passed.

She knew her amber eyes stood out against the mocha of her skin, knew that despite the Brotherhood's best efforts, her cropped black hair still framed her feminine features, and that even beneath her whites, her curves were proportioned to attract notice.

But she also knew that noticing such things was a shortcut to suffering.

She avoided the shadow's eyes, and headed to the dragon cages.

Jade entered the live supply wing to find the dragons understandably agitated; it had been only a few days since their last vialling. But where before they'd been crammed into cages that were small enough to reach in and grab them, now they were in enclosures big enough for the dragons to make more trouble for their captors.

The red — the one Jade thought of as the Alpha — clung to the bars across the top of his full-height cage, hissing down at the unfortunate acolyte charged with his sample.

Meanwhile, the delicate silver was being pinned by two burly acolytes in her cage.

And Jade felt one of the bonds inside her shiver in pain.

She'd never felt anything from the dragons before, their presence nothing but a soft hum in her heart reminding her that she wasn't alone.

But now, her tether to the silver trembled, and it wrenched something deep inside her.

"Stop." She strode to the cage door. "You're hurting her!" Hands grabbed her from behind — her shadow pulling her away. She knew she'd be punished for interfering, knew that there was nothing she could do here, but she couldn't stand by either. The silver looked up, bronze eyes widened by fear, blood seeping from the corners like red drops of pain.

"Stop!" Jade pulled against the hands that held her. "Leave her alone!" Through the bars, the other dragons took up her call, screeching their protests, beating their wings, and hissing venomously. Acolytes fell over themselves scrambling from the cages, slamming doors shut behind them. All eyes turned to the skirmish unfolding around the silver's pen.

Jade wrenched one arm free, and slipped from her shadow's grasp. She threw herself against the bars of the silver's cage. "Let her go! You're hurting her!" The silver trembled beneath the weight of the two men pinning her. Her bronze eyes swivelled desperately around the room, taking in her frantic siblings, shrieking for her release, the fearful acolytes backing away from the cages, and finally turned to Jade, her hands wrapped around the bars with a white-knuckled grip.

Along the bond, Jade heard her own words repeated back to her.

Don't be afraid.

Then the silver fought back. The normally gentle female — who preferred to sit quietly rather than wail and hiss — bucked and reared, jerking her wings open and slamming them shut in an effort to throw the men from her. She threw her head from side to side, snaking her neck, flicking her tail, lashing her body until the acolytes had no choice but to release her. Her elegant, triangular face was contorted in rage, chasing her captors into a hasty retreat. The one nearest the door dived for safety. As the second fled from the cage, she spun to face them, and her clawed wingtip sliced across his shoulder, drawing blood. He stumbled, and fell through the door while his brother slammed the bars shut.

Jade's shadow dragged her away from the cages again, and she didn't know if it was to protect her, or prevent her from making things worse, but she didn't care.

The cries of the dragons echoed off the stone walls, their claws clashing against the metal bars of their cages as they threw themselves about, jaws open to display every one of their sharp teeth.

"What is this?" Brother Gerard stepped into the room, his own escort of acolytes flanking him. The dragons increased their clamour, hissing and snaking their heads, their eyes gleaming with hatred.

Brother Gerard's eyes flashed. "Enough!" He stepped forward and gripped Jade's arm, wrenching it at an angle hard enough to force her to stumble. "ENOUGH!"

The dragons fell silent, the only sound that of their claws against the bars.

Brother Gerard yanked at Jade's arm until she was inches from his face, his breath hot against her cheek. "Your presence seems to be making things more difficult here." He made a sharp gesture to one of the acolytes, and Jade heard one of the pens open. The sounds of a scuffle followed, along with a panicked shriek. Inside her, a bond trembled. The green.

She tried to turn to see what was happening, but Brother Gerard gripped her chin so hard it hurt, and pulled her face even closer until she could see the burst blood vessels on his bulbous nose.

"Perhaps if you aren't feeling in much of a helpful mood, you aren't the one that needs encouragement." He sneered at her, his eyes darting over her shoulder only long enough to nod at his underlings before he returned his attention to her.

A sudden keening sound filled the pens, a high-pitched wail of pain, and the bond within Jade shimmered, yanking mercilessly at something deep in her gut, demanding an answer.

She struggled against Brother Gerard's grip, trying to turn, to see what they were doing, but his hold on her was unyielding. His lips twisted into a dark smirk the more she fought him, and the horrible keening noise continued unabated over her shoulder.

Tears spilled over her cheeks as the sound of unrelenting pain surrounded her, ricocheting off the walls to come at her from all sides. And the bond inside her twisted in agony.

Ignoring Brother Gerard's sneering face, she screwed her eyes shut, as if that could make it any better, and reached for the bond that radiated pain. She stroked it, caressed it with her touch, soothing it the only way she knew how.

Don't be afraid, she sobbed along the bond. *Stop fighting. I'll stop fighting. And they'll stop.*

She took hold of the other five bonds. *Stop fighting*, she pleaded them.

And then for the first time, she heard a response.

No. Her breath stopped in her chest at the single word that rang through one of the bonds. From the Alpha. *We will not stop fighting.* In her mind's eye, she saw the swirling bronze of his eyes, distinct in their own way from those of his siblings.

Then they won't stop hurting you. Jade squeezed her eyes against more tears. *I can't stop them.* Her shoulders slumped, and she went limp against Brother Gerard's grip. Behind her, the heart-wrenching sounds of torture stopped. She was released, and she whirled to see what they'd done.

A sob escaped her lips before she had a chance to slip on her mask of impassivity, long since abandoned in her distress.

The tip of the green's left wing was bent at the wrong angle, the bones broken and wrenched out of place. The dragon was collapsed on the ground, an acolyte pinning his neck while his chest heaved in pain. Despite all of that, not a single drop of blood was spilled.

Get off him, Jade wanted to snarl. She bit the inside of her cheek to stop herself before the words could come out. It would only make things worse.

"Finish vialling them," Brother Gerard snapped at the acolytes. "Now." He stepped in close to her side, and leaned down to breathe in her ear. "I think we'll have to have words with the Sorcerer Supreme, you and I." She swallowed bile, hearing the sick pleasure he took in that promise.

Inside, she took hold of the six bonds that meant everything to her.

I'm sorry, she whispered. What else was there to say? She wasn't strong enough. She couldn't fight back. Sure, the Brotherhood used the dragons to punish her, and vice versa. But even if they could break out, if they could somehow fight free of this place, there was a reason the acolytes had a ready supply of their blood on hand.

She fingered the seventh bond of oil and blood inside her, the one that wasn't welcome there. The constant reminder that she could never be free of this place.

We won't stop fighting. She looked up to find the red's eyes boring into hers. *Do not give up on us.* She looked around. Despite submitting to the acolytes, all six of her dragons were watching her. All six gazes held a determination that could fell mountains. And it rocked her to her very core.

Do not give up on us. Because if she gave up, it wouldn't be just her subjected to this life. It would be all of them. And these dragons, these creatures that held her heart, they deserved to *fly*.

She plucked at the bond inside her again, the one they all had. Pulled at it, and let it drop.

She met the eyes of the red again, and nodded. Just once.

He dipped his head. And across the pens, all five of his siblings followed suit.

Brother Gerard stiffened beside her. "That's enough," he snarled, and yanked her from the room.

Inside her, Jade's dragons hummed with anger.

And a promise.

20

THIN ICE

Brother Gerard didn't waste any time. He dragged her straight from the bowels of the Sanctum up to the Sorcerer Supreme's Atrium.

Jade was hauled from the cool, dark stone maze into the dazzling sunlight streaming through the open sides of the atrium, the dry heat of the desert suffocating as they swept in through the gilded doors.

The Sorcerer Supreme lounged in a chaise to the side of the chamber, dressed in his customary white, long silk curtains protecting him from the glare of the sun's rays. He lowered the papers he'd been perusing and straightened as Brother Gerard barged into the room.

The Brother hurled her into the atrium, and she stumbled down the steps to sprawl across the floor.

"Explain yourself." The Sorcerer Supreme stood, stalking towards them, his voice like ice despite the desert sun.

"I... I..." Jade scrambled to her knees. But what could she possibly say that would make this situation better?

"Not you." He cut her off with a slash of his hand, and turned his black gaze to Brother Gerard.

Brother Gerard seemed to miss the danger in the Sorcerer Supreme's voice. It was subtle, like a sharp knife slipping under ribs; deadly, and quiet.

"Xid is impeding the replenishment of essential supplies," the Brother blustered, oblivious to the thin ice he stormed across. "She is inciting rebellion in the supply stock! One of my acolytes was injured today in a routine vialling."

The Sorcerer Supreme fixed Brother Gerard with a flat stare.

"Did you get the samples?"

Brother Gerard blinked. "Yes." He straightened, and the colour drained from his face. He glanced down at Jade, where he'd so carelessly flung her, finally realising his position.

"Are the supply stock safely enclosed?" The Sorcerer Supreme stalked across the atrium. Slowly.

Brother Gerard swallowed thickly. "Yes." A light sweat broke out across his brow.

The Sorcerer Supreme came to a stop before the Brother, close enough to kiss. "Then why is my control asset bleeding on my floor?"

Jade glanced down, and saw a flower of blood blooming across her knee through the white of her trousers. She stared at it. When was the last time she'd bled without someone there to collect it? Even her monthly bleeds were collected and taken gods-knew-where. At first it had been mortifying. Now, it was just another facet of her life.

Brother Gerard dropped to the floor, pressing his head into the tile, his arms stretched out, palms either side of the Sorcerer Supreme's feet.

"Forgive me, Supremacy," he grunted into the ground. "I thought only to teach Xid the importance of the samples we collect."

"Stand." The Sorcerer Supreme's voice was a blade, hovering over the the Brother's heart. Jade wondered how many people had found themselves in the path of his mercy and lived to talk of it. From the cold fury in his gaze, she suspected the number was pitifully low. Brother Gerard scrambled to his feet. "Get Jade a healer." He bowed deeply, and turned to see to his commands.

"Brother Gerard." He turned back, eyes widening expectantly.

The Sorcerer Supreme, lightening quick, reached forward, took hold of the Brother's face in his hands, and wrenched his head around with a *crack*.

Jade gasped as Brother Gerard slumped to the ground, his expectant eyes now forever unseeing.

The Sorcerer Supreme looked up to Jade's shadow, hovering in the doorway. "The healer."

"Of course, Supremacy," came the hurried reply, and then her shadow was gone too, leaving Jade alone with the most dangerous man in the Sanctum, possibly in all of Pharro.

Who now turned his attention to her.

Jade shuffled on her knees, wincing as the bleeding skin scraped against sandstone. Gritting her teeth against the sharp sting of pain, she bowed her head. "Supremacy."

His sandalled feet stepped into her field of view. "Stand up, Jade." His voice had lost its knife-edge, but it still slithered under her skin, and she suppressed a shudder as she rose. "Come. Sit." The words were inviting, but his tone left no room for misinterpretation. They were a command, and Jade knew better than to refuse. She followed him back to the chaise, and perched on the end when he indicated she take a seat.

He eased back into the cushions at the other end, and regarded her with his black gaze.

Jade fought the urge to fidget under his scrutiny. It felt like they sat that way for long minutes before his lips kicked up, and he leaned forward.

"I think it is time we talk about why you are here."

Jade started. Now? After six years in ignorance? Her confusion must have shown in her face, because the Sorcerer Supreme nodded. It felt somewhat incongruous coming from him. One didn't hope for understanding from the Sorcerer Supreme. He demanded obedience from everyone. There wasn't room for anything else.

"I can see you are confused," he said. "Let me explain." He shuffled some of the papers left on the low table beside him, and pulled out one covered in lists and numbers. "These are soldier counts for the troops provided by the Noble Houses for the Eminency's conquest in the north." He glanced up at her. "You do know about our efforts in the north?"

Jade shook her head. She had no reason to know anything that went on outside the Sanctum.

The Sorcerer Supreme made a frustrated sound in the back of his throat. "From the beginning then. Our Eminence — you know who that is yes?" Jade nodded. Of course she knew the Eminence. He was the ruler of Pharro and the Greater Thamibian Empire. "Good. Our Eminence has set his sights on the fertile lands north of the desert. He has succeeded in bringing all Thamib's nations under one empire, and seeks to expand further still." He waved a hand as if dismissing the importance of such a move. "There are advantages: better soil for crops, more land, materials we cannot source here in the south..." He flicked his hand impatiently. "In order to conquer this land, His Eminence requires an army. More than his own personal forces. So the Noble Houses have been called to supply soldiers for the campaign." He jabbed the papers pointedly.

Jade nodded blankly. She still didn't understand what any of this had to do with her.

The Sorcerer Supreme eyed her shrewdly. "Do you know what we do here, Jade?"

She blinked. "In the Sanctum, Supremacy?"

His black eyes gleamed as he nodded.

She shook her head. "No, Supremacy." Even after six years, she couldn't fathom what it was that the Brotherhood did here. She'd always assumed it was some sort of sadistic worship. She didn't know of any gods that demanded blood sacrifices, but that didn't mean there weren't any.

The Sorcerer Supreme smiled, but it was cold.

"Magic."

Jade's eyes widened. Magic?

"Did you never wonder at my title?"

She hadn't. She hadn't dared to. Although now she thought about it, the rank of Sorcerer should have rung alarm bells. Is that what all the Brothers were? Sorcerers? Her mind raced. A thousand thoughts jostled for position inside her head, all blurring together in a storm of white noise.

Eventually, she shook her head. "I don't understand, Supremacy."

"Please, call me Kohl."

Jade blinked, and scanned the Sorcerer Supreme's eyes for any sign that she should expect the imminent arrival of death.

"You're confused."

Jade nodded. So confused she wondered if she'd knocked her head when Brother Gerard had thrown her to the floor, that she lay there still and that this was all the workings of her addled brain.

"Let me explain." He straightened in his seat. "The dragons are growing to an... unmanageable size. We need them to be more cooperative." His eyes fixed her with a pointed look. "We need *you* to be more cooperative. Perhaps it is time you understood what it is the dragons are needed for." He paused, seeming to wait for a response.

"Yes, Supremacy." He raised an eyebrow. "Kohl."

The Sorcerer Supreme's lips curled up at one side.

"All magic demands a price, Jade." He stood and paced to the wide balcony overlooking the city of Pharro and the desert sands beyond, hands clasped behind his back. "One can't have something for nothing, after all. The most valuable currency in magic, is blood."

Jade started. Blood. And like that, everything made sense. But the Sorcerer Supreme wasn't finished.

"The more powerful the source, the more potent the blood. So you can imagine how much we value dragons as a source. They are arguably the most powerful beings that still roam this earth. And your unique... attachment to them gives you a special kind of leverage to gaining their cooperation." He turned to face her, his profile outlined against the orange glow of the Thamibian sands. A dry, hot breeze whispered in through the open sides of the atrium, ruffling the strands of his inky black hair. Jade supposed he was quite an attractive man, if he didn't send chills down her spine with almost every word he spoke, every dark glance he sent her way.

"With dragon blood, we can strengthen the Eminency's forces, protect the soldiers against harm, even speed their travel across the desert. We can make the empire truly great, expand its reach across the continent, and become the unrivalled power over all nations. All because our spells, our magic, have one of the most potent power sources the earth can deliver." He stepped back inside, stalking back towards her. "So you see, Jade," he leaned in, bracing his hands on the back of the chaise, trapping her in a cage of his arms. She bristled, and fought to keep her features neutral. "We need the dragons to cooperate. Our Brothers need free access to their blood, as and when it's needed. For the success of the empire." The intensity of his gaze filled her vision. He was so close to her face that for an instant, it was like she was drowning in those twin pools of pure black. Her breath caught in her chest. His lips twitched, and he straightened, releasing her from his prison. "And when we take the north, the burden on our loyal, *obedient*, beasts will finally relent. We may even be able to release them."

Jade knew without question that there was no way her dragons would ever be released. Never be free to stretch their wings and fly. Whether the Brotherhood had a dozen, or even a hundred dragons to replace them.

But there were no more dragons.

They would never be free.

Even Ixio had cautioned her about crossing the Brothers in the red robes, years ago. No good ever came of a deal with the Brotherhood, he'd said.

Yet he'd still sold her out to them.

And he'd died for it.

Something must have shown on her face, because the Sorcerer Supreme frowned down at her.

"It would be best, for all of us, for all of *you*, if you agree to work with us Jade. I would hate to have your dragons put in shackles along with you."

Jade flinched at the idea. Cages were bad enough. Shackles would kill them all — if not in body, then in spirit.

She didn't know why she said it, why she'd want to bait him, but the words were out of her mouth before she could stop them.

"Why don't you just spell us to obey, when you have all of our blood?" She could have slapped herself, but she had to know. Had to know why that oily bond inside her had never been used to control her. Unless it already was.

The Sorcerer Supreme smirked, and sent chills under her skin. "I'd much rather use my most valuable assets to further our goals in the north." He leaned in again, and gripped her chin so hard she gasped in pain. "It takes power to control a living thing, and I control enough important ones already. Especially when we have other, more effective ways to ensure your cooperation. Honestly it's almost too easy. Hurt the dragons, rein you in. Hurt you" — he jerked her chin to the side roughly and brushed his lips to her ear — "and the dragons fall right in line."

Jade tore herself free of his grip and whipped her head round to stare daggers at him.

The Sorcerer Supreme breathed a laugh. "Go on," he said, inches from her lips. "Tempt me. It's been a while since I leashed someone new to my will. It would be so sweet for my next one to be you." He trailed a finger down her cheek. Jade flinched.

A knock came from the towering gilded doors.

The Sorcerer Supreme didn't move. "Yes."

"The healer, Supremacy." A voice came from beyond.

"Ah yes," the Sorcerer Supreme murmured against Jade's ear, glancing down at the blood stain on her knee. "Wouldn't want any of that precious

138

blood going to waste. Or falling into the wrong hands." He straightened, shooting her one of his black stares. "Enter," he called, then strode back to his balcony.

The healer entered with Jade's shadows in tow, and immediately bustled over to her. While the Brother tended to her knee, a clean pair of trousers was laid on the chaise beside her.

"Escort Jade back to her rooms as soon as her blood is sealed," the Sorcerer Supreme said, addressing no one in particular, his back turned to the room. "Then report for vialling." Jade stilled as he turned to give her an icy glare. "We never can have too much on hand, after all."

His gaze caught on Brother Gerard's lifeless body. "And remove that."

21

CONTROL

Fae trained with the High Magi for a week.

Madja continued juggling water and earth while Fae tried reaching for them any way she could think of. Luca wielded his elements to the point where Eah'lara trembled, in the hope that it would shake something loose. Demilda was an Aurora-Mizula dual wielder, and tried talking Fae through how air and water felt to her senses. She brought a wide, shallow dish with her that she called a scrying bowl, explaining how water had memory, and could sometimes be used to see patterns.

Terrence was a Theras-Mizula dual wielder like Madja, and a welcome presence of stolid dependability. But he surprised her with insisting they meditate.

"No point trying to force the issue if your mind isn't ready for it," he grumbled, taking a seat on the lowest ranks of arena steps. So they spent their time working through the blocks in Fae's subconscious. She learnt more about how much her fear was holding her back in those sessions than she had ever figured out on her own.

Kallis's tactics were even more dramatic than Luca's. He was an Umbra-Incendus dual wielder, and drowned the arena in darkness the second he entered, lighting his path with columns of flame. His hair gleamed blue-onyx in the firelight, and his copper eyes glowed as he prowled towards her with languid, feline grace.

"Hello, Fae dear," he drawled.

"Kallis," Fae replied warily. While he prowled about like Luca did, Kallis's movements were lazier. Luca watched, ready at any moment to pounce; Kallis regarded the world through half-lidded eyes with no intention of involving himself, a jungle cat content to sprawl in his tree while everyone else scurried around beneath him.

She was honestly surprised he'd bothered to come to these sessions at all.

"I wonder if you've noticed how the elements each have their own personalities," he said, twirling a flame around his fingers the same way she'd seen Luca do it. Kallis arched a lazy eyebrow at her. "Earth is sturdy, reliable, and *boring*. Air is flimsy and mostly useless." Fae snorted. She already knew that wasn't true. Kallis ignored her. "Water is fluid and adaptable, but it can also be ice — brittle, and cold. Fire" — the columns of flame flared — "fire is passion, hot and wild, and hard to tame." He stalked closer. "Light is useful," he admitted grudgingly. "But dark is the element of secrets, lovers, and assassins." The flames guttered, and the darkness in the arena deepened. Between his control of his elements, Kallis surrounded them with a velvet black so intense she could almost touch it, but for the fire he held in his eyes, inches from her own. "It's the element where your demons live, and where your darkest desires hide."

Light bloomed from the side of the arena where Luca maintained his customary watch over her lessons.

"*Kallis*," he admonished.

Kallis rolled his eyes and straightened, reeling the darkness back like a cloak. He left two columns of flame alight behind him, and stepped back towards them.

"High Magi Fialli may try to teach you control over the fire," he said with a wave to where Luca sat as he sauntered across the shale floor. "But I would suggest you try relinquishing it instead. Fire is fickle." He pivoted upon reaching his flames, and shot her a look that was pure temptation. "Let go."

"Might I remind High Magi Alum that letting go is precisely how Fae has found herself in this situation in the first place?" Luca remarked dryly from his perch.

Kallis's face darkened. "Must you preside over every session, Luca?" He scowled to the side.

"Yes," came the flat response.

Fae covered her mouth as she fought a grin. It was clear Kallis was unaccustomed to being challenged. He was, undeniably, a beautiful man — seduction personified. She found herself wondering how many had fallen for his charms over the years.

The week passed in a blur of such lessons, and she fell into bed each night more exhausted than the last. But despite their efforts, none of the High Magi had managed to coax so much as a puff of air from her. And try as she might, Fae still couldn't find where the Source Magic was supposed to be coming from.

She'd just returned from a particularly frustrating session with Terrence, during which she had utterly failed to focus her thoughts on anything useful at all, when Irya appeared at her door.

"Knock knock," the Echo trilled as she walked right in and threw herself down on the mattress beside Fae. "How's training going?"

Fae, staring up at her ceiling, groaned and flung an arm over her face. "It's not," she lamented. "I've tried everything they've told me to try. Madja even had me stand barefoot up to my ankles in mud the other day." Neither of them had been convinced it would work, but nor had they wanted to leave anything to chance. "I've held my breath until I thought I was going to pass out," she continued ticking fingers off, "I've played with fire until I questioned my sanity—"

Irya snorted. "Let me guess: Kallis?"

"What gave it away?" she answered darkly.

"Luca would *never* suggest playing with fire," Irya said, her face schooled into an expression of utmost seriousness. Then her lips twitched, and she dissolved into gales of laughter.

"Oh don't look so glum!" She gave Fae a shove. "Irya is here to save the day!"

Fae's brows knitted in confusion. "I thought you'd be mad at me."

"Why? Because Luca asked my father to help you?" Irya shook her head. "That's not your fault, and whatever happens because of it won't be either." Her lips twisted into a wry smile. "My father will do whatever he sees fit, regardless of anything I have to say on the matter. If Luca hadn't gone to him, he might well have asked you anyway."

"Then why were you so angry with Luca?"

Irya pursed her lips. "Luca has a chip on his shoulder about protecting us all, since even before the war." She paused, thinking. "Sometimes he thinks he has to take it all on himself, and makes decisions without considering that maybe we might be more capable than he thinks. He'd already decided that you needed my father's help without asking you, or thinking about what that meant for him."

Fae mulled it over. "I'm sure that's not all there is to it."

Irya shot her a deeply cynical look. She reached over to give Fae's hand a squeeze. "You're trying," she said. "And you'll get it." Her mouth kicked up into a determined grin. "And I'm going to help you." She laughed at Fae's groan. "Tomorrow. Right now, you look as if a strong breeze could knock you over." Indeed, that's exactly how she felt, but there was a nervous energy in her, urging her on.

The next day, Luca met her at the arena, a familiar face by his side.

"Ah, fair Fae! How I hoped we would meet again." Alexi swept out a bow, his wide smile beaming as his striking eyes glimmered in the morning sun.

"Alexi!" Fae returned his smile. He wore the same sleeveless leather jerkin she'd seen him in before, and she subconsciously tugged her coat closer around her. "What are you doing here?" She glanced towards Luca, who stood watching their exchange. "Alexi saved me from the Warrens, my first morning here." She turned back to him. "I've not seen you around since though."

Luca answered. "Alexi's been running patrols this last week," he explained. "But now that he's back, I've asked him to help with your training."

"Oh! What element do you wield?" she asked.

Alexi's smile broadened. "Oh no, I'm not a Magi," he corrected her.

"He's our combat trainer," Luca supplied. "There's no one better to teach you to fight." He gestured to the weapons racks against the wall.

Fae frowned at him. "But... Why do I need to learn to fight?"

Luca stepped up to her. "We've thrown a lot at you this week, and your focus is all over the place. Alexi is going to train you until you learn to think with only your body." He leaned in, and tapped a finger to her temple. "You need to clear your mind." Straightening, he retreated back to his customary spot. "Then, you and I will train."

Alexi was still smiling when she turned back to him.

He strode over to the weapons racks, and gestured to the ranks of weaponry arrayed there.

"Have you done any combat training before?"

Fae swallowed. "Of a sort," she hedged.

Alexi nodded. "Alright. What weapons are you familiar with?"

Fae's eyes flicked to the twin swords at the end of the rack. "None in particular," she said, dragging her gaze back. She hadn't danced in over a year.

If Alexi noticed her hesitation, he said nothing of it. Instead, he selected the hardwood staves Luca had chosen the first time he'd brought her here, and handed one to her.

"Then we shall begin with the Bō," he said. "It is blunt and simple enough to hold, but good for teaching balance and focus." He moved back into the middle of the arena. "I will teach you some sequences first. Then we can put them together, and that is when the fun really starts." He flashed her a white grin that gleamed against his olive skin, and then his lesson began in earnest.

She was glowing with sweat by the time they were finished, her coat long since abandoned by the weapons rack.

"You move well, fair Fae!" Alexi boomed when he called the lesson over. "You understated your abilities! You must tell me how you learned to move like that!"

Fae hauled down a breath, her chest heaving, and gestured limply that she needed a minute.

Alexi just chuckled, the sound rumbling around the arena. "Alright, keep your secrets. But next time I will be better prepared to test your mettle!" He shot her a wink, then waved to Luca. "I will leave you for now, High Magi!" Turning back to her, he leaned in. "Until tomorrow, fair Fae."

Fae whimpered as he strolled from the arena, not even slightly winded. She wasn't sure if her muscles would even hold her upright after the exercises he'd put her through.

"Would you like to try Source Magic before or after lunch?" Luca drawled as he drew level with her.

"You're trying to kill me," she gasped incredulously. "That's the only possibility. You plan to torture me in the name of training, and hope I drop dead in the process."

The corner of Luca's mouth twitched. "Why would I bother going to all the trouble of training you, when I could have just left you out in the snow?"

Fae's blood went cold at the starkness of his words. "Alright, no need to get crotchety," she mumbled.

"Fae! Just the person!" Irya sashayed into the arena, her auburn hair swinging from a high tail tied at the crown of her head. She halted a few feet away, waving the air in front of her face. "Oof, what happened to you? It smells like you went twenty rounds with a snow bear!"

"Luca's had me training with Alexi," Fae replied, grateful for Irya's interruption.

Irya hissed. "Sadist."

"Alexi's not bad!" Fae jumped to his defence.

"Oh no, Alexi's lovely," Irya amended. "He just doesn't operate on the same level as us mere mortals."

"But he's not a Magi."

Irya waved the comment away. "Semantics, my dear. He's still stronger, faster, and better at almost anything physical than anyone else here. Anyway" — she turned her blind eyes toward Luca — "I'm going to take Fae for some lunch — and a bath." She gingerly reached out to steer her to the exit at arm's length. "I'll return her to you refreshed and ready for... whatever it is you're doing here."

Fae turned to shoot Luca an answer over her shoulder. "After lunch. See you later."

He just watched her go, his dark gaze as unreadable as ever.

22

NEW APPROACH

Irya shoved Fae unceremoniously into her bathing room and waited all of five minutes before banging on the door again.

"Come on! I can only wait so long!"

Fae dragged herself from the tub and towelled dry, opening the door a crack while she pulled on some clean clothes.

"You'd have thought, that after five hundred years, you might have learned some patience!" she grumbled.

Irya barked a laugh. "Ha! You wait half a millennium and then see how patient you feel."

Fae emerged, weaving her ash-blonde strands into a braid that now fell past her waist to the lower curve of her spine.

"Excellent!" Irya clapped her hands together, and then patted the bed beside her, shuffling over to make room.

Fae frowned. "I thought we were getting lunch." Her stomach growled its assent.

"We are." Irya smiled sweetly. "But we're taking my way."

Fae cocked her head questioningly.

Irya tutted, and patted the bed again. "Sit. We're going to use Eah'lara to guide us, and I don't want you falling and knocking yourself out at the first step." She help a hand up when Fae opened her mouth to speak. "No arguments — this is what we're doing. So look into Eah'lara, and I'll teach you how I navigate it."

Fae clamped her lips shut on the questions she had, closed her eyes, and did as she was bid.

The Spirit Realm was as beautiful as always, the shimmering pastel nebulae drifting about as serenely as the motes of spirit dust spinning gently through the ether. Glittering spider-silk threads criss-crossed the endless space, spearing off to distant lifeforms, connecting everything together.

"Right." Fae jumped as Irya materialised beside her. "I've never tried teaching anyone else how to do this so it'll be a game of trial and error for both of us, okay?" The Echo's white eyes were dusted with colour here, and they watched her, waiting for a response.

Fae opened her hands out. "I am your student."

Irya nodded. "Alright. First thing's first: I know you can see the auras of *living* things, but you need to see inanimate objects too, or you'll end up falling flat on your face." She gestured around them. "See the dust?" Fae nodded. "Watch it. It drifts through the space. But it... sort of... stills, when there's something in the way." She grasped at the air, as if searching for the right words, and shook her head. "It's almost harder here, because there is life in the mountain itself, so the dust moves through it the same as it moves through the air, but you can spot the walls with a bit of practice. Here—" She pointed in front of them. "The door to the bathing room. It's made of wood, which is dead now that it's no longer connected to the tree, so the dust moves differently around it compared to the walls either side, and the air around it. Can you see?"

Fae squinted at where she knew the door to be. "Yes..." she said hesitantly. If she focused hard enough, the tiny motes seemed to slow, falling into a current of sorts — around what could be the outline of the door. "It's like the dust would rather avoid going through the door." Some of the tiny particles did, carried by their own momentum. But most sidled around, like river water around a rock.

"Excellent, now tell me what else you can see."

Fae looked around. She found the edge of the wardrobe, and the door to the corridor beyond. The table and chair were harder, but they were there too. "I can't see the walls though."

Irya rose. "That's alright, I can help you with that bit and you'll get used to it. Now, without leaving Eah'lara, remind yourself of where your limbs are, and stand up."

It was harder than she thought, but eventually, Fae found the feel of the bed under her legs, the palms of her hands against her thighs, her feet on the ground. She stood.

Irya clapped her hands together. "This is perfect!" she squealed. "You're so much better at this than I expected! Right, take it easy. Let's go to lunch."

Going from sitting to standing, to walking across La'sa and into the busy kitchens seemed like a leap, but Fae was determined to succeed at something today. She followed Irya across the room, trying to remember what obstacles were between her and the door.

"Alright, now remember where your hand is, and reach out to where you know the door handle is," Irya coached. Using her spiritual sight to guide her physical body was an exercise in concentration unlike anything else the High Magi had tried with her so far, but she managed to place her hand on the handle. The cool metal of the doorknob felt like a memory as she turned it, and opened her door. "Excellent!"

"Not that I'm not grateful to finally be learning something," Fae said as they left her room, "but how is this going to help me master Source Magic?"

"Well," Irya tapped a finger against her lips as she led the way through the Warrens. Magi auras approached like ships in the mist and passed without incident, clearly visible and easily avoided. "I can't teach you like the High Magi can," she said apologetically. "My strength lies in here. Kind of like a seventh element." She cupped a hand to the side of her mouth, and stage-whispered, "But they don't like us calling it that." She straightened and traced a finger along an Aethyrial thread running alongside them. "It's all connected. But Eah'lara is all you have access to at the moment. So I figured, if I can teach you how to relate this to the mortal, physical world" — she spread her arms to indicate what they were doing — "then maybe it will help your body to reconnect itself to the Source." She shrugged, and shot Fae a knowing glance. "You of all people should know the importance of connections, being Aethyr-born and all." She winked, just as Eah'lara brightened and took on a whole new spectrum of colours. Inside the mountain, the Spirit Realm had adopted the hues of ice and rock — all glittering blues and crystal whites, silvers, and greys.

Outside, in the open air of the Core, Eah'lara mirrored the multi-faceted nature of the people who lived here. The undertone was still icy and blue, but there were splashes of reds and golds, greens and pinks mixed through the sparkling nebulae. It was beautiful.

And it made the dust motes almost impossible to keep track of.

"Don't worry," Irya muttered slyly in her ear. "Just follow me." And she skipped off to dance through the threads and spirit particles like she could walk through walls.

Fae was half-tempted to open her eyes. This was impossible.

And then she remembered how this was the only thing she'd succeeded at so far, and she refused to give up. If Irya could do this, so could she. And Irya didn't have the option to just open her eyes and see where she was going.

Fae took a deep breath, sending the spirit dust spinning as she blew it out. She watched it go, and saw how the dust seemed to catch in a sign-post-shaped spider's web to her right, but danced freely through the air dead ahead. Taking a tentative step, she walked into the bustle of La'sa's Core.

The movements of the auras helped her more than she'd expected. Where people moved, she could also move. In the gaps where they didn't go, the spirit dust slowed to skirt around solid objects. Occasionally, she saw Irya flitting between auras and nebulae, keeping watch with a glint in her eye, but the Echo left her to work her way through on her own.

Once, she was sure she spotted another Echo — another figure who appeared as clearly in Eah'lara as in the mortal realm — but then they were gone, and Fae was left to regain her bearings.

Finally, she made it to the gardens outside the kitchen, where spirit dust fluttered about like butterflies, as if it was happy to be in this place.

Irya reappeared at her side, and flung her arms around her.

"That was amazing!" She squeezed her tight, and when she let go, there were tears in her eyes. "Open your eyes."

Fae did, and immediately squinted in the brightness of the midday sun. Irya reached out to grasp her hand, and crushed it between hers.

"You have no idea how much I have wanted to..." She hesitated, uncertainty pinching her brows together. "The other Echoes aren't like us," she said instead. "Their connection to Eah'lara takes something from them." Fae nodded, thinking about the elf Whisperers back in Arolynos.

Irya squeezed her hand again, and let it drop. "It's good to play with someone who knows how to play back." She smiled, almost apologetically, and without another word, she strode into the kitchen.

After the morning she'd had, Fae had no qualms about loading her plate up with flatbread and a stewed lentil dish that resembled elven *dahka*. Suspecting she might need it, she filled a generous mug with *kahveh*, spilling liberal cream and sugar into the bitter drink. Irya helped herself to steamed vegetables, a mixed grain Fae didn't recognise, and some rich, dark sauce from a bowl on the side. She took a mug of tea, and strode confidently through the tables to one at the far side of the room, already occupied.

Rylan stiffened at her approach. "Irya," he greeted nervously, a far cry from the swaggering youth Fae had met a few days ago. "What can we do for you?" The other two diners turned in their seats — Taniq and Arissa.

"Fae!" Arissa shoved Taniq aside to make room, and patted the bench beside her. "Come join us!"

Irya grabbed a stool with unerring accuracy, pulling it over to sit at the end of the table. "Wonderful," she said, as if she'd been invited as well.

Taniq and Rylan exchanged uneasy glances, Arissa shooting them a glare until they resumed picking at their food.

Irya waved her fork to take in the three Magi. "Sheree told me she introduced you," she said, and tucked into her meal without delay. "And I thought" — she swirled some sauce through the grains — "you could practice recognising auras with these three." She shovelled a forkful into her mouth, glancing around the table as she chewed. "Call it another exercise in Eah'lara training." She threw a wink at Fae, spearing some vegetables on her fork.

"You're training in Eah'lara?" Taniq asked, impressed.

Fae tore off a piece of flatbread and dipped it in the stewed lentils. "I'm training in everything at the moment. This morning I was working with Alexi."

"Condolences," Rylan muttered. Arissa grimaced. Taniq grinned sympathetically. It seemed they'd all suffered at Alexi's goodnatured hand.

"Why are you training with Alexi though?" Arissa asked. "He can't help you with Source Magic."

"Says who?" Irya spoke around a mouthful of food. She swallowed. "There's more to magic than throwing the elements around, you know."

The other three froze, as if they didn't quite know how to respond to her. Irya merely shrugged, and carried on with her meal.

"Luca says it will help to clear my mind," Fae answered. "But so far it's just made my arms feel like jelly." Her legs weren't much better off, but after over an hour of twirling and thrusting the six-foot-long staff, her arms were definitely worse.

Irya's fork clattered to her plate. "Right then, I'll be off," she said suddenly, rising smoothly and nudging her stool under the table. "Remember to practice while I'm gone." She smiled sweetly down at Fae. "Same time tomorrow?" Then she turned and left without waiting for an answer.

A collective sigh of relief went around the table.

Fae glanced at each of them. "What?"

"She's just so... odd," Rylan said with a shrug that suggested he couldn't describe why.

"All the Echoes are," Arissa explained. "But Irya's... well, she's different."

"It's the eyes," Taniq suggested. "I don't know what she can see and what she can't."

Fae frowned. "Well she's been nothing but nice to me."

An awkward quiet fell around the table.

"How's your other training going?" Arissa asked quickly. "Any progress?"

Fae shook her head woefully. "No. It's all just" — she grasped at the air — "beyond my reach. I can't sense any of what the High Magi are trying to teach me."

"Maybe we can help," Rylan offered, scowling at Arissa's snort of derision. "What? We've all had to come up with different ways to develop our magic — maybe we've thought of something the High Magi haven't."

Fae's interest piqued. "Like what?"

But Rylan and Arissa seemed to be trying to stare each other down, until Taniq finally cleared his throat.

"Being as we are, suspended in time, the development of our magics halted along with our age. No matter how much we practice, our abilities don't increase in power. So we've had to get a bit inventive with how we use them. For example, Arissa is limited by how much water she can wield, but she's learned to do some pretty clever tricks with small amounts.

Rylan's discovered that several well-placed smaller fires can often achieve the same results as one big one. Especially when he combines it with air."

"And you?" Fae prompted.

"Don't let Taniq undersell himself," Arissa interjected. "He's come up with really intricate frameworks that enable him to use the earth to move the earth. It would be easier to show you than for any of us to describe it to you." Taniq's caramel skin flushed crimson, but a small smile pulled at his lips.

"That's amazing!" Most of the magic the High Magi had shown Fae had focused on showcasing their power. Perhaps it was time for a new approach. "Can I see?" She could examine their auras while they worked, so she could learn to recognise *them* from Eah'lara too.

"Of course!" Arissa agreed. "When?"

Fae thought of her session with Luca at the arena. "Tomorrow? I'll meet you after lunch."

They agreed upon a time, and then had to go their separate ways: Taniq was working on a project with a Master Craftsman in the workshops Fae had yet to discover; Arissa was a healer, a revelation that sent a thrill through her — how long had it been since she'd practised healing?

Rylan had kitchen duties, and bemoaned his ill fortune all the way to the pot-wash station.

Fae left the kitchen smiling. After a week of dead ends and no progress, it felt good to explore Eah'lara with Irya, and have lunch with... new friends.

A stab of guilt reminded her of her family back in Throldon. What were they going through, while she trained in the safety of La'sa? She hadn't taken Madja up on her offer to send a message, she didn't know what she would say. If she was honest with herself, a part of her was clinging to the chance that she'd figure out this Source Magic and get back in time to protect them.

Another part of her was terrified that she never would, that she'd be leagues away from them all when she should be by their side.

And what would she do? Stand powerlessly by as the walls shook and crumbled, knowing she should have been able to stop it? No. If there was a chance she'd be able to do anything to help, that chance was here. And it was in training with these Magi.

The cloud of Fae's thoughts chased her back to the arena.

Luca was still there, as though he'd never left.

He was bare-chested, his shirt discarded on the arena seating, and was going through a sequence of exercises like the ones Alexi had been trying to teach her, only Luca's movements were smooth and effortless, where hers had closely resembled those of a newborn foal. The muscles of his arms and torso bunched and straightened as he moved — slow, and controlled, and strong. The broad expanse of his back gleamed a deep caramel colour in the sun.

"Are you going to stand there and gawk or shall we begin your training?" he said with a hint of amusement in his tone.

Fae shook herself. "You're the one prancing around with no shirt on," she muttered, snatching up said shirt and throwing it at him.

She could have sworn she saw a smirk grace his lips before his face resumed its inscrutable facade.

"I shall remember that, next time I notice your focus slipping," he noted dryly, sliding his arms into the sleeves, before slowly fastening the buttons. Fae felt her cheeks heat, but schooled her face into her best impression of haughty indifference, and took up a position in the centre of the shale floor.

The early afternoon sun hovered over the western wall of the arena, its glare catching on the mineral deposits scattered throughout the stone seating. Luca came to stand before her, his arms relaxed by his sides.

"Today, we're going to try something different," he said, but his voice had changed. It was cold and distant, and it made her senses prickle in anticipation.

"What do you mean?" she asked uneasily, trying to ignore the ice sliding down her spine.

Luca's eyes flicked over her shoulder. "I've asked for some assistance." Fae turned to see Terrence, Madja, and two other Magi she hadn't met enter the arena, all looking decidedly puzzled. Madja's face became thunderous when she saw Luca and Fae.

Fae turned back to him. "Why? What are you going to do?"

Luca's indigo gaze slid back to hers.

"I'm going to provoke you."

23

NIGHTMARE INCARNATE

Fae blinked.

She almost laughed. The idea that he could provoke her into doing anything dangerous was ridiculous.

Then Madja marched up and placed herself squarely between them.

"You cannot be serious," she hissed.

Luca arched an eyebrow. "Deadly," he said, completely unperturbed by the rage rolling off Madja like steam. Thinking about it, it might actually have been steam.

"I assume you want us here for structural support?" Terrence sidled up beside them, his hands shoved deep into his pockets. Luca nodded. Terrence returned the gesture, and turned to the other two Magi. "Alright, take up positions at east and west compass points. High Magi Sorrento and I will take north and south."

"I refuse." Madja stood her ground.

Luca shrugged, but the motion suggested it would be her who regretted her decision.

Madja whirled on Fae. "You don't have to do this Fae," she said earnestly. "You can walk away and no one will think any less of you for it."

"I don't even quite understand what 'this' is yet," Fae replied honestly.

Madja ran a trembling hand through her silver mane. "He wants to try and force your powers to surge, by provoking you. By poking and prodding at anything that will elicit a reaction that might open the floodgates to your magic." She shook her head, shooting a glare at Luca. "It's dangerous, and it's reckless, and I would urge you not to go through with it." Her blue gaze bored into Fae's, brow knitted with worry.

Fae glanced up at Luca. "Do you really think this will help?"

Luca shrugged again. "It might be the first opportunity you've had to experience Source Magic running through you while being conscious of what's happening."

She thought about it for all of a second before meeting Madja's gaze again. "I have to try."

A flash of hurt crossed Madja's face, but it hardened in an instant. She nodded curtly to Luca, and turned on her heel to march to the north corner of the arena.

Fae looked up at Luca again. "What about the Dreamweaver?"

"He's been warned."

"Alright then." Fae swallowed. "What now?"

Something flickered behind Luca's eyes. "Kallis!"

And that's when Fae's nightmares came to life.

Darkness pooled in the air above her, a single red glow at the centre. The wind surged, picking up the snow and shale dust, whipping it around her, cutting her off from Madja and the other Magi.

Fae's throat closed up, her eyes widened with remembered panic. She knew the darkness was Kallis, wielding his element from somewhere nearby. She knew that the storm tearing around her was Luca, the same as before. But it was her nightmare incarnate. That day come back to life.

Her muscles locked up, her fists clenched until the bite of fingernails into her palms was the only thing keeping her grounded in the real world. But the grip of fear held her poised between the two.

From behind her, Luca whispered in her ear.

"Do you remember how it felt? When the well ran dry? When you had nothing left to give?"

Lightning forked through the snow clouds gusting around her, bright and frightening.

"How useless you were. How powerless."

Fae felt her old fear rise up inside her. She shrank from it. It was instinct.

And then she remembered why she was here. She was here to feel the fear.

"You're scared that if you learn this power again, that it will be torn from you again. And you will be left vulnerable and helpless. Powerless again."

The darkness above loomed closer, leaning in to suffocate her, the red glow leering down at her worthless attempts to control her own power.

"You're scared that you were never worthy of it in the first place. That you aren't strong enough to hold it. That it'll consume you, and you'll wind up even more broken than you already are."

A sob caught in her throat. How could he know her so well, know the hidden depths of her fear, when she'd never spoken so openly about it to anyone?

The wind tore around her. Lightning flashed. Darkness smothered.

"No point being scared of it. You're powerless now."

The darkness swooped down over her, blotting out everything else.

And her fear took over.

It was a mindless thing — another thing over which she had no control.

Powerless, helpless, broken. Luca's words echoed around her head. She couldn't breathe.

There was nothing in the darkness. No light, no air, no life.

And she was going to die here.

Under her feet, the earth bucked. It heaved as if it too, relived her nightmares.

Distantly, she heard the cries of the Magi.

"Hold it!" Terrence yelled.

The wind dropped, but the darkness stayed.

The earth rolled.

"Feel the power move through you." Luca's voice changed, and she felt him move to stand in front of her. "You can control it."

Her nightmare still hovered in the darkness, but Fae wrenched her mind away from it to focus.

Luca said the Source Magic flowed *through* her — she had only to find it.

She delved deep into herself, shrinking from the shadows hovering in the corners of her mind.

She searched and searched. Felt the earth rumble beneath her feet. Heard it shake the walls of the arena. Heard Terrence's bellowed instructions.

There was power in her somewhere. Enough to move mountains.

Then the earth shuddered its last, and fell silent.

In one last-ditch attempt, Fae threw herself into Eah'lara. But aside from the swaying threads, there was no trace of her power surge.

She opened her eyes.

She stood inside a ring of shale dust with Luca. The Magi at the four corners brushed themselves off, all four casting wary glances her way.

From halfway up the arena seating, Kallis slunk down to meet them. She hadn't even seen him come in.

"Well that was fun," he drawled. "I haven't seen Terrence that ruffled in centuries."

Luca ignored him. "Fae?"

She didn't know what to tell them. Nothing. She'd felt nothing.

Her hands shook, and she balled them into fists.

Tears of frustration burned behind her eyes. She ducked her head to hide them.

"Fae?"

She couldn't face them. Couldn't tell them she'd failed again. Couldn't admit it aloud.

She was failing. Over and over again. And she would never be able to go home and help save Throldon as she'd once done.

If she was lucky, they'd put her down and save themselves the trouble.

Someone dropped a hand on her shoulder. She shook it off angrily. She didn't want their pity. Or their sympathy. Didn't deserve it anyway.

Without meeting anyone's eyes, she pushed past Luca and Kallis, and all but ran from the arena.

After the day she'd had, the nightmares were too close to the surface. They swooped in the second her head hit the pillow.

She lies broken on the floor.
  She rises to fight again.

Anson's dark shroud hangs above, his hideous smile grinning down at her.

And she throws herself at him. All of her.

The very fabric of herself comes apart at the seams, and she pours every last piece into the broken god.

He screams, and drops to smother her with his darkness.

But there is nothing left to smother. She is gone.

In the dream, there is nothing but a black pit. And she is falling. Falling. Forever falling.

This is it. This is the end.

And then a gentle voice comes out of the darkness.

"I'm sorry, my dear. I hope you will forgive me."

Then she is rising through the darkness, rising toward a light.

And there are no more shadows in her mind.

Fae sat bolt upright in her bed.

Luca burst into her room at the same instant. She stared at him, eyes wide.

"Ath!" She scrambled out of bed, reaching for her boots. Because that had been the Dreamweaver she'd heard in her nightmare. Which meant...

Luca put a hand on her shoulder. "There's nothing you can do now," he said softly, his voice aching. "Sleep."

"I have to go and see him!" She pulled one boot on, tucking the flannel of her pyjamas into the leg.

Luca watched her, his expression shuttered.

Fae laced up her boots and leapt up, grabbing her coat as she swept from the room.

She wasn't confident enough in her ability to navigate the Warrens all the way to the opposite side of the mountain, so she went through the Core, Luca trailing behind.

It was the dead of night, the sky inky black, but the town was still awake. Strings of tiny lanterns winked in the windows of cabins like captive fireflies, some were even lucky enough to have the use of Luxo Lamps, hanging clustered in bowls from the eaves. But Fae saw none of it as she ran from one end of the Core to the other.

She raced up the sloped passageway towards the Dreamweaver's rooms, and banged on the door.

"Ath!" she called through the wood. "Ath, are you okay?" She remembered Irya's protests against her father taking the nightmares in the first place, and she was filled with dread at what she might find. She banged on the door again. "Ath!" Luca stood back, like he already knew what awaited her.

The door swung open, light spilling into the hall, and the Dreamweaver stood before her.

Gone was the welcoming, cheery face she'd met only a few days before. The Ath that stood before her now looked tired. His eyes were foggy, the bruised circles beneath them cutting grooves into his face. His short, white hair stuck up at odd angles, like he'd been tossing in his sleep. And as she watched him, he twitched, flinching from something only he could see.

Her heart fell. How had this happened in the minutes since she'd woken?

"Ath," she said gently, "Are you alright?"

The Dreamweaver blinked.

"Fae." He smiled, and the fog lifted from his eyes for a moment. "I'm well, I'm well." He flinched again, casting a furtive glance at the ceiling. Fae's stomach clenched. She knew what it was he saw there, hovering above like death waiting.

"It's not real," she said quietly, reaching for his hand. And then, "I'm so sorry."

"Oh it's alright, my dear," he said, his voice wavering between strained cheeriness and a frailness that didn't belong to the man Fae had met that week. He patted her hand with his, and let it drop. "If you don't mind, my dear, I'm rather tired." His smile was heavy and worn.

"Of course," Fae stepped back from the door, and came up against Luca, standing behind her. The Dreamweaver's eyes flicked up to him, and hardened.

"Goodnight, Fae," he said. Then the door closed between them.

She stood in the dark, nothing but silence and the sound of her own breathing to comfort her.

"I'm sorry," Luca whispered, his chest hard against her back. She whirled, and in the tiny sliver of light leaking from under the Dreamweaver's door, she could see the tension humming through him. "I

shouldn't have pushed you today. I shouldn't have forced this on you."
And there — in his eyes — that flash of self-loathing she'd glimpsed before.

But she wasn't in the mood to comfort him this time.

"No," she hissed in the dark. "You forced this on *him*." She jabbed her finger at the door behind her. "You didn't need to ask for his help. *You* put him in this position. *You* did this to him."

He did not break her glare, taking every drop of venom she threw at him.

"You can push me all you want. It's my power to master. But you had *no right* to drag him into it."

Luca didn't argue back. Didn't even try to justify his actions to her. She knew he'd had his reasons. She even knew they'd been good ones. But she didn't wish her nightmares onto her worst enemies. And now a good man was living them, in a prison built from the hell of her own mind. She felt sick to her stomach. She wanted to scream.

She had no more words for Luca. She pushed past him, and stormed from the eastern quadrant.

And in the dark behind her, Luca stared at the Dreamweaver's door.

24

ONE STEP AT A TIME

After a fitful night of half-sleep, Fae crossed the Core again for her morning session with Alexi.

In the light of day, the effects of the quake the night before were apparent. Cracked windowpanes glinted in the sun, a food vendor righted a cart shaken free of its props, and in the mountain itself, fine lines spider-webbed up one section of rock. The tremors were getting worse.

A shiver that had nothing to do with the cold ran through her.

She understood why Luca had decided to take her nightmares out of the equation. She understood why the Dreamweaver had done it.

She cast her eyes up at the cracks in the mountainside. Maybe she even agreed with them.

But those nightmares were her burden, her reminder. She hated them, but they were a part of her broken self. And now, a man with ghosts of his own was carrying them for her.

Fae scowled at her reflection in a fractured windowpane, and turned her steps towards the arena. She ached from head to toe after the previous morning, and every step felt like walking through water, but she needed to vent her rage — at Luca, at her continued failures, at her whole damned situation. Sparring with the seemingly unflappable Alexi seemed as good a way to work out her anger as any.

The arena was empty when she got there. She was early by about an hour, not having had the stomach for breakfast. She debated waiting for Alexi to arrive, and then her eyes caught on the twin swords in the weapons rack.

She hadn't danced in *so* long.

She shucked her coat onto the lower rank of seats, pausing before pulling her boots off as well. She swept a patch free of shale until her feet stood on cold, bare earth.

She closed her eyes, and breathed.

The elven dancing forms had always been her way of coming back to herself. At least, they had been... before.

Fae didn't know what had happened to her after the fog had lifted from Throldon. Once, she'd danced, she'd healed, she'd even taught others to do the same. But now...

She breathed again, letting her tangled, knotted thoughts fall away.

She began with *Bin'dera* — the dance of contemplation. Her balance was off, her form rusty, but she remembered the motions like they were woven into every fibre of her body. The flow of *Bin'dera* was designed to clear the mind; to bring a turbulent cascade to a quiet, still lake.

She stepped out wide, snaking her arms out, easing her body left and right, bending forward and arching back, before bringing herself back to the centre. To start with, her movements were hesitant; she didn't feel safe stepping out wide. Didn't feel as if she had any right to. But with each step, with each sweeping arc, she moved out further, reaching, straining to feel worthy again.

She repeated the motions, twisting and stretching to take up as much space as her body allowed, before coming back to her centre again. Once she could pull herself out no more, the motions became smaller and smaller, until her feet barely parted, and the furthest her arms extended was to the sky directly overhead, her shadow no bigger than her footprints on the ground. She brought her hands back to her heart, and exhaled long and slow.

Her mind was as still as a pond, her thoughts idle lily pads floating on the surface.

She would normally follow *Bin'dera* with *Thallak*, the dance of logic. But she didn't need to work out what was bothering her. She knew that. What she needed now was strength. Strength of body, and strength of mind. And so she moved into *Re'yal,* the movements firm, determined.

They left no room for doubt, no space for hesitation. They were either done, or not.

She stepped out, angling her foot sideways, and placed her hands exactly where they needed to be. A wayward thought snaked into her mind and she wondered what Alexi would think of *Gestral*, the dance of combat.

She let the thought pass through her, allowed it to tug a small smile onto her lips, and then moved into the next pose, bringing her focus back to the dance.

Alexi arrived towards the end of *Re'yal*, but he didn't interrupt, instead waiting by the entrance until she finished.

He grinned broadly when her feet finally came to a stop, her breath heavy in her chest.

Alexi stepped forward, his applause echoing around the walls.

"You have been holding out on me, fair Fae!" he boomed, his eyes sparkling in the sun. "You did not tell me you are a dancer."

Fae winced. "Was," she said. "Once."

Alexi shook his head. "Not only once," he corrected. "You are a natural. No wonder you move so well. I will have to stop going so easy on you." He winked knowingly down at her.

Fae groaned. "Yesterday was not easy!" she protested.

Alexi laughed. "Perhaps not. But now you will have to show me if you can still move when you are breathing like a winded horse."

Fae laughed, and if it sounded a little hysterical, Alexi didn't seem to notice. He crossed to the weapons rack, and took up the twin swords that hung there. Fae tensed as he turned back to her, blades resting across his open palms.

"I saw you eyeing these the other day." He held them out. They were straight, and narrow. A little heavier than she was used to, and not as sharp, but they were well-oiled, and gleamed in the light. "Why don't you show me what you can do with them."

Fae took a small step away from the swords. She wasn't ready for that. *Aleralys* had always been her favourite dance. But it didn't belong to her anymore. She was too broken for that. Too sad. She didn't have the grace left within her to do it justice.

She shook her head. "No."

A tiny crease appeared in Alexi's brow, the first deviation from boundless joy that she'd seen in him yet. For a fleeting moment, she thought he might push the matter. But his eyebrows merely lifted a fraction, mildly surprised, before he returned the swords wordlessly to the rack.

"Alright then," he said, striding back to where she stood, still barefoot in her little circle cleared of shale. "Put your boots back on, we're going to do some barehand combat today and I don't want you to slice your pretty feet on this shale." He gave her a look that suggested she was mad for taking them off in the first place.

Fae ignored it, but reclaimed her footwear as asked.

Luca did not appear to take his usual place halfway up the arena seating, for which she was endlessly grateful. The session that followed was brutal, and Fae learned that Alexi had indeed been going easy on her. She dodged, ducked, and weaved between his touch-strikes. The lightness of his blows didn't make them any easier to avoid — the La'sa combat trainer was whip-quick, and more often than not, Fae felt his tap on her shoulder, her chest, her head.

He called it a day when she lay in a puddle on the ground, the shale digging into her back.

Alexi's face came over her, blocking her view of the sky above. "You did well!" he grinned, offering her a hand up. She waved it away with a limp shake of her head. She wasn't sure her body would stay upright after what she'd put it through that morning. Alexi hauled her to her feet anyway, laughing when she swayed.

She shot him a watery smile, shoving away the strands of hair that had escaped her braid to cling to her face. She was beyond exhausted. But Alexi's training had had the desired effect: she was no longer wallowing in a futile rage.

"I will see you tomorrow, fair Fae," he said, white smile flashing against his olive skin. He gave her a wave, and strode from the arena, passing Irya coming the opposite way. The Echo wrinkled her nose immediately.

"Urgh, you stink," she said, wafting the air in front of her face.

"I know," Fae replied woefully, contemplating collapsing back to the ground again.

"Well come on then," Irya said impatiently, waving for her to follow. "Don't ask me to carry you. I may be fierce, but feats of physical strength are not part of the deal. Alexi gave up with me centuries ago."

Fae huffed a weary laugh. "Lucky," she grumbled, but she dragged herself along in Irya's wake.

After a long soak in the huge copper tub, she emerged to find the Echo sitting cross-legged on the bed, eyes closed, hands folded together in her lap. Fae cocked her head, wondering what in Eah'lara she saw.

Just as she pulled the door to the bathing room shut, Irya opened her eyes, likely having noticed her staring from within Eah'lara.

"What?" She lifted a hand to her head. "Is there something in my hair?"

Fae smiled. "Where did you go?"

Irya waved a hand. "Here and there," she answered enigmatically. "Got to make myself useful somehow around here, and keeping tabs on the outside world is how I do that."

"Will you show me?" Fae asked, throwing the towel over the back of the chair.

"One thing at a time," Irya said, unfolding from the bed to stand beside her. "First, let's take a walk." She winked, and closed her eyes.

Fae sighed, closed her eyes, and looked into Eah'lara.

As before, Irya stood unchanged beside her but for the slight colouring in her eyes. As before, she identified the subtle shifts in the flow of spirit particles, revealing the room's outlines.

"You know, I have — what was it Luca called it? Oh! Wisping — I have wisped before," Fae said, reaching for the door handle, feeling the cool smooth surface of the metal beneath her fingers when all she saw was a cluster of spirit dust.

"I know," Irya responded blandly. "And don't get me wrong — that's impressive. I don't think anyone else here can. But" — she waggled a finger against the backdrop of Eah'lara — "you've been working instinctively. Everything you're learning here is new. So" — she pointed ahead — "one step at a time."

Fae turned back to the vague shape of the corridor tunnelled through the mountain. The spirit dust flowed through the rock and ice the same as it did through the air... and yet, it didn't. The particles moved effortlessly between the elements, but their patterns changed from one material to the next. Through the air, they floated serenely. Through the mountain walls, their motions followed the structure of the ice and the rock: in straight, jagged lines. The differences were difficult to spot, and

Irya rescued her from breaking her nose against the walls more than once.

When they reached the open air and wash of new colours that indicated the Core, Fae glanced over at her friend.

"I didn't think you'd want to come today... after last night." After she'd lost control of her nightmares, and Irya's father had been forced to take action.

Irya just shook her head. "What do I have to say to get you to hear me?" She shot her a look of exasperation. "I don't blame you. My father will always do what he believes is right, regardless of what I have to say about it. Or the High Magi, come to think of it, so don't be too hard on Luca about it either."

Fae eyebrows shot up in surprise. "I thought you were mad at him for suggesting it?"

Irya winced. "I owe him an apology. He only did what he thought was right, just like my father has." She twisted a strand of hair through her fingers.

Fae hesitated. "How does he do it?" she asked eventually. "Your father."

"He's very good with auras." Irya waved to one as it passed, careful not to touch. "His speciality is in the finer details. The threads that make up a person's psyche." She shook her head, a small smile playing across her lips. "Meddling with auras can be dangerous — they're fragile things, easy to damage. I've never been able to work at that level. I'm all about the bigger picture." She spread her arms wide and spun through the butterfly-dust that filled the kitchen garden. "And yes," her eyes glinted shrewdly, "I will show you how that works too. But not today."

Fae opened her eyes just in time to catch Irya's uncertain glance through the glass doors of the kitchen.

She reached forward and gripped her hand.

"Sit with me today," Fae urged. "Properly. I'm spending the afternoon with the others anyway. They won't mind."

Irya's frown suggested her request was unwise. "You don't want that."

Now it was Fae's turn to frown. "Why not?"

"They're... unsettled by me."

"Why?"

Irya sighed, and ran a hand through her autumnal hair, sending the waves tumbling over her shoulders. "Because I'm different. I don't fit into their nice little Echo box. We're supposed to be... brittle. Most Echoes need constant care, or some kind of special treatment. Imagine growing up, knowing that's your fate. Knowing that at some point, you'll stop recognising the people around you, and become half-lost in the Spirit Realm. Everyone expected me to be the same, but I'm not, and they still don't quite know what to do with me." She shrugged. "There's a... a price for all magic. It takes its toll on some more than others. I escaped the fate they expected for me. Maybe this is my price."

Fae snorted. "Well, I don't believe that for a second." She raised a skeptical eyebrow. "You can navigate the world using the Spirit Realm because you can't see in the mortal one. I think it's more about balance, not prices. But then" — she spread her arms to the sides — "what do I know? I'm nothing."

Irya smiled, a little incredulous. "You're not nothing. You're turning into a damn fine Echo."

"I'm supposed to be a Magi," Fae reminded her.

Irya considered her. "Be both."

Fae laughed cynically. "There's got to be a price for that."

Irya squeezed her hand. "I think you already paid it."

Fae's heart swelled in her chest. She smiled, and tugged at Irya's hand. "Come and have lunch."

Irya smiled back at her. She squeezed her hand one last time, and let it drop. "I'm okay. *Really*," she added when Fae went to insist. "I'll see you tomorrow." And she turned and left the garden.

25

BALANCING ACT

Fae entered the kitchen and was immediately waved down by Rylan and Taniq, sitting by the windows. She helped herself to a roasted vegetable pie from the counter and headed over to join them.

"Where's Arissa?" she asked, sliding into the seat beside Taniq.

"She got caught up at the Healing House." Rylan slurped at his *kahveh*, another empty mug already discarded by his plate. Dark half-moons clung to the smooth skin beneath his green eyes. "She'll join us when she's finished."

"It can't be that busy there?" Fae compared the relatively compact community of La'sa with the sprawling one of Arolynos, and couldn't think of many occasions to need a healer here.

Both Magi barked a laugh. "I must show you the workshops sometime," Taniq said, grey eyes dancing. "There are more ways to injure yourself in there than there are stars in the sky."

"And we're *Magi*." Rylan drew out the word. "You know, wielding elements like fire and ice and earth. We can get into plenty of trouble just sitting at home some days."

"I heard it was one of the Echoes," Taniq said, lowering his voice. "Went drifting through the Spirit Realm and saw something he didn't like. And now he's gone into some kind of shock."

Fae tried to imagine what it would be like to grow up knowing that was your fate. She shook her head. It must be awful.

"Anyway, eat up." Rylan gestured to her half-eaten pie, and downed the last of his *kahveh*.

Taniq raised an eyebrow. "Late night, Rylan?"

Rylan lowered his mug to the table with a loud *clunk*, and massaged the corners of his almond-shaped eyes. "I was in the Archives researching more dual-wielding methods." He held his eyes open with his fingers. "But I was in there so long I don't know if the blurred vision is from reading in the dark, or because when I looked up, it was dawn."

Taniq picked up the discarded mug and shook it at him. "Or from drinking so much *kahveh*!" he laughed.

Rylan batted the suggestion away. "Anyway, I found some examples of Therasae working with Mizulae to encourage crop growth, Auroras and Mizulae combining their elements to manipulate weather, and — of course — Incendi and Auroras controlling fire with pinpoint precision. I even found an example of Therasae and Incendi working together to control lava flow. Fascinating."

"And why all the research?" Fae asked, pushing her empty plate to the side.

Taniq rolled his eyes. "Boredom. He's looking for inspiration to see what else he can do with Source Magic. He has fire and air at his disposal, so he can get a bit more inventive than most of us."

Rylan tapped his finger against the table. "Yes, but what if I could convince another wielder to work with me? What do you reckon, Shalla? Fancy playing with lava? I wonder what we could do with earth, fire, *and* air."

Taniq shook his head, pushing his short, black waves back when they dropped over his face. "Oh no. No thank you. I will need at least another five hundred years before I look for those kind of risks. I've seen what carelessness causes with*out* Source Magic, I'm quite happy leaving *lava* out of the equation."

Fae laughed as Rylan shrugged. "Suit yourself," he said airily. "You could have been part of something great."

"Shall we go?" Taniq asked pointedly, surveying the table.

"Yes." Fae stood, carrying the plates to the pot-wash. "I've been looking forward to this!"

Instead of the arena, Taniq and Rylan led the way to a small park at the western edge of the Core. The glittering rock of the mountain reared up at their backs, a wide stretch of moss and hardy grasses edged with paving and other winter planting extending out before them.

"Go on then, Rylan," Taniq said, perching on the edge of a raised bed. "You first."

Rylan rubbed his hands together. "Alright then." He stepped forward, and the sun caught on the copper in his hair. "If I'm ever able to reach physical maturity" — he gestured to his adolescent frame — "I should be able to light infernos that rage ten feet high, consuming anything up to the size of a house." To the side, Taniq rolled his eyes at the dramatic tone in his voice. Rylan ignored him. "As it stands, the biggest I can manage is this." He thrust his hand forward, and a cheery flame around a foot tall appeared in the middle of the park. Rylan let the fire burn for a moment, then clenched his fist, and watched as is hissed out.

Fae applauded his display. It was more than she could manage; his ability to summon the fire at will alone was impressive.

Rylan held up one finger. "But if I light a number of fires together..." Five of his flames flickered into life in a small circle on the lawn. They coiled around each other like vines, snaking higher than the first had, until they reached perhaps two feet high. "Then add some air into the mix..." He eased his other hand towards the fire, and a gentle breeze blew across the ground, fanning the flames higher still. "Then I begin to achieve something akin to my potential." His fire now burned almost four feet high, the flames licking around each other and giving out a welcome heat.

Rylan held his hands out towards it, like he was holding it together by willpower alone. Sweat beaded on his brow, and his arms began to tremble. Finally, he dropped his hands, and the fire disappeared with a hiss.

"Showing off again, Rylan?" a voice called from the edge of the park. Fae looked over to see Arissa crossing the lawn towards them, a satchel slung over one shoulder. "Sorry I'm late."

"Don't worry, you didn't miss much," Taniq replied, his eyes lingering as she bent to retie her bootlace.

"I thought it was very impressive," Fae said.

"*Thank* you." Rylan dropped to sit on the low stone wall beside her. "Go on then, Taniq, let's see your trick."

"Oh no, ladies first." Taniq gestured to Arissa, a bashful smile tugging at his lips.

Arissa shoved her blonde hair behind one ear. "Let me catch my breath! Some of us had responsibilities to attend to today." Indeed, she wore the pale blue tunic that marked her healer status. Something mournful pinged inside Fae.

Rylan looked about to say something unwise, so she interjected.

"If Magi are conduits for Source Magic, why did you seem to run out after a while?"

Rylan twirled a fallen twig through his fingers. "There's a pay-off with any kind of magic. With Source Magic, as long as you let it run *through* you, the price is mostly physical exertion. It's like there's a valve inside. You can hold it open wider with maturity, and with practice." He flicked the twig away, and it burnt to cinders in a burst of flame. "Our valves are jammed half-open, so there's only so much we can draw through at once." He waved a hand to the scorched ground where his earlier fire had burned. "I probably drew slightly more than my reserve could replenish there, which is why I couldn't hold it." He shrugged. "It's all a balancing act."

"Do you have different reserves for the different elements?"

He shot her a lopsided grin. "You're a sharp cookie aren't you? Yes. You'll often find that dual-wielders will have larger reserves for one of their elements than the other. For example, my primary is fire, so I'm Incendus-Aurora weighted. High Magis Sorrento and O'Toole are good examples." It took Fae a moment to remember he was referring to Madja and Terrence. "High Magi Sorrento is Mizula-Theras, while High Magi O'Toole is strongly Theras-Mizula weighted. His earth-wielding is very powerful."

"Right, enough of this dual-wielder swaggering now." Arissa stood. "Let me show you what a pure Mizula can do."

"It would only be fair to remind Fae that you *are* older than us," Rylan pointed out, his attention still on Fae. "Her reserve was already more mature before we all got stuck like this." Fae nodded her understanding.

"Are you done making excuses, Rylan Green?" Arissa stuck her hands on her hips and regarded him with such haughtiness that Fae had to laugh.

Rylan simply sat back, and waved for her to continue.

Arissa huffed disdainfully, and turned her shoulder to him.

"Mizulae mostly work with existing bodies of water," she began. "They can pull rivers off-course, divert rainfall, freeze bridges across lakes, that sort of thing. I have to work on a smaller scale. I can freeze a smaller raft, and move the water immediately around it to propel it along. I can't pull a whole river, but I can coax smaller trickles away to relieve pressure." She lifted her hands into the air. "What I've become particularly fond of doing" — water droplets appeared, suspended around her like frozen rain — "is drawing water out of thin air."

Fae gasped, and clapped her hands in appreciation.

Arissa smiled, her cheeks colouring. "Most Mizulae like to work with water in its natural form." The droplets began weaving together to form a large globule floating before her. "But when you're limited by quantity, you start to think about how many different ways you can use what you've got." The globule pulled and stretched, and shaped itself into a chain before freezing solid. Then it was fluid again, moving and shifting until it was a key, frozen in ice. Then again, the water flowed and changed shape. Arissa played the water into different forms over and over, freezing and thawing it into dozens of different uses. A bowl, a blade, a lens, a stool, a cup.

Eventually, she opened her hands out, and the globule separated into drops again, and misted back into the air.

Arissa smiled. "I can make almost anything that needs to be solid. I'm lucky: most of my creations will stay frozen in this climate. Otherwise I would have to feed them with magic constantly to keep the water solid."

"That's amazing!" Fae cooed with delight, and Arissa took a small bow before returning to sit beside them on the wall.

"You haven't seen anything yet. Wait until Taniq shows you what he can do. At full strength, I wouldn't be surprised if he could rival High Magi O'Toole."

Taniq blushed furiously, the caramel of his skin flushing bright red as he shrugged deeper into his coat, mumbling something into the collar.

"Enough modesty Shalla." Rylan punched his arm. "You know you're good. Come on, show us what you've got."

The hairs on the back of Fae's neck stood up in warning.

"What is this?" An ice-cold voice spoke behind them.

Rylan, Taniq, and Arissa leapt to their feet, spinning to address the man standing there, their faces white with fear.

"H-High Magi," Arissa stuttered.

Fae stood, and turned.

To find Luca standing behind her, his face a mask of fury.

26

WILD THING

Everything in Fae screamed at her to run.

"Can I help you?" she said instead.

Luca's eyes flared.

"Do you think this is a joke?" His voice was deadly quiet as he stepped around the wall and strode towards her.

Out of the corner of her eye, Fae saw the others back slowly away.

"What's wrong?" she asked. He'd been sullen and broody ever since she'd arrived, but he hadn't been this... *angry* before. But as she watched him approach, the anger didn't seem to be entirely directed at her. There was frustration in the tension of his arms. Guilt even, in the angle of his scowl. He'd been quiet last night after Ath. And he hadn't been to her training that morning as usual.

Luca stalked closer until she had to tip her head back to look him in the eye.

"What's wrong," he breathed, fire smouldering behind his gaze, "is that instead of training, instead of working to fix a problem that could kill us all, you're out here... *playing*." He glanced up to take in the other three, hovering a safe distance away. His eyes narrowed.

"Hey!" Fae hauled his attention back to her. "I am *trying*!"

"It doesn't look like it to me." There. That hint of something else in his gaze. Regret?

173

"I am doing everything I can to try and make this work," she snarled at him. "Do you think I don't understand? If I don't master my elements, the earth will continue to shake itself into a pile of rubble, with all of us buried beneath it! I get it!" She shoved a strand of ash-blonde hair out of her face. "And on top of that, there's an army marching on Throldon that I might be able to help stop, if only I can figure this out!"

She thought she saw Luca flinch, before his eyes shuttered. "You can't go to Throldon."

Fae swore even the wind stilled at his words. "What?"

"You can't go back to Throldon," he repeated, his tone as unyielding as the mountain around them.

Fae's heart stuttered. "Madja said I wasn't a prisoner." Her voice lowered, daring him to challenge her.

Because on this point, she was absolutely prepared to stand and fight.

"You have a responsibility, as a Magi, to protect our people here." Luca remained unmoving.

"And what about *my* people?" Fae demanded. "What about my family? The innocent people with a damn *army* on their doorstep? What about them?" Her eyes flashed, the amber ring around her usual ocean-green flaring gold.

"There are more important matters at stake," he replied flatly.

"They are *both* important!" Fae was shouting now, the roaring in her ears drowning out everything but his next word.

"No."

Fae erupted.

Flames burned across her body, flickering from her fingertips, weaving through her hair, whipping the strands into a fiery corona around her head.

And in an instant, she knew where she'd been going wrong all along.

The magic didn't flow through her, as they'd thought.

She *was* the magic. The power cascaded from every cell in her body in crashing waves, the swell of it more than enough to drown her.

It could easily have dragged her under, those waves, but Luca was there in front of her, a shield of his own flames between them.

"Pull it back, Fae," he instructed, his voice firm and insistent.

She snarled at him, and the fire snapped out a fraction more, a lion prowling at the edge of her control.

The flames flared, and she allowed herself a small smirk of satisfaction when he inched back a step.

"*Fae.*" This time, his tone held a warning. And a hint of something else.

Fine. She'd made her point... somehow. She only hoped she would remember how to call the fire again, without Luca having to threaten her freedom.

But when she went to reel the flames back in, they wouldn't obey her. They licked gleefully across her skin, wild and free.

And they weren't interested in being leashed.

Sweat broke out over her body that had nothing to do with the heat.

"That's enough Fae!" Luca growled at her.

"I can't stop it!" she cried. The magic poured from her — fuel for her flames. "How do I stop it?!"

Fire danced behind Luca's eyes, lighting them up from within. "You need to pull it back into you." The wall of fire he held between them flashed as her own flared again. "Draw the magic back into you, and the fire will follow."

"I don't know how!" Fae's panic swelled, and all logic fled. She was a wild thing, caged and fighting for her life.

She heard Luca swear through the roar of the flames. "Fae, just breathe." But she was trapped in a vortex of fire, and there was no way out. She was going to burn up in an inferno of her own creation.

She was going to die here.

Her heart pounded inside her chest, punching at her ribs. Her panicked breathing only pulled the hot, arid air into her lungs, burning on the way down, and dragging great choking coughs from her at every breath.

"Breathe, Fae!" Luca urged, and his voice was coloured with... fear?

She gasped a breath, and her mouth filled with fire. It seared down her throat, scorching her from the inside.

And all conscious thought vanished as she screamed.

Then she was gasping for a different reason.

She couldn't breathe deep enough. Couldn't draw enough air into her lungs.

The fire guttered.

Her ribs worked like bellows, trying to draw breath, but nothing came. Spots danced before her eyes, and her vision darkened at the edges.

The flames receded until they licked sullenly across her skin.

"Hold on, Fae." Luca's voice sounded muffled, as if there was a wall between them. His fire was extinguished, and he stood, hands outstretched, as if readying to catch her.

She clutched at her throat, gasping like a fish out of water.

The fire winked out.

"Hold on." Luca stepped closer without touching her.

As her world shrank to a pinprick view, the glowing orange embers at her feet dimmed, until with a hiss of protest, they finally faded to ashes.

And Fae passed out.

She woke to a pounding in the back of her skull.

Her eyes felt like they'd been rolled in sand, her eyelids stuck together like glue. Her throat tasted of ash.

She ran her tongue along the roof of her mouth and cringed.

"Here." A hand slipped behind her head, a cup lifted to her lips. The trickle of water was sweet and crisp, and she gulped it greedily.

"Easy," a familiar voice said. Fae cracked one eye open.

She was lying in a light, airy room, with windows that looked out onto neat gardens and glittering mountain walls. Her bed was made up with clean white linen, and in the chair beside it—

"Luca," she rasped.

He leaned back in his chair, cradling the cup in his hands.

"Feels like all the water has been sucked out of your mouth doesn't it?" He nodded before she even replied. "I remember."

Fae tried clearing her throat, and Luca reached over to give her another sip of water.

"Where am I?" The rasp improved to a croak. Luca put the cup on the bedside table.

"The Healing House." He took a breath, eyes closed, a small crease between his brows. When he looked back at her, it was with that regret she'd seen him carry around so much. "I'm sorry about earlier. I was out of line. I was frustrated and I took it out on you." He sat back and clasped his hands across his waist. "I had to draw the air away from your fire to smother it." He looked down at his hands. "Unfortunately, that meant having to... well it meant you were suffocated too. Temporarily."

Fae nodded. That's exactly how it had felt. Like all the air had been sucked out of the world, and there was nothing left to breathe. She didn't think she could blame him though.

"I couldn't control it," she whispered.

Luca shook his head. "None of us can to start with." He leaned forward. "The difference is that you've come into your powers at full strength, or near enough. The rest of us grow with it, usually surrounded by a community of Magi who know what they're doing." His lips lifted at the corner. "Most of us would have wished to have it your way, but I'd bet you'd have it otherwise."

He sighed, and ran a hand through the dark strands of his hair. "But, just like the rest of us, you must learn to shape the magic as is moves through you." The indigo of his eyes seemed bottomless when they met hers again. "You could be an artist, or a hammer, depending on how much control you learn."

Fae hesitated. "What if the magic doesn't move *through* me?"

Luca frowned. "What do you mean?"

Fae pushed herself up to sit, grabbing the cup of water for herself and taking another sip.

"What if the magic is already in me? No..." She paused, trying to find the right words for what she'd felt in the fire. "It's like it's part of me. The fire was fuelled by power coming *from me*." She glanced up to see Luca's brow furrowed in confusion. "What does that mean?"

Luca hummed pensively, his hand coming up to cup his chin. "I... I don't know." His gaze lifted to hers. "We should try it again."

Fae started. "Are you mad?" she asked frankly.

"Possibly." Luca shrugged. "But I don't think so." He looked her over, assessing. "Do you think you can?"

She gaped at him. "I — I don't know. It's not like I knew what I was doing last time." But this power was in her, whether she knew what to do with it or not. Her throat was scratchy with it, the taste of ash lingering on her tongue. Her heart pounded in anticipation.

She nodded. "Okay."

"Okay?"

She nodded, more certain the more she thought about it. How else was she going to learn?

Luca stood, and offered his hand. She ignored it, and swung her legs down from the bed. They felt like water beneath her, but they held.

"Shall we try the arena this time?" Luca suggested. "As a slightly more controlled environment?"

"I don't think the location will matter," she replied honestly. "You seem able to piss me off wherever we are."

Luca snorted, his lips kicking up into an actual smile. The expression changed his face so much that Fae was momentarily taken aback. He caught her looking, and it shifted to a smirk.

"Don't get used to it," he murmured. They left the Healing House, and his enigmatic facade fell back into place.

Frost-tipped gardens separated the Healing House from the Warrens behind it, and from there it was a short distance before they were following a well-worn path back to the arena.

Luca strode through the archway, across the shale floor, and turned to face her.

Fae hesitated. "What happens if..." she wrung her hands nervously "... if I lose control like that again?"

Luca cocked his head, considering her. "I can always knock you out again."

"What if I block you?"

"What?"

"You blocked my fire," she pointed out. "What if I block you?"

"That takes control," he replied dryly. "Which you don't have."

Fae scowled. He was right. But that wasn't the point.

"So," he began. "What was it that ignited your fire?"

She didn't have to think long about that. "You told me I couldn't go back to Throldon."

He stilled. "You can't."

"My family is there," she levelled at him. "In a city with next to no defences — a city that has only just started rebuilding after thirty years of anarchy."

"That doesn't matter."

Her nostrils flared as she sucked in a breath. *This* was why she'd lost control. "There is an *army* marching on thousands of *innocent* people, and all you can say is *that doesn't matter?*"

Something flashed across Luca's face, but he answered her with the same dispassionate tone. "There are bigger issues at stake here."

"They are *both* big issues." Her body thrummed. Her hands shook. How could he be so callous? Hadn't he defended the innocent once, too?

But his gaze was flat and expressionless as he stared at her. "No."

Fae felt it this time. She felt the pressure build in her very cells, until her skin felt as though it would shatter like glass.

She tried focusing on her hands. Tried to push that feeling down her arms until the skin of her palms burned with the tension building beneath.

And then fire burst from her palms.

Flames licked over the surface of her body like a coating of liquid fire, but she'd managed to contain the strongest outburst to her hands. Somehow.

"Good." Luca stepped closer, while still maintaining a safe distance — in case she erupted again, she suspected. "Now don't try anything with it. Just feel it. Feel where it's coming from."

"I told you," she ground out through gritted teeth, "it's coming from me."

Luca nodded, frustratingly calm. "Alright, but where? Where would you draw it from again? Find that place so that you know where to go looking next time."

Holding the fire in her hands was taking almost all of Fae's concentration, but she closed her eyes, and sent her attention inward.

She'd done this once before, while accepting her Aethyr guides into herself. But this was different. She felt like she was looking for a leaky tap in a castle that was already flooded to the roof.

"It might not be one defined place within you," Luca continued. "It could be something more diffuse. Like a blanket you have to throw off rather than a switch to flick."

"That's not helpful," she sniped. He fell silent.

She breathed. *Forget Eah'lara,* she told herself as her mind instinctively reached for the Spirit Realm. This power was within her already, she just had to find — *there.*

It was like her cells flickered between two different states. Like the fire in them was just another version of herself, jostling for the alpha position. Like a shadow stepping into the light...

She waited, watching the flickering within her. Watching as the fire took a form...

Her control slipped, and she fought to pull it back before the flames could run rampant. She willed the pressure back into her skin, pushed it under and into herself, like a folded page into an envelope.

And as she tucked that heart of fire back in beside her own, she caught an impression of a burning mane.

She opened her eyes, and smiled.

27

MONSTER IN SILK SLIPPERS

In the belly of the Brotherhood's Sanctum, Jade sensed a change in the atmosphere.

Normally, she was surrounded by hushed silence — her shadows were silent beyond the occasional barked instruction, and acolytes lowered their voices or sealed their lips in her vicinity. Her whole world was reduced to her room, her dragons, and blood.

But something had changed enough for the acolytes to speak more freely, the shadows at her door to exchange the odd clipped comment.

The Brotherhood was preparing a small company to join the Eminency's forces, and the halls of the Sanctum echoed with whispered discussions over who would be going.

Jade lay back on her bed, working the blood bond in her mind. She plucked at its tether, easing the smallest fraction of slack into it, and let it drop.

In the months — or perhaps even years — of working at the bond, it had loosened from a shackle at her throat, to a loose leash. And over the last few days, she had redoubled her efforts to weaken the hold the Brotherhood had on her and her dragons.

Perhaps with the Brothers away, they'd be left alone.

She snorted inwardly. The viallings had only become more frequent since the Eminency's efforts in the north began, for whatever purposes the Brotherhood needed their blood for.

We will not stop fighting, Alpha had promised, so neither would she.

Although what they did next, she had no idea.

A commotion in the hallway caught at the edge of her hearing, and she sat up to peer at the shadows guarding her door. One of them nodded to someone out of sight before turning to her.

"Sorcerer Supreme requires your presence."

Again? Goosebumps rippled up her arms and she suppressed a shudder. What could he want her for now?

But she nodded, and fell into step behind the acolyte sent to fetch her.

Murmured whispers followed her through the halls. Eyes followed her at every turn, their touch an itch under her whites.

Too soon, she was back at the gilded entry to the Sorcerer Supreme's Atrium. The doors stood open today, the heat of the desert blowing through them into the cool halls like a summer storm. Inside, a dozen Brothers stood around the sunken circle at the centre of the room, the Sorcerer Supreme standing above them, framed by the pillars of his balcony.

Her escort knocked tentatively at the door. The Sorcerer Supreme glanced up, his black eyes instantly finding hers.

"Jade Xid, Supremacy." The acolyte practically shook down to his slippered feet, confronted by so many Brothers in one place. Every member of the Brotherhood wore the blood-red robes that ruled Jade's life. But where the attire of an acolyte was simple and unadorned, the robes of a Brother were long and flowing, made of finely woven linens, and bore thick, embroidered borders of deep purple at the hem and cuffs.

The Sorcerer Supreme though, wore his customary silver-edged white. His sun-bronzed skin contrasted sharply against the brilliance of his attire. His robes were tailored to accentuate his features; the open front exposed the top of his chest, highlighting broad shoulders, and the wide sash at his waist drew the eyes to his hips.

And yet despite all of that, there was no warmth in him at all.

Jade's blood chilled as his gaze swept over her. Apparently satisfied, he returned his attention to the Brothers before him.

"Be ready to leave at dawn," he said. "I will not delay any longer."

A chorus of "Yes, Supremacy," and then the Brothers were filing past her, leaving Jade alone once again with the Sorcerer Supreme.

He strode towards her. "Great news, Jade!" He gripped her arm and steered her into the atrium. There was a mad gleam in his eyes that sent chills down her spine. "The Eminency's army has reached the northern borders. It is time for the Brotherhood to join with our forces, and ensure our victory over the north!"

Jade kept her face neutral. If enough Brothers were leaving the Sanctum, perhaps she could find an opening to finally escape.

The Sorcerer Supreme turned his cold smile to face her. "And you'll be coming with us."

She froze. *No.*

"We leave tomorrow — the dragons too. We'll need to keep well stocked for the inevitable resistance the troops will face." He rolled his eyes and in that simple gesture, Jade saw heads rolling too. "This empire would be nothing without me and my Brothers."

"Of course, Supremacy." It had felt like the right thing to say, but when the Sorcerer Supreme's gaze swivelled to meet hers, Jade felt like she'd miscalculated horribly.

"Do you understand why, Xid?" His voice dropped dangerously low, and she had the distinct impression of being baited. "Do you know what I have done to ensure the triumph of this empire? What has been taken from me? What I have built from?"

Jade shook her head frantically. Somehow, the conversation had taken a perilous turn, and she didn't like the maniacal glint in the Sorcerer Supreme's eyes.

"Of course not," he hissed. "Because I have worked from the shadows. Thwarting those who would thwart me. Bolstering the fortunes of those who would further mine. Hunting allies, burying enemies, sowing secrets to reap power. I have fought, throttled, and killed to make Thamib the empire it is today." His lips curled back to bare his teeth in a snarl. "Without me, our *Eminence* would never have amounted to more than another merchant in the square, and Pharro would still be an unremarkable port on the southern coast of a forgotten desert." He straightened, smoothing over the front of his robes, his cool mask slipping back into place.

"I should thank you, Jade." He brushed his hands together. "You and your beasts are the reason I've been able to advance our plans to conquer the north. And once we do" — he stepped in close, and ran the back of his hand down her cheek — "I will have no further need of your whelps, and I can release them to fly off into the sunset. But until then..." The cuff of his robe slipped down his arm, revealing a gold bracelet at his wrist, seven ruby charms glinting in the light of the atrium. And inside, the leash that Jade had painstakingly loosened over months, years even, tightened until it was a noose around her neck. She gasped as her throat closed around nothing, her breath collapsing like a sail on calm seas. She clutched at her throat, half expecting to find it wrapped in rope.

The Sorcerer Supreme smiled. "Until then, my dear, I will not be letting you or any of those pathetic creatures out of my sight." He fingered the rubies on his bracelet. Jade stared at them. Not rubies.

Blood.

He caught her gaze, and held out his wrist for her to see. "You like?" He gave the chain a little shake, and Jade saw the rubies were in fact tiny vials, filled with blood and sealed into beads that hung from the bracelet like gems. Spots danced across her vision as he withdrew his hand. "Just a little insurance, my dear. You understand." The vice around her throat released its hold, and air rushed into Jade's lungs as her chest expanded again. She coughed in great gulps, breathing past the sparks floating in front of the Sorcerer Supreme's smirk.

"I hope you hadn't forgotten where you belong, Jade." He strode over to the chaise where they'd sat before, and relaxed back into the cushions. "Your former employer understood, but he forgot the rules of engagement." He casually pulled the cuffs of his robes back down over his wrists. "In here, the currency is blood. I paid for you with his. And I own you with yours."

Jade stared at him, her hand still at her throat as she heaved in breaths like she had to store them up, her own mask of impassivity long since abandoned.

"Yes, Supremacy," she gasped.

The Sorcerer Supreme tipped his head to one side and regarded her from beneath a reproachful brow. "I have asked you to call me by my name, Jade."

Jade barely managed to conceal her incredulity. "Yes, Kohl."

He nodded. "Good. We're going to be spending a lot of time together in the next few weeks, Jade. I would hate for us to be anything less than friends."

Jade wrestled a semblance of composure from somewhere. "Yes, Supr — Kohl." Her throat felt like someone had poured half the desert down it, and she blinked back tears. She'd never had her mortality put in such stark relief.

The Sorcerer Supreme — the monster in silk slippers — smiled without it ever reaching his eyes.

"Rest up, my dear." He picked up a report from the table beside him, and scanned it. "We leave at dawn, and I expect you to be there to assist with the beasts. Everyone needs to be on their best behaviour for our trip."

Jade stared at him as he read. "Yes, Kohl."

His eyes flicked up to meet hers before returning to his report, and Jade stifled a shudder at what she'd seen in his gaze.

She turned, and walked from the atrium.

Hunger, she thought as she eased the gilded doors closed behind her.

It had been hunger in his eyes.

Jade barely managed to control her pace as she made her way through the maze of stone corridors, her silent shadows a step behind. She wanted to break into a run, but there was nowhere to run to.

Back at the relative safety of her rooms, she turned on the threshold.

"A moment," she said, to the shadow with the dark eyes. "I need to tend to a private matter." Before he could refuse, she pushed the door closed in his face.

She turned her back to the cold, iron surface and slid down it to sit on the floor.

Then she let the tears fall.

She wrapped her arms around her legs, and buried her head against her knees as silent sobs wracked her.

All those months, those *years* of working on the blood bond that had been forced on her, undone in an instant at the Sorcerer Supreme's will. At *Kohl's* will.

Why did he want her to use his name? Was it to forge some sort of relationship between them? Was it to garner some level of trust from her?

She shook her head against her knees. He was a monster, and they would never be free of him. She didn't believe for an instant what he'd said about releasing them when they reached the north. No, when he was done with them, he'd kill them all.

Despair rose up and threatened to drown her. She bit her lip to stop the sobs from breaking free, and tasted blood.

She sat up with a gasp, touching a finger to her lip. It came away red. She sucked it clean, pulling her lip into her mouth before it could drip onto her whites.

It had been years since she'd been punished for bleeding. Would they still punish her? She'd learned the hard way that there were plenty of ways to inflict pain without drawing blood. That there were ways to whip a person without breaking the skin.

She ran a hand up the arm of her tunic, felt the ridges under the skin where the whip had drawn such welts that the swelling alone had scarred.

She sucked at her lip until she no longer tasted the metallic tang of blood.

The cocoon of wings and talons inside her shifted uneasily, and she stroked a hand down the bonds that held her heart.

I'm okay, she reassured them, feeling the hum of concern from her dragons. The wings settled again, but the slightly heavier thread of the Alpha didn't seem convinced. She marvelled at the feelings emanating from the bonds now. Days ago, when she'd fought back, she'd heard their voices in her mind, hadn't she? She might have imagined it — but she didn't think so.

She ran a hand through the threads tethered to her heart. *Can you hear me?*

The bonds thrummed a chord, and it felt like joy.

28

HAUNTED

The streets of Throldon were a mess.

They'd had to rewrite the maps for the war efforts. Scaffold lay across roads and alleys, blocking access to the inner city. Makeshift bunkers made from rubble and sandbags had sprung up on cobbled intersections, and traps crouched ready and waiting for any would-be invaders.

Hal walked through it all, Ty at his side. The elf had withdrawn more and more into himself over the two weeks since the council meeting. Hal worried for him. Ty's worry for Fae was constant. It was a living thing clawing inside him. But his duty to this city and to Arland as a whole anchored him here.

They passed another half-constructed bunker, and Hal nodded his approval to the Reformers knee-deep in earth and grit, packing the sides and reinforcing them with broken boards. On the one hand, the work gave them all something else to think on. But the hollows under Ty's eyes spoke volumes on how it ate him up not to be scouring the wilds for Fae.

Hal knew the feeling well. And he could do nothing to fix it. Not for himself, not for Ty. Not for Laina.

They were all hurting. One way or another.

"Eh, Ty! Hal!" A hand waved them over from the midst of a small group digging a trench across a particularly rough street, earmarked for repair. Aren and Stef were among the workers.

187

"Do you like what we've done with the place?" Aren straightened to lean on his shovel, mopping the sweat from his brow, his usual sun-kissed ebony hair grey with dust and grime. Hal shouldn't have been surprised to see the brothers there. Everyone was pitching in where they could. Aren gestured to the trench. "George here says he can get some planks to lay across the opening that we can pull back as needed." He eyed the pit forming across the breadth of the street. "When we're done no human will be able to cross this point without help. It's a good bottleneck."

Hal nodded his approval again, a gesture he was becoming rather familiar with. He recognised a few of the men and women digging the trench. More than one had been Survivors before the liberation. Now reformed folk, they were carrying more than their fair share of the efforts in preparing Throldon for the incoming army. "Good work." He made sure his voice carried over the lot of them. "Make sure someone fetches you all something to drink. Must be thirsty work, doing all this. And I know you've been hard at it."

As if on cue, a girl of no more than ten appeared, lugging a bucket sloshing with water, three ladles hooked over the sides.

"Yessir! Already taken care of sir!" Aren snapped a grinning salute, and Hal couldn't stop the smile that pulled at his lips.

As the workers paused for a well-earned drink, Hal pulled Aren and Stef to one side.

"Really appreciate you boys helpin' out like this." He watched as one of the women poked fun at the men, a roar of laughter going up from the group in response. "Keeping morale up is more important than they realise. I've seen how you are with them. It helps. Just wanted you to know."

Aren smiled. "Boys? I'll have you know we're definitely older than you."

Ty hummed in agreement. "By a few decades at least."

Hal laughed. "You elves may be older in years, but you're younger in body. You're still strapping lads, while I grow creakier by the year."

Aren clapped him on the shoulder. "Not so creaky yet, Councilman. But certainly wise beyond our years." He glanced over to the workers, and sobered.

Stef followed his gaze. "They're good people. They've been through a lot, but I think they'll do you proud."

Hal blinked away a tear. "Aye, I think you have the right of that." How many times had he seen soldiers haunted by what they'd seen — what they'd done — and then come back stronger, better people because of it? He couldn't count.

"Hey, bean-poles!" A call came from above, and they turned in time to spot Jesse leap from a nearby rooftop. She caught a lamppost on the way past, swinging around it to slow her descent, and landed cat-like on the ground before them. Behind her, Max scrambled down the brickwork, her boots long-ago abandoned in favour of barefoot escapades across her old Sky-Roads.

Hal had to smile. He knew what Kagos thought of his charge capering about Tholdon's rooftops. He also knew Aiya turned a blind eye, well aware that Max would just sneak off to do it anyway. Besides, the girl had been teaching others how to navigate the city from above, an advantage their attackers wouldn't have.

Aren whistled his appreciation at their antics. "Didn't know you had it in you Jesse. Has the student surpassed the master?" He arched an eyebrow at Max.

Max jogged over, adjusting the dragon-shaped bundle in her coat. "Pig slows me down!" she moaned. "Well, you do!" she added at the indignant squawk that emanated from the hatchling.

"You know," Jesse interjected, "before I came here I *danced* up the Gatekeepers every day for guard duty? Years of training. They don't let just anyone do that." When her statement was met with bemused expressions, she mumbled something about not being properly appreciated.

"Of course your skills are highly valued, Jesse." Hal was quick to allay any brewing discontent. "*You* are indispensable. How thankful we are that Lord Graem sent you to council in his stead."

"Alright, alright." Jesse blushed furiously, something he'd never seen her do before. "That'll do." She straightened and gestured to Max. "We were mapping out the Sky-Roads today, thought we'd check out the University, seeing as that wasn't here last year."

Hal nodded his approval. He was going to develop neck cramp at this rate. But something about the way Jesse hesitated made him pause.

"What did you see?"

The slightest thinning of her lips made his blood run cold.

"Scouts spotted to the south, Councilman," she said, and Hal recognised the return to formality for what it was — her way of dealing with the brutal reality of their situation, of separating her emotions from the oncoming horror. They could joke and laugh in the moment, on home soil, among friends. But these streets would soon become a war zone. A fact many of them were having difficulty facing.

He nodded again, and his neck twinged in protest. "The army won't be far behind the scouts. Likely we have a few days at most." He glanced at Aren and Stef. "Get those trenches dug, lads. Give me as much as you can to protect this city."

"On it." The elves turned back to their crew and leapt into the pit. Sprays of earth flew out a second later, and the men and women around them returned to work in earnest.

"I will need to check in with Sheha and your healers," Ty said. "Make sure they have everything they need." Laina had of course taken the lead on their medical preparations, setting up an infirmary in the castle bailey, where fortifications were the strongest. Sheha had slotted right into place at her side, and the two of them had organised a group of herb gatherers and healers to stockpile as much as they could in readiness.

"Yes, let them know of the situation. Meet us back in the map room in one hour." Hal turned back to Jesse and Max. "You two, come with me. Gather the council. I need an update from every corner of the city.

"Our time's nearly up."

29

A SPARK

It turned out that the Brothers had never intended to ride with the army for a variety of reasons, not least because the sorcerers were a little-known secret, and Kohl wanted to keep it that way.

Another, more obvious reason, was that a convoy of wagons bearing shackled dragons was likely to draw attention from anyone, friend or foe.

The entire company consisted of the dozen Brothers Jade had seen in the atrium, with as many acolytes scurrying around at their barked orders. Jade's shadows, for once, were being left behind.

Kohl stood at Jade's shoulder as the dragons were loaded onto simple, flat-bed wagons, each pulled by a two-horse team. Alpha fixed the Sorcerer Supreme with a sullen glare as he was bullied and shoved onto the wagon, but the beasts submitted to the acolytes' harrying, as if they too recognised the threat standing at Jade's side.

They'd been dragged out of the Sanctum in the dregs of night, dawn but a promise on the horizon, and yet their gaze brimmed with the reverence of a lost soul coming home when they beheld the inky sky. The bronze of their eyes gleamed with dew in the flickering torchlight, and Jade could have sworn she saw tears fall from more than one.

Seeing them outside at last, exposed and vulnerable, she felt the familiar burn behind her own eyes.

Shackled and chained two to a wagon, the dragons were pale, gaunt, and broken. Alpha was the largest of the six, the red now around eight feet long from snout to tail, his wings still healing from where they'd rubbed against the bars of the smaller enclosures.

The silver, who she'd named Delita, looked the worst of them all, her shimmering scales dull and flaking, her sides rough and raw. Beside her, Chary, the nervous green, seemed to have recovered from his ordeal at Brother Gerard's orders, but his left wingtip still sat at an odd angle. Jade wondered if it would impact his ability to fly.

The blue, Brave, crouched atop her wagon, glaring at anyone who approached, but her eyes kept flicking to Jade — to Kohl at her shoulder — and she kept her peace. Envy, on the other hand, hissed a constant stream of protest from where she sat beside her sister, her scales of dark purple and bronze appearing almost black in the pre-dawn gloom.

The runt of the family was Fearless. Only around five feet long and pure, matte black, she was barely visible beside Alpha but for the quiet glow of her eyes catching in the Brothers' torchlight. Alpha extended one battered wing over her, instinctively protecting the smallest member of his family, if only because he couldn't do the same for Jade.

A lump formed in Jade's throat. She'd named her dragons by their characters, her own private way of acknowledging each one individually. They were hers alone. The Brothers certainly had no interest in knowing them. They'd likely whip her for attempting such attachments.

The wings around her heart shivered in anticipation, the bonds humming within her.

Then a strong hand dropped onto her shoulder, and the bonds fell silent. Watchful.

"Time to go, my dear." Kohl's voice rumbled through her, like whispered secrets between lovers. She resisted the urge to shrug him off. There would be nowhere to run from him, no room to hide in. She would have to play by his rules. Jade glanced sideways at the hand on her shoulder, and the gold chain peeking out from beneath robes as white as her own.

It struck her then — together, they must look a pair, the only two among the company to be attired in white. But where her clothes were white to control her, Kohl's robes were a symbol of power.

He dropped his hand to her lower back, and moved her forward. Unyielding.

He steered her to one of the horses, a heavily built stallion that pawed impatiently at the ground. She'd never been anywhere near a horse before, let alone ridden one. The beast towered over her, its nostrils flaring wide as she approached.

"Don't worry, Hallar will not bite." Kohl reached around her to rub the horse's neck. He stepped in close, adjusting the stirrup, although Jade was certain the acolytes had already tended to such things. Then, without warning, he gripped her hips and lifted her straight up and into the saddle.

Swallowing a squeak, Jade gripped the pommel in front of her. She felt completely unbalanced, and feared toppling with every shift of the horse's back. Beside her, Kohl kept hold of the reins in one hand, while the other rested on her thigh. She was utterly pinned; a rabbit caught in a snare, while the wolf stared her down.

"The latest missive stated that the armies were within a week of the capital." Kohl addressed his Brothers. "We travel in the twilight hours, and ride hard to meet them before they engage." Then he did the last thing Jade expected — the Sorcerer Supreme put his foot in her stirrup, and swung himself up to sit behind her on the horse. "Let us not delay!" With a sharp kick to the horse's flanks, he spurred Hallar on. The Brothers fell in behind them, the wagons taking up the rear of the procession with two acolytes to each.

Jade sat as straight as a rod, trying to maintain an element of distance between herself and the Sorcerer Supreme, but it was impossible. His body brushed hers with every jolt of the horse; his chest pressed against her back, his knees bracketed her thighs, his arms reached around her to grip the reins.

Minutes after leaving the Sanctum behind, she felt him brush his lips against her ear.

"I told you," he murmured, "I do not intend to let you out of my sight." He pressed his arms in around her. "Not for a moment."

Jade fixed her eyes forward, focusing on the slow lightening of the horizon as the sun finally deigned to show itself, and tried to swallow the nausea pushing bile into her throat. She squeezed her eyes shut against the threat of tears.

She may have been one of the lowly worker class for as long as she could remember, but she'd never once been forced upon. Her body had always been her own. Since being taken by the Brotherhood, she'd had to relinquish tiny pieces of herself that she'd never imagined she'd have to give up, but not once had she had to surrender her body in that way.

But as the heat of the Sorcerer Supreme's body permeated the chill in hers, she couldn't shake the utter hopelessness of her situation — the Brotherhood was taking her north to bleed her and her dragons dry in their conquest to expand the empire.

And there wasn't a thing she could do about it.

After riding through dusk with only two crescent moons to light the way, their company made camp on the desert sands.

They'd stopped just before the sun reached its peak, pitching stilted canvases to rest and water the horses during the worst of the midday heat. But now, it was full dark, and the temperature had plummeted so far, Jade's teeth chattered.

Kohl's tent was the first to be erected, and he disappeared inside with two of his Brothers, leaving her with nothing to do but watch as the acolytes unpacked the rest.

One pulled out a sack of cooked chickens, and began throwing carcasses up onto the wagons, one for each of the dragons. The chains were left on, red sores already showing on Delita's pale legs. She nuzzled at the shackles with her wedge-shaped head, and warbled in pain.

"Shut up!" A Brother grabbed the slack on her chain and whipped it over the bed of the wagon with a *crack*. Delita startled, and Chary shrank away from them. The Brother cast them a look of such disgust that Jade had to fight the urge to snarl at him. He turned to the acolyte assembling his tent and snapped, "Hurry up! I'll be standing here all night waiting for a bed at this rate! And where's dinner? Get on it!"

"Yes Brother Leroy," the acolyte murmured with a bow.

Brother Leroy turned his sneer back towards the dragons. "Gods, these animals stink! Why do we have to drag them along with us in the first place?"

"The armies have moved too far." Another Brother Jade vaguely recognised sidled up to him. "It's simple mathematics at this point. The further the magic has to travel, the more energy is required for it to reach. Either the magic must be stronger — by source or practitioner — or the distance must be shortened."

"Ah Brother Amand, always with the ready answer." Brother Leroy leaned back against the wagon, waving to the dragons perched atop it. "I thought these were supposed to be the most powerful creatures on earth? Surely if anything was going to give our Sorcerer Supreme the reach, it would be the blood from one such as them?"

Brother Amand smiled, the expression one of humouring a child. "These are only young — barely hatchlings when they came into the Sorcerer Supreme's ownership. The real power lies in the dragons in the north. The ancients. One was spotted by our scouts just this year. Why do you think the Sorcerer Supreme enables this campaign so willingly? He doesn't care for the northlands. He wants the peninsula. He wants a *real* dragon."

Jade covered her gasp in a hand. Until she'd stumbled upon hers, she hadn't thought there were any dragons left. But if what the Brothers were saying was true, then there *were* more of them. In the north. And Kohl was hellbent on capturing one for himself. It all made sense now.

She looked to her dragons, shackled and broken, and understood exactly why he wouldn't need them upon conquering the north. If he had a fully grown dragon, a true ancient, her little family of juveniles would be beyond superfluous. They would become a burden.

But if there were dragons in the north, they could help her. She could warn them.

They could save each other.

If only she could get to them first.

The idea of yet more dragons being held captive the way hers were twisted her insides into knots. She could not — *would* not — let that happen.

She glanced up to find Alpha's eyes fixed on her, like he knew exactly what the Brothers were talking about, and exactly what she was thinking. His head dipped.

We will not stop fighting, he'd said to her.

The makings of a plan began to form in her mind. Nothing but a scrap. It had holes and gaps and questions leaking from it, but it was a spark of a plan, and she was determined to give it wings.

30

AFRAID

Now that Fae knew what to look for, finding the elements was easy.

Each one, she discovered, responded differently to the various aspects of her personality. Fire was only the most overt of them: brash and vibrant.

After corralling the fire back into herself, she had Luca wield his own, so that she could compare the two. He obliged wordlessly, mimicking her earlier feat by holding flames in the palm of his hand, albeit with significantly more control.

She stepped closer to him, reaching out — almost as if she intended to take the fire from him — and stood, hands hovering to either side of the flames.

And she Listened.

Not to Eah'lara, but to the essence of the fire itself. To the heart and soul of the element Luca wielded.

She cocked her head to the side, focusing in on the flames, the flicker and dance of them as they twined around each other. And once again, she had the distinct impression of a mane of fire, shedding sparks and glowing embers as it roared.

Fae dropped her hands, and nodded to Luca.

His fire flared and winked out.

"Now draw air," Fae said, holding onto how it had felt to sense the essence of the element itself.

Luca raised one eyebrow, but lifted his hand once more, and summoned a whirling ball of wind into his palm.

Fae held her hands out to either side of it, and Listened again.

Air was fleet and subtle, whispering where fire roared. But there was a strength in it too, and it was in that strength that she caught glimpses of a tiny, jewelled form flitting about, quick and nimble.

She dropped her hands, and took a step back, looking deep into herself for that small, whispering flicker.

She found the fire easily this time, smouldering within her, ready to lash out and play. And now that she knew where to look, she noticed the others, lining her insides like overlapping nesting dolls, no one bigger or smaller than the others.

And there, fluttering freely between them all, was air.

It took a minute for Fae to will the air to the fore; fire was still keen to play. But eventually, after some gentle coaxing, her body tingled with a kiss of wind, pressing outward from under her skin.

As before, she pushed the pressure down her arms, willing the magic into her hands. But when air emerged, it moved more freely than fire, and escaped her before she could think of how to contain it. A small gust of wind twirled between her hands, and then it was gone.

A current ran across her whole body, her hair blowing about in a gentle breeze, while the air she was trying to hold in her hands simply billowed out and away.

Luca dropped his hand, and smiled. "Air is fickle," he said. "That one might take a bit more practice." But something warm shone in his eyes.

Fae willed the quick, nimble element back under her skin — it was easier to do than it had been with fire. Air was trickier to control, but it was happy enough tucking in alongside the other element-aspects within her.

Fae slumped where she stood, her arms hanging loose at her side, but her grin was wide and wild.

Over the next few days she worked on water with Madja, the element darting and slippery in its natural state. Terrence wielded earth for her, which was solid and wholesome, but eluded her when she went to draw it out herself; stubborn.

"Then we shall continue our meditations," he declared solemnly, and the rest of her session with him was spent in quiet contemplation. Despite her disappointment, she understood the reasons behind his methods more, having touched the essence of earth. Meditation was grounding, and she always left Terrence's lessons feeling more connected to the physical world around her.

And in between all of these, her morning training with Alexi continued. She was improving, he laughingly told her after besting her in a bout of staves.

Then he suggested they move onto knife training.

"Ooh, he honours you," Irya said later, playing her autumnal hair through her fingers while sprawled across Fae's bed. "Knives are his weapon of choice." She winked at her. "Good luck with that."

Fae groaned and flopped onto the mattress beside her friend.

It had been a week since Ath had taken her nightmares from her, and she was starting to feel the benefits of more regular sleep. While it was still far from perfect — there were plenty of other things that conspired to keep her awake at night — it was much more than she'd been coping with before.

But she couldn't help but worry about how the Dreamweaver was doing.

She plucked at the bed sheets. "How's your father doing lately?"

Irya stilled. She leaned up on her elbow, and fixed Fae with a white stare.

"Why do you ask?"

Fae shrugged. "I was thinking of paying him a visit."

Irya's eyes narrowed. "You don't want to see him like this."

Guilt bloomed deep in Fae's gut. Her hands smoothed the wrinkles beneath her fingers. "Maybe I need to."

"It won't make you feel better."

Fae gave her a hard stare. "I'm not looking for absolution," she said, and the words came out stiff and clipped.

Irya held up a hand. "I didn't mean that," she soothed. "What I mean is..." She hesitated, choosing her words carefully. "I don't want you to feel bad about it, is all. He knew what he was doing, and he made his decision of his own free will. He wouldn't want you to feel bad for him either."

Fae's lips pressed into a line. "Please."

Irya considered, and Fae thought for a moment that she'd refuse. Then the Echo nodded.

They made their way through the Warrens rather than going through the bustling Core; Irya didn't want anyone making a fuss of their visit.

And Fae soon found out why.

Irya knocked gently on the door to the Dreamweaver's home, and let herself in.

Light from the midday snowscape flooded in through the expanse of crystalline ice along the far wall. The furniture was neatly arranged, as before. Someone had even brought in a vase of flowers, although Fae couldn't fathom where from.

But the living area was quiet. Empty.

"Follow me." Irya picked her way across the room, down an open hallway, and stopped at another door.

"Father?" she called softly. "We just came to check on you, see if there's anything you need..." Slowly, she pushed the door open.

Inside, it was pitch dark, the only light spilling in from the hall. The room wasn't large, perhaps only wide enough for two to sleep abreast, and as bare as an empty cupboard. A thick, cushion-like pad covered the floor, sinking deep underfoot. And in the corner, the Dreamweaver sat staring into the middle distance, arms wrapped around his knees, knuckles white where they gripped the fabric of his shirt.

"Ath?" Fae crouched down opposite him. She'd seen people in shock before. This looked a lot like that. She glanced up at Irya. "Why is he in the dark?"

Irya leaned against the door, holding it open to let the light in. "He finds it easier to tell the dreams apart from reality this way." She gestured to the room. "That's why he comes in here."

Fae faced the Dreamweaver again. He was a shell of the man she'd met less than two weeks ago. His eyes were ringed by shadows, his face gaunt, and his clothes hung off him as if he hadn't eaten in days.

"Ath." She reached out, and gently pried his hand from his arm.

"He lives in your nightmares," Irya said, her voice strained.

Fae nodded. "You're not alone," she whispered to the Dreamweaver.

"And you're not powerless." As the words came out of her mouth, she wondered whose benefit they were for. "I defeated him, in the end. He's gone. He can't hurt you." She squeezed his hand. "You're not alone."

The Dreamweaver's hazel eyes blinked slowly, the fog lifting from them like a veil. His gaze focused first on his hand, clasped tightly in hers, and then on her face.

"Fae." His voice was a croak, like he'd not used it in days, or like he'd screamed, alone here in the dark. "You're afraid."

It took her a moment to realise he meant in her dream. He was right, she was always terrified there.

"I was afraid," she said. "But I'm not anymore."

He blinked, the fog creeping back into his eyes. "Your fear is crippling."

A tear ran down Fae's cheek. "I know," she breathed.

In a flash of clarity, the Dreamweaver smiled. "But there is a light, in your darkness."

She frowned. There had been no light in her nightmares. Only endless dark, and a pit of shadows.

The Dreamweaver leaned forward to tap her on the chest.

"It is in you. You need only to find it." Then he recoiled, shrinking back into the corner. The veil fell back over his eyes, and his arms came around to grip his knees once more. His head whipped from side to side, seeing a nightmare that had once plagued her instead. He rocked in place.

"Come on," Irya's hand touched her shoulder. "He won't be back for a while."

Fae eased to her feet and padded from the room, the door sliding closed behind them with a muffled *snick*. Wordlessly, they walked back through the apartment, and Fae saw the neatness with new eyes.

"Who's looking after him?"

"I am," Irya replied, then dipped her head to the side. "And Luca drops in sometimes."

The revelation surprised Fae, but she simply nodded. "He looks awful."

Irya's eyes flickered towards her. "You didn't look so great when you first got here either, you know."

"I wasn't sleeping."

"Do you think he is?" They reached the door and Irya pulled it open.

Fae chewed at her lip. "It didn't look like it."

"That's because he isn't." Irya regarded her starkly, and waved her through the door. "I told you, don't feel bad about it. He took your nightmares, because you couldn't handle them. And the consequences of *that* were worse than if he couldn't." Stepping in the corridor beyond, she took Fae's hands in her own. "My father has walked in the dreams of others longer than I've been alive. He'll be okay."

Irya's words of comfort were sincere, despite the quiet pain behind her eyes. But seeing her own nightmares on the Dreamweaver's face had lit a fire inside Fae.

"Alright," she said, an idea forming in her mind. "Have you still got time for lunch?"

"Of course," Irya's smile chased the pain from her face. "But we're still going my way. I'm not about to go easy on you."

Fae chuckled. "Of course you aren't." She was counting on it.

31

ANYTHING IS POSSIBLE

Using only Eah'lara to guide them — as usual — Fae and Irya made their way through the eastern quadrant, the nebulae of the Spirit Realm a serene, shimmering wash of blues.

"Huh." Irya stopped as the blues gave way to the multi-hued backdrop of the Core. "It's snowing."

"It is?" Fae's eyes darted around, instinctively looking for white flakes.

"Look." Irya pointed up, to where glittering clusters of spirit dust tumbled through the ether. Just like— "Snow."

Fae stared. She'd never seen anything translate so perfectly from one side of the veil to the other. Because there was no other way to describe what she was seeing. It was snowing in the Spirit Realm.

"It's so..." She fumbled for the right words.

"Accurate?" Irya arched an eyebrow at her dryly. "The elements have a funny way of doing that. They have no other way of being — they just are. Whether you see them from here, or the other side." She frowned up at the lazy flakes, the swirling colours of her eyes glinting. "I thought we'd seen the last of the snow for the year..."

Fae glanced across at her tone. "Does that worry you?"

Irya watched the snow suspiciously for a breath longer. "Not specifically..." She blinked, and shook herself. Turning back to Fae, she shot her a lopsided grin. "Any chance you've started messing with the weather and not told me about it yet?"

Fae barked a laugh. "I can barely harness a gentle breeze, I doubt I could direct the weather. Besides, this would be water, right?" Irya did not deign to answer that. "I can *just* about sense water. I'd be hard-pressed to summon it in any capacity, let alone make it snow."

Irya shrugged, and continued towards the kitchens. "Just thought I'd ask. Seems like anything is possible with you these days."

Fae spluttered, and narrowly avoided walking into a shop awning. "What do you mean, 'these days'?"

"You know..." Irya waved a hand airily. "Shaking the earth, bursting into flames... You said yourself that you've summoned storms before."

"That was before! And none of it has ever been controlled!"

Irya rested a hand on her arm, and pulled her to a stop. "I'm only teasing." But the look she levelled Fae with now was anything but. "These abilities are in you, Fae. Stop doubting yourself and you might stand a chance of owning them." The Echo fiddled with a wayward strand of hair. "My father said your fear cripples you. I think he told you that for a reason."

Fae didn't know what to say. She'd spent a year believing herself powerless, to then be told that she'd been channeling power all along, and in doing so, slowly broken the earth. Of course she didn't trust herself with it.

At Fae's continued stunned silence, Irya sighed and pushed her hair over her shoulder.

"Come on, I'm famished."

They sat together at a table with a view of the gardens, watching as the snow slowly blanketed the beds and covered Eah'lara in a layer of fluffy spirit dust, outlining everything clearly to their spirit-sight.

In Irya's presence, Fae had taken to using the Spirit Realm to navigate the mortal one for more than just walking to the kitchen, and she was quietly pleased with how much easier it was becoming.

So much so, in fact, that she even thought she recognised the aura walking across the garden. She focused in on it.

Auras were walking tangles of whisper-thin connections sparking in a language of light and constant messages. The threads that spun through Eah'lara were strong enough to hold, strong enough to follow from one end to another. But the ones that made up a person's aura were so delicate, they broke apart on a breath of wind.

How on earth the Dreamweaver was able to manipulate them, Fae couldn't even begin to fathom.

"Hi Fae, Irya."

Fae opened her eyes and smiled. She'd recognised Arissa's no-nonsense, fun-loving energy even in Eah'lara. "Hi Arissa."

The Mizula slid into the seat next to Fae, propping her feet on the one opposite with a groan.

"Long morning?"

Arissa arched her back with a *crack*. "A group of juveniles went sledding down the mountain crags in the snow, and half of them came back with broken bones. I've been setting idiotic arms and brainless legs all morning."

Fae winced in sympathy. "Isn't everyone here old enough to know better?"

"Some juveniles never grow up," Irya answered flatly. "Regardless of how old they were when time stopped."

"Isn't that the truth!" Arissa nodded her solemn agreement. Fae chuckled.

"It wouldn't be half as bad," Arissa continued, "if, after breaking themselves once, they took better care of their terminally breakable bodies the next time. But no, they waltz into the Healing House with a smile, get themselves fixed up, and go straight back out to do it all over again."

"Magi," Irya stated sagely, "have an inoperable invincibility complex."

Arissa conceded her point with a tip of her head.

"*You're* a Magi," Fae reminded her.

"Oh I know. Don't worry, I've made my fair share of unwise calls in the past. And it's true, we do have a tendency to use our magic as a safety net, and hope it'll catch us when we fall." She jerked her head to Irya. "You don't see half as many Echoes in the Healing House injured out of pure stupidity."

Irya coughed pointedly. "I'd go so far as to say you won't find *any* Echoes in the Healing House after an ill-fated trip down the mountain on a rickety pile of sticks."

A laugh bubbled from Arissa. "That's true." Then she turned to Fae.

"I hear you're having more luck with your magic now? Since..." She trailed off.

"Since I burst into a human torch?" Fae suggested helpfully. If Luca's anger had unsettled her fledgling friends, her sudden transformation into a standing pyre appeared to have scared them off completely. She hadn't seen Rylan or Taniq since.

Arissa glanced uneasily at her now. "Well, yes."

"She's doing well with combat training too," Irya supplied. "Alexi wants to move onto knives next."

Arissa's eyebrows jumped an inch. "Oh? He must really like you. He doesn't trust just anyone with blades."

"So I hear." Fae shot Irya a glance.

The Echo just gave a shrug, draining her *kahveh* in one last swig. "Well, must be going," she said, pushing her chair back. "This world won't keep an eye on itself." She shot Fae a wink, and stood. "Same time tomorrow?" She left without waiting for an answer.

Fae was due for a session with Kallis, who was still trying to show her dark, as well as hone her fire-wielding. She groaned as she pushed her chair back as well. She was getting tired of being shown what she *couldn't* do.

"What's on the menu for today?" Arissa asked, correctly guessing the reason for her reluctance.

"It's Kallis today," Fae answered with a grimace. She had nothing against the High Magi — in fact, he often provided a little light relief after Luca's moods — but his methods were a little... theatrical.

"Have you had any luck with dark?" Arissa asked.

Fae shook her head. "No. Nor light. And earth still won't come either, which is the one I really need to master."

"Maybe you were never meant to wield light and dark," Arissa suggested. "Four is already a large number, even for a Power."

Fae dropped her head into her hands. There was that term again — Power. If there was ever a way to describe how she felt in La'sa, her apparent magical potential was the perfect oxymoron.

Arissa patted her on the shoulder. "It's not that bad, is it? You've figured out three of them already!"

"Barely," Fae muffled through her palms. She dropped her hands to look at her friend. "I can summon fire, and almost air. Water is slippery, but I can feel it there. Earth is stubborn and won't budge." An idea came to her. "You can help me with water! Oh please, if I have to listen to Demilda recite the properties of water again I might finally form an icicle just so I can stab myself in the eye."

Arissa erupted with snorts of laughter. "Oh she means well, but I know what you mean. She's very detail-orientated."

Fae clasped her hands before her. "Please help me. Madja's been so helpful but it's like I've hit a block."

Arissa smiled, but shook her head. "If your magic is as powerful with water as it is with fire, I can't help you." She wrapped her hands around Fae's. "I work on a small scale, because I have to. You're going to have to learn to control the elements on a much bigger stage."

"But," Fae reached desperately, "I might not be as strong with water. Like Rylan's air isn't as strong as his fire."

Arissa shook her head again. "I don't think even you believe that." She patted her hands, and stood from the table. "You'll get it, Fae. I know you will. You just need to find the right reason." She jerked a thumb across the gardens. "Do want some company?" One side of her mouth quirked up knowingly.

Fae groaned and stood, her chair matching the sound as it scraped across the floor. "No, I'll be fine. But thank you."

"Alright then." Arissa flicked her pale hair over one shoulder. "Good luck!"

Fae lifted a hand in farewell. "See you around."

The snow had stopped falling by the time she stepped outside, La'sa now covered in a thin blanket of white. The town looked particularly magical, with its cozy wooden chalets iced in snow, the windows laced in frost. Cold lamps and lanterns strung between the deep cabin eaves caught the sun and glinted even in the day, like strings of diamonds. Magi and non-Magi alike wandered the cobbled streets in brightly-coloured coats and scarves, shouting greetings to each other across the squares and sharing steaming chocolate from drinks carts.

Fae sighed, and stepped onto the path that was so familiar, it ought to carry her very footprints, she travelled it that often. She was beginning to think she could be dropped anywhere in La'sa blindfolded and still make her way to the arena. She wondered idly if she could get a cot set up in one of the empty rooms adjacent.

She was just dropping her coat into its customary place on the lower seats when the arena was plunged into darkness, blocking even the sun from above. She let out an exhausted sigh, and turned to the entrance, where two solitary columns of fire burned.

"Well, Fae dear," Kallis prowled across the space, the flaming columns flipping over themselves to follow him. "Let's see what you've got for me today."

Fae reached inside herself, and let fire out to play.

The session with Kallis hadn't gone too badly, all things considered.

She'd held the fire in the palm of her hands with minimal spread over the rest of her body. She'd even learned to extend that ball into flickering twin daggers, and even if drawing them out to the length of a sword resulted in the flames snaking out in mutinous tendrils, she was happy to call that small step a success.

At the end of their session, Kallis condensed the dark into a dense, smoky ball, holding it out for her to sense. Extending her hands to either side of it, as she had with all the other elements, she Listened. They'd agreed that this would be her last try. If she still couldn't sense dark after today, it was unlikely she ever would.

At first, as with every other time they'd tried this, she felt nothing.

Her shoulders slumped as she resigned herself to failing this as well. But she kept her hands outstretched, Listened a moment longer. Just to be sure.

A gasp escaped her when, for the first time, she felt the whisper of shadows flit beneath her skin, quick and silent. She tried to follow the shadow as it sighed between her cells, vanishing as if it had never been, nothing more than a mirage. If water was slippery, dark was nebulous — as tangible as a dream. She had no hope of summoning it with her current level of control.

But it was there.

She grinned up at Kallis.

"Dark is a very shadowy mistress, Kallis." And she felt the kiss of dark slip to the surface.

Kallis's eyes widened, his gaze darting over her before a lazy grin spread across his face. "Indeed she is, Fae dearest."

Fae glanced down, and found her hands wreathed in shadows that flickered over her skin like black flames. She gasped, and lifted her hands to examine them closer. As soon as she moved, the shadows retreated, disappearing back into her skin, the dark element-aspect vanishing as if it had never been.

Kallis slung an arm around her shoulders. "And that concludes our lesson for today." He began walking her to the archway.

"That's it?" Fae stared up at him.

He laughed. "Fae. Darling. You held blades of fire in your hands, and the elusive dark deigned to grace you with her presence. Yes, that's it. For today at least." He tugged at a strand of her hair, and there was pride in his voice that brought heat to her cheeks.

That was when Luca entered the arena.

His eyes flicked from Kallis to Fae, flashing as they took in Kallis's arm over her shoulder, and the strand of Fae's hair woven between his fingers.

His gaze settled on Kallis, the indigo so dark it was almost black.

"Did I miss something?"

32

OUT OF TIME

"Luca!" Kallis drawled. "Fae has seduced the Lady of the Night herself." He pulled her closer, squeezing her shoulders. "I guess this makes yours the last element to the party."

A muscle ticked in Luca's jaw, but either Kallis missed it, or he chose to ignore it. He planted a kiss on the top of Fae's head, and finally released her.

"I look forward to when next we play, Fae dear." He shot her a wink, his copper eyes glinting, and swaggered from the arena.

Leaving her alone with Luca.

The atmosphere was so thick Fae felt the breath stall in her chest as Kallis's footsteps faded into the Warrens, the air between her and Luca unnaturally still.

"If you're done with fire, shall we work on air?" Luca swept past her, and strode to the centre of the arena, his back ramrod-straight.

Fae pivoted to follow him. "You don't want to show me light?" she asked, clearly feeling brave. He'd never openly declared his third element, but she'd seen enough over the past few weeks to figure it out. What she couldn't work out, was why he hadn't showed her yet.

"Not particularly."

Fae cocked her head to the side. "Why not?" If she had dark, it stood to reason that she probably had light as well.

Luca's eyes darkened. "Because I'm not interested in getting into a pissing match about whose is bigger. Now," he clasped his hands before him, as if he had all the time in the world. "Draw air."

Fae's lips twitched at the image of the languid Kallis and uptight Luca getting into a pissing contest, but she said nothing as she planted her feet, and reached into herself.

Fire was right under the surface, as always, ready to play, its mane of sparks and embers flaring bright and tempting. Water was close as well, but it was slippery, twisting out of reach, taunting her. Earth sulked beneath them both, hulking and solid, but ever the stubborn one. And now she could feel the whisper of dark as its quiet form prowled in the shadows.

She imagined light would be bright and clear, happy to be front and centre. But she still couldn't sense it, despite now knowing how the elements resided within her.

The Dreamweaver had said there was a light inside her. Was he talking about the last of her element-aspects?

Shaking her head free of wandering thoughts, Fae coaxed air from where it flitted between the other elements, darting and quick. She breathed deep and, like the sun emerging from behind a cloud, she let her air-aspect out.

Immediately, the element tickled across her skin, her body enveloped in a gentle breeze. Her heart sang, and the wings within her grew until they were no longer tiny and darting, but wide and soaring. Beautiful. Majestic. Her chest lifted, as if she could pull herself into the sky with only the air in her lungs.

"Bring it to your hands," Luca reminded her from across the arena. Fae smothered the urge to tell him where to stick his suggestions. Once she had control of her magic, she could do what she wanted with it. But until then...

She pushed it down her arms, willing the magic to her palms, drawing the fickle element out with the promise of fun.

Wind rushed through her veins, rustled in her hair, and then her hands were holding the air itself.

"Good." Luca's voice pierced the magic of the moment. "Now shape it like you do with fire."

This was the part that continued to elude her. Fire, she could direct. Air didn't like to be told what to do.

A bit like her.

She gritted her teeth, and urged the air to form a ball between her hands. But as always, the element wasn't inclined to listen. It billowed from her fingertips, and whispered away on a breeze.

She let out a sound of frustration, and dropped her hands to her sides. Luca considered her for a moment.

"Try using the air, to shape the air," he said. "The currents are commanded by you, but without direction they're escaping as soon as they leave your body. Try giving them something to do."

Fae frowned over at him. Then she remembered what Arissa had said about Taniq's magic. How he used the earth to manipulate itself.

She took a breath, and shook her hands out, then brought them up once more. This time, she curled her fingers around, and when the air emerged, she pushed it into a curve so that it wrapped around itself. The breeze held a small vortex before escaping again. She adjusted her position and tried again.

The air danced and cavorted between her palms, and she felt the push against her skin as it ricocheted from one to the other, the currents she generated corralling the air into a rough sphere.

She cried out joyously. "I'm doing it!" Her focus slipped, and the air escaped once again.

She glanced up at Luca, her eyes shining. His expression, as inscrutable as ever, remained unchanged.

"Again."

But even his moods couldn't dampen this moment for her. Again, she drew air into her hands. Again, she curled her fingertips, directing the flow into a sphere. The wind buffeted against her palms, and a wisp of air escaped between her thumb and forefinger.

Determined to hold it this time, she brought her hands in towards each other, feeling the pressure build in her tiny storm.

"Give it room," Luca said. "Air needs to breathe."

Fae gritted her teeth. "Give me a minute." She'd sensed the pattern before, she'd just lost her focus. But now, if she could just get the air to flow the right way...

The pressure pushed against her, and her hands shook.

"Fae."

"I said give me a minute." Sweat beaded on her lip. Then — *there*.

She extended her arms out in front of her, and slowly parted her hands.

Between her palms, a perfect ball of air swirled around itself like a storm in a glass bauble. She moved her hands further and further apart, until she held a tempest wider than her shoulders.

Her eyes widened in amazement. She'd done it. Now just to hone it.

Already, she trembled with the effort of holding it. Following nothing but instinct, she threw the ball into the air, where it dissipated with a thunderous *whoosh*.

Panting with a mix of exhaustion and exhilaration, she looked over to where Luca stood, arms folded. And she could have sworn the ghost of a smile graced his lips.

"Again."

She was training with Madja when the next quake hit.

Fae had just managed to hold a floating droplet of water between her hands when the floor bucked underfoot, throwing her to the ground. As she lifted herself off the shale, the earth rumbling beneath her palms, a worrying groan issued from the mountain walls around them.

She glanced up at Madja. "This isn't me!" she yelled over the din.

"I know." Madja eyed the trembling rows of seating around them as pieces of the rock shook loose and tumbled down the steps. "We must find the others." She waved for Fae to follow, and hurried from the arena.

The tremors echoed through the Warrens, ice and rock dusting them as they went. As before, Madja led her to the Meeting House, where Terrence and Demilda waited on the porch. Kallis appeared from the opposite direction, his features set into a grim mask.

"Terrence?" Madja asked as soon as they reached the steps.

The Theras High Magi nodded gruffly. "Another rift has opened in the earth's shell."

Kallis swore loudly. "Where is Fialli?"

"Fetching our best intelligence officer." Luca strode across the plaza, half-dragging Irya with him. Stopping at the bottom of the steps, he pulled Irya to the front. "Tell them what you saw."

The Echo didn't hesitate. "These tremors are being felt across the entire north-eastern continent. Avalanches throughout the Edge

Mountain range, tidal waves sweeping over Yneshia, and sinkholes appearing all over Arland. Yneshia's the worst hit. They're an island kingdom. They have some defences but it'll take them years to recover." Her white eyes angled harshly. "This is the worst one yet."

"We always knew this wouldn't stop until we found a way to fix it." Kallis turned to Fae, one eyebrow raised hopefully.

Fae felt every single one of their gazes on her as she shook her head. "I am trying," she promised, although they felt like empty words when the earth shuddered beneath her again, and the sounds of things shattering and breaking repeated across La'sa. "I'll try harder. I'll get it. It's in me, I just... I'll try harder."

"Well you might want to get a move on, darling," Kallis suggested, his copper eyes darting around the trembling chalets.

Fae opened her mouth to reply, when the earth finally stilled.

The High Magi released a collective sigh of relief.

"Shore up the damage and prepare some defences." Terrence stomped down the steps, taking the lead without hesitation. "The quakes will start coming thick and fast now that the rifts in the earth are worsening." He reached the bottom step, and stared hard up at Fae. Despite his shorter, dwarven-esque stature, in that instant, he managed to make her feel even smaller. "We're changing tactics. I will see you at dawn, before your session with Alexi. Right now, I must see to our people." Fae managed a nod, and he left without another word.

"I'm afraid there are things I must tend to as well," Madja said, running a hand through her silver mane. "I'm sorry. We'll have to continue our session another time."

"Of course." Fae accepted the murmured farewells of the other High Magi, not entirely sure what to do with herself. La'sa would be occupied with taking stock of the damage. The best she could do was to keep out of the way.

"I'll walk with you." Irya appeared at her side, looping her arm through Fae's. She cocked an eyebrow at her. Fae offered a weak smile in return, but closed her eyes, to see through Eah'lara.

The threads of the Aethyr swayed, as they did when there had been a large outburst of power, the nebulae all muddied, as if they'd been tossed about like leaves in a storm.

"It's a mess isn't it?" Irya frowned at the tumbling spirit equivalent of dust and debris. "Don't worry, it'll settle, just like everything does eventually." She tugged Fae onward, guiding her through it all.

Finally, they reached the cool blue of the Warrens. Irya leaned close.

"Did you realise that when we talk here, we're not talking aloud?"

Fae glanced at her. "No. But I suppose it makes sense." She thought back to when she'd possessed her Aethyrial powers, and had the ability to speak into the minds of her friends.

"Speaking aloud from here is like commanding your body to move. You have to concentrate. Project." Irya gripped her arm, and Fae stopped, expecting another lesson. But there was tension in Irya's eyes, like she was warring with herself.

"What's wrong?"

Irya hesitated. It was like watching two personalities fight for the right to speak, and Fae wondered if the Echo had finally cracked.

"When I scanned through Eah'lara just now — to survey the damage from the quake — I looked everywhere." She fidgeted in place, her fingers twining together.

"Okay..."

Irya's colour-dusted eyes flitted about nervously. "I have to check. To see if there's more to it than we can sense from here. To make sure we haven't missed anything. You know, like you."

Fae's eyes narrowed. "Irya, what are you trying to tell me?"

The Echo ceased her restless shifting, and lifted her gaze to Fae's.

"I checked Throldon. The Thamibian Empire has reached the city, and they're camped across the river. It... it doesn't look good." She reached forward to grip Fae's shoulders. "We knew about the army, Fae. I'm so sorry. You needed to focus on mastering your magic, and the High Magi didn't want to distract you with something you could do nothing about. But I couldn't just..." She shook her head, as if there was too much to say, and not enough words to say it. Eventually she settled on, "I would want to know. If it was my family."

Fae stared at her.

The army had reached Throldon.

She'd run out of time.

"I have to go," she said.

Irya shook her head again. "You can't go, Fae. It would take you weeks

214

to travel. And then what would you do? Light a few candles? Your magic is unpredictable at best. You're needed here, where we can train you, so we can fix the rents in the earth." She dropped her hands, and stood uncertainly before her. "I just... thought you should know."

Fae nodded dumbly, her mind circling.

The army had reached Throldon.

She had run out of time.

And the Magi had been keeping her in the dark on purpose.

Her eyes whipped back to Irya.

"How long have you known?"

Irya flinched at the sudden bite to her words. "We've been keeping an eye on all the major nations for centuries. We had to—"

Fae cut her off with a slash of her hand. "No more lies. *How long.*"

Hurt flashed across Irya's face. "We knew about the army as soon as it left Pharro. Weeks ago. Before you arrived."

Fire and dark whispered beneath her skin, begging to come out. But even in the rage that stirred inside her, Fae kept them leashed.

"You've known about this for weeks." Her voice dropped dangerously low. "Knowing it threatens my family, and yet you chose to keep it from me so I would play the good little student for you all. So I wouldn't be *distracted.*" She hissed the last, so disgusted with what she was finally understanding.

"You have to understand," Irya begged, "the High Magi thought if you could be free from distraction, you'd be more clear-minded. They thought—"

"They *thought* to make yet more decisions on my behalf," Fae snapped. "Tell me, if I was fully in control of my magic and the earth was all nice and mended, would they even have let me go then? I've heard Luca's opinions on this, I know what he'd say."

"Fae, please..."

"No. No more." Fae opened her eyes to storm away, and turned straight into the solid muscle of Luca's chest.

The indigo of his eyes flashed as he steadied her. "What's going on here?" he asked, looking from a distressed Irya, to the rage evident in Fae's entire body.

Years ago, she'd learnt about the body's instinctive response to a threat.

But in the peaceful branches of Arolynos, it seemed she herself would never experience such things.

Now, her skin hummed with tension, her hands balled into tight fists, and her heart pounded in her ears. Now, that possibility was alive within her.

The only question was whether she would fight, or flee.

33

SACRIFICES

"What's going on here?" Luca repeated when neither of them answered him.

Irya looked as if she was on the verge of tears, but Fae couldn't muster any sympathy for her.

She whirled on Luca. "When were you going to tell me about Throldon?" The gold ring in her eyes flared dangerously. "Or did you plan to keep me in the dark until all my family were dead?" Her voice lashed out with venom barbs, but Luca's face remained as cooly impassive as ever. His eyes flicked to Irya, who shrank away from his gaze.

"As the events of this afternoon have clearly demonstrated" — he turned his attention back to Fae — "you are needed here. The lesser conflicts of the nations on this earth are of little consequence if the very foundations on which they are built turn to dust."

Fae lifted her chin and stepped even closer. "And I've told you before, it is *all* of consequence." The bite of her nails into the palms of her hands grounded her as fire lashed beneath the surface of her skin. "Don't you get it? I followed the Aethyr to save Arolynos, and my family there. I will not abandon them so I can learn party tricks up here with you!"

Luca's eyes narrowed, and his voice lowered to a murmur. "There's more to it than that and you know it."

"But what *you* don't seem to realise is how much I lose if I can't save them." Fae's heart stuttered at the admission. "I can't help you save the earth if I can't save them." She choked on the words, and she realised in that moment how much she meant them. Arissa had mentioned needing a reason. Her reason was her family — the chance of being able to save them again.

She'd already been through so much to protect them. And she'd do it again in a heartbeat. If they died when she might have prevented it... she didn't know if she would come back from that.

Luca's gaze softened, and his head dropped towards hers, until their noses brushed.

"Sometimes," he breathed, the words heavy between them, "sacrifices have to be made."

Pain lingered in the midnight of his eyes, but Fae shook her head.

"I don't accept that."

Luca straightened, breathing deep, as if to draw strength from some inner well.

"I'm sorry, Fae, but you're going to have to."

The fire inside her finally cooled, her mind made up.

Fae stepped back from him, a pang of regret tainting her resolve.

"I'm sorry," she said, her eyes flicking to Irya as the threads of Eah'lara sprang up across her vision.

Arissa had been right. She'd just needed the right reason.

She met Luca's eyes again.

"But I can't."

She grabbed hold of one thread among the thousands of silvery connections — one that glimmered with gold. The one that would guide her home.

And she wisped from La'sa.

34

GONE

Luca rounded on Irya.

"Where did she go?" His chest was banded in iron. He couldn't breathe.

The Echo's face had gone as white as her eyes, which were round as saucers.

"Where did she go?" The light in his veins stuttered and went out. If anything happened to her...

Irya's throat bobbed.

"Throldon." Her voice was barely more than a whisper.

Luca's knees threatened to go out from under him. The ground was slipping out from beneath his feet and it had nothing to do with the quakes.

Fae had wisped herself into a war zone, armed with nothing but barely usable magic.

"Bring her back," he rasped, his voice choked along with his breath.

Irya's stare was one of horror. "I can't."

He thrust both hands into his hair. He knew she couldn't. No one here could wisp. He hadn't been lying when he'd told Fae it was rare.

La'sa had just suffered the worse quake yet, was still reeling from it, and Fae, their only hope at stopping them from getting worse, was about to throw herself in front of the biggest army on the continent.

And yet he couldn't think about the quakes.

All he could think about was her.

Light sent out a questing beam from where it remained curled up in his heart.

She's not here.

"We need to tell the others." Irya's quiet voice dragged him from his turmoil.

She was right. Pulling the fractured pieces of his thoughts together, he straightened again, running a hand across his face before smoothing the front of his shirt.

"Send for the High Magi," he said, his voice distant in his own ears. "Have them come to the Crystal Chamber."

Irya nodded, and ran back down the hallway. She had a better chance than anyone of finding where the High Magi had dispersed to, able to search through Eah'lara in a fraction of the time it would take him to hunt them down on foot.

Luca turned his steps toward the room they left for matters they didn't want overheard in the Meeting House. The people of La'sa were welcome to all that the High Magi discussed — he would hide nothing from them after they gave up so much to come here.

But some news needed a cushion.

He barely noticed the turns he took, letting his feet guide him all the way to the room with its view over the freshly snow-covered Ice Fields. Dropping into his deep armchair, he leaned forward over his knees, and stared into the crystal that sat at the centre of the circle of chairs.

When they'd first arrived here, each of the thirteen seats had had someone to occupy it. But by some cruel perversion of fate, so many of those members had succumbed to the ravages of time, despite his efforts to maintain the stasis around La'sa.

He passed a weary hand over his face. How he sorely wished for some of their counsel now. He'd been a soldier in the war. A damn good one, but never meant to lead. And even after five hundred years of protecting his people as a High Magi, he still felt like that soldier, freshly escaped from the obliterated front line, his comrades all dead behind him.

Demilda was the first to find him.

"Luca," she said, concern jarring her musical voice, braids swaying as she angled her head to pierce him with her pale gaze. "What's wrong?"

He waved her to her seat, his hand ten times as heavy as it ought to be. He only had the strength to say this once.

Kallis strode in next, his normally languid prowl converted to clipped paces that heralded a rare bout of taking things seriously.

"What is it Fialli?" he snapped. "We all have enough to be getting on with without you pulling us away." The Umbra-Incendus was always the quickest to temper among the five of them — Luca was long used to his moods.

Fortunately, he wasn't the only one.

"Peace, Kallis," Demilda hushed him. "Wait for the others."

Kallis growled, and moved to the far wall to pace across the view.

Madja and Terrence arrived together. They'd undoubtedly been coordinating emergency measures with the other Therasae.

The instant Madja laid eyes on Luca, she froze in place. "What is it?" Her voice already trembled with dread.

Luca drew in a breath, and steeled himself.

"Fae's gone."

The room was silent for a heartbeat. Two.

And then it exploded.

"What do you mean, she's gone?"

"What have you done now, Fialli?"

"What happened?"

"Where is she?"

"She can't be."

He let his fellow High Magi's questions wash over him as they all fought to be heard. It didn't matter which one he answered first, his words would be the same.

He'd failed them.

"Luca." Terrence strode forward and planted himself before him. "What do you mean, she's gone? Where has she gone?"

Luca lifted his gaze to meet the eyes of each of his comrades.

"Throldon." His eyes came to a stop at Madja, for whom this news would tear open old wounds. "She's gone to Throldon."

Madja slumped into the nearest chair, and Demilda rose to comfort her. Terrence blew out a long breath, and ran a hand over his hair.

Kallis stared at him, slack-jawed.

"Shit."

35

FOR THE EMPIRE

After days of hard riding, the Brotherhood's company reached the Eminency's armies.

They'd covered the distance in a third of the time, thanks to fresh horses left for them in the army's wake.

But while the horses were fresh, Jade was so sore she could barely walk. Every jolt was like a hammer to her thighs and sit-bones as they cantered through camp. The Brothers that suffered likewise had brewed themselves remedies to dull the crippling aches as they travelled — a luxury she was not afforded.

Her eyes stung from squinting against the sand and road-dust that flew up around the horses' hooves. Her arms ached from gripping the pommel of the saddle. Her back ached from holding herself upright, as far from the Sorcerer Supreme behind her as possible.

Jade's whites were saturated with grit, and certainly no longer white, while Kohl's robes had somehow retained their gleamingly purity. She wondered how he did that. She decided she didn't care, as long as she never had to see another horse again.

The northern city sprawled along the banks of a river, its outer buildings crusted in a skeleton of planks and poles, as if it was still being built. Jade stared at it. This city didn't even have any walls.

She glanced back at the sea of forces the Eminency had sent to take this land, and a cold sweat broke out along her spine.

These northerners didn't stand a chance.

Suddenly her spark of a plan felt like dry straw held over a flame — brittle and hopeless.

Jade's muscles cried out with relief when the horse finally stopped before the command tent: a marquee-style canvas set atop a rise with views over the plains and the city beyond. Kohl swung down from their mount with feline grace, leaving her straddled atop it, and handed the reins to one of the acolytes. "Wait here." Without a backwards glance, he strode inside.

Jade risked a glance back at her dragons.

It wasn't just Delita suffering with welts around her legs now, all of them had at least one limb rubbed raw by their shackles. But despite that, the open beds of the wagons had allowed the dragons to stretch their wings, to sun themselves in the open air as they travelled, and the improvement in their countenances was palpable through their bond.

They weren't free, but the journey had been a short reprieve from the cages back in Pharro.

And if Jade managed to pull this off, things would only get better.

Or they'd get terminally worse.

Still, death would be preferable to what Kohl had planned.

While she waited, Jade cast an eye about the camp.

The Eminence's troops were strictly ordered; everything appeared to have a place and a purpose. But it was still a war camp. The ground was churned up from the passage of thousands of feet — human and equine — and the air stank of horses and sweat and steel and leather. The ring of weapons and voices calling across the camp was unbearably loud after the ominous quiet of the Brotherhood's Sanctum. At least it was cooler here, the dry heat of the desert having left them behind days before.

Behind her, the dragons had drawn a small crowd of soldiers. Just as one particularly brave grunt stepped closer, the tent flaps whipped back, and Kohl emerged, sending the crowd scurrying.

Even here, they knew not to meddle with the Brotherhood.

"We will need somewhere to stable our animals," Kohl said to a greying man with slanting eyes and a bushy moustache. Judging by the gold stars on his uniform, Jade marked him as one of the Eminence's generals. "And our own lodgings, of course." He shot the general a smile that didn't reach his eyes. Jade knew that smile — it was one that expected obedience.

The general grumbled into his moustache. "You have arrived rather late in proceedings, General." Jade started at the alternative honorific given to the Sorcerer Supreme. "There is room for you here, as a commanding officer, but your men and beasts will need to find space wherever it's going spare."

Kohl's smile thinned. "Oh no, I don't think that will do, General Tahe."

The general blustered. "It will have to, General Reksus. We attack at dawn — I can't go rearranging camp for a handful of priests." Jade wondered what he'd be saying once the Brothers finally revealed their hand.

Kohl leaned in close, his tall frame towering over Tahe. "You will see, at dawn, just how vital my Brothers are, General. I would *strongly* advise you reconsider."

Whatever Tahe saw in Kohl's bottomless eyes caused him to swallow thickly. He waved a nearby soldier over.

"Move Lemur Company to the east front," he instructed, his slanted eyes not leaving Kohl's. "Have the general's men and beasts stationed in their place."

The soldier snapped a salute, and rushed off to perform his duty.

"Excellent." Kohl flashed Tahe another of his cold smiles before turning to his Brothers. "When the ground has been cleared, set our camp and prepare the beasts for vialling immediately. I want everyone well-stocked before the assault tomorrow."

A chorus of "Yes, Supremacy," echoed through their company, accompanied by a few unnerving sneers in Tahe's direction.

General Tahe muttered something about the Eminence and favourites before disappearing back into the command tent.

The soldier who'd been sent to relocate Lemur Company reappeared a moment later.

"If you and your men would follow me, General."

Kohl's answering smile sent him skittering backward. "Most kind. I presume it isn't far?"

The soldier shook his head. "No General. Just beyond the command centre, sir."

Kohl gave a wave of his hand. "Lead on, then."

Their escort brought them to a space within shouting distance of the command tents, where a group of battle-hardened soldiers were breaking camp to clear the way for the Brothers, shooting the robed "priests" looks of disgust as they moved out.

"Set camp." Kohl gestured sharply to the acolytes, who sprang into action. "Brother Amand, if you would."

The Brother Jade recognised from before stepped forward. He drew a slender dagger from the sleeve of his robe, and ran the tip of his index and middle fingers along its edge. Blood immediately welled from the cuts, and he crouched to trace symbols in the dirt, murmuring strange, unintelligible words. The symbols formed a sort of triangle, encompassed by a circle of dirty blood. He finished the process by standing and touching his finger to each of his Brother's chins, just beneath their lower lips.

The bloody smear left by his fingers gave them all a feral, primitive look, but once he'd marked all thirteen of them, he murmured something else, pressing his palms together, and then he was silent.

Kohl began to speak, but no sound passed his lips.

The Brothers nodded, and replied silently.

It took a minute before Jade wrapped her head around what was happening.

Brother Amand had spelled them to be audible only to each other. Jade shuddered to think what they were discussing that would warrant such measures. They were here to help the army.

Weren't they?

Eventually the Sorcerers nodded as one, and Brother Amand dragged his foot across the symbols in the dirt. The Brothers' voices surged back to her, as if she'd just opened a heavy door into a crowded room.

"Prepare what you need for tomorrow," Kohl said, the flat black of his eyes gleaming. "Let us make quick work of this." He added, "For the empire." Although Jade had a feeling it was nothing to do with the empire at all, and all to do with the Sorcerer Supreme's own agenda here in the north.

Still perched on her horse, Jade gazed across at the city that was due to be sieged.

There were no signs of any dragons.

She glanced over at her own. These six were only a few years old. What would a fully-grown dragon — a true ancient — look like?

Kohl's hand touched her thigh, and she fought the instinct to flinch as she turned to face him. He lifted her down without asking, setting her on her feet before him, his hand lingering in a way that made her stomach clench in revulsion. Behind him, the acolytes made quick work of erecting their tents, arraying the wagons and their shackled cargo in the centre of their camp.

"Come." His voice was a purr — silk set over a razor edge. "Let's ensure the beasts behave while we're here." Pressing his hand firmly against her lower back, he steered her over to where the remaining acolytes were vialling the dragons for fresh samples.

Six pairs of eyes watched warily as he approached, pushing Jade ahead of him, rested his hands on her shoulders, holding her close: a not-so-subtle reminder of who held the power here.

Alpha's eyes narrowed at the Sorcerer Supreme, but all six of them held steady for the acolytes.

The key, she'd heard the Brothers discussing late one night on the road, was to take just enough blood that it would easily be replenished without draining the animal's reserves. The information had made Jade want to vomit. Just another reason that her plan *had* to work.

But first she needed a distraction.

She hoped the battle tomorrow would provide it.

They were woken before dawn by a great rumble from the ground itself.

Jade jolted awake. The sound was deafening. The earth shuddered beneath her. The canvas above snapped angrily, but there was no wind, only the thunderous roar that sounded unsettlingly like the cave-in that had trapped her underground with an orphaned clutch of dragon eggs.

She pushed herself upright, saw Kohl do the same across the huge tent. It could easily have slept at least six, but had been reserved for the Sorcerer Supreme alone. And his precious *control asset*.

Thankfully, the tent was the only thing he'd insisted on sharing with her.

She'd heard the Brothers snickering at her expense. Speculating on why the Sorcerer Supreme had taken such an interest in her.

Apparently they didn't consider her use as a means for controlling the dragons reason enough.

The earth bucked as she went to stand, throwing her back to the ground before she could get her feet under her.

"Stay down." Kohl's voice in the near-dark was rough from sleep, and still brimmed with power.

Jade curled around herself, her arms wrapped around her knees. In the distance, the sound of crumbling walls mixed with nearby cries of alarm, both chording together with the groan of the earth until she knew she would dream of this moment for years to come, the sound imprinting itself in her mind.

She squeezed her eyes shut. A few feet away, separated only by canvas, her dragons keened in worry.

Jade threw out both hands to steady herself as the very ground tilted beneath her again. Fear escaped her lips as a whimper.

Kohl seemed unperturbed by the whole affair, head cocked, listening intently.

What felt like hours later, the earth finally shuddered to a rest, like a bird ruffling its feathers before settling down to roost.

Kohl pushed to his feet, pulled a robe on over the trousers he'd worn to sleep, and belted it at the waist.

Outside the tent, voices called back and forth across the camp, the army emerging into the day.

Kohl ducked his head through the tent flaps, then returned to crouch before her.

"It's time, my dear," he said, his black hair sliding across his forehead. "To show you what you and your dragons have enabled us to accomplish."

An ice-cold stone of dread settled in her stomach.

But first, "What was that just now?" She'd never felt anything like it before. Her stomach still roiled from the motion of the earth, her legs wobbling like those of a newborn foal as she tried to find her feet.

Kohl smirked. "The north has been experiencing these quakes in the ground for some time now. Hopefully they will work to our advantage."

Jade blinked. "How so?"

Kohl leaned in, his eyes gleaming in a way that made her lean back. "Because while we sleep under the open sky, the northerners are surrounded by walls. Walls which need stable ground on which to sit.

Walls which will crumble around them, while our forces descend to pick the carcass of their city clean." He whipped out and gripped her elbow, pulling her towards him, his fingers digging in so hard she gasped. "And then the north will be ours."

Jade didn't think now would be a good time to ask how they intended to occupy a city if it was crumbling to the ground, so she kept her lips clamped shut, nodding when he paused for her to respond.

He snarled, a sound halfway between triumph and frustration.

"Come." He dragged her from the tent.

The acolytes were already up and milling about their little camp. They were to stay and mind the dragons while the Brothers dispersed themselves among the troops, although to do what, Jade still didn't know. All she knew was that they each took a sickening stock of dragon blood with them.

Kohl led Jade to the command tent, the open side offering an uninhibited view of the battlefield.

A single moon hovered in the slowly lightening sky, its sister setting to the north as dawn leaked over the horizon.

Ahead of the Thamibian forces, the land flowed downhill to a wide plain that ran right to the river's edge. And across the river, the northland city.

She'd heard that the city was called Throldon. That, until just over a year ago, it had been under the rule of... well, anarchy, by the sounds of it. Which would explain its ramshackle appearance along the river's edge. Perhaps some of it could be explained by these quakes. The mix of old and new. Collapsed and repaired.

Either way, none of it was defensible.

The only defence the city had on this side was the river itself, and Jade had already seen the machines the army would use to lower wide, wooden bridges into place over the water.

Kohl stepped into position between General Tahe and another commanding officer — a colonel, marked by the gold bands on his arm. He acknowledged neither of them.

"My Brothers are in position among your troops, General," he said by way of greeting, his eyes fixed on the distant city as if he could see over the walls to whoever was coordinating their defence.

Tahe bristled at the impertinence, even if he had acknowledged Kohl as having equal rank.

"I don't see what use your priests will be in the midst of battle, General." His bushy moustache quivered as he spoke, his lips downturned enough to convey his thoughts on the matter.

Kohl's mouth slanted up at one side, his cheek dimpling. "You and I have never had the pleasure of standing side by side in battle before, so I'll allow you your ignorance." He turned to face the general, and his eyes were cold as chips of black ice. Lethal. "But after today, I expect you to understand why I have been at the Eminence's side for as long as I have."

To his credit, Tahe did not avert his gaze, even as his impressive facial hair drooped.

"I'll take that under advisement."

Kohl's eyes crinkled. "They told me you were a shrewd one." And he turned back to the view.

Tahe stared at him, his slanted eyes wide with a confusion that bordered on horror. Like he was only now beginning to question what kind of monster he'd given a bed in his camp.

"Pass the order." Tahe's colonel began shouting orders that echoed down the lines.

Jade stood beside Kohl as if hewn from stone. As if moving would draw unnecessary attention to herself.

She still questioned why exactly he'd brought her. Her usefulness with the dragons didn't call for her to be present in the command tent of all places.

"Watch, Jade." His voice skittered under her skin as the armies began their march towards the city. "Watch what we can do."

So Jade watched in horror as Thamib's forces — Kohl's forces, it felt like — marched on a defenceless city.

Her breath caught in her chest.

This is what she was for.

She was an audience.

To witness his power.

36

READY

As dawn bleached the sky of colour, they came.

The last tremor had been the worst one to date. And yet, miraculously, Hal thought they'd come away from it relatively unharmed. Some of the archways through the base of the University wall were now filled with rubble where before they'd been weaknesses to make allowances for. In other places, the walls had completely collapsed, opening up new gaps in their very limited defence.

One of those places was a section of wall to the west of where he stood, now a great gaping gateway into the city.

Hal was just glad there hadn't been any casualties. He couldn't spare the time or resources to investigate the extent of the damages. They'd have to hope the city would hold long enough to survive this.

And pray to the gods they didn't get hit with another of those damn quakes.

Atop the still-standing astronomy tower of the University, Hal and Laina watched the southern armies march inexorably towards them.

Thousands of feet stomped over the plain across the river, those huge wooden machines rumbling along in the midst of men.

The southern soldiers were garbed in tan leather armour and pointed helmets, the front ranks bearing poleaxes and wicked shortswords, those behind carrying bows and bristling quivers of arrows.

To Hal's soldier's eye, it was an impressive display. One that Arland hadn't seen since the Rebel Unity tore apart any political or social structure the once-kingdom had.

Beside Throldon's skeletal forces, the southern army was a leviathan of astronomical proportions. It stole the breath from him, even after seeing its extent for himself those few weeks ago. The sight had filled him with cold dread then, as it did now.

In the time since, he'd managed to pull together an answering force of five-thousand, although where they'd even come from, he had no idea. Some were veterans of another time and place, keeping their heads down while the Unity incited anarchy across the land. Anarchy that perhaps spoke of some fundamental issues in the monarchy's ruling up until that point, even if a god with a grudge had helped the rebels along somewhat.

Some were reformed former members of the Unity itself, ranging from everyday thugs to highly capable fighters. During the brief tenure of the Survivors shortly after, Tamra Walker, then known as Lady Black, had trained her people with brutal efficiency, and while Hal would never admit it — and certainly hadn't thought so when he'd first arrived back in Throldon — he was mighty grateful for it now. They made up a good third of his forces, and would likely end up carrying the rest.

The rest were men and women so green they barely knew which end of a sword to hold, and he'd used the little time they had to train them in the bare essentials of warfare.

"They just keep coming." Laina's voice was a mere breath beside him, so quiet he almost missed it.

"Aye," he murmured. And that they did. Fifty-thousand soldiers was a lot to see all gathered in one place. Numbers which left Hal under no illusions of the intentions of that army.

He turned to the gangly boy standing by to relay his orders to the men and woman peppered across the southern edge of Throldon. Men and women that had adapted to the change in their defences without qualm. He hesitated to call them soldiers — so few of them had seen real battle like this — but today, that's what they were. "Ready archers," he said, and the boy scurried away, another child stepping into his place for the next order. On Laina's other side, Ty, Aren, and Stef unslung the elven longbows from their shoulders, and checked the stocks of arrows at their feet for the hundredth time. Jesse watched the approaching army through a long glass intended for use by students in the very University on which they stood, her eyes not as sharp as those of the elves she stood amongst.

On Hal's other side, Kagos and Aiya stood with Max, her tiny dragon curled around her shoulders, watching events unfold with whirling, copper eyes.

At first, Hal had questioned the wisdom of having a child up on the makeshift ramparts. Then he remembered that Bek had been a similar age when he'd travelled across Arland with Fae. Sure, he'd been an Aethyr with eons of experience tucked inside his mind, but Max had had to grow up before her time too, living on the streets of Hapton, and she'd gotten them out of plenty of scrapes before without being babied.

The enemy camp was only a mile over the river, the front lines of which had already covered half that distance, clearly unperturbed by the quake. They would be at the river's edge in a matter of minutes, and Hal now had some suspicions about the purpose of those machines.

"Shields on the riverbanks," he said to the red-haired girl standing by for his next instructions. "And prepare for crossings."

Her eyes widened in fear, but she nodded, and darted off to pass the word.

"Fire on anyone trying to bridge the water." Hal took his eyes off the field to check the elves understood him. Ty met his gaze with a nod; he'd been unusually quiet since reaching the top of the wall and seeing what lay before them. Aren and Stef grunted their understanding, their striking eyes catching the rising sun to glow with unforgiving focus. Aren raised his bow to sight along the shaft of an arrow, the fletching brushing against his tapered ear, the muscles of his raised arm bunched as he held it ready.

"They're assembling trebuchets further back." Stef's voice punctured the silence as they waited.

"Aye, and we can't do a damned thing about it." Hal growled in frustration. "They've got all the time in the world while we'll be fightin' four-to-one in the streets, and they've got the numbers to spare." His eyes fixed unblinkingly on the advancing force. "Them Reformers better be ready to make it count."

The former Unity thugs and Survivors were scattered among the rest of the Throldon defence, heading up squads of three or four a-piece. The traps and bunkers they'd littered the streets with created defensible positions where before there had been none.

In short, they had proven to be worth their weight in gold.

"They will." Aren drew his arrow back an inch further, the string as taut as the air. The brothers had been here when Fae liberated Throldon; they'd seen the change in the men and women when the fog lifted from their eyes. And in working with those who'd once been poisoned to destroy their own city's heart and soul, they'd found a well of people with a tireless drive to right past wrongs. Nothing was too much; they worked day and night to do what was needed. And in doing so, they found fast friends in the elven scouts.

The front ranks of the southern army hit the river a minute ahead of the second lines, and they immediately set about lowering those great wooden towers over the water. Bridges.

Aren's arrow flew without so much as a flicker of movement from the elf, and a man fell.

"Archers!" Hal bellowed, his voice carrying far enough for the call to relay down the lines. Once the din of battle overwhelmed the city, he would need to use his messengers again, but while there was breath in his body, he would let his people know he stood with them.

A hail of arrows flew across the river, and the southerners operating the machines were forced to take cover.

Aren and Stef nocked two arrows apiece and let fly, all four finding marks across the river. Ty's arms transitioned smoothly from one shot straight into the next, a constant stream of motion.

Kagos and Aiya watched, their vision infinitely better than Hal's, while Jesse manned the long glass. The dwarf had been keen to fight in the streets with the Reformers, but Hal had insisted she remain with the rest of the Council. Because, of everyone in this gods-damned city, he trusted no one more than those who stood beside him now. There would be a time for them all to join the fight — he knew Laina was already itching to join the other healers in preparation for it — but, somewhat selfishly, he wanted to keep his friends from the worst of it, as long as he could.

No matter that they were also the only ones here he would trust to have his back in a fight.

Arrows continued to fly, the enemy employing a few of their own, but their focus was on lowering those bridges, and they had the numbers to make it happen, regardless of how many bodies piled up beside their machines.

Inevitably, the first bridge fell, hitting the bank with a *crash*. It was a monstrous thing, wide enough for ten men to march abreast, which they did the instant it touched land. The timbers groaned as the first group of enemy soldiers thundered across, helmets glinting in the watery sunlight like a river of metal spikes aimed straight for the city.

"Infantry, ready!" Hal roared, and the call could be heard echoed along the walls.

The University walls were never designed to be defensive, and were peppered with gaps and archways through to the streets of the River Quarter even before the tremor had collapsed more sections, not to mention that they didn't run the perimeter of the city. The enemy had only to march a bit further around and they could walk straight through Throldon's outskirts.

They'd have to hope that they were as yet uninformed on that particular point.

At Hal's call, bands of Reformer-led "soldiers" readied themselves to inflict as much damage as possible from the bottlenecks they'd created in the walls.

Another bridge dropped into place with a *boom* that echoed off the walls to fill the short battleground with the sound of more soldiers marching towards them.

"I've got their commander." Jesse passed the long glass to Hal, and pointed. "Looks like there are four of them, but I'd put money on the ones in white."

Hal looked. He found the group she'd spotted, watching over the field from a command tent not dissimilar to one Lord Marl would have used back when he'd been garrisoned in Bredon. Two of the occupants were uniformed in tan as their soldiers were, but the cut and fit was far more becoming of a commanding officer, the gold accents further marking them.

The other two were dressed all in white: one man, and a young woman. The man was taller than the others, his black hair gleaming in the sun, his white robes spotless, and his expression fixed in a zealous snarl. The woman however... her face, invisible to the man at her back, was a mask of horror.

"Do you think I could make the shot from here?" Aren asked idly, sighting along the shaft of a fresh arrow.

"It's over a mile," Stef replied flatly.

"You're right, I'll probably overshoot." Aren adjusted his aim.

Laina gaped at him. "You can't be serious!"

"Shall we find out?" Aren drew back, ensured his aim, and released.

They held a collective breath, and tracked the path of the arrow through the sky.

Hal took up the long glass again.

Jesse shaded her eyes. "No way..."

The arrow flew true.

It soared toward that command tent.

The white-robed commander's eyes snapped up, and he waved a hand, as if batting a fly.

The arrow crackled with red sparks and stumbled mid-air, dropping like a stone to bounce harmlessly on the carpeted floor of the tent.

The commander bent, and plucked it from the ground.

From over a mile away, across a teeming battlefield, the commander of the southern armies met Hal's gaze with one of pure black, and with one hand, snapped the arrow in two.

Aren made a sound in the back of his throat. "Cheat."

Laina gaped. "Was that... magic?"

Aiya shot a glance at Kagos, whose brow furrowed deeply. "Yes." His own obsidian eyes narrowed. "And that's not all." He angled his body to Aiya, who'd forgone her usual flying attire in favour of leather trousers and a tight-fitting leather jerkin over a linen shirt, her long, black hair braided tight to her skull. "Do you see, to the left of the command tent, between the canvases?"

Aiya stepped forward, squinting. "Pass me the glass." She held her hand out towards Hal, who obliged with a puzzled frown. Raising the long glass to one eye, she scanned the horizon until she found what she was looking for. Adjusted the focus.

The warmth in her creamy brown skin drained in an instant, her mouth dropping open. "It can't be..."

Kagos's lips pressed into a line, her reaction confirming his observation. "And yet."

Aiya lowered the long glass, her hands shaking.

Another bridge slammed into place, and the ring of steel chimed across the walls.

"Now's not the time for guess-what," Jesse barked. "What is it?"

Kagos turned to face her. Between his customary black silk robe, ebony skin and obsidian eyes, he was the picture of ominous portent as he said, "They have dragons as well."

37

THE WORST OF THEM

"Breach!" The call went up, heralding the enemy in the streets. But the group atop the battlements remained where they were, staring at Kagos.

Jesse's arms slackened at her sides.

"We're screwed then."

To everyone's surprise, Kagos shook his head.

"They are younglings, no bigger than a large dog or a small pony." His eyes flashed with fury. "They are chained like beasts, shackled like slaves." His slitted nostrils flared, and for an instant he looked as if he might breathe fire in his humanoid form.

Max clutched at Pig, her eyes wide with horror. "How could they do that?"

Kagos's lip curled. "Some monsters belong to your nightmares. But the worst of them walk the earth and wear human skin."

A shiver ran down Hal's spine at his words. He'd seen enough horrors at the hands of his own kind to know they were true.

"Right then." Jesse unsheathed the curved daggers at her sides. "If the dragons on the hill aren't a concern, can we start dealing with the southern pricks at the door?" As if to punctuate her question, another bridge thumped onto the riverbanks, followed by the thunder of boots across the planks, and the answering ring of steel.

Hal glanced over the wall to see his men engaging the enemy outside the walls, trying to push the tide back beyond the city limits.

"I know I said I would stay out of your way." The sound of mountains crumbling infused Kagos's voice. "But I must see to these dragons. We thought there were no more of our kind outside Hearthstone. That these are here..." He trailed off, his thoughts too dark to voice. "I must enter the battlefield. But not as myself. I would not have these southerners recognise what I am."

"You can't seriously be thinking of walking through that?" Aiya gaped at him, the whites of her eyes telling him just how insane she considered him to be in that moment.

Kagos shrugged blandly. "It's such a lovely day for it."

Aren's silver eyes gleamed. "It would be a shame to let it go to waste. And these considerate fellows have even built us a bridge — or five."

Kagos narrowed his eyes as he turned to him. "I do not need accompanying."

Aren released one last arrow, and shouldered his bow. "I'm well aware." He braced his feet, and folded his arms.

"He'll go whether you will it or no," Stef said with a wry smile, thumbing the long knife at his side. "We'll make a trip of it."

Hal jerked a nod, the clash of weapons below calling to him. But his duty was to stay, to lead. It grated against every instinct in him. "Fine. But do us all a favour — don't die." He included them all in that statement, shooting the rider a look as well, as if she had any ability to rein in her dragon.

Kagos's lips curled up on one side. "I never knew you cared so much."

Hal grunted a laugh. "Go."

"Don't need to tell me twice." Jesse leapt over the wall, and darted nimbly along an adjacent roof ledge. "See you on the other side!"

Max watched her go with wide eyes. Even in her street urchin days, she'd never managed to move that sure-footed across the Sky Roads' terrain.

Laina cleared her throat, her voice shaky as she said, "I should head to the infirmary. I'll be needed soon enough."

Kagos turned to Max. "Go with Councilwoman Woods. Help where you can." Before, Max would have revelled in the chance to help. To use her knowledge of Throldon's Sky Roads to help them weave mayhem for the southerners. But with Pig wrapped around her shoulders, she couldn't risk it. And she knew it.

Max threw her arms around Aiya's waist. "Stay safe," she said, her voice wavering but firm. She glanced up to meet Kagos's gaze. Unspoken words passed between them, the girl nodding quickly before she followed Laina from the wall.

Hal held out his hand to Kagos. "Meant what I said," he reminded the dragon. He'd seen enough friends die in his lifetime.

Kagos grasped his arm firmly, his black eyes gleaming. "You worry too much, old man."

Hal nearly choked. What was it with beings hundreds of years old — maybe even thousands — calling *him* old?

"Let's go!" Aren hopped from foot to foot. "I want to see how fast these southerners are." Likely not very, especially up against elven reflexes. Let alone whatever Kagos had up his sleeve.

"Don't do anythin' I wouldn't," Hal said.

Aren arched an eyebrow. "I've seen you fight, Halbert. That's hardly sound advice."

"Come." Kagos swept towards the steps. "Let us see what flavour of monsters would shackle the young."

Their departure left Hal with only Ty for company. The elven Eldra had been remarkably quiet since the army had begun its march down to the river. Hal glanced across to see a look in the elf's grey eyes he'd recognise anywhere: fear.

"I've never seen war before," Ty admitted with a whisper, snatched away by the wind and drowned by shouts down below.

"Aye." Hal sidled up to stand beside him, scanning the battlefield, assessing. "Ain't pretty, no matter how many times you see it."

"Before last year, I'd never even seen conflict." Ty shook his head. "Aren and Stef — they've been out in the world a bit. I've been a scholar, a healer, and an Eldra."

"Why don't you help in the infirmary then? There's going to be plenty o' need for it."

"Sheha's down there." Ty watched the black-haired heads of Aren, Stef, and Aiya weaving through the battle below, flanking Kagos in his black, cowled robes. "I wanted to try and *prevent* the casualties, rather than stepping in once the damage is done."

Hal nodded, his gaze sweeping the battlefront from east to west. He frowned at the looming shapes of the southern army's trebuchets, rolling ponderously into position. "Don't suppose you've got a solution to prevent those?" He pointed across the field. "'Cause we ain't got nothin' to match them."

Any colour left in Ty's cheeks drained as he shook his head. Without pushing the front line back, their forces had no chance of getting close enough to disarm them.

"Maybe we should have surrendered the city," Hal was muttering to himself. "Avoid all this." His lips formed a hard line beneath his beard.

"You've worked too hard to free these people from one tyranny to give way to another."

"Aye, but is death a price the people are willin' to pay?" His jaw clenched, eyes taking a grim cast. "'Cause for some, that'll be who comes collecting."

Below, the paltry Throldon forces pushed their way onto the battlefield. In the River Quarter, skirmish crews lay in wait for any southerners that dared the streets. But outside the city limits, chaos of the kind only seen in war reigned.

38

ORBS

The nebulae of Eah'lara blurred past as Fae threw herself along the golden thread that would lead her home.

Please don't be too late. Fae didn't know who she sent her prayer to. The gods, formed of nothing but hopeless wishes? The overly self-involved Aethyr? Perhaps the spirits, woven through the world without a care?

Maybe the stars above, who'd once been plucked from the sky to become true gods. Would they hear? Would they listen?

Fae urged herself onward, opting to cast her prayers skyward. To the stars Aethyreomma had chosen to be her children. To the first defenders and destroyers of earth. She cast her hopes to the celestial fates, and left them in their eternal safekeeping.

The world flew past in shapes and colours pressed into spirit dust. She knew the instant she passed into Throldon by the still-healing purple tinge to the Spirit Realm's usual white backdrop.

But the golden thread she held speared on, through the tethers connecting the Aethyr back into this area. Tracing the glinting spider-silk through the city, she passed flashes of colour, shimmering outlines of nearby auras, their spun-cloud threads sparking in a language of light unique to them.

Then Fae saw it.

She came to an abrupt stop in an open space filled with flashes of motion. All around, tiny Aethyrial orbs were popping back through the veil, the stitches of Eah'lara unpinning at a terrifying pace. The Aethyr only appeared in the Spirit Realm as orbs when there were no lifeforms available to inhabit.

This region was full of orbs. And more kept appearing.

Ahead, the golden thread she held dived through a stitch in the veil separating Eah'lara from the mortal plane. Fae steeled herself for what she was sure to face, stoked the fire-aspect within her.

And leapt through.

She materialised just beyond the University walls, into a mêlée of action and noise.

The air was muggy and warm after the crisp cool air of La'sa. Leather-clad soldiers with pointed helmets swarmed the riverbank, the river itself so obscured by wooden planks lashed together that it was as if it had been buried. And beyond it...

An army bigger that anything she could have imagined covered the plains in a sea of weapons and bodies poised to kill, the troops interspersed by hulking machines lumbering towards the city on creaking wheels.

Her grasp on fire faltered, and it slipped away as she beheld the impossibility before her.

Soldiers fought man-to-man, sword upon sword. Shouting, grunting, screaming. The ring of steel and the thump of flesh. All she could see was bodies and blood, and the fast-churning mud underfoot.

A flash of steel caught her eye. A group of Throldonian soldiers clashed against their southern counterparts, one of them swinging his weapon — a halbert — in a wide arc to take his opponent in the chest.

A streak of clarity cut through the din in her mind.

Hal would know what to do. She needed to find Hal. And her mother.

She retreated until she felt the stone wall hard against her back, and inched her way along in search of one of the many archways she knew lined the University walls to allow people free access between the River Quarter and the river for which it was named.

The sounds of the battle enveloped her, the smell of gore and metal filling the air. Her heart thundered so hard in her chest it felt as if it might break free and fly away from this new nightmare. The rough stone behind her felt slick under her sweat-soaked palms.

Blood sprayed.

A woman cried out in fury.

The clash of steel. The thud of flesh struck.

Violence flashed around her, too much and too fast to process.

Eons later, Fae's fingers wrapped around a corner in the stonework, and she turned to hurtle down a passageway into the city.

But the passageway had caved in on itself, rubble from the walls to either side and the archway above piled into an insurmountable heap in the middle, blocking the thoroughfare completely.

She glanced back at the madness outside the wall, considered working her way further along to the next opening, when a fighter stumbled and fell into her.

The weight of the soldier threw her into the rocky mound of the passageway. She flung her hands out, and pain barked up her arms, into her knees. Her head struck stone. The world spun drunkenly, like a child's spinning toy, and she went to lift herself away from the rubble.

But the man was still lying over her, and he wasn't moving. She shoved against him, and realised with horror that he was dead.

Pushing and heaving with everything she had, she managed to roll the soldier off her, and free her torn and bloodied body free of broken masonry. She tried not to look at him as she surveyed the mound, her mind noting only that his face was perversely unmarked while his body remained irrevocably broken.

Forcing her eyes to scan the wreckage of the passageway, she plotted a route up and over. There was no way she was going back out into the mêlée. There was a path into the city right here, and she intended to use it. Even if the world did insist on swaying so.

Fae blinked her eyes, and something warm dripped onto her cheek. Lifting a hand to her face, she wiped at the wetness, her fingers coming away red. Stars danced across her vision, limning her fingers in light.

She dabbed her hand to her head, and now her palm was covered in red. Her hair was sticky with it.

Damn. Her thoughts were muddy. That couldn't be good. Especially not with the ground tipping beneath her feet as well. She staggered sideways, and approached the mountain of rubble.

Placing a hand on one large fragment of stone, and a foot into the gap between two others, Fae hoisted herself up, and began to climb.

One step at a time, one precarious grip after another, she half-crawled, half-scrambled up the wreckage. Gravity betrayed her more than once, and at one point the world pitched so violently that she fell sideways and rolled down the rubble again. But finally, she hauled herself over the top, and slid down the other side.

The slide down was not as smooth as she was hoping, and she earned herself more bruises to her back and legs in the process. But she was on the streets of Throldon.

"Halt! Who goes there?" A voice bellowed behind her. She winced at the noise and staggered to her feet. Turning, she found two young men of no more than eighteen staring at her with open confusion, one holding a sword that was really too long for him, the other aiming a crossbow at the wall to her left.

The one with the crossbow gasped and lowered his weapon. "That's the Saviour!" he said with reverential awe.

Fae wanted to roll her eyes, and then thought better of it. *Countless Gods, Eah guide me, spirits save me, stars in the sky above watch over me.* She snorted. There really were too many places for people to lay their problems and hope for divine intervention.

The boys stared at her.

She schooled her face. Right, not funny. *Probably concussed though.* She cleared her throat and ploughed through her dizzying thoughts. "I need to find Councilman Johnson and Councilwoman Woods," she managed half-convincingly.

The boys nodded slightly too enthusiastically, and called for someone to cover their posts before leading her out through the city.

They took her past improvised ambush points, makeshift bunkers fashioned from bags of sand, and even trick walls, all constructed to make the most of the River Quarter's winding roads and crooked houses.

Finally, they came back into the University buildings.

"Councilman Johnson is on the astronomy tower," the boy with the sword told her, gesturing up the stairs with his weapon.

She nodded her gratitude. "Thank you." And damn it if the boys didn't *bow* to her before running back the way they'd come.

Fae glared at the tower steps, and started to climb.

The view from the top was even worse than what she'd glimpsed from outside the walls.

Her gasp was snatched away by the wind, her hair ripping out behind her like a flag the colour of ash.

From here, the ground shimmered an oily red, churned up like waves on a stormy sea beneath booted feet from both north and south. Spiked helms flooded the plains, glinting in the sun like countless winking eyes, watching her. From here, she could see the camp on the rise, and the swathes of canvas that stretched away without end. The tan of the southern soldiers' armour seemed to bleed from their camp, the canvas of their tents a dull, uniform shade of sand. The few exceptions were the open-sided canopies at the front of the camp, and the gleam of sunlight catching on a shimmer of colours behind them.

She squinted, her eyes drawn to that splash of colour half-concealed behind the first row of enemy tents.

"Fae!" She turned to see Ty stepping towards her with long, easy strides, his choppy, blond hair blowing back from his face in the wind that whipped about the tower. He gripped her shoulders before wrapping her in an embrace that stole the breath from her. "Where have you been? It's been weeks!" Holding her at arms length, he looked her over, his storm-grey eyes catching on the smear of blood across her forehead. "What happened?"

"I fell." She blinked at him, her gaze lurching between the concern on his face, and the horrors below.

Ty's brow knitted as he dabbed at her head with his sleeve. "Laina will be beside herself. We feared the worst."

Behind him, another figure standing vigil atop the tower caught Fae's attention.

"Hal!" Fae brushed Ty aside to run to the ranger's side. "What can I do to help?"

Hal's eyes widened when he saw who stood beside him, a thousand expressions crossing his face before it hardened again into the mask of a commander of armies. A defender of cities.

He turned his attention back to the section of battlefield almost directly below them. A stretch of wall just to the west of the tower had collapsed, and the fighting there was thick and brutal. Bodies of both forces covered the ground, friend and foe alike stumbling over them to attack and defend.

"Get to the infirmary." Hal's voice was hollow and aching, his eyes devoid of life. "There'll be plenty need of your help there, Fae."

Fae reached forward and gripped his arm. "I can fight," she said, a fervent gleam in her eyes, the gold ring burning around her ocean-green. "Just tell me where you need me."

Hal looked her over, as if seeing her for the first time. But he saw the Fae that had haunted Throldon before they'd heard of an army marching from the south. The Fae that was Spiritchild in name alone. The Fae that was powerless.

The Fae that was already battered and bloody, and swaying slightly on her feet.

He shook his head. "I don't need you on the field, Fae. Need you with the other healers. Need you to get my people to another day." A crash below drew his attention back to the battlefield, where the southerners had moved the planks from one of their many bridges onto the ruined wall, forming a new bridge over the rubble, and into the streets.

"Ready the streets!" Hal bellowed, and Fae saw a small figure peel from the back wall to scurry away down the stairs.

Just as she watched the tiny messenger go, Jesse leapt over the parapet, nimble as a cat.

"They're overwhelming us with numbers," she reported without preamble. "We need to stop them coming over those damn bridges but they've got them covered with archers."

"I can help." Fae spun back to Hal.

"Fae..." Ty came to stand beside her. "You can't go out there."

Jesse blinked at her, recovering quickly to say, "No offence, but you don't look in the best shape already."

Fire curled through Fae's veins. But it wasn't fire she needed. Not yet.

Pulling air up through her skin, she pushed it into her palms, and leapt from the wall.

39

RIVER WITHOUT A DAM

Air rushed past as she fell, and Fae shoved more out through her hands before she could collide with the ground.

She braced her arms, the force of the air pushing hard against her palms, and stumbled to a landing at the foot of the astronomy tower.

Without letting herself think about the carnage happening around her, about the clash and screams coming from the section of collapsed wall to her right, she focused air to her fingertips, bending them into claws as she willed those majestic wings to soar between her palms.

The air obeyed, curling in on itself to form the sphere she'd only just mastered. But Fae knew the pattern of air now; it lived inside her, it danced to her song.

She wove streams of air into the ball between her hands now, laced them around each other like a weaver at a loom until the storm she held in her palms was heavy and dense as lead.

She waited until her arms were shaking with the effort of holding it, before easing her hands apart, spreading her arms wide until a tornado swirled before her, contained only by her will.

The battle faltered around her, soldiers from both sides staying their hands long enough to watch.

A flicker of movement to her left. Ty's strangled cry from above.

And Fae dropped her hands.

The storm exploded outwards from where she stood, throwing soldiers like leaves tossed about in the wind.

Drawing on her training with Alexi, she didn't wait to see what the Throldon forces would do, instead striding straight for the river, and the planks laid across it.

In the wake of her storm, the ground was clear, her winter boots wading through mud and other things to reach the banks of the Amedi. Only weeks ago, citizens of Throldon would come here to fish, to collect waterroot for stews, even to swim. She glanced down at the pink waters, at the bodies floating downstream to lodge along the banks further down.

She doubted if anyone would swim here again.

Easing air back under the surface, she let fire loose. The element needed no encouragement, and leapt to the fore, licking across her skin, eager to be free.

Concentrating the fire into her hands, she formed the twin daggers she'd wielded against Kallis. She reeled them out, letting the fireblades get longer and longer, until they lost cohesion and became more akin to forked whips in her hands, the ends snaking out wildly to taste the air of their own volition.

Gritting her teeth in an effort to hold her focus, Fae heaved one arm over her head, bringing a lash down across the two bridges to her right. The timbers gave way with an audible *crack*, the planks ripping down the middle, splinters flying.

She repeated the process on the other side, the two bridges to her left tumbling into the river to be washed away.

A ragged cheer went up behind her, the defenders immediately realising what she'd accomplished. But the work wasn't done yet.

Turning, Fae ran west along the wall, ignoring the way the ground still pitched beneath her feet.

She reached the next set of bridges, and cut them down as she had done the first. But by the time she reached the next stretch of river, her fire was fading, flickering in fits and starts in her hands. Instead of bringing her lashes down across the timbers, she simply held the fire to the wood, waiting for it to catch, reestablishing the river as a physical barrier between the southern army and the city.

But now she stood unarmed on the battlefield. And while she had destroyed a number of the bridges, it was far from all of them. She may have slowed the enemy force, but they were still coming.

Fae reached inside herself and gripped water, slippery and quick.

Madja and Demilda had both warned her against drawing water from her body. They always had a flask with them for whenever they intended to call it forth. Air was all around, and easy to replenish. Fire had a mind of its own. But water needed to come from somewhere.

Fortunately, she stood above a ready source.

Leashing the quicksilver element and hauling it to the surface, Fae pulled on the water from the river. It thrashed and slipped between her fingers, but she held on, and willed it to be still.

A stream of ice flowed up to her, the water below feeding into a frozen current that rose straight into her waiting hand.

Fae stared in disbelief as she continued to pull, shaping the water as it flowed upward, until she held a sword of ice, slender as an asp and sharp as steel.

And then the fighting found her.

Southern soldiers on this side of the river arrowed towards her, weapons raised, while the Throldon defenders did likewise, shouting ridiculous battlecries like, "To the Saviour!" And "Stormbreaker returns!" But Fae didn't have time to argue with them.

The first of the southern soldiers to reach her wielded a shortsword that cut through the air with a hurried breath before she was forced to jump back, throwing her ice sword up to block it.

Steel met ice with a *crack*, lines spiderwebbing through her hastily constructed weapon at the first blow.

Her eyes widened in horror as she instinctively dodged the next swing, ducking away to the side and leaving her opponent lurching into the space where she used to be. Fae spun and gripped her sword near the weakened midpoint. She winced as the edge bit into her palm, but snapped the blade in two. Willing the ice to soften enough beneath her hands so that she held two rough daggers, she crossed them in the air to catch her assailant's blade as it came arcing towards her again.

Between the training Alexi had so ruthlessly made her endure, and her natural grace, Fae danced around the lumbering soldier, ducking and slicing out at him until she finally managed to snake out and run her blades across the backs of his legs.

He dropped like a stone, and Fae was already wheeling to face the next opponent. She caught another southerner across the arm just as he was about to land a finishing blow to a Throldonian swordsman. The next whipped a spear about his head, and Fae dashed under his reach to stab up into his armpit, forcing him to drop his weapon.

She twisted and danced and flew between the soldiers, incapacitating enemies at every turn and every pirouette.

And then her luck ran out.

A great beast of a man charged across the battlefield towards her, throwing soldiers out of his path to reach her. His leather armour was smeared with blood until it looked as if he was dressed in red, his pointed helmet lost somewhere amid the carnage. About his head he swung a great sword the size of her entire body.

The warrior brought his sword down with a challenging bellow, forcing Fae to leap backwards. The enormous blade bit deep into the ground, but her challenger pulled it free without taking his eyes from her, and swung it again.

Fae's ice daggers were no match for the weight of this weapon, and she was reduced to dodging and ducking and weaving away from it, knowing that a single blow would eliminate her in an instant.

Alexi's voice whispered in her ear. *If you're outmatched, find a way to bring your opponent down without engaging them.*

Fae scanned the beast before her, leaping to the side again as his great sword swung for her feet. The only way she was going to bring him down and keep him there was to kill him.

Her stomach lurched, and she instantly rebelled at her own misgivings.

This is war, she rebuked herself. But — she'd never killed before.

He came at her again, and the next moments were reduced to instinct alone as he increased the ferocity of his attack. One swing flowed into another until she didn't have time to think, didn't have time to calculate. Only react.

And then, an opening.

He swung the great sword over his shoulder, bringing it down towards her in a move designed to end the fight.

She sidestepped. Just enough to see the flash of her reflection in the steel as it passed.

The instant the blade drew level with her, Fae leapt. The swing was committed. Far too late for him to reverse it.

She hooked her arm around his neck, gripping the opposite shoulder of his jerkin to hold herself in place.

And drew her other dagger across his throat.

There was an instant in which the world stood still — Fae hanging onto the back of the biggest man she'd ever seen, blood pouring from the neat line she'd opened across his neck, hot and thick over her hands.

His own hand reached up as if he might hold the blood in, as if he might beg it to stay. The sword fell from his grip as he dropped to his knees, the bloody sludge underfoot splashing up to hit Fae in the face.

And then, with a final gurgle that sprayed yet more blood into the gruesome mix on the battlefield, he tipped forward into the mud, and lay still.

Perched on the back of a dead man, Fae's stomach revolted, her breath coming in heavy pants as she heaved.

But there was no time to take stock. The southern army had sent reinforcements around over the bridges she hadn't been able to burn, and now a dozen soldiers ran at her from either direction.

She heard the cries of dismay from the Throldon forces, already tied up fighting their own battles behind her, and knew there would be no help forthcoming.

Water was still under the surface, and she drew hard and fast from the river, not giving it time to slip from her grasp before she willed it to still.

A glittering curtain of icy darts flew from the river, parting to arrow towards the soldiers bearing down on her.

One moment, two dozen armoured men were rushing at her, snarls of aggression contorting their features until they resembled nothing so much as a horde of creatures born of the worst faerie tales.

The next minute, two dozen men were clutching at the holes puncturing their bodies. One bore so many through his legs that it didn't seem possible he was able to hold his weight up as long as he did. Another's face was unrecognisable as human. Yet another appeared remarkably unharmed until blood bloomed across his hardened leather chest plate.

To a man, they fell.

To either side of Fae, men fell like stacked dominoes, their bodies a circle of carnage around her.

The battlefield had been a horror to start with. Now it superseded her worst nightmares.

She stared into the eyes of a gasping soldier, the flow of blood from a hole in his neck a sluggish pulse as the life left his eyes.

The sounds of battle raged far away.

But around Fae was a deathly silence.

She was a healer. Not a killer.

And yet...

She bent to close the eyes of the soldier who stared at her even in death.

A hail of arrows fell as southern archers fired on her from the opposite bank.

Pain lanced through her shoulder as one struck home.

Acting on instinct, she pulled air to the fore, and threw up a wall of wind, knocking the arrows off course before any more could find their mark.

A cry went up to her right, and she wheeled to see the arrows falling across the battlefield, Throldon fighters going down all along the riverbank where she'd destroyed the bridges.

Cursing her short-sightedness, she gathered her legs under her. By bringing down such a wide section, the southern army had resorted to distance fighting, something the limited resources of Throldon were ill-equipped to defend against.

The instant she went to step from her circle of death, another arrow found her, piercing her arm.

She cried out in pain, her wall of air faltering, and another arrow hit her leg. She went down hard, her knees hitting the pile of bodies around her with such force that they shifted even under her slight weight.

Then one of them... *moved.*

She blinked.

A shout went up, and she glanced up to see a group of red-robed figures walking down the slope with calm deliberation, muttering in a drone that reached her even from across the river. They painted symbols in the air with hands dripping with... was that *blood*?

The bodies beneath Fae's knees shifted again. She scrambled off them, finding a clear patch of churned earth on which to make a stand. Her wounded leg buckled, and she gritted her teeth through the pain, forcing her body to straighten through sheer will alone, just in time to see what was happening.

The soldiers she'd felled with her magic lurched to their feet, their eyes glazed and empty. They came towards her in disjointed, broken movements, as if their bodies sought to obey a command they were no longer able to execute. The one whose legs were riddled with holes dragged himself along the ground to reach her.

Horrified, Fae stumbled back, reaching for water to drag it to the surface again. But her grasp was uncontrolled, and the element twisted out of her grasp and slipped away.

A roar filled her ears as the dead closed in around her. Her thoughts scattered. She reached for air, but she didn't have the focus to weave its patterns. Instead of channelling fire, its flickering form eluded her.

Her heart pounded in her chest, in her head, the beat thundering through her entire body. Her limbs were not her own. She wanted to run, but her legs wouldn't obey.

The drone of the red-robed group drifted over to her, the dead soldiers eerily silent.

She was sinking into that dark pit again, the endless black swallowing her without hope of escape.

And her fear was ice cold inside her.

Light receded from her vision.

Her element-aspects recoiled inside her, curling up beside her heart, as if it would protect them.

She was going to die here.

Darkness surrounded her.

And something inside...

Snapped.

Power rushed through her.

The Magi had been telling her she was a conduit. They were wrong.

She'd been a dam.

But now the dam was broken, and the magic rushed through her without check.

Magic poured from her in an endless surge.

It exploded out of her, a force of nature incomparable to anything seen before.

Fire and air combined into an inferno that shot into the sky.

The river thundered from its bed to form a solid wall of water between her and her enemy.

The earth groaned as it heaved beneath her feet.

Darkness twined around her arms.

Her eyes glowed incandescent. Her hair spiralled above her head.

Power cascaded from her. A tidal wave no dam could hold.

Her mouth stretched into a scream no one could hear.

Her skin began to split under the strain, light pouring from the cracks. She was coming apart at the seams, her control but a feather against a flood.

Then, as soon as it had happened, the dam slammed shut again. The magic dissipated, a freak storm blown out as quickly as it had come in.

The fire went out. The river dropped back into its channel with a crash.

Ashes fell from the sky in a soft rain, as if she'd scorched the clouds themselves.

And around her, pieces of human flesh lay strewn about in a bloody splatter, with her at the centre.

The soldiers were gone. The robed figures across the river had ceased their droning.

The battlefield was still at last, its players standing about in a state of dumb shock.

The world blurred. Fae staggered to her knees.

Her vision tunnelled to the cracked, blackened earth before her.

A trickle of blood ran into the scorched circle of char beneath her fingers.

Fae's body spasmed, and she vomited bile, her throat burning, eyes tearing.

She heaved again, as if her body attempted to purge itself of any trace of the violence, of the sheer brutality of what she'd just done.

The retching tore through her, not even breaking enough to allow her to draw breath.

The earth pitched abruptly, almost throwing her flat to the ground. It rippled out from her in waves that defied reason. It rolled and heaved with her body, as if the earth felt her horror. As if the earth itself was horrified by her.

When it finally subsided, the earth and her body finally quiet, her arms trembled with the effort of holding herself up. She wanted nothing more than to just fold to the ground.

Her head hung between her shoulders, sweat dripping down her temples as she sucked down deep, cleansing breaths.

When she'd composed herself enough, she pushed back to sit on her heels, and tipped her head back to the sky.

A blinding pain burst through the back of her skull.

And she was slammed into black.

40

NOW

The Thamibian camp was in uproar.

Jade gaped at the place on the battlefield where, a moment before, a pillar of fire had touched the sky.

The Brothers had prowled together on the battlefield, drawing shapes in the air with blood-drenched hands, Jade's stomach lurching at the sight.

Their hands dripped with *dragon* blood. *Her* dragons' blood.

Seeing it run down the Brothers' embroidered sleeves had filled her with a revulsion she hadn't realised before. But then, she hadn't fully understood what the blood was for — until now.

The bonds inside her shuddered, echoing her thoughts.

A thick pulse of magic crackled across the field, and she felt the dragons recoil from it.

You feel that? she asked down the bond.

It is unbearable, came the answer, and over the din of battle, the plaintive cries of her dragons could be heard, piercing and pained.

That's when the river rose up, and fire speared the heavens.

At first, she'd thought it was the Brothers' doing, but then she heard the confusion in the hurried words exchanged behind her, felt Kohl's grip tighten on her shoulder, saw the Brothers stumble back from the wall of water. And then the ground moved beneath their feet.

And she'd known then: this power belonged to the northerners.

Kohl delivered clipped orders to a pair of Brothers who'd returned to the command tent, his voice radiating fury... and his attention finally averted from her.

Jade turned, just in time to see a runner enter the tent in the wake of the Brothers. The soldier cast the red-robed "priests" a nervous glance, his eyes darting to the blood crusting on their hands before nodding a respectful greeting.

"General." He snapped a salute, addressing Tahe.

"Report," Tahe grunted impatiently.

"Heavy losses around that final blast, sir."

"I saw that for myself, soldier," General Tahe barked, his irritation almost as bristly as his moustache. "When the air cleared it looked like they detonated some kind of explosive. Took out some of their own too, if I'm not mistaken."

"Yes sir," the soldier continued. "But there's a squad returning from the front line reporting that they've apprehended the one responsible for the blast."

General Tahe's eyes widened at that. "Excellent work! Have him prepped for interrogation at once!"

Kohl cleared his throat pointedly. "I rather think my Brothers would be best placed to obtain a full report from this individual, General." His voice was smooth as silk, and lethal as poison.

But the general stared him down, lifting his chin to look Kohl straight in the eye. "See here, *General* Reksus. This is *my* camp, and *my* men risking their lives for the Eminency and the Thamibian Empire. It will be *my* men who interrogate the reason why *their* brothers won't even be returning home in a matchbox." His moustache quivered with barely contained indignation as he held Kohl's gaze.

Kohl's face remained impassively serene, the gleam in his eyes unreadable. "As you will, General," he said, and his tone made Jade's hairs stand on end.

General Tahe turned back to the runner. "Send word that they are to take this individual to the interrogation tent. Let's find out what he knows that our intelligence missed."

The soldier bobbed a curt nod, a sheen of sweat beading his brow as he ducked from the command tent.

General Tahe turned back to Kohl. "Your Brothers can ask their questions once my men are finished."

Kohl's lips curled into a mocking smile, even as his words were the picture of respectful. "You are most kind, General."

Tahe watched him with open suspicion, before marching from the tent, his colonel and attending staff falling into place behind him.

Kohl waited a breath, before sweeping out himself, leaving Jade to follow in his wake.

No hand on her shoulder, on her back. No whispers in her ear. No reminders of the hold he had on her.

He was distracted.

Now, a voice in her head urged. Now was the time to act.

The bonds inside her thrummed. They knew it too.

She followed Kohl back to the Brothers' circle of tents, avoiding the six gazes she felt upon her the instant she stepped into sight.

Playing the part of the obedient, submissive little girl, she kept her head down and stayed out of the way as the Brothers gathered to discuss the events of the battle, and the latest item of interest.

Jade's blood cooled at the thought of the Brotherhood getting their hands on someone with the ability to cause that much destruction.

She needed to get herself and her dragons out of here.

Brother Amand performed his spell of silence once more, and an unnatural hush fell over them, their conversation masked to anyone but those marked to hear it.

Jade recalled the words Amand had exchanged with Brother Leroy on the road — about how distance impacted the effectiveness of their blood magic. All she needed to do was to get far enough away from here that they couldn't use her or her dragons' blood against them. And after the battle, they were sure to be low on supplies.

She only hoped Kohl's bracelet didn't hold enough to make a difference.

The Brothers' discussion appeared to be a heated one, the tension palpable even from where Jade stood, the acolytes exchanging uneasy glances nearby.

Kohl ended the debate with a visible snarl. A few of the Brothers blanched, but all nodded to his authority, the words "Yes, Supremacy" shaped on their lips.

Brother Amand dragged a foot across the symbols in the dirt, and they broke from their meeting.

"Brothers Nadir and Garra, station at the interrogation tent. I want to be informed on everything that goes on inside." The black in Kohl's eyes flashed with impatience. He looked like a beast dressed in maiden's clothing, pulling at a leash within. His gaze snagged on Jade, standing demurely, exactly where she was supposed to be.

He stalked over. "You are to stay here." His finger tipped her chin back so that she was forced to meet his eye. "Do not disappoint me."

Jade smothered the nausea that roiled in her gut and plastered a superficial smile across her face. "Of course, Kohl."

He nodded his satisfaction, and released her. Barking instructions at the acolytes, he strode from their camp.

And Jade's smile became real.

41

BLOOD MAGIC

Hal held up a hand to halt the constant stream of information coming at him.

"Can *nobody* tell me what in the hell happened out there?" He looked around the room.

He stood in the University's very own map room, currently set up as his war room. The castle was too far from the front, smack in the middle of the city. A great position to retreat to, but right now he needed visibility of the field; it was just how he preferred to work.

Another section of the University's walls had collapsed not far from where they now sat. Hal knew more of the city would have fallen in that last quake, but he didn't have time to assess the damage. He'd have to send someone out to report back on it. And even then, he wasn't sure what on earth they were going to do about it.

Around him gathered the most experienced of his troops — his generals, of sorts.

David had been with him since the liberation of Throldon the year before. A former captive of the Survivors, the man had a ferocious dedication to protecting the city that even some of the more experienced fighters lacked. Norman sat back in his seat, hands laced across his middle. As a veteran soldier from the days before the Unity, he seemed to delight in reminding Hal how ill-equipped he was to deal with defending a city.

He was gruff and coarse, but knowledgeable. Yvonne leaned against one wall, arms crossed, her bow within easy reach. She was one of Hal's best archers, her brother Garrett one of his best swordsmen. Both commanded their own divisions. Perched on the back of a chair, Jesse was cleaning under her nails with the tip of one dagger. She'd become invaluable in assessing the city's defences, or lack thereof. Hal wondered if he could convince Lord Graem to loan her out on a more permanent basis, if she'd stay.

Laina had stayed in the infirmary to manage her patients, sending Sheha up in her stead. Hal's lips tugged up at the corners. That woman was incapable of delegating when it came to the care of her people.

Last to arrive were Kagos, Aiya, Aren, and Stef. The turmoil of Fae's arrival on the battlefield had prevented them from crossing to investigate the dragons. The way Aiya kept watching Kagos from the corner of her eye made Hal think that perhaps this dragon wasn't best pleased with their lack of success.

"Fae." Ty finally spoke from his position staring blankly out of the window. He hadn't said a word since both sides had called their retreat, each force peeling from the battlefield like receding tides. "That was Fae. And now they have her."

Hal nodded. "Aye, I saw that part." He hadn't worked out how to tell Laina that her daughter was not only back, but now in the hands of their enemy. How, after diving over the tallest tower on the south side of the city, she'd disabled those bridges with fire, then hurled herself into battle with significantly more fighting prowess than he'd ever seen from her, even before Anson. And then, after she'd bested the worst the southern army had deigned to throw at her, she'd pulled yet more power from somewhere and lit up the sky. "What I meant was the rest of it." The part where the dead had risen to keep fighting her.

"Blood magic," Kagos said blackly. He stood, unbelievably unmarked by his excursion onto the battlefield, his hands tucked into his sleeves.

Hal turned to him. "What in the hell is blood magic?"

Kagos's nostrils flared with fury. "A black art that ought to have been wiped off the surface of this earth centuries ago."

"Aye but it wasn't, was it?" Hal leaned forward over the huge table gracing the centre of the room. "So enlighten us. *What is blood magic?*"

Lines bracketed Kagos's mouth. He took a breath to answer.

But before he could, the air in the room hollowed out, and the door slammed open.

On the threshold stood a man Hal had never seen before. He wore a fur-lined coat and rugged, worn boots, like he'd come from the mountains. His dark brown hair was in such a state of disarray it was as if he stood in the midst of a storm. Eyes of midnight indigo flashed dangerously.

A gust of wind blew past him into the room, rippling through the curtains and sending loose pages fluttering from the table.

Everyone who bore a weapon had it levelled at the newcomer in an instant. Disregarding them all, he scanned the room, pausing only slightly upon marking Kagos, before his gaze finally settled on Hal. "Where is she?"

"Who the fuck are you?" Yvonne demanded from behind a nocked arrow.

The stranger's gaze swept the room once more, realising the impression he'd made. He relaxed his stance, and raised his hands before him. "I'm a friend." When no one appeared convinced, ire flickered across his face. "I'm here to help Fae. Where is she?"

"Sorry, *friend*," Ty stepped forward. "You'll have to get in line. And you didn't answer the lady's question."

"My name is Luca Fialli." His eyes narrowed at Yvonne, and another gust of wind blew the bow right out of her hands, the arrow thunking harmlessly into the floorboards. "And I don't take well to being threatened."

"Magi," Kagos breathed.

Luca pinned Kagos with a stare. "Dragon."

"Does anyone want to explain what's going on?" Jesse reclaimed her perch, idly playing her free dagger over her fingers

Luca wheeled back to Hal. "Fae said she would return to Throldon, but there are much larger dangers than the one you have camped out there." He pointed south. "I need to find her. Is she here?"

"Fae's been captured," Hal said. "She ain't here."

"*Shit*," Luca growled. He turned back to the door.

"They have blood sorcerers," Kagos warned him, as if he already knew what the man was planning. "And dragons." Hal glanced between the two, feeling as though he was missing half a conversation.

Sure enough, Luca jerked his head round to stare wide-eyed at the dragon. "*Shit.*"

And without warning, he spun and strode from the room.

Hal rounded on Kagos. "What the hell was that?"

Kagos drew himself up to his considerable height, and inhaled a deep, steadying breath.

"Sorcerers use incantations and runes to cast spells and manipulate magic. The use of certain artefacts can amplify a spell's power. That, in itself, is not inherently evil. Blood, however, is a perverse but effective power source. The stronger the source of the blood, the stronger the magic they wield." He paused, and a conflicting array of emotions flashed across his normally stoic face. "Centuries ago, during the War of the Races, a group of desperate sorcerers attempted to use dragon blood against us. We did not take kindly to it. The blood sorcerers were wiped out. Or, they were supposed to be."

The room fell silent.

"Eah," Aiya swore quietly, staring at her partner. "They mean to use Fae for her blood."

Ty blanched.

Aren looked queasy. "With that demonstration out on the field, they know exactly how powerful she is."

"But where did *that* come from?" David asked, his eyes darting between them. "She's not done anything like that since Black."

"No," Ty shook his head quietly. "She thought she'd lost it all."

"Clearly, she got that bit wrong." Jesse arched one eyebrow, her dagger balancing on her fingertip.

Kagos nodded. "They've likely been using the smaller dragons we saw up until now. But if Fae is back to her former strength, the power in her blood will dwarf theirs."

"We've got to get her back." Ty's voice trembled slightly but there was no missing the resolve in it.

"I think the magic man might already be looking into that." Jesse flipped her dagger up and pointed it at the door.

"He can't possibly charge into that camp and pull her out unaided." Norman spoke for the first time to inject the conversation with his unique brand of derision.

Kagos shifted where he stood.

Hal glanced his way. "Yes?" Anger and worry and the painful weight of helplessness turned the word sharp.

The dragon looked up to meet his gaze, a small smile playing across his lips.

"I wouldn't discount the Magi just yet."

42

SOMETHING OTHER

Fae gasped awake, cold and dripping wet, her head full of wool.

A voice began yelling but it was muffled in her ears. Shapes loomed in front of her, fuzzy and insubstantial.

She blinked slowly. Her view tipped sluggishly to one side. Then swung laboriously back the other way. Lights winked in and out in the periphery of her vision.

Water dripped from her eyelashes to splash onto her cheek, the sound unnaturally loud when she could barely hear the man shouting in front of her. At least, she assumed it was a man, gesticulating with sharp, angry motions.

The shape to his right shifted, and she was soaked through again with cold water.

Fae inhaled sharply, coughing when some of the water got into her throat.

Her vision sharpened enough to identify the men standing before her, although the world still pitched recklessly from side to side. The shouting sounded clearer, but she still didn't understand the words.

She spluttered, water dribbling from her mouth. The man who'd been shouting — dark-skinned with cropped, black hair — wrinkled his face in disgust. He muttered something else she didn't understand.

"Sorry," she slurred, the fog slowly lifting. "I don't understand."

The man adapted instantly, switching to a thickly-accented attempt at the common tongue.

"Your weapon. What is?" he demanded, thrusting a long finger out, presumably in the direction of the battlefield. "Tower of fire. Wall of water." He leaned in until she could count his scowl lines. "What weapon?"

Fae shook her head, stopped when her surroundings couldn't keep up with the motion.

"I don't know what you're talking about—" Her thoughts waded through syrup. She didn't have any weapons. Was the University on fire? Throldon had no walls.

She went to lift a hand to her head, but came up short by the shackles around her wrists, chained behind her to the chair.

Her head whipped up again, a sharp pain lancing through her temple. She looked at the two men again.

Hardened leather armour. Two spiked helms sat by the entrance to the tent in which they stood. A tent of sand-coloured canvas.

The dark-haired man cocked his arm, and slapped her full-force in the face.

Fae's head snapped to the side, tears springing to her eyes, the skin of her cheek burning.

"What weapon?" he bellowed in her face.

The other man chose that moment to step forward, placing a hand on his compatriot's shoulder. He was smaller than his dark-haired colleague, paler too, his hair a sandy colour that blended into the tent.

"You don't want to answer my friend?" His common tongue was better than the other's, his accent still thick and rolling. He shrugged, as if the outcome of their conversation didn't affect him either way. "Maybe you answer my questions instead." He pulled a stool over from the corner, and Fae's gaze was drawn to the tools set out along one side of the tent.

The sandy-haired man smiled a cold smile. "Yes. You see my questions are maybe not as nice, yes? Maybe you answer my friend's questions?"

Fae stared at him, her mind slow to catch up. She played over the last few minutes.

These were southerners. They thought Throldon had some secret weapon they hadn't anticipated, and that she could tell them what it was.

But there was no weapon. There was only her.

If she told them that, they would surely kill her. Or put her in a cage. She hesitated too long.

Her interrogator reached over and selected what looked like a pair of long, crooked tweezers, inserted them into the arrow-wound on her leg, and twisted.

Pain shot through her body, and her thigh muscles bunched, instinctively trying to prevent further damage. With her feet shackled to the chair, she couldn't move away, was forced to endure his ministrations. Her back arched as much as the chain around her waist would allow, her head thrown back, teeth gritted against the onslaught. He pushed the wicked tool further into her leg, twisting the tissues as he did so. A scream burst from her lips, feral and beyond her ability to leash, and through the pain, she felt something tear with a wave of nausea that threatened to rip her from consciousness again.

The man gripped her upper thigh with his free hand, twisting savagely into her leg, a fresh onslaught of agony shocking her from impending blackout.

"You tell us this city's defences. Then this stops." He pulled his tool free with a jerk, and threw it on the table. He moved his hand from her thigh to her shoulder, his thumb resting beside the hole where the first arrow had hit.

Fae's insides tensed painfully, anticipating his intentions. The man's fingers danced across his tools, lingering longer on some more than others, before he hefted a small, metal mallet.

"Our intelligence did not mention river defences," he said, standing to move around her. He unlocked the shackle around her left wrist, leaving her right still bound to the chair. "Or anything like what we saw today." He pulled her arm out straight, standing just behind it. She felt the cool metal of the mallet rest against her skin, and closed her eyes. "Tell me. What weapons is this city hiding?"

Fae clamped her lips together, pressing her tongue to the roof of her mouth.

The man tutted his disappointment behind her. She sensed him shift, and then white hot pain exploded through her as he swung the mallet. Her shoulder dislocated, bones shattered.

The sound that came from her throat wasn't anything human. Her teeth ground together but at least she didn't bite her tongue.

Nothing within her roused to come to her aid — her element-aspects remained silent.

Her interrogator left her arm to hang limply at her side, and replaced the mallet on his table.

As he deliberated over what instrument of torture to select next, another figure entered the tent. It was one of the red-robed men she'd seen on the battlefield. The ones who'd appeared just before the dead had risen to fight her again.

Panting through her pain, Fae fought down bile at the reminder of what had happened out there. What kind of magic were these southerners wielding? She hadn't seen anything remotely like it in La'sa.

The robed figure looked young, his face an even paler version of the interrogator's, as if he spent his life indoors. His eyes took in the tools, the interrogator, and finally rested on Fae. A muscle in his clean-shaven jaw ticked.

He spoke in the language that Fae didn't understand, addressing the soldiers with a sharpness to his tone that they clearly didn't appreciate. They became more agitated as the robed man spoke, their arms waving in increasingly wild gesticulations, their voices rising until they were all but shouting while the man in robes maintained an infuriating level of calm before them. Finally, the dark-haired soldier threw his arms up and stormed from the tent, the interrogator following close behind.

The man in robes glanced over Fae one more time, his expression oddly disconcerted, as if he was disturbed by what had been done to her. Or perhaps simply disturbed by *her*.

When his gaze met her eyes, he recoiled, and she wondered what it was exactly that he saw there.

Jade peeked out from behind a stack of crates.

She tried not to think about what Kohl would do if he found out she'd followed the Brothers here. She planned to be gone before it mattered.

She ducked back behind her cover just as Brother Garra stumbled backwards out of the interrogation tent, his face paler than its already pallid shade.

"What is it?" Brother Nadir leaned in, voice low. The men from Sphinx Company — the army's intelligence corps — had stormed off in search of some senior authority to eject the Brothers, incensed that the "priests" had interrupted them.

Jade resisted rolling her eyes. Had they not seen the same battle she had? How did they still think the Brothers were priests?

Then again, she'd lived in the Sanctum for years and never suspected that the Brothers... well, she'd never considered *this*.

Brother Garra was shaking his head. "Thank the gods they have her in iron, even if they don't know why. Although I'm not sure even iron will hold *that* power." His eyes darted about, as if concerned with being overheard. "I wonder if the Sorcerer Supreme knows what he's doing this time?"

Brother Nadir made an urgent shushing gesture, his eyes darting around as Garra's had. "What on earth are you talking about?"

"That woman is not... she's not normal. Something moves in her eyes."

Jade froze statue-still. What exactly was she dealing with here? But the Brothers were talking again.

"You forget yourself, *Brother*," Nadir's tone left no room for misinterpretation. If Garra didn't get a hold of himself, he'd likely find himself in a similar situation to the soldiers who'd gone up against whoever was in the tent. He was younger than the others, and it showed.

Garra nodded. He pulled his shoulders back and straightened, schooling his face until there was no longer any hint of the terrified schoolboy beneath.

"She will need cleansing," he said, his voice returning to proper formality. "She's been pierced with steel, and that Sphinx butcher was digging around in her flesh with his tools. There will be iron in her bloodstream. Not to mention contaminants from the battlefield."

"Fetch what you need," Nadir said with a nod of approval. "I'll inform the Sorcerer Supreme that we've secured the asset he sought."

Garra hesitated. "Shouldn't someone watch her?"

Nadir shot him a look, and pulled the tent flap back, standing between Jade and her view of the person inside. He dropped the canvas with a derisive grunt. "She's not going anywhere. And if Sphinx come back, we can just have the same conversation again, with the Sorcerer Supreme present."

Garra gave a nervous titter, and the two moved away.

Jade didn't waste any time. The second those embroidered hems whipped out of sight, she dashed from behind the crates, and ducked into the tent.

On the way here, she'd found a pile of discarded steel pins outside what she assumed was an armourer's station — straight, twisted, bent, there were enough different shapes to make perfectly adequate lock picks.

Pulling them from where she'd tucked them into her headband, she set her eyes on the prize Kohl seemed willing to give up his entire plan for.

The woman didn't look like much. Petite, bordering on scrawny, she wasn't exactly imposing. The hair that hung lank about her shoulders was a shade of blonde so colourless it reminded her of pale ash. Added to the deathly cast to her skin, it looked as if she'd been leeched of colour entirely. She bore open wounds to her shoulder, upper arm, and leg, and her left arm hung loosely at her side in a way that told her the woman couldn't move it. She was covered in mud and gore, and was soaked through. She looked like a drowned rat. And that was being unkind to the rat.

"Um..."

The woman's eyes snapped up. Jade staggered back. She could see what Brother Garra meant. There was something not quite human in the way this woman looked at her.

"I've come to help." Jade stepped forward, keeping her voice low. She'd learned enough of the common tongue while working for Ixio with all his illicit trading that she'd recognised it immediately upon overhearing the Sphinx interrogator through the canvas. She held up her improvised lock picks.

The woman's eyes narrowed, assessing her. Jade took another step forward, and crouched at her feet. The locks were made of dark iron, the same metal that made the door to her cell back in the Sanctum.

"What's your name?" Angling the first pick into the lock, she manipulated it to slot into the back tumbler. Then in went the second. The skill came back to her as if she'd practiced it yesterday.

"Fae." The quiet rasp startled her, and she fumbled the second pick. Wedging her tongue between her teeth, Jade inserted the pick again, and applied just the right pressure...

A reassuring *click* announced the release of the first lock.

"I'm Jade," she said, moving over to the other one.

"Why are you helping me?"

Jade worked the second lock. "Because the Sorcerer Supreme cannot get his hands on you." It sprang open.

Standing, she found herself looking straight into those remarkable eyes. On the outside, they were a subtle, ocean-green with a ring of pure gold around the irises. But behind them... Garra had been right, something *other* hovered behind Fae's eyes.

"Tell me you can get out of here." She had hoped for help getting *herself* out, along with her dragons. But one look at this woman told her she'd be no help at all in her current state. If anything, Jade would have to be the one to help *her*.

Fae studied her, and Jade had the distinct impression of being weighed. "I'll figure something out."

Jade stared at the woman, bloodied, broken, and defeated. But the determination in her eyes was like flint.

She nodded. If there was anyone more motivated to escape this godsforsaken camp than her, it was Fae. Jade decided that if she had such a thing, she'd put money on her.

She edged around to pick the lock restraining her right hand, when she heard noise outside the tent.

Jade stiffened, listening, like a startled dear.

She knew those voices.

"I've got to go," she whispered. The voices were approaching too quickly for her to slip out the way she'd come in.

In a panic, she dropped to the ground and rolled under the canvas side. It was pegged tightly to the ground, and there was a moment where she was sure her mad shuffling would give her away.

Then she was out, lying in the dirt, looking up at the pale northern sky.

Inside the tent, Kohl purred, "And there I was, thinking the Magi died out."

43

SO MANY LIVES

Fae fought the urge to snarl at the man who looked at her like a jungle cat — like she was prize prey, a fat rabbit, cornered and his to toy with.

He wore white robes edged with silver — impossibly pristine in what must be a filthy war camp. His sun-bronzed skin, almost a match for Luca's, glowed in contrast. He would have been beautiful had his eyes not gleamed with black malice. Kagos had eyes of pure obsidian, and yet his were innocent as a doe compared with these.

"I am Sorcerer Supreme of the Thamibian Empire." His smooth voice, hinting only softly at the southern accent, raised the hairs on the back of her neck. The air crackled with static, like there wasn't enough space in the tent to accommodate his presence. He pulled over the interrogator's stool, and sat across from her. "And I have waited a long time for an opportunity such as this."

Fae glowered at him. White-hot fire poured from her shoulder down the length of her arm. Her leg muscles spasmed erratically against the pain of her mangled thigh. Lights continued to flare too bright across her vision, the image before her occasionally doubling and sliding back into focus.

And inside her, nothing roused to her aid.

She swallowed an agonising breath and rasped, "Thought you just said the Magi were all dead."

He laughed, the sound raking claws under her skin.

"I did say that didn't I?" He leaned forward, as if she was an interesting specimen that warranted closer inspection. "Indeed. What I mean to say" — he reached forward, and she jerked from his touch — "is that I have waited a long time for a source powerful enough to bring my goals to fruition."

Her stomach hollowed out. What did he intend to do with her? The girl, Jade... she'd said the Sorcerer Supreme couldn't get his hands on her. Well, here she was. At his mercy.

Even with her legs freed, her arms were useless. Broken or bound, neither was going to be any help in getting out of here. And there was still the chain around her waist, pinning her to the metal chair.

The sorcerer looked her over, his gaze stripping her bare.

"So much power in such a small body." Fae suppressed a shudder at the echo of Luca's words, uttered so long ago. "Enough to rival a dragon's? I wonder..." He was muttering to himself, his expression as bland as if he were appraising a work of art. And then his eyes caught on her left arm. Skipped over the mess of her leg. He recoiled, nostrils flaring.

He snapped his fingers. "Come."

Behind him, two red-robed adolescents stepped forward, one holding a wide, shallow dish, the other a basket of assorted items.

The sorcerer stood. "I see my countrymen have been less than hospitable. No matter. My acolytes will have you cleaned up in no time. Your blood must be pure. This" — he gestured to all of her with a flick of his wrist — "will not do."

The acolytes set down their items and stood to the side.

The white-robed sorcerer glanced down at their supplies, nodding his satisfaction. "Ensure the sage burns for a full hour."

"Yes, Supremacy," the boys echoed.

The sorcerer's gaze travelled back up Fae's body, a cold smile gracing his lips when he finally met her eyes.

"Worry not, my dear. Your blood will be purified. And then, you and I will achieve great things together. You'll see." He turned with a flourish, his robes swishing about his ankles. Pausing at the tent flaps, he spoke with someone outside. "Notify me the instant she is ready."

He was answered by another paired, "Yes, Supremacy," and then he was gone.

Still chained to the chair, there was nothing Fae could do as one of the boys lit a stick of white sage, wafting the smoke around the tent before setting it in a shallow bowl to smoulder. The other poured water from a glass bottle into the wide dish, adding more sour-smelling ingredients from the basket before reaching for a stack of clean, cotton cloths.

She hissed at him when he reached forward to bathe her wounds, and he flinched. When he went to touch her again, she reacted instinctively, kicking out with her injured leg, forgetting that it was supposed to be bound.

And that it hurt like hell.

Her cry of pain mingled with the acolyte's startled yell, and the next thing she knew, the two that had been standing guard outside the tent were holding her down, one pressing on her legs, the other wrenching her shoulders behind her. A wave of black rolled over her vision before it cleared again. These men were older than the boys, and wore robes of finer cloth, embroidered with deep purple. She recognised the pale one who had called her interrogator away.

The other guard was older, with rough black hair, and snapped angrily at the boys in a language Fae didn't understand, gesturing sharply to the open shackles by her feet.

He grabbed for the chains, gripping her ankle roughly as he brought the two together.

Fae struggled. She couldn't stay here. She was no good to her family here.

She was no good to the Magi either.

The guard reached up and slapped her hard across the face. Her head snapped to the side for the second time since she'd woken in this hell, her joints cracking in protest. A gasp escaped her lips.

She squeezed her eyes shut against the hot burn of tears. Tears of fury, of humiliation, of helplessness.

Again.

A breeze rustled through the tent, and it smelled of crisp, mountain air.

Fae's heart stalled.

The tent flap corners flipped open at the bottom. Just enough to reveal black trousers tucked into worn, heavy-duty boots.

The southern army dressed in tan, not black.

The guard at her feet used her moment of hesitation to clamp the shackles back around her ankles.

He straightened, fixed her with a glare, and gestured for the boys to continue their work.

They didn't make it a single step towards her.

A vortex of air speared into the tent, throwing all four of the sorcerer's people to the ground.

And then he strode in.

Luca's eyes whirled with fire as he took in the scene before him. He marked the threats with a single glance before his gaze finally came to rest on Fae.

Danger! Fae's senses blared. But this time, the power that prowled behind his gaze wasn't for her.

The boys scuttled as far out of the way as the tent walls would allow, leaving Luca facing the two guards.

Guards who found their feet, and began tracing symbols in the air, their voices a drone that filled Fae's ears like a swarm of bees. Together, they drew knives from the sleeves of their robes. But instead of using the blades to fight, they sliced into the muscle of their forearms in a disturbingly synchronised motion, dipped fingers into their own blood.

A scene flashed before Fae's eyes, of a group of such men approaching her across the battlefield, hands dripping with blood.

"Luca, watch out!" But he was ready for them. He threw up a shield of hardened air, then sent bolts of fire that flared brighter and hotter as they passed through the barrier.

The flames caught quickly on the canvas, and within moments the entire tent was ablaze.

The boys ran from the fire, screaming as they went. Soon the whole enemy camp would be on top of them. There was no way Luca could carry Fae out of here and survive it.

The pale sorcerer drew a complex series of shapes in the air, but Luca's fire whipped out to interrupt his incantation before he could finish. The black-haired one was faster, and his spell lashed out in an explosion of red sparks that knocked Luca flying though the burning canvas.

"Luca!" Fae screamed, her voice hoarse and breaking.

But beyond the thick smoke rising from the crumpled ruins of the tent, Luca stepped through the flames. He snapped his arms out to either side, and they became wreathed in fire.

The sorcerers threw up a net of magic in front of them: a shield behind which to incant their next spells.

A shout went up nearby, and Fae watched in horror as dozens of southern soldiers sprinted towards them, four more sorcerers among them.

"Luca!" Fae called. "Luca!"

He lifted his arms, and a wall of fire erupted around them, immolating anything that might dare to come close. He braced his arms out to either side of him, the muscles bunching under soot-streaked skin as he strained with the effort to push that wall outward...

Screams pierced the air beyond the flames. The smell of cooked flesh and burning hair nearly made her gag.

Then his gaze turned to her at last.

The raw power behind his eyes stole the breath from her. It was wild and alien, and a glimmer of something else that a hidden piece of her reached across the void inside to answer.

"There are more coming," she gasped out, the flames sucking all moisture and oxygen from the air.

Luca's eyes snapped up, as if he could see through the solid wall of fire around them.

Then he was a flurry of motion. He snatched the keys from the amongst the tools of torture and had her freed in an instant. Helping her to her feet, he swept her up into his arms before she could stumble on her bad leg. She nestled against him, careful of her bad shoulder.

"Hold on," he said, his voice a deep, primal growl. Fae looped her good arm around his neck, clutching the fur-lined collar of his coat.

And then they were rising above the flames, Luca flying them over the enemy camp, using air to propel them through the sky.

Fae peeked over her shoulder to see the sorcerers shrinking away beneath them, their arms waving uselessly at them.

Luca carried them up and over the endless sea of sand-coloured canvas, the southern army milling about like so many ants.

His arms were bands of iron around her as he pressed her into his heat, his voice unusually soft as he brushed his lips to her ear. "I told you not to come." Not mocking. No, his words carried something more like sadness in them.

He took them north, back over the battlefield.

When the tents finally gave way to what should have been a blanket of green, time seemed to slow.

The ground had been trampled by thousands of feet until it looked like a hammered sheet of dull bronze. The river was still pierced by the bridges Fae hadn't been able to tear down, like a jagged wound ripping its stitches, the red waters clogged with bodies and splintered timber.

And beyond the river...

Fae didn't want to see, but she couldn't look away.

Between the riverbank and what remained of the University walls, a black crater stained the land. And around it, like a grotesque poppy flower painted across the field, a corona of charred red. Smoke still issued from the earth, the smell of burning flesh and hair reaching into the sky to choke her.

She'd stood there, in the centre of that, and her power had torn apart anyone too close to escape. Friend and foe. Ripped to paper shreds.

No bodies remained to litter the ground. Just endless red.

So many people, to stain the earth like that. So many lives.

She ought to cry. She ought to be sick to her stomach. She ought to scream.

But there was nothing left in her.

She stared at the scar in the earth, and nothing inside answered.

44

CREATURES OF THE SKY

Jade had been resolved to free Fae at any cost, even if it had meant sacrificing the freedom of her and her dragons.

And then the man who wielded wind and flames like they were merely extensions of his body had come crashing through the tent and set it ablaze.

The way Fae had called out to him, it had been clear he was a friend, and Jade wasn't stupid enough to think she'd be any help in a fight of magic against magic.

So she ran, using the smoke and tents as cover to get back to her dragons.

The entire camp was in turmoil. Soldiers sprinted in every direction: reporting, rushing to aid, running for water and sand to douse the flames.

No one paid any attention to Jade.

She didn't see Kohl in her wild dash for freedom, for which she thanked the gods over and over as her feet pounded across the dust and dirt, each step thundering through her body in tandem with her racing heart.

Her dragons keened desperately at the panic in the camp. The Brothers were nowhere to be seen, only a handful of acolytes milling between the sorcerers' tents, unsure whether to help or stay.

Alpha spread his wings wide over the wagon he shared with Fearless as soon as he spotted Jade. She ducked quickly from the shelter of the supply crates to the cover of the wagon wheels.

We must go now. His voice was a command.

"You think?" she hissed. Fumbling with her makeshift lock picks, she forced her hands to steady as Alpha sidled to the edge of the wagon, bringing his shackled legs as close as the chains would allow. Jade flattened herself to the planks as she reached across to work at the locks, Alpha spreading a wing to conceal her from view.

In minutes, the cruel manacles fell away, thudding to the wagon bed louder than she'd have liked.

Stay there, she said. This would go better if the acolytes remained oblivious of their escape until they were all free.

Alpha turned a whirling bronze eye on her. *You think?*

Jade almost laughed, and moved over to work on Fearless's chains. The smaller dragon covered her as her brother had done, crouching low so that Jade would not be seen.

It took agonising minutes to insert each pick, to find the tumblers inside the lock, to line up the next pick, apply pressure, turn...

The *click* of each lock giving way under her ministrations lifted a weight off her chest, until she turned to the next one.

As she freed Envy's front legs, one of the acolytes spotted her.

"Hey! Hey!" the cry went up. "*What are you doing?*" And then they were all running at her.

"Shitshitshitshitshit." She bit her tongue as she concentrated on the second set of shackles. Even if she was stopped, she would see at least some of the dragons free.

Now? Alpha asked dryly in her head.

The lock clicked. Envy's shackles fell to the floor. Jade looked up at Alpha and Fearless, who hunched, poised and ready above the acolytes as they dashed past their wagon.

Now would be good.

With a roar that nearly deafened her, Alpha unfurled his wings to their full reach, and snaked his head down to snap at the acolytes running towards her.

Jade blinked up at him. Free from the confines of a cage, he was bigger than she'd last guessed, his wingspan easily twenty feet from tip to tip.

The acolytes, seeing that Alpha was no longer chained to the wagon, stumbled back, just as Fearless leapt down in pursuit, hissing vehemently.

Envy reared up, throwing her smaller wingspan wide, her brown-and-purple colouring catching the sun like a bruise against the sky.

Jade didn't waste the time she was given, ducking beneath Envy's sweeping wings to tackle Brave's restraints.

Somehow, despite the chaos now reigning around her, she got Brave's legs free in no time at all, and then she was dashing to the final wagon, no longer worried about being seen.

She winced at the angry sores around Delita's legs, the silver scales completely ripped away to expose sensitive flesh beneath. Jade worked carefully around the wounds, and was rewarded with a nuzzle from the dragon's triangular head when the shackles fell free.

A voice bellowed a question from beyond the Brothers' little section of camp.

And one of the acolytes screamed for help.

Fearless ripped his throat out.

Jade stared at the blood shining on the smallest dragon's maw. At the motionless body splayed before her.

Chary, the injured green, warbled beside her.

Tearing her gaze away, Jade threw herself at the last set of chains.

Shouts were getting louder as the acolyte's call for help was answered, and Jade didn't know if it was soldiers or Brothers who came.

Her fingers slipped on the picks, and she dropped the lock.

Growling her frustration, she scooped up the lock again, and jammed her picks back into the mechanism. She forced herself to take her time — time she didn't have — lock-picking was not something that could be rushed.

Just as she heard the reassuring *click*, strong arms grabbed her roughly from behind, and a cold line pressed against her throat. She glanced down without moving her head, caught sight of simple red robes.

The acolyte breathed heavily in her ear, his knife hand shaking wildly as he held the blade to her skin. A small flare of pain speared through her shock.

Jade slowly raised her hands up to either side. "Alright. Alright." Years of practice with the Brothers helped her to keep her voice calm. "Easy. No one needs to lose a head here." Least of all her.

"Tell that to Jahmal!" The acolyte's voice broke into a hysterical shriek. In front of her, all six dragons advanced on her and her captor.

Don't corner him. She held Alpha's gaze — where he led, the others would follow.

The dragons halted their stalking.

"If you kill me, they'll kill you. Plain and simple." Jade kept her voice level. Honest. "And if you bleed me, which I'm pretty sure you already are" — she felt a trickle run down the hollow of her throat — "the Sorcerer Supreme will have your head."

The acolyte stilled behind her. She could almost hear his brain turning over the options. She knew which option he'd be better off taking. The one she hadn't voiced. Let her go, and the Brothers might not think to take it out on him. After all, the dragons had already killed one of them.

Of course, Jade knew better than that.

He was dead either way.

And as he pondered his choices, the knife eased away from her neck. It was all she needed to throw her head back into his nose, knocking the knife from his hand in the same moment.

As he howled in pain, she dashed across the space to her dragons. As one, they spread their wings, ready to take off.

You can fly? She'd always worried that years confined in cages would hamper their ability to do so.

A ripple of scorn travelled down the bonds within her. *We are creatures of the sky.* Alpha's eyes mocked her gently as he delivered his simple statement. *Come.* He bent a foreleg so that she could climb onto his back, to sit just in front of his wing joints.

Around them, the others launched themselves into the air, drunkenly at first, and then, as they accustomed their muscles to motions that they were indeed designed for — *born* for — their wings levelled out, and they *soared* over the camp. Even Chary, whose wing bones had been so cruelly broken, managed a lopsided gait through the sky.

Alpha waited until they were all aloft, then extended his wings to their fullest extent, beating them once, twice, three times before bunching his legs and throwing himself from the ground in a storm of dust and dirt and wind.

There was a hairy moment when he caught the trailing edge of one wing in a flapping tent panel, pitching them both sharply to one side. But then he was clear of the tents, his wings free and unimpeded by the makings of men.

And they *flew.*

Above the camp, Jade saw the utter destruction Fae's friend had wrought in their escape. Black smoke billowed over smouldering canvas in a plume that covered a visible portion of the camp.

And as her dragons limped away from it, she saw a figure in the air above, borne away on a gust of wind, a smaller figure with ash-coloured hair cradled in his arms.

Jade allowed herself a small smile before glancing back at the circle of tents around three large wagons.

And the white-clad sorcerer standing as a stone amid a sea of red robes.

Her stomach turned to lead.

Jade flattened herself along Alpha's neck.

Fly, she urged them all. *Fly.*

And whether they saw him too, or sensed the urgency in her tone, they beat their wings with every ounce of strength contained in their abused bodies, to carry them away from that life of captivity and torture.

A tug on the bond of blood that had been forced on all of them.

"*FLY!*" Jade screamed.

The Sorcerer Supreme watched them go. Those beasts that had brought him so far.

Then he turned his eye to the Magi that carried his prize away on the wind.

A smile pulled its way across his face. He snapped his fingers, not particularly caring who answered, just that someone did.

"Supremacy." Brother Leroy stood at his shoulder. Always eager to please.

"Bring me General Tahe." His eyes never left the speck of two figures leading him to a treasure trove. "And get someone to vial the blood at the crater."

He would have that power for himself.

He would have power.

PART II.

45

SPIRIT OF A WANDERER

Thousands of miles away, in Equi'tox.

The fires of Immrith's memorial pyre jumped and danced against the night sky, the colours bright to celebrate the light his life had brought to the world.

Coloured salts added to the pyre made the flames flare vibrant red, blinding yellow, and deep, slumbering purple.

A flash of cobalt blue signalled that the flames had reached the heart of the pyre, and the sparks it threw out mingled with the others to paint the sky's dark canvas with the colours of Immrith's life.

This would be the last time he would be remembered like this. The souls of the dead walked the earth for one full turn around the sun after their funeral pyres were lit, before moving on to the next life. This was their final farewell.

Fanrell tipped his head back to watch the sparks drift away on the cold northern winds, a trail of coloured stars leading his brother to the heavens.

He'd only just made it in time for the ceremony. The tremors that shook the earth these days had brought down a bridge in Arland, forcing him to track along the river a day longer than he'd intended in order to cross. Then a great gash had opened up in the Northern Tundra, miles from any civilisation, again forcing him to plot a new route around. He'd arrived home — to the clan of the Little Bear — in time to paint his torso and flanks in the ceremonial paints to honour his brother: red for bravery, purple for honour, and the rare blue for the spirit of a wanderer. A band of black was daubed across his eyes, and he knew he looked like a demon staring from it. Then had come the wild gallop into the cold, uninhabitable wilds beyond their village, to the pyre that had been built the night before.

He watched until the last of the fire died out, the last sparks drifting away with his brother's spirit.

"Farewell, brother," he murmured to the sky, and he swore a star glimmered back in answer. So unlike when his parents had passed. The Wildlands were harsh and unforgiving, and claimed many who dared to live upon them. But Immrith had stood beside him when they burned their parents, and bid them farewell a year later. Now, he stood alone.

The embers glowed at his feet for a long while after the last of his clan filtered away. He sighed, his breath drifting away like smoke. He hadn't even reported to the clan Elders yet. Hadn't had time to greet Philomena's father, the male who had taken the position of Clan Leader after Fanrell's own father had passed.

Dawn leaked over the horizon. He turned his back on the ash of Immrith's memorial pyre, and began the sombre trek home.

Home. Was it anymore? He had no more family here. Even by centaur standards, Fanrell was aloof and detached from his peers. He'd had friends, but it had been Immrith who'd balanced his solemn tendencies.

But Immrith had had his own problems fitting into the life the fates had dealt him. Too caring, ruled by his emotions more than harsh logic, and with a true wanderer's soul. It was no wonder he'd left when Bravargh had arrived in their village so long ago.

The Elders hadn't trusted the nomad the instant he'd appeared. But he'd won over the younger centaurs with his stories of the wider world.

Fanrell thought of Fae, who now carried Bravargh's memories in her own, and wondered if she remembered how glad Immrith had been of the chance to leave here.

When he'd first gone south to stand in Immrith's place on the Council of Races, he'd thought to hate those who had contributed to his brother's death. But he'd found another family of mismatched sorts, mourning Immrith more intensely than his own people had. And in the year since, he'd come to see a glimmer of why Immrith had left the village.

He'd been right. The centaurs needed to step into the world of races. They were dwindling fast in the north, their numbers being cut every winter like wheat to the scythes he'd seen in Arland's fields. They wouldn't last another generation up here.

And yet, the army approaching Throldon's fragile borders threatened to do the same to the human capital.

Fanrell scowled as he passed the outskirts of Little Bear Village. Huts leaned away from the constant winds, some in such a state of disrepair that they'd been abandoned in favour of homes left behind by families not strong enough to survive this life. Between harsh winters and clan warring, it was a miracle the centaurs weren't lost to the world already.

Once, they'd made up for their unforgiving lives in numbers. But they were no longer the hordes they'd once been.

Fanrell trudged into the centre of the village, to the hall with the high, vaulted roof and the fire at its centre beneath a small opening to the sky. The floor was bare, rushes pushed to the edges in an effort to keep the drafts out.

As he expected, the Elders sat with their long, awkward legs tucked up under their bodies, long, grey hair falling all the way to drape across the dusty floor.

There were three ancient Elders, white and grey hairs flecking the colours of their lower bodies. Sangrell had once been a fearful black, his lower body matching that of a pure black stallion, his upper body the tall, strong form of a warrior. Now his long hair was grey, the hairs of his tail flecked with steel where once it had gleamed all-black. Greghar had been a dark bay, the black of his hair and tail contrasting against the rich brown of his coat and deep tan of his skin. Now his colouring had faded as if left out in the sun too long, the pigment slowly bleeding as if he might one day simply fade away.

The last of the Elders sat in the middle of the two males, her position at the head of the hall one that Fanrell had never seen belong to anyone else. Rochelle was a female of pure white — hair, flanks, and skin. Whether she had ever been another colour before, Fanrell did not know.

Her eyes — an unsettling shade of palest blue — tracked him as he crossed the hall. She knew why he was here.

Oracles were rare among the centaurs, but not unknown. Philomena had been gifted with the Sight by the spirits at her *Ateth Legarrh* as well. Perhaps she would one day become a village Elder.

If the centaurs survived that long.

"Fanrell Megarson." Rochelle's voice was deep and clear, belying her age. The males to either side of her practically withered before Fanrell's eyes. How had the Oracle retained so much of her vigour? "How was your journey across the Barren Lands?"

"Troubling, Elder." Fanrell would not trot around the issue. And she didn't expect him to. "The land breaks apart, and a southern army marches on our friends in Throldon." He looked her in the eye. "I've come to seek aid from the clans. To ask the centaurs to rally, to take their place in the world again."

"Ha!" Rochelle's laugh was whip-crack in the space. "And why would we do such a thing?" She arched a disdainful brow at him, the hair braided across her forehead shifting with the motion. "I am surprised you would come to us with such a request having only just made your final farewell to your brother."

"My brother died for something our friends in Arland understand." Fanrell held her unsettling stare, unwilling — unable — to back down from this. "Throldon is a city of people who once fought against each other. They rebuild a nation torn apart, together. And it is working. Humans work and learn alongside dwarves and elves. It is a vision worth defending." It is one that, had the centaurs thought of it only ten years before, would have saved his family. Would have kept him from utter isolation among his own kind.

Rochelle made a derisive sound in the back of her throat. "No great feat."

"The dragons join them," Fanrell said, enjoying the hint of surprise that passed over the Elder's face. "It was them who brought the news of the army."

Greghar lifted his head to fix him with a watery gaze. "The dragons withdrew into isolation far before the clans did. Their race dies out, as ours thrives." Fanrell didn't know what version of the past the Elder thought they existed in now, but his perception on the state of the clans needed refreshing. He didn't bother correcting his assumption about the dragons either. "We do not involve ourselves with humans." The disinterest in his tone was final. There would be no help forthcoming from here.

A muscle feathered in Fanrell's jaw in a rare sign of irritation. He'd gone with the elves a year ago to represent the centaurs in their Council of the Races, and to uncover the truth behind Immrith's death. But he'd known even then that the Elders of his race would never agree to be a part of their collaboration. They were too set in their ways, too accustomed to their cold halls and bitter winters to think that there might be something better. Far too fiercely territorial to consider *sharing*.

They were no better than temperamental toddlers.

Rochelle held a hand out towards Greghar, her eyes fixed on Fanrell in an expression that clearly said, *there you have it.*

Fanrell kept his face schooled despite railing inwardly against their shortsightedness — no, their *blindness* — to the fortunes of the centaurs. To the benefits of uniting them with the other races of the world. To how critical it was that they do so.

"Your wisdom has been heard, Elders," he said stiffly, bowing his head just barely enough to be respectful.

Rochelle eyed him with a shrewd glint as he left the hall, but whatever thoughts passed behind her gaze, she kept her counsel to herself.

Despite the weariness that pulled at his bones, his hooves all but dragging along the ground before setting down again, Fanrell had one more stop to make.

Those hooves made a hollow sound that echoed the feeling in his chest as he clomped up the ramp to the Clan Leader's house. He knocked on the heavy wooden door, ignoring the way villagers stopped in the midst of going about their daily tasks to watch him. He hadn't been popular before — he hadn't expected a warm homecoming.

The door swung open to reveal a female a few years younger than him, and one of the few centaurs who treated him with any sort of kindness.

"Fanrell!" She shot forward to wrap slender arms around him, her long fingers pressing into his upper back. Usually shy among company, Philomena had always worn a smile for Immrith and Fanrell, and the knowledge warmed his heart. Her lower body was coloured a chestnut pinto, with small brown spots dappled over her mostly white flanks. The skin of her torso, warm against his chest, was a creamy gold which freckled in the sunlight, and strawberry blonde hair hung down her back in gentle waves. She pulled back and regarded him with eyes of bright blue. "You made it! I didn't see you at the ceremony." Most of the clan had come out to see the pyre lit, it would have been easy to miss him in the dark. And he'd always made an effort to avoid almost all of them.

Almost all.

"You look well, Philomena." The wrap she wore across her torso left her waist and shoulders bare, perfectly appropriate among his people who often wore nothing at all.

She blushed furiously. "You haven't changed a bit."

"It's only been a year."

"Precisely! It's been a whole year!" She reversed her steps to make room for him. "Come in. Father is out in the workshop."

Fanrell dipped his head in thanks, and stepped into the house.

Centaurs, as a rule, preferred the open skies to having a roof over their heads, but practicality dictated that some things be covered. The sleeping areas were always sheltered, but even the eating area ran out from under the cover of the house and into the central courtyard, the inner walls of the building traditionally absent.

The Clan Leader's house was larger than most, set in a long U-shape, the workshop built off one arm of the structure.

Fanrell walked through the living area and straight across the courtyard to the workshop, where the sounds of hammering matched the rhythm of his steps.

The space was — like the rest of the house — part-roofed, the tools set along the far wall over the work bench. The flash of the hammer caught his eye before he spotted the hulking form of the centaur who wielded it, his powerful arm flexing as he brought the tool to bear.

Philomena's father had the same patterning as his daughter, but that is where the similarities ended. The dappled pattern across his flanks were black on sooty-grey, which is why Fanrell hadn't seen him at first — he blended into shadows eerily well. The Clan Leader's black hair was tied back from his work with a thick cord, the strands clinging to the sheen of sweat across his broad, tanned back as he straightened at last.

"Chief." Fanrell cleared his throat. The male turned, his black tribal tattoos twisting with the motion.

"Fanrell." His booming voice rattled Fanrell's bones. "I've told you to call me Jeorgen more times than I can count." Jeorgen exited the workshop to clap Fanrell on the back hard enough that his feet shifted to maintain his balance. "Doesn't feel right, you calling me 'Chief' when it wasn't that long ago you were all stumbling around my yard while your father and I drank mead together."

Fanrell's jaw clenched unconsciously. Jeorgen saw it.

"The fires burned bright for Immrith last night." It was as close to *I'm sorry for your loss* as the centaurs would ever get. Fanrell nodded. "Now" — another thundering clap to his back — "what can I do for you?"

Fanrell spent the rest of the morning relaying everything that had happened to his Clan Leader.

Jeorgen folded his arms across his bare chest, biceps bulging so much it was a wonder they even allowed him that motion.

"You bring grave news, Fanrell," he rumbled, running a hand across his jaw. "Especially after your brother—"

"I know." Fanrell cut him off before he could remind him again, his tail flicking his grief away. Coming back here had brought more memories to the surface than he had been prepared to face. "But I believe the human city worthy of saving. And I believe it time the centaurs join the world of many races." He felt like a sullen teenager saying it but, "It's a lot better than the lands we squabble over so pettily."

Jeorgen scowled, and it was worse than if he'd given him a full dressing down. "Do not speak ill of the generations before you. They fought and died so that this land would be yours. Do not speak ill of your parents."

Fanrell's face burned. "I meant no disrespect." His hooves shifted uncomfortably on the packed earth floor. "But our people are failing out here. The other races thrive together. They build great institutes just to learn from one another. They share knowledge, resources, ideas. They build a future. Together. And they have invited us to join it with open arms, because of what Immrith did." His eyes burned with the conviction of his words. He swept an arm out to encompass the bleak clan lands. "We are dying out here." Jeorgen held a hand up, and Fanrell's words died on his tongue. Despite taking on the responsibilities of the Clan Leader, this male remained the closest thing he had to a father, and for that, and that alone, he had Fanrell's respect.

"What you speak may well be truth. But you have seen the Elders already. They have spoken."

"But if you spoke to them..." The Clan Leader had more sway with the Elders.

Jeorgen shook his head. "They have spoken," he repeated. "And without their support, you will not get any further with the other clans."

Fanrell clenched his jaw to keep from saying something disrespectful. Stupid, backward, self-centred people he had the misfortune to call his own. It was the mindless clan wars that had killed his parents. The tenuous treaties they held restricted each clan to strict borders, prevented them from becoming stronger together.

"Do not look at me like that, Fanrell." Jeorgen's voice rumbled through the room. "You know our ways. We have survived for generations. It has been... hard, these past few years." And Fanrell knew he was talking about the loss of his own wife as well. Philomena's mother. "But we will rise again. We have more youngsters walking the *Ateth Legarrh* this season than we've had in a long time. You'll see. We will rise." He drew himself to his considerable height, his black hair brushing the high beams. "Only the centaurs are strong enough to prosper in these lands, and we make them our own. It is a feat to be proud of."

Pride will be the death of you. Fanrell's face showed none of his frustration as he nodded respectfully to his Clan Leader. "Then I will return to Throldon, Chief."

Jeorgen's face drooped almost imperceptibly but Fanrell saw it, and it was like a punch to his gut. Jeorgen's piercing blue gaze studied him, and Fanrell shifted his weight across his hind legs, trying to avoid the way it felt as if he saw right through him.

Finally, the Clan Leader nodded. "I understand." He turned to resume his work and paused, his head tipping to one side. "When will you leave?"

Fanrell blinked. "As soon as possible." He didn't want to think about how Throldon fared even now.

Jeorgen made a sound low in his throat. "Wait until after the *Ateth Legarrh*. Philomena has missed you. The wolf moons are only three nights

hence. There may be other wanderers who emerge with visions of travel."
Like Immrith.

The unspoken words hung in the hair between them. Fanrell stared at the other male's broad back.

At what he was saying without saying.

Finally he remembered how to work his mouth.

"Yes, Chief."

Jeorgen jerked another nod. And hefted his hammer again.

46

RAISED AMONG WOLVES

The plains south of the Amedi River were empty, the camp on the hill eerily quiet.

Ty stepped up beside Hal, his features drawn. "What are they doing?" He and Sheha had taken Fae's capture particularly badly. They'd all breathed a sigh of relief when they saw the Magi — Luca — carry her from the enemy camp, but Ty's gaze had held an edge of wariness when they didn't return to Throldon, disappearing instead toward the northern horizon.

Hal grunted. "They're waitin'."

"Waiting for what?"

Hal's jaw clenched. "I don't know."

They used the respite to collect their dead, although no one entered the giant bloodstain soaked into the earth where Fae had fought, as if they feared the ground would burn them where they stood. There were no bodies to collect there in any case.

The bridges were collapsed, pyres built for the bodies the enemy apparently had no interest in clearing from the field, and Hal was finally able to take stock of the damage.

"The River Quarter was the worst affected by the quakes," David reported later that day. It wasn't surprising. The River Quarter had always been where the poorest citizens scraped a living, and where repairs were always the most haphazard. "But the builders' guild says it looks like the University weathered most of the damage. Like the epicentre was, well..." He pointed out to the battlefield. "Out there."

Hal nodded. He'd seen. Seen how Fae had called wind, and fire, and water. How the earth had *rippled* beneath her.

"Sir, there's something—" David leaned forward over the parapet, squinting at the sky. "Look!"

Hal followed the line of his arm as he pointed skyward. There, against the clouds, a cluster of shapes moved towards them. At first glance, it could easily have been a small flock of birds. But as it got closer, it was clearly anything but.

And it was coming straight for the city.

Hal grabbed for the long glass and lifted it to his eye.

"Get Kagos and Aiya!" he barked. "Now! Go!" He didn't turn to see if David carried out his order. Couldn't tear his gaze from the small group of dragons limping its way towards him, not one of them flying true. And on the back of the largest — a red with a body no larger than that of a horse — the girl he'd seen standing beside the enemy's commanders.

He was still watching their perilous descent towards the city when Kagos arrived on the tower, Aiya in tow. Max clattered up the steps behind them, Pig clinging to her shoulders.

Aiya turned a scowl on the girl. "I told you to stay below."

Max snorted. "And when has that ever worked?"

Whatever words Aiya had lined up to deliver died on her tongue, and she pressed her fingers into her eyes. "Fine, just... stay back."

Kagos approached the parapet, his obsidian gaze fixed on the dragons. They were so small compared to Kagos's true form, Hal suspected they were no more than a few years old.

Still watching the group through the long glass, Hal spotted the moment the dragons, aiming vaguely for the University walls, suddenly arrowed sharply towards them.

"I have instructed them to land here." Kagos spoke calmly, but it was the icy calm laid over quiet rage. His eyes flashed as one of the dragons — the green — careened abruptly to the side, as if the sudden change of direction had thrown it off. "They are young. Untrained. And injured."

"How can you tell they're untrained?" Hal asked.

"It is like talking to a child that has been raised among wolves. Be prepared. They will not be as civilised as I am." Aiya raised a quiet eyebrow, but said nothing. Max stared intently at the incoming dragons.

"They're all hurt." Her face twisted in distress.

Kagos's face darkened further. "This is why we wiped out blood sorcerers centuries ago."

"Well, looks like you missed some." Hal backed away from the parapet. "Here they come."

The dragons tumbled out of the sky onto the tower roof, landing in a tangle of wings and talons. There were six of them, not one the same colour as another, and all different sizes, ranging from about five feet long, to the ten-foot-long beast that carried the girl on his back.

Kagos reached for the girl, but was forced to retreat when the red snapped at his hand. He hissed in reproach, but the red only snarled back.

"Sanctuary!" the girl cried, sliding down from her mount, chest heaving. Her thick black hair was cropped short, revealing a heart-shaped face a shade of mocha many people of the desert south shared. A headband that had once been white crossed her brow, now smeared with streaks of soot. "Please! We seek sanctuary!" Her accent was thick, but her words were clear.

"And why would we grant sanctuary to one who holds dragons captive and sends armies against this city?" Kagos's voice lowered to a rumble that echoed of boulders tumbling into bottomless ravines.

"Kagos..." Hal warned. But the dragons replied with their own cacophony of snarls and hissing.

The girl placed her hand on the largest dragon's neck, and as one they quieted, the only sign of hostility the swirling storms in their matching bronze eyes. Sweat ran down her face, as if something was causing her pain.

"This is my family." The girl met Kagos's obsidian gaze with one of steadfast amber. "We have been held captive, together, by the Brotherhood." She stroked a hand down the dragon's neck. "As stock." She glanced back at the group assembled behind her. "They are injured. The Brotherhood have never cared for their wellbeing, as long as they could bleed us." She looked to Hal, her eyes hazing slightly. "Please. We only want to be free of them. Allow me to care for my family, and we will be on our way."

Kagos made a derisive sound in the back of his throat. "Dragons belong in Hearthstone."

"How 'bout we work the details *after* you've seen to your dragons?" Hal glared at Kagos, willing him to drop the hostility.

"I know where there's room." Aiya stepped forward, her hand subtly brushing Kagos's arm as she passed. "Max, fetch some supplies from the infirmary and meet us in the botany courtyard."

Max leapt forward, Pig squawking a protest from her shoulder.

The girl's amber eyes tracked her across the roof until she disappeared down the steps.

"What's your name, girl?" Aiya asked, ignoring Kagos's scowl burning a hole into her back.

The girl breathed as if she'd just sprinted across the battlefield. "Jade."

"Well, Jade," Aiya held out her hand. "Welcome to Throldon."

Hal blew out a breath when they finally left to tend to the new dragons, taking their undercurrent of tension and distrust with them. He ran a hand through his disheveled hair, scanning the skies for any more surprises. Laina was still tending to their own wounded in the infirmary. How was he going to tell her all of this?

He needn't have worried. Rumour took care of that for him.

Laina found him in the map room later that night.

"Fae was here?" His head whipped up so fast his neck cracked. In the flickering candlelight, the shadows under her eyes looked as if some divine sculptor had carved them there. Her skirts were streaked with blood, but her hands were scrubbed clean. She leaned against the doorjamb, her shoulders slumped with exhaustion. This was a side that she would never show anyone else.

Hal took all of her in, and saw the steel glinting behind her weary gaze. He nodded.

She folded into a chair, dropping her head into her hands. "Is she alright?"

Lines bracketed his face as he watched her: a mother who'd had to give up her only child once before, who'd seen that child throw herself into danger to save her people, and who could no longer do anything to protect her.

"She's not in the southern camp anymore," he said. He didn't know if Fae was alright. He hoped so.

Laina let out a sound that could have been a laugh as much as a sob. She looked up at him, silver lining her eyes in the candlelight. "Is everything they're saying true?"

Hal nodded. "Probably. Seen some strange things today, Laina. How 'bout you?"

She waved a hand. "As you'd expect." She leaned forward over the table. "Tell me about Fae."

They stayed up until pink stained the sky, Hal recounting everything he'd seen. Laina's hands came up to cover her face when he told her of Fae facing a giant of a man alone on the field. But she stopped him when he described how the ground had rippled beneath Fae at the end.

"The quake came *from* her?"

"Aye." Hal ran a hand across his beard. "Which begs plenty more questions."

Laina shook her head, eyes wide. "Not at all — it explains everything." Hal raised a questioning eyebrow, and she held up a finger before he could ask how. "You wouldn't remember, because you were busy bleeding out on the floor, but when Fae faced Black, a storm filled the Great Hall, with wind and lightning. And that was when the earth first moved."

Hal nodded. He'd heard the stories, even though he hadn't been conscious to see it himself. "But she said she lost her powers."

"Clearly not." Laina stood, and paced to the window. The first rays of day reached in to paint her face with golden light. She thrust her hands through her unbound hair, letting out a growl of frustration. "Where is she now?"

The question wasn't directed at him, but he rose and came to stand behind her, gently disengaging her fingers. "I don't know. But she's safe as she's going to be for now." Laina whirled, scanning his face, and he shrugged. "Kagos seemed to think the Magi knew what he was doin'. And he did pull her out of that camp. Not sure I know anyone else as could've done the same."

Laina nodded, her eyes drifting in contemplation. "The Magi... Luca, right?" He nodded. She turned to rest her head against his shoulder. He brought his arms up around her.

"I let her go once before," she murmured into his chest. "I can't stand to lose her again."

Hal closed his eyes. "I know." He held her close, until the sounds of the city waking pulled them back to their duties.

After three days of waiting for the other shoe to drop, a flurry of activity was sighted in the enemy camp.

Hal bounded up the stairs to the tower, almost snatching the long glass from Yvonne on watch.

"They're packing up." Kagos stood with his hands tucked into his sleeves by the wall, his superior vision having no need of the glass. Aiya and Max had taken on caring for the southern girl, Jade, and her dragons. They'd commandeered an empty livery yard on the outskirts of the Trade District to house the beasts, and the girl had insisting on staying with them.

Bringing the long glass to his eye, Hal stepped up beside Ty, silently watching the enemy camp.

Aren and Stef stood to one side, keen eyes tracking the activity. They'd spent the last few days helping wherever they could: shifting rubble, rebuilding walls, carrying bodies. They shouldered the burdens of Throldon's people as if they were their own.

"Doesn't make much sense." Jesse crouched atop the parapet, daring gravity to snatch her. Laina was trying not to watch. "Why march all the way here, only to leave after one day of fighting?" Her dark eyes narrowed. "They've got the numbers, and the advantage. We're sitting ducks here." The dwarf turned and lowered herself to sit facing them on the wall, her legs swinging a good few inches from the floor. "What gives?"

Hal studied the camp through the long glass. "I don't like this."

Kagos rumbled his agreement.

"Where are they going?" Laina asked, rubbing her arms despite the sun's heat reflecting off the tower stones. "They're not going back south."

Indeed, as the canvases slowly dismantled, the column of troops did not retreat back the way they'd come, but began to snake across the horizon, curving west around the city.

"They found something bigger to conquer." Hal frowned, his jaw working. "What?"

"Our own Spiritchild." All heads turned to stare at Kagos, the dragon's obsidian gaze fixed on the moving army.

"Okay." Aren drew out the word, exchanging a glance with his brother. "But how do they even know where she went? I suppose we all saw the Magi take her north, but beyond that...?" He held his hands out to either side with a shrug. "She might as well have disappeared."

Kagos breathed deep, as if unwilling to admit what he was about to share.

"Kagos." Ty's voice held an edge Hal hadn't heard there before.

Finally, Kagos turned. "Blood magic." He waited a second for the implications to sink in. They'd all heard a version of Jade's history, although even her knowledge of the Brotherhood's operations was patchy at best. "They're tracking her from her kills." He gestured towards the giant bloodstain that no one dared enter.

"They can do that?" Aren's face paled, silver eyes darting to the scar in the land.

"They can do much worse if they get their hands on a Magi." Kagos buried his hands deeper into the sleeves of his robe. "There are different ways of manipulating magic. Blood sorcerers use the power contained within the blood of a living thing to power their spells. The more powerful the source, the more powerful the spell." His face flashed with rage. "Once, the most coveted source would have been a dragon. I imagine that is what drew them from the desert in the first place. Hearthstone has long been known as home to the last of the dragons, and an adult of our kind, never mind an ancient, would put the power of those six younglings in the shade. But a Magi? One with the power our Spiritchild demonstrated on the battlefield? I doubt anyone could stop a sorcerer with her blood at their disposal. And if what that southern girl claims is true, and we are facing their strongest practitioners..." He trailed off, and for the first time, Hal saw a flicker of worry behind his eyes.

"We need to find her!" Laina sounded on the edge of hysteria, her calm facade cracking at this new horror.

"*How* do we find her?" Aren said, voicing the single biggest obstacle.

"I can take you."

They turned to find Jade standing at the top of the steps, Aiya and Max at her back.

47

A BRAID OF SEVEN THREADS

The old dragon hissed at her, actually *hissed*, his disapproval clear.

She didn't know how Alpha had known the tall, dark-skinned figure who looked both like a man and also nothing like one was a dragon, but he assured her he was. A question for another time.

Either way, Jade didn't have time to indulge him. She'd underestimated Kohl.

The blood bond pulled at all of them: the dragons, and her. Everything was an effort. Her limbs dragged as if she walked through water instead of a city of paved streets and free people. Sweat beaded on her brow now despite the cooler northern climes. The effort of speaking, of *breathing*, felt as though an anvil pressing down on her chest.

But she'd escaped. They'd escaped. They were free of him. Even if this weight plagued them for the rest of their lives, it was worth it. Even if it had already taken them two days to adjust to the new burden of their unwanted tether.

It was as well that they had each other to lean on, a braided rope of their seven threads tied together to pull against the one of blood and oil.

Fire flashed across the dragon-man's eyes of purest obsidian. "If you think I will allow you to use those younglings beyond what they have already endured at your hands, then you have not understood my intentions clearly enough." His slit-like nostrils flared in fury.

"I have told you already, they are my family." The words came out laboured, her teeth gritted. "I have no more compelled them to my side than a flower has compelled the sun to shine on it."

"Then tell me how you come to have not one, but six at your disposal." His voice lowered to a dangerous rumble, as if he'd found the hole in her story.

Jade's legs shook, and she slid down to sit on a stone ledge beside the stairs. "I was there when they hatched. They are as much mine as I am theirs."

The woman behind her gasped — Aiya. She'd been nice to her. Had helped her care for her family.

Max, the girl, glanced at her sharply. "Does that mean...?"

But Aiya was looking straight at the dragon-man. Kagos, if Jade remembered correctly. She'd been almost delirious with the flight and the maddening pull of the bond upon her arrival. As soon as they'd reached the stables the dragons now rested in, she'd seen to it that they were safely taken care of, before collapsing in the straw.

Aiya's creamy brown skin paled as, quietly shaken, she said, "I would hear her story."

Kagos's face was unreadable, but he made a gesture that might have been a shrug.

Max certainly took it as such, and crouched beside her. "What happened to you?" The tiny dragon that normally clutched at her shoulders scrambled onto the ledge to curled up in Jade's lap, wide copper eyes whirling curiously.

Jade absently scratched beneath the hatchling's jaw, and those eyes closed with a hum of satisfaction.

"As long as I can remember, I've been working one way or another," she began. "My family was the other children who worked beside me to afford the next meal. It was always a transient group. Always changing." She took a heavy breath, pushing against the pressure that squatted over her chest. "My last employer, before the Brotherhood, dealt in crystals and gemstones. The most valuable of these are always the hardest to reach. There was an underground cave system he suspected of having rich gemstone deposits. It was tight. I was the only one small enough to make it through. The cave collapsed while I was inside." Sweat slid down her temples, even though the memory had long ago lost its hold over her. In the initial months after getting free, she had woken in the night drenched in sweat, believing herself to still be trapped down there.

She swallowed thickly, using the pause to take a breath. "The rockslide revealed a hidden cavern, untouched for decades. Maybe longer." Her fingers stilled as she recalled the moment she first laid eyes on the clutch. The draw she'd felt to the eggs, as if they called to her.

The hatchling in her lap chirped a protest, and she resumed her petting of it. "The second I saw the eggs, I couldn't keep away from them." She lifted her eyes to meet those of the girl beside her, the one who'd undoubtedly been through the same thing, given how the tiny dragon clung to her. "The instant they hatched, I knew they were mine to care for. And I would have turned over heaven and earth to do it." A small smile crept across her face at the memories of those early days. Just her and her strange new family as they struggled to get to grips with their tiny bodies, tripping over their wings and leaping off rocky ledges to glide across the cavern. "It wasn't long before they were hungry. I'd run out of things to hunt for them in the caves — insects and the like. But we were trapped."

She looked up at Kagos then. "It was Fearless who found the way out. A hole in the rocks that skinned my entire back to get through. But we got there. They could have left me at any point — they were small enough to get through without me. But they stayed. *They* saved *my* life." Pride that didn't belong to him flitted across the old dragon's face. Her gaze skittered away again. Those were the best days.

"My employer found us." Jade shuddered, and it was nothing to do with the cold. "He took us to the Brotherhood. I never worked out if it was because he didn't know what to do with the dragons, or if he thought he'd cut his losses, or make some quick money." She cringed at the memory of his bloodied body sprawled across his office desk. At the warehouse bloodbath that had been the rest of the workers, witnesses to what the Brotherhood now had in their possession.

"The first thing they did was take our blood. But it didn't take them long to realise they could just threaten one of us, and the others would fall into line." She tipped her head back. She didn't think she would ever tire of seeing the open sky above her. "We've been kept in the Brotherhood's Sanctum since that day. Me in a windowless cell, with an iron door. My family locked in *cages*." She snarled the words, as if even uttering them was intolerable. "Underground. Barred from ever seeing the sky they were born for." A true tear slid down her face at how they had been denied their instinct to soar. How Delita had never had the sun glint off her silver scales. How Chary and Brave had never played in the rain. "We were all vialled for our blood. I never fully understood why. Until the Sorcerer Supreme decided to bring me here."

Bringing her gaze back to Kagos, she let the truth of her next words blaze through her eyes even as her breath was as laboured as if she'd run up the steps at her back. "We have dreamed of being free of them for *years*. I made a promise to my family that we would. And I will do what I need to give them back the skies." Finding strength from somewhere, she pushed to her feet, even if her legs shook to stand. "Do not presume to know me, old one. I have faced worse than you."

A stunned silence fell over the tower roof.

"Well damn," Max's quiet declaration coaxed a smile from one of the elves — the one with silver eyes.

The bearded human's gaze flared with a cold fury. "How long?" he rasped. "How long were you their prisoner?"

Jade shrugged, the gesture aching at her shoulders. "Six years. Give or take." She'd stopped counting some time ago, but even in the belly of the Sanctum it was impossible to ignore the passing of seasons.

"Six..." He ran a hand through his hair, his face caught between outrage and horror.

A hand touched her shoulder, and she turned to find Aiya beside her again, but the elf's grey gaze rested on Kagos. "She's a rider." Her tone indicated that this should be obvious to him.

Jade kept her thoughts to herself. As evidenced by her intensely uncomfortable ride across the Thamib Desert with the Sorcerer Supreme, she was anything but a good rider, but it seemed to mean something different to the dragon-man with an inexplicable interest in her family's wellbeing.

Kagos frowned, making a disgruntled sound in his throat. "Riders partner to *one* dragon. Not an entire flight."

"Flight?" Jade glanced between him and Aiya, unfamiliar with the term.

Aiya broke Kagos's gaze and turned to face her. "A group of dragons. Normally a family unit, but not always siblings. Your... family... we'd class them as a flight." She turned back to Kagos, folding her arms. "And that doesn't mean she isn't a rider."

"Coercion is more likely." Kagos drew himself up, his arms buried deep into his sleeves.

Aiya looked as if she might scream at him. "How?" She took a step toward him, her long, black braid swinging behind her. The others stepped back. "How can you see this as anything other than what it is? Those younglings *defend* her. They wouldn't do that if she was their captor."

Kagos's lips pressed into a thin line. His eyes narrowed, and Aiya frowned.

Jade knew that look. They were talking mind to mind, the way she did with her... flight. The word felt foreign but it fit well, even if hers had only taken to the skies the once.

One of the elves — tall, with golden-yellow hair and storm-grey eyes — edged closer to her. "Do you mean it?" His brows knitted tightly together, something like anguish darkening his gaze. "Can you find where she went?"

Jade stared at him. Someone shifted behind him, and she glanced up to see the human woman watching them intently. There was something in the shape of her mouth, the angle of her eyes. Fae's mother, perhaps. Beside her, the bearded man hovered nearby, watching.

Her eyes sketched across all of them: the humans like her, the elves, the dwarf.

She belonged to none of these people. But they all seemed to belong to each other somehow. The way she had once with the other children of Pharro.

She could not allow Kohl to get his hands on Fae. And if this mismatched group wanted to help her...

Jade nodded, dragging her gaze back to the blond elf before her. "I can — the dragons can track the sorcerers' magic. If they're using it to track Fae, we can follow the... disturbance in turn." The crackle in the air. The unbearable grate against the senses that Alpha had mentioned.

Her eyes flicked to Kagos. "I'm surprised you don't feel it."

The dragon-man stilled. As one, the others on the roof turned to look at him.

Aiya lifted a brow. "Kagos?"

He scowled at her tone, but said, "I'll admit that when the sorcerers stepped onto the battlefield, their incessant droning got under my scales. Felt wrong." The liquid obsidian of his eyes slid to Jade. "But I will not endanger Hearthstone by exposing myself to them."

Jade struggled to contain her dark laugh. "It's too late for that." She took a step towards him, her legs dragging through molasses. "Kohl has had his sights set on Hearthstone since before he left Pharro. Likely before the Eminence even thought to march on the north. He wants dragons. Old dragons. Powerful dragons, so that he won't need mine anymore." She didn't bother to hide the shudder that ran through her. "He wants power. And he won't stop until he has total dominance." She'd felt it the first time he'd used her blood against her. How he revelled in his control over her. How he only hungered for more.

"How did you get away?"

Jade stumbled to a halt.

Kagos stalked towards her, a gleam in his eye. "You can hardly stand, you're sweating, and panting like a race horse." He stopped barely two paces from her, his eyes narrowing as the dampness on her brow chilled. "It might have been a century or two, but I'll never forget what blood compulsion looks like." He leaned in, and grimaced as his nostrils flared. "And you're right — I can smell it on you. So tell us: how can we trust you?"

Jade swallowed thickly. Sweat dripped down her back. She balled her hands into fists in an effort to stop them trembling, squeezed her eyes shut to try and reclaim any semblance of control over her body, but it was as if acknowledging the blood bond had strengthened its hold over her. Simply standing there seemed an impossible feat.

"Kohl has my blood," she gasped. "A tiny vial he wears on a bracelet. He has one for each of us. I didn't know how hard it would be to fight. To walk away." But the reason she fought, those precious six bonds within her, reminded her why she stood here, in front of a crotchety old dragon-man. She opened her eyes. "But I made a promise. So I fight."

"How do we know this isn't exactly what this Kohl wants?" A single, darkly arched brow.

She let out a heavy breath, exhaustion almost drowning her voice as she answered. "Because there's no way he'd give up his best power source. Just walk away. Not unless he had his sights set on something better."

Turning to the others arrayed behind her, she reached out a hand. "You said you wanted to help Fae. I can help you find her. What more do you need?"

"Why do you want to help?" The dark-haired elf with polished steel in his eyes stepped forward.

Jade sagged. "Because besides not wanting anyone to suffer through what we have suffered, Kohl won't stop with Fae. He won't stop until he has *all* the power." She turned back to Kagos. "He'll still go after Hearthstone." She remembered his fervour when he'd talked about them back in Pharro, and couldn't suppress the shudder that ran through her at the memory. "I wouldn't wish the last six years of my life on anyone. He is twisted and dark inside, and if he begins collecting more power... I would spare the world from his brand of horrors."

The rooftop fell quiet at last, the only sound the gentle sigh of wind in her ears.

Max jiggled impatiently on the balls of her feet, looking as if she wanted to explode with her opinion on the matter. Aiya and Kagos appeared to be having an intense, silent aside. The bearded man reached out to touch the woman's back. The dwarf watched them all with cunning dark eyes, waiting for the rest to reach their decision.

The tall, golden-haired elf exchanged a look with the others, his grey gaze meeting with each of theirs before he turned back to her.

"How many can you carry?"

48

DORMANT

It took three days for Luca to carry Fae back to La'sa.

He called the winds to bear them hundreds, maybe thousands of miles without rest. Fae slept in his arms, his body strong and warm against her cheek. They stopped only for water, and to relieve themselves, exchanging barely more than a glance before taking to the skies again.

Luca hadn't uttered another word since they'd flown over the battlefield. Fae didn't have any words to give him anyway.

In her waking moments, her mind replayed the gush of blood over her hands as she slit the first soldier's throat, the sound of a hundred ice darts striking flesh and armour, the look in a soldier's eyes as the life left them.

In her snatched moments of broken sleep, she felt the power rush through her again and again, her own efforts powerless to stop it. Powerless to stop the slaughter.

She saw Throldon's walls crumble around her. Felt the heat of her inferno. Heard the roar of the river as it rose up like a great water dragon beside her. And saw blood bloom across the landscape like a giant flower of death.

She woke drenched in sweat every time. If Luca noticed it — or the way her body thrashed awake in his arms — he didn't mention it. He held her wordlessly, his presence a solid reassurance against the wide open sky all around them, their only witnesses the stars and moons above.

The green plains of Arland became rolling hills, and then scratchy tundra, before finally, the snow-dusted Ice Fields stretched out ahead.

Luca brought them down outside the gates of La'sa, the silver and steel shimmering almost golden in the setting sun.

Madja waited for them, her silver mane wilder than usual, as if she'd run fretful hands through it over and over again, her eyes red-rimmed and puffy. She dashed over the instant Luca set down. Arissa followed closely behind with two healers Fae didn't recognise. They carried a stretcher between them, and assessed her condition with practiced eyes.

Fae wasn't ready to be given over to their care. Wasn't ready to leave the blissful quiet of the skies yet.

Wasn't ready to face what had happened.

What she'd done.

As if reading her thoughts, Luca's arms tightened around her.

"I've got her." His voice echoed in her ear, pressed against his chest. Someone argued, she didn't hear who. Luca's answering growl quieted any further disagreements. His steps didn't slow, and soon they were enveloped by the cool blue ice of the mountain.

He took her straight to her room, as if he knew.

Knew that she couldn't answer the questions that would surely follow. That they would send her back to that unstoppable power spiral.

And the corona of blood.

He sat her on the bed, where she stared vacantly ahead, not seeing the people who gathered around her. Not able to explain it to them.

How could they even want her back here when she'd caused so much death?

Strong fingers tipped her chin back until she was looking into eyes of deepest indigo.

Luca held her with his gaze, searching the depths of her own.

The power that normally prowled behind his eyes lay dormant. Watching her too.

Then he stood, breaking the contact, and she was left drifting.

Voices conversed in subdued tones beyond her door.

"No questions." Luca's low voice rasped against her senses. "I've done what I could, but her injuries need reassessing."

Something in Fae registered his words as if from a distance. *What had he done?* They hadn't stopped to bind her leg, or set her arm. If she thought about it, none of it hurt as much as it should. She'd put it down to shock. There'd certainly been enough of that.

Someone mumbled a response, and then Luca crouched before her again.

"Drink this." He handed her a cup of something that smelled bitter and chalky at the same time. "It'll put you out. So the healers can look at your wounds." She gulped it down, barely registering the awful taste. If it stopped her mind spinning, stopped the battlefield from haunting her, she'd drink it a hundred times over.

Wordlessly, Luca took the empty cup from her, then helped her to lift her legs onto the mattress.

She lay back onto the pillows, and waited for the sedative to sweep her under.

And the last thing she saw, before the soothing blackness enveloped her, was the naked worry on Luca's face.

Fae spent days drifting in and out of pain. The torn mess of her leg burned like fire. The arrow wound in her arm itched horribly. But her shoulder ached so intensely that waves of nausea roiled through her with every breath.

She deserved it. She deserved worse.

She woke one morning to find she wasn't alone.

At the end of the bed, her feet propped on the covers, Irya leaned back in the chair, her blind eyes trained on the ceiling, autumn hair hanging in loose waves behind her.

Fae watched her friend, wondering what, in Eah'lara, her gaze was fixed on. The question floated to the front of her mind. She opened her mouth to ask it.

And stopped.

What would she say, when Irya inevitably asked how she was? What happened? Was she alright?

Was she alright?

Fae closed her eyes.

No. She wasn't alright.

. . .

She woke again to the pain in her shoulder, now radiating down her arm to pulse in her fingertips. Unlike before, the ache did not allow her to drift off again, but throbbed an unrelenting drumbeat down her entire left side.

Fae shifted in an attempt to alleviate the pain. Hissed when a sharp flash forked across her chest instead.

The door opened just as she attempted to shimmy up the bed, the task made all the more difficult by only having half her limbs functioning.

Arissa entered, nudging the door closed with her hip, a tray occupying both hands.

"Fae!" She exclaimed softly, setting the tray down and rushing over to help. Careful of Fae's injuries, she helped her into a sitting position, propping cushions behind her back. "I'm so glad you're awake! I was beginning to wonder if we'd gotten your dose wrong." She dragged over the chair to perch on its edge. "How are you feeling?"

Fae winced as twin spears of pain shot across her chest and down her arm. "Like someone sawed my arm off and did a piss-poor job of sewing it back on."

Arissa grimaced. "Your shoulder was a mess when you got back. We had to remove three splinters of bone that were shattered from your shoulder blade. But the rest has started healing nicely around the injury. The pain should improve soon." She nodded to Fae's bandaged thigh lying atop the sheets. "How about the leg?"

Fae flexed it experimentally, feeling only a dull ache, deep in the muscle. "Surprisingly good." Her stomach twisted as she recalled what had been done to it. As her mind replayed the sound of muscle tearing under the interrogator's tools.

Arissa nodded. "You might have a delay to full function with that one. The damage was quite... extensive." She smiled reassuringly. "But the *assvissi* in the tincture we've been giving you will help." Reaching across to the tray, she passed over another cup of foul-smelling liquid. "Here." Fae wrinkled her nose, and she laughed. "I know, but it has incredible healing properties."

Taking the cup with a dubious scowl, Fae toasted her. "Cheers." She knocked back the tincture in one swallow, shuddering as the taste lingered in her mouth. "Eah, that is vile."

Arissa took the cup from her, replacing it with another. "That's why I brought some chocolate as well."

Fae hummed with pleasure, and cupped the steaming mug between her hands. "I knew you were my favourite." She took a sip, eyes drifting closed to better appreciate the rich flavours of the chocolate. Resting the cup in her lap, she caught Arissa's watchful gaze. "What?"

"Nothing," she said too quickly.

"Arissa."

Arissa's face twisted.

"What is it?"

She hesitated a moment longer before saying, "Luca said we're not to ask."

Fae stilled. "Oh." Was it because he didn't want them to know she was a murderer now? That she'd killed friends as well as foe? Was it because she'd willingly thrown herself into a situation where she had no hope of controlling her magic? Where she'd surely only made the fractures in the earth worse?

The cup in her hands suddenly felt ice-cold and her head filled with the drone of a thousand flies as guilt, shame, and horror swarmed her.

Arissa reached over to grasp her hand. "We've all been so worried. I'm just glad you're alright." She fidgeted, as if she was desperate to say more. "If... If something happened with your magic... You know you can talk to us. Taniq, Rylan, or me. Right?" Her pale blue eyes were wide and earnest as they held Fae's.

And Fae didn't have the heart to tell her she couldn't.

49

DARKEST MOMENTS

Fae endured a slew of visitors once it became known she was awake.

Madja arrived shortly after Arissa, and immediately burst into tears. Alarmed, Fae reassured her that she was alright — a lie — and apologised repeatedly for worrying her.

Taniq and Rylan dropped by whenever Arissa was busy at the Healing House, and updated her on the latest gossip around La'sa, despite Fae not knowing most of the people they talked about. She pinned a smile on her face, nodding at appropriate points in the conversation, counting down the minutes until they had to leave. They were trying to help, but she didn't deserve it.

When Sheree bustled in to change the bed sheets, she brought with her a children's game.

"I'm not a child," Fae said when she explained what it was, and arched a curious eyebrow.

Sheree smiled with tired eyes. "I know, dear. But you are still new to the magics." She waved at the contents of the box as Fae emptied it out onto the bed. There was a large wooden board carved with a circuit of winding grooves, and a smaller box that opened out like a drawer, divided into five sections. "Most Magi children grow up with games like this to practice control of their elements. I thought you might find it interesting."

Fae plucked each item from the drawer to inspect, one at a time. Her

313

eyes widened as she understood. Returning her attention to the board, she identified the divots — one at each of the four corners, and two nearer the centre — rounded out to hold a miniature representation of each element from the drawer: a stoppered thimble of sand for earth, a small vial of water, a tiny tinder and flint to light a fire, and a downy feather for air. A central groove was for the last item: a mirrored disc. The mirrored side would face the corner in which the tiny fire would be lit, reflecting light. The back of the disc would then be cast in shadow, for dark.

"The aim of the game is to trace the grooves in the board with your chosen element," Sheree explained simply. "The first to complete a full circuit without leaving the channels, wins. If you lose control of your element, you must start again. That's the skill. The more adept the players, the more tactics get involved." She smiled. "It's quite fun really."

It was beautiful.

But the idea of drawing any of her elements to so much as lift the feather made Fae want to retch.

She smiled weakly up at Sheree. "It's lovely. Thank you."

Sheree simply nodded. "You need anything, you know where I am. You'll need to exercise those legs soon if I'm any judge of these things."

She was right, and Fae was avoiding it. It had been two days since she'd woken fully. Her thigh was healing so well she forgot about it until she went to stand, and then all she felt was a wrench in the muscles. Painful, but not debilitating. The pain in her shoulder was becoming more manageable too, and she'd stopped taking Arissa's tonics for it. The wound in her arm had healed before she'd even woken.

As the door slid closed behind Sheree, Fae swung her legs off the bed and stood, bracing for the twinge in her thigh.

Limping across to the bathing room, she ran a tub of hot water, and eased herself into it. The heat was blissful as it permeated her muscles, her skin tingling like tiny needles as she soaked. But even the steam couldn't chase away the dread and tension coiled inside her. She rested her head back against the edge of the tub, playing her fingers through the water to break the quiet that reminded her too much of the stunned silence of the battlefield.

By the time she hauled herself from the bath, the water had cooled. She wrapped one enormous towel around her body, using another to wring the water from her hair.

She stepped back into the bedroom to find some fresh clothes.

And found Irya sitting cross-legged on the bed.

The Echo cocked her head, but said nothing, waiting for Fae to speak first.

But she didn't know what to say to her. Irya already knew where she'd gone. What she'd faced.

She settled on, "Have you spoken to Luca?"

Irya straightened, unfolding her legs. "I have. And he's told me the same thing he's told everyone else."

Fae snorted. "No questions."

"Mhm." A pause while Fae rifled through the wardrobe. "Are you alright?"

Fae froze.

Power rushing through her.

A giant bloody splatter around her. Pieces of human flesh.

The eerie stillness of the battlefield.

"No."

She pulled out some clean leggings, and an oversized jumper that cocooned her in warmth and softness. It was grey, just like her mood.

Irya waited while she pulled the clothes on. The leggings were tight but supportive around her leg. The jumper was soft against her shoulder.

"Can I help?"

Fae combed her fingers through her hair, and began braiding it from her crown.

Irya had done nothing wrong. In fact, she was the only one who'd thought to even tell her about what was happening in Throldon.

But she couldn't bear the thought of how her friend might look at her if she knew.

Fae tied off the end of the braid.

"No."

Irya let out a breath and ran a hand through her own hair, loose down her back.

"Okay." She stood to leave. "I'm here. If you need."

Fae nodded. "Actually..." A thought occurred to her. One that had her chest constricting in panic. She tried to breathe around it. "Can you find people? Can you tell if they're alright?"

Irya's blind eyes saw right through her. "They're alright, Fae." She stepped forward, reaching out to squeeze Fae's good arm. "I watched until you were clear. Your family is safe."

Fae flinched at Irya's words. That meant she'd seen. But she'd also thought to check on her family for her. "All of them?" Irya nodded, and she didn't question how she knew who they were. The Magi had been watching Fae long before she got to La'sa. "And the army?"

"They've retreated for now."

Fae heaved a sigh. At least she'd bought them some time. "Thank you."

Irya watched her. "What will you do now?"

Fae's rueful smile was more of a grimace. "No questions, remember?"

Irya's laugh came out soft and quick, a tiny puff of wind. Then she flung her arms around Fae.

"I'm so glad you're okay."

Fae's arms came up slowly to hold her friend.

Her hands felt filthy despite the bath, her conscience far from clear.

Fae waited until Irya left her rooms before she hobbled her way into the Warrens.

Arissa had left her a walking stick, which she leaned on gratefully. Even so, her leg throbbed within minutes.

She was desperate for some fresh air. To see the sky. But she couldn't stand the thought of facing the stares, the questions that lingered in their eyes even if they wouldn't voice them aloud. She turned back down the corridor, following it deeper into the mountain until it brought her to the quiet eastern quadrant.

Knocking on the Dreamweaver's door, she gazed out over the unblemished white that stretched as far as the eye could see beyond the clear ice wall. A wintery gust blew curls of snow across the landscape, the flakes glittering in the sunlight.

Fae rested her forehead against the ice, letting it cool her even as her skin warmed the surface, melting small droplets to run down the wall.

It was so peaceful. She could see why Athanasius had chosen quarters here, as far from the bustling population of La'sa as he could get.

She sighed, and pushed open the door to his apartment.

Light streamed in through the ice. Fresh flowers bloomed in a vase on the counter. The fireplace was cold and swept. The tea pot and cups were clean and stowed neatly away on a shelf.

Ignoring it all, Fae limped through the living area, and down the hallway branching from it. The door she was looking for was wedged open, a scrap of cloth stuffed beneath the corner. She leant her stick against the opposite wall, and slowly pushed the door open.

The Dreamweaver was where she'd last seen him, huddled in the corner of his padded room, his knees drawn up to his chest. But when his hazel eyes flicked up to her, they were clear.

A sad smile pulled at his lips, and he opened his arms to her.

Without a word, Fae lowered herself to the floor, and tucked herself into his side.

The Dreamweaver held her close, cupping her head to his shoulder.

And in the quiet, in the dark, the tears poured in rivers down her face, and a high-pitched keening clawed its way out of her chest.

"Shh." Athanasius stroked her hair, rocking them side to side. "There now. It is in our darkest moments that our souls find the strength to face the demons within. And there, at the very bottom, is the stage on which we might fight them."

Fae's sobs tore through her in jagged rasps. She knew what demons haunted her. Her need to help, to protect, had led her to hurt, to kill.

And she couldn't see how she would ever wash the stain of char and blood from her soul.

She stayed with Ath until the sobs dried out, her throat scraping like sand when she went to speak.

He patted her knee where it leaned against his, and she lifted her head to meet his gaze.

"Your fear consumes you again, but it is different this time." He cocked his head, bird-like, his collar bones cutting like blades against his skin. His eyes slid out of focus, as if he was seeing *through* her. "The threads are tangled. Like a serpents' nest, all coiled around each other, choking and squeezing." His sunken eyes came back to meet hers again with piercing intellect. "What happened?"

Fae drew in a great, shuddering breath. "I lost control." Her eyes squeezed shut against the memory of being once again powerless while her magics slipped her grasp. "People died."

"Ah."

Behind closed eyes, Fae trembled at the pity in his tone. Almost like he'd expected this of her. Her brows knitted together in an effort to quell the wave of shame that crested over her.

And then a gentle finger lifted her chin. "Look at me." She opened her eyes.

"If you allow this fear to consume you, death will follow. You must become stronger than it. Own your fear. Make it cower before you, or you will become the very thing you fear to be."

The steel in his words took the breath from her. His eyes, clear and bright, saw right into the heart of her, and plucked the core of her fear out for her to look at. She wanted to protect her family, the way she hadn't been able to as a child. But she couldn't bear the idea of becoming like the animals that had beaten her father to death and driven the Aethyr to wisp her away from her mother. The thugs that had shot Immrith in the back. That had nearly killed Hal. Nearly killed her.

The Dreamweaver tipped his head back and gazed at the ceiling as if he could see through it to the sky. A small smile pulled at his cracked lips. "The sun and stars may shine above, but true light comes from within." He leaned forward and jabbed her in the chest. "Find your light, Spiritchild. And make it shine." His gaze shone with such fervour that she nodded even though she didn't have the faintest idea how to do what he was asking. Or what, exactly, he meant.

But before she could ask him, the fog drifted over his eyes, and he retreated back into the existence of her nightmares.

50

LOCKED DOORS

Despite the Dreamweaver's words, Fae couldn't bring herself to face the outside world. Sheree brought her meals from the kitchen. Arissa brought her tonics from the Healing House. Madja came and fussed over her at least twice a day.

Luca stayed away.

Sheree's game set rested on the desk at the foot of her bed. Every now and again, she found her gaze pulled toward it like a lodestone, as if something inside her wanted — needed — to try. But every time, she recoiled from the idea of letting her element-aspects out. Of releasing the most dangerous parts of her.

So she sat in the dark, and wondered what light Ath thought a monster like her might find.

She was massaging one of Arissa's ointments into her leg, when Terrence barged into her rooms.

"Come on," he said without preamble. "We've waited long enough. Madja may be content to coddle you, but I will not."

Fae jerked upright at his tone. Terrence was always composed. His training consisted of breathing and meditation. Until now, it seemed.

"Come on," he repeated at her shock, waving impatiently, apparently unfazed by the bare length of her exposed thigh.

She replaced the ointment jar on the side and eased her leggings back up over her hips. "What's the rush?"

Terrence frowned incredulously. "You're joking."

Fae stood and grabbed the walking stick from where it leant against the bed frame. "Sorry...?"

The High Magi let out a sound like a disgruntled horse, his beard shifting around his lips. "Follow me."

He led a brutal pace through the Warrens, unconcerned for her limping along behind, and took them to the Core.

Where she stopped dead.

She hadn't seen the town centre since Luca carried her through. And she'd been in no state to notice then.

"That last quake echoed through existing fractures in the earth, causing unprecedented aftershocks that reached across the world. We checked. This isn't the worst of it."

Fae stared slack-jawed at the remains of La'sa.

A black fissure the shape of a lightning bolt had almost completely cleaved the northern quadrant from its eastern neighbour. Rubble was piled up against the mountain walls, the splintered wreckage of cabins mixed in with the stone. All across the Core, structures had collapsed under the repeated movements of the ground beneath their foundations. Fountains lay crumbled into the frozen pools they once stood over. A shop roof was caved in over there. An uprooted tree had crushed another where it fell.

Fae's ears hollowed out. She had done this. Simply by not being strong enough to leash the power in her.

"Let's go." Terrence's gruff voice broke her from her shock.

She planted her feet. "No."

He turned. "What?"

"Every time I summon earth it ends in disaster." She waved a hand around at the damage. "How can you possibly still believe that I'm the solution?"

Even as short as he was, the look he gave her then made her feel six inches tall.

"Because we have *no other options*." He advanced on her, the golden brown of his skin that spoke of some ancient southern heritage flushed with... Anger? Frustration? Desperation? "Either we do nothing, and the earth falls apart anyway, or we do something. Anything." He thrust a finger in her face. "*You* do something."

Fae shook her head. "I can't wield earth. You know that. The only times I have, are when I lose control. I could kill someone." Saying it out loud made her feel physically sick.

Terrence frowned. "That's fear talking."

Fae gasped. What had the Dreamweaver said to her? *Own your fear. Make it cower before you.*

Do not become the thing you fear to be.

If she didn't try, more people would die. And she would still be a killer.

Clenching her hands into fists so tight she could feel her fingernails cutting into her palms, she nodded, not trusting herself to speak.

"Alright then." Terrence turned, and strode between the ruins of La'sa, through the Warrens, and into the arena, where three more Therasae waited for them. Two Fae recognised from the last time Terrence had brought "structural support", and Taniq.

Fae stopped in her tracks. "Where's Madja?"

"Busy." Terrence avoided her gaze as he took up position at the one compass point not occupied. "We're going to try something different today. I want you to send your awareness straight into the earth itself and see if you can sense the rifts. And if you can, pull them together." He crouched, placing both palms flat against the ground. The Therasae at the other three points mirrored him. "We're here to offer support, but it's your power that will make the difference." He glanced up, eyes as brown as the earth he wielded finally meeting hers. "Ready?"

No. "Yes." This was too quick. She wasn't ready at all. She wasn't even fully healed.

And she was terrified.

But they were running out of time.

She glanced over at Taniq; his eyes were closed, brow furrowed in concentration, a wave of black hair fallen over his forehead.

Own your fear.

She pulled in a long breath. Shook her hands out. Threw her walking stick to the side, and crouched, awkwardly extending her injured leg out in front of her.

Inside, she rifled through her element-aspects like a deck of fortune cards, looking for the right one to draw. Huddled together deep within her, they pressed in close to her heart, as if each one hoped she'd pick another.

As if they knew this was a bad idea.

Earth's form was as clear to her as all of her element-aspects: hulking and solid; slow and stubborn.

Forgoing all attempts at coercion, Fae reached inside herself, grabbed hold of earth like it was a weed, and pulled.

It resisted. It dug in its huge, heavy feet and refused to budge. Earth still didn't trust her.

Fae slammed her hands to the ground, ignoring the bite of shale against skin.

You don't need to trust me, you just need to help me fix what we *broke.* And then instead of pulling her earth-aspect to the surface, she pushed it through her palms, into the ground, sending her awareness with it, searching, seeking.

Earth was much happier being in its native element, but it still fought her all the way, wanting nothing more than to curl up and be left alone. Fae gritted her teeth and kept pushing, shoving her awareness into the ground, into the earth.

She felt every clod of dirt, every buried stone, every tiny piece of sand and silt that made up what lay beneath her feet, each bit slamming against her senses as if she were physically tunnelling down through them.

All the while, earth pulled against her, trumpeting in alarm for her to stop.

And then she felt it.

Great chasms deep in the earth opened up before her senses, huge fissures in the fabric of their world, aching apart, trembling with the effort of trying to hold itself together.

Stifling her shock, Fae threw herself at rifts Terrence's warnings had not adequately prepared her for. But she couldn't wield earth. Never had. Not consciously. The element-aspect she needed most remained unyielding within her, a locked door, and she didn't have the right key. She could press her ear to the door, could peek through the keyhole, but she couldn't walk through. She'd forced it to show her the fractures causing the quakes, but she still couldn't draw it to the surface, to use it as she did the other elements.

Another crack forked away from the largest fissure, another chasm burrowing deeper into the earth, and the tremors intensified.

Distantly, she was aware of voices yelling. Someone calling her name.

As she watched, the fissures widened, the trembling ratcheting up until a deep *crack* thundered through the earth.

She flailed wildly at the rents in the earth, desperately willing them back together.

A hand on her shoulder dragged her roughly back to herself.

She blinked her eyes open, the world rushing back, one sense at a time.

At first, it was just Madja's face in front of her, her blue eyes so wide she could see the whites around them, silver mane powdered in dust.

Then the arena around her came into focus. The walls shook violently. Stone peeled away from the mountain like strips of bark from a tree. Clouds of dust billowed across the floor from where a section of seating had collapsed in a heap of rubble, leaving a valley between the sections left standing.

Sounds came back to her as if she was rising to the surface of a lake.

Madja was shouting.

"—got to get out of here! Move! Now!" She tugged on Fae's arm, half pulling, half lifting her away while Fae reeled. "Go, go!"

On one side of the arena, two of the Therasae limped to the entranceway, their hands held over wounds leaking blood that glared impossibly red against the grey dust hanging in the air. Demilda stood in the archway, beckoning them with urgent arms, her pale green gaze fixed on the trembling walls.

Fae's eyes scanned back across the space, the scene crossing her vision too slowly. The rumble of the earthquake filled her ears. It sounded like a great creature groaning awake after eons of sleep.

Then her gaze snagged on what her subconscious had known was missing.

Terrence and Kallis bent over half a figure lying prone on the ground.

Taniq.

51

NO MORE

Fae wrenched free of Madja's grasp and stumbled into a run. Her feet slid across the shale as she skidded to a stop at the foot of the rubble. Taniq's body was wedged from the waist down beneath the weight of stones that continued to roll down from the mountain walls. His black hair was grey with dust, blood streaked across his temple. Pain ravaged his features.

And then Madja was beside Terrence, their hands outstretched as if to push the rocks away. Magic rippled over the stone in a wash of colour. They stood that way for an eternity while Taniq's face contorted with unimaginable agony. An animal groan scraped past his gritted teeth.

Fae dropped to the ground beside him and found his hand. His grip was an iron clamp around her fingers, but her pain was nothing. Words were worthless. *I'm sorry. Hold on. I'm here.* Nothing seemed adequate. So she held his hand, and let him crush hers.

Finally, with a scraping that reminded Fae of how it sounded when Kagos transformed, the rubble rolled back just far enough for Kallis to pull Taniq free.

Fae gasped at the sight of his legs. Through the tatters of his clothes, fragments of bone protruded in jagged shards from a mess of gritty blood and torn flesh. It made her own leg wound look like a paper cut.

Luca appeared with two healers in tow, and they quickly shifted Taniq onto a stretcher. The sounds of his agony twisted a knife deep into Fae's chest.

"It is time to leave now, fair Fae." Alexi's strong hands steered her from the chaos and into the passageways of the Warrens.

Therasae had interspersed themselves equally along the corridors, their magic shimmering green and bronze over the surface of the ice, holding it steady so the others could escape the arena. How long had her focus been buried underground? How long had these people been here helping?

Alexi walked her out of the nearest exit, and finally the tremors faded, leaving a shocked silence in their wake.

The arena wall that had collapsed was shared with a park on the south side of La'sa. The mountain of rubble appeared even bigger here, stopping only a few feet from the nearest chalet. Inches from destroying yet more of this community that had survived for hundreds of years before she arrived.

Horror filled her veins with ice.

Every time she used her magic, the rifts in the earth worsened.

Every time she used her magic, people got hurt.

People died.

No more. Ignoring Alexi's warnings about structural integrity, ignoring the way Luca's eyes followed her from where he spoke with the healers, Fae marched back the way they'd come.

Terrence and Madja were in the middle of a blazing row in the arena, heedless of the destruction surrounding them.

Upon seeing her, Madja's face softened.

"Fae, thank goodness—"

But Fae was glaring at Terrence.

"I'm done." Her body shook with... adrenaline, anger, guilt, horror. "Enough."

Something like relief passed over Madja's face.

Terrence took a breath to argue.

"No." Fae lifted a tremulous finger at the avalanche of rubble visible through the haze of dust still hanging in the air. "I've tried your training. I've tried helping." She leaned in, her breath a rasp in her ears. "*I am not your solution.*" She straightened, her eyes going once more to the proof of her inability to control earth. "You can't fix me." Turning on her heel, she found herself face to face with Luca. Something like sadness passed behind his eyes, his face otherwise unreadable.

Fae held up a hand before he could speak. "You can't fix me."

She stepped around him, and walked away from the High Magi that had tried to mould her into what they needed her to be.

"No more."

Fae returned to her room, wondering if it was some perverse irony that had kept the mountain from collapsing on top of her already. It was a miracle that Taniq was the worst of the injuries from today.

She dropped her head into her hands. *Taniq.* A steady presence between Rylan's moods and Arissa's fierceness. Humble, calm Taniq, who was quietly but clearly in love with Arissa.

His legs — gods, his *legs.*

She surged to her feet again. She had to see him. Had to know how bad it was. She swallowed thickly. Even in Arolynos, she doubted he would be able to walk again. But the healers here achieved things she'd never been trained in. There was hope. Hope that she hadn't just ruined his life.

Nobody stopped her as she limped across the Core, all too busy with clearing the signs of damage from the town, or knee-deep in repairs.

No one approached her as she stood on the threshold of the Healing House, suddenly unsure if she would be wanted inside. Healers bustled past. A gentle breeze sighed through the herb garden to one side, the only mark of the quakes a few broken windowpanes lying forgotten in the grass.

She was about to turn back when two raised voices made their way around the path towards her. As they drew nearer, she identified their owners.

"I had to try something, Madja!" Terrence's voice was rough with anger. "The longer we sit here waiting, the worse it's getting."

If Terrence was angry, Madja's voice was a study in cold fury. "When has forcing an untrained Magi *ever* achieved anything positive?"

Not wanting to find herself in the middle of this confrontation, Fae stepped over the planted border, wobbled slightly on her bad leg, and tucked herself behind a giant lavender bush.

"She's not untrained," Terrence was saying. "She's had success drawing at least three elements. Kallis even brags that she's touched on dark, although I doubt that's of any consequence."

"Drawing the elements is *not* the same as being competent in wielding them and you know it." Madja's voice dropped to a hiss. Fae flattened herself to the ground, shuffling closer to the herbs. She'd never heard Madja talk to anyone this way.

"I was there to help guide her."

"But you weren't, were you?" Their voices stopped just outside the Healing House, exactly where Fae had stood moments before. "She went too deep even for you to follow. Navigating blind. And the worse thing is that she doesn't even know how alone she was." Fae jammed a fist into her mouth to stop her sharp intake of breath from giving her away. But Madja wasn't finished. "You can't wield her like you wield earth, Terrence. Stop trying to create another High Magi."

"If there were more of us, we wouldn't need her." Terrence's voice held the jagged edge of grief, and Fae recalled the empty seats in the Crystal Chamber. "But there aren't. We're the only ones left. And as long as we stay here, no one can rise to take a place at the table. We're stuck safeguarding the future from the mistakes of the past. But I can't help but feel that we're losing ourselves in the process. And this time it won't just be the Magi that pay for our loss."

A pause. "You can't force her to be powerful, Terrence."

"She *is* powerful." Then Terrence's voice softened. "She isn't Sasha."

The silence that followed was so brittle Fae feared breathing lest she shatter it.

"I know she isn't."

"Do you?"

For a moment, the air was so still Fae thought perhaps she had imagined them being there at all. And then the door to the Healing House opened and closed. A heavy sigh carried through the sweet-smelling lavender, footsteps scuffed the gravel path and crunched away.

In the silence that followed, Fae lay in the grass, the soil of the flowerbeds rich and loamy beside her head, the conversation she'd overheard spinning ever-increasing circles through her mind.

"Comfy?"

Fae jolted so violently, tiny buds of lavender tumbled from the shrub above into her hair.

Irya grinned down at her from the path.

"You know, there are easier ways to spy on someone," she said as Fae extricated herself from the herbs.

"I wasn't spying."

One elegant brow arched. "I was."

Fae glanced at her. "You heard?" Irya nodded. Fae limped around to the path. "Are they right?"

"Which one?" Irya puffed at an errant strand of hair that had fallen over her face. "In case you missed it, they weren't in agreement."

"About me."

Irya hummed evasively.

"Irya."

Irya threw her hands up. "What do you want me to say? Yes, they were arguing about you. Yes, things would be a lot easier if we had a full circle of High Magi, but we don't. No, you don't know what you're doing half the time, but you already know that. Yes, you are powerful enough to make a difference." She let out a long, exasperated sigh. "But you can't force these things. Madja's right. That way lies only disaster."

Fae hesitated, unsure if she should ask. And then, "Who's Sasha?"

Irya smiled sadly. "That is for Madja to tell you."

Fae nodded. She'd known that simply from the way Terrence's tone had changed when he said her name. The way Madja's had caved in on itself.

"Have you heard about Taniq?"

Irya nodded. "Do you want me to check on him?"

Fae's voice wavered. "I just want to know that he'll be alright." Then it caught. "He has to be alright."

Irya's eyes flared in sympathy. "Wait here." She swept into the Healing House, leaving Fae to wrench herself back under control, until she was no longer at risk of falling apart.

Irya emerged a few minutes later. "The healers are working on him now. Arissa is there." She paused, hesitant. "He'll pull through."

"And his legs?"

Irya pressed her lips together. "They don't know yet."

The hard knot in Fae's chest tightened. She nodded her thanks.

Irya reached out and clasped her hand, twining her honey-brown fingers between Fae's pale ones. "I know you're going to beat yourself up about this, but it's not your fault."

"It feels a lot like my fault." The quakes, the destruction, the deaths.

She turned to head back to her room, wanting nothing more than to be left alone. To bury her magic back where it was before the Magi started teaching her how to use it.

But that was when the quakes first started: when she had no idea what she was doing. Better to teach herself not to *use* the elements, but to throttle them, so that the magic had no chance of slipping her leash again.

"You know, there's a story" — Irya tipped her head back, as if sifting through her centuries of memories — "that describes the earth as a great celestial beast that curled up and went to sleep among the stars."

Fae stopped. And blinked. "Huh?"

"I was just thinking, if the earth is in fact sentient, albeit asleep, then I wonder how it feels about us ants crawling around up here drawing its magic..." She pressed a finger to her lips, contemplating. "Are we annoying? Like a fly that won't leave you alone? Or are we performing a necessary function? Like a release valve, or those tiny fish that clean sharks in the ocean."

Fae breathed a laugh. "I've never heard that story before."

Irya looped her arm through Fae's, and started back along the path. "An old Echo once told me, before all of this." She waved a hand around at La'sa. "She liked to remind me that we're none of us permanent. That the only things to truly endure are the earth, the moons, and the stars."

"What about the sun?"

"What is the sun but another star that got too close?" Irya scuffed her feet through the gravel, and her voice drifted into the dusty shelves of her life before La'sa, and the war that drove them here. "She used to say that dragons are the only true children of the earth, the ones that heralded a more fleeting, fragile kind of life."

"I've heard that one." A fragment of a larger epic, buried somewhere in Fae's faded Aethyrial memories. "You're distracting me."

A small smile tugged at Irya's lips. "Ah, but it's working isn't it?"

Indeed, they were back at her door. With a heavy sigh, Fae reached for the handle.

"Don't blame yourself, Fae," Irya pleaded, her eyes slanted with worry. "We all have a piece of that to claim."

Fae returned her small smile. "Ah, but no one else is tearing the world apart, are they?"

Before Irya could say anything else, Fae slipped inside, letting the door close behind her.

52

SHADOW

Philomena wasn't dreaming.

She was Seeing.

Twin full moons gleamed over the flats of the clan lands: pools of spilled silver in the sky, gilding the hardy grasses with their light, glowering down at the world like a wolf's gaze in the night. The single annual occurrence of the wolf moons was a banner for the *Ateth Legarrh*, when the veil between spirits and the mortal realm was at its thinnest.

Fanrell watched her with growing unease. He'd never seen an Oracle at work, those rare few who came out of the *Ateth Legarrh* with visions of futures not belonging to them; the gift of Sight went beyond the single coming-of-age spirit quest undertaken by all juveniles on the cusp of adulthood.

She'd asked him to sit with her, to watch this year's juveniles gallop off into the night. And it had been just as the last hoof beats faded into the distance, that she stiffened.

Her eyes clouded, reflecting the moons' glare with a strange yellow-green glow, as if *she* were the wolf. Her face was utterly relaxed. If her eyes had been closed, she could have been sleeping.

Fanrell wondered if he should fetch someone. How long had it been? He touched a hand to her arm. "Phil—"

Her hand shot out to grab his forearm with slender fingers, her grip unbelievably strong. With a huge gasp, as if she was coming up from underwater, she blinked the clouds from her eyes, and her gaze finally met his.

"We have to find father."

They found the Clan Leader in the village hall with the Elders.

"Elders." Philomena bowed her head. Fanrell followed her example. In that moment, he realised he'd lost all respect for their judgements, but it would do no good to antagonise them before Philomena could say her piece.

"Philomena, what's this about?" Jeorgen turned to face them, huge hooves scuffing on the packed earth floor.

"I have had a vision." She strode forward without hesitation, fully confident in her right to be heard. "A storm of fire and a wall of water. I saw a human in white, but he is black inside. I saw an army of metal and blood marching from the south. And I saw the clan lands, and everyone within them, crushed beneath it." Her voice choked at last, her confidence faltering in the face of whatever it was that she'd seen. Her eyes flicked to her father, and then back to the Elders.

Rochelle watched her, calculating. "They will not come here," she said simply.

Fanrell kept his expression schooled. Of course she'd known. Rochelle was an Oracle too. And far more experienced than Philomena.

Then why was she lying?

Sangrell and Greghar maintained their silence, allowing her to make their decisions for them, as always.

But Philomena pressed on. "If this army reaches its goal, it will mean an end to all we know. A shadow over the land. One that follows wherever they go." She glanced between the Elders, her eyes coming back to Rochelle. "I saw it. We have to stop it."

A small smile curled at Rochelle's lips, but it lacked warmth. Lacked anything.

"We do not involve ourselves in the affairs of humans." Sangrell parroted back the same rhetoric that had come from Greghar's lips a few days ago. "We have kept our clans alive by staying away from the other races." He turned his gaze towards them, his eyes milky with age. "If the Oracle says they will not come here, we would be fools to put ourselves in their path."

Philomena gaped at him. At Rochelle.

Again, that empty smile from Rochelle. "Unravelling the messages of the spirits is a skill that ages well. You are young." Fanrell wanted to growl at the condescension in her tone. "Sit with your vision a while, girl. Perhaps you will gain a clearer view of what is to come."

Philomena looked about to argue her point when Jeorgen spoke.

"Thank you for your sage advice, Elders." He shot his daughter a look, his gaze taking in Fanrell as well. "Your wisdom is heard."

The Elders inclined their heads, and turned, dismissing them without a word.

Philomena shook as they emerged into the night outside the hall.

"Not here." Jeorgen gripped his daughter's arm, steering her away. A jerk of his head had Fanrell following along behind them.

As soon as the door to the Clan Leader's house closed, Philomena whirled on her father. But Jeorgen simply held up a hand.

"Before you start, I will remind you that I am Clan Leader, and those are your Clan Elders." His tone brooked no argument, and she deflated instantly, but Fanrell saw the simmering in her glare. Jeorgen held the fire in her eyes and continued. "It would appear the army you came seeking aid against will indeed spill blood onto our lands, Fanrell."

Fanrell stood silently in place. Jeorgen was getting to something.

"Tell us what you saw."

Philomena blinked, her surprise evident in her wide, blue stare.

Then she took a breath, and collected herself. "I saw lines of human soldiers, stretching as far as the eye could see. They march across the world from the south, over Arland" — she glanced at Fanrell, and he knew she was thinking of Throldon, and the friends he'd made there — "and up into the Ice Fields. I cannot see what they seek — it's like there's a smoke screen around it. But whatever they achieve, the stain of blood will destroy everything in its path. Starting with the clan lands. And once Equi'tox is drowning in blood, it will spread further still." She closed her eyes, shaking her head, her strawberry-blonde waves drifting over her shoulder. "It *will* reach here. I am sure of it. There was a... a solidity to the vision. Like this outcome is already carved into time." Opening her eyes, she looked back up at her father. "Rochelle is wrong in this. And her determination to turn a blind eye will kill us all."

Jeorgen watched her, and for the briefest moment, Fanrell could have sworn he saw wetness lining his eyes, a sadness in his gaze. Then he blinked, and it was gone.

"You cannot defy the Elders."

"Father—"

Jeorgen held up his hand again. "You cannot defy the Elders." His eyes darted to Fanrell, and held his gaze. "And even they cannot defy the spirits."

"But the spirits are telling me—"

"And our Oracle has interpreted that this does not threaten us."

Philomena looked as if she might breathe fire. "*I* am an Oracle."

Jeorgen placed his hands on her shoulders, and bent his head to meet her eyes. "You are. And you know the importance of the messages of the spirits. It is why we have three dozen juveniles out completing their *Ateth Legarrh* right now. It is why Immrith went south, and why Fanrell now builds bridges with the other races of the world." He lifted his eyes to shoot a pointed look at Fanrell. "Despite how insulated our Elders would have us be." Jeorgen straightened, looking out across the courtyard, to the lightening sky beyond.

"They should be returning soon. You should go and see them in. We can discuss this more after the welcome feast." He gave Philomena's shoulders a squeeze, and turned down to his workshop, disappearing into the room without another word.

"Come." Fanrell reached out to take her hand. "I think you father believes there is something we should see." He'd hinted at it before, but Fanrell wasn't sure to believe it until he saw it for himself.

Philomena ignored his hand, and stormed out of the house, her hooves thumping along the ground far harder than they had any need to. "What does it matter, if they would all rather sit here and be mowed down like crops beneath the scythe, than do something that has never been done?" She uttered a sound of derision from the back of her throat.

Fanrell did not try comforting her. Instead, he fixed his eyes upon the horizon, waiting for something he almost didn't dare hope for.

"Maybe we'll die out before that army ever reaches us." Philomena continued her tirade as they went. "We've been slowly bleeding out our strongest people in *stupid, mindless, idiotic* clan wars anyway." Fanrell didn't bother pointing out that her choice of words all meant the same thing. She had a point. The same one he'd been silently railing about since before he'd even left Throldon. "You know, I think there was a reason the spirits guided Immrith south, and it wasn't to die." She wagged her finger in front of her, as if reproaching the wind. "It was to guide our people south. To show us that we can be a part of the larger world." She turned abruptly, thrusting a hand out to stop him, her palm pressing into his chest. "You believe me — don't you?" Philomena looked up at him with wide, urgent eyes, her whole body tense, ready to fight if she had to.

Fanrell looked down at the place where her skin touched his, the contact arcing across his chest like lightning. He lifted a hand to close over hers.

"Of course I believe you." Relief swept over her face, softening her features again. "But your father is right. We cannot defy the Elders." A figure on the horizon caught his eye as dawn flooded the land. "But we might not have to."

Philomena raised an eyebrow, then turned to follow his gaze, her body lining up beside his, their flanks brushing against one another, tails tangling in the breeze.

As the wolf moons sank behind the world, the newest adult members of Little Bear clan galloped back into the village.

And came straight to Fanrell and Philomena.

They ran almost in formation, slowing to a canter, and fanning out to stand arrayed before them as if they expected a lecture.

A female with roan colouring and hair that glinted like fire in the rising sun stepped forward.

"We will wander with you." She spoke as if answering a question Fanrell hadn't even asked. Casting a glance behind her, she was met with a collection of nods. "I am Helena. The spirits have shown us all a future beyond the borders of our clan territory." She turned back to Fanrell, bowing her head slightly to Philomena. "With an Oracle to guide us, we can become a new village. A new clan. One that does better for all of our peoples." A hint of doubt flashed behind her eyes. "If you'll have us."

Fanrell did a quick head count. Of the three dozen that had departed for the *Ateth Legarrh*, a full thirty stood before him now. He turned to Philomena, to find her staring open-mouthed at the group waiting for her to lead them. Waiting for both of them to lead them.

He nudged her with his flank, and she turned to look up at him.

"There are more." A voice spoke up from the back of the group.

Fanrell straightened, trying to find the speaker. "What do you mean? Come forward."

A male with dark bay colouring pushed to the front, his peers parting to let him through. "The spirits showed me more than this." He gestured to the thirty assembled. "They showed me the clans coming together."

And sure enough, the distant sound of hoof beats rumbled towards them. Fanrell grabbed Philomena's arm, and together they trotted to a small rise at the edge of the village.

From three different directions, more centaurs galloped towards them.

Fanrell whirled on the male that had spoken. "How many did you see? How many clans?"

The response was immediate, without a hint of doubt.

"All of them, Chief."

Fanrell looked down at Philomena. There were at least thirty clans, sprawled across Equi'tox. If as many of their new adults were wanderers like these, they would have more than a new clan on their hands.

They had the beginnings of a new nation. A New Equi'tox.

Philomena gazed up at him, wonder shining from her eyes. "The will of the spirits," she whispered.

And as such, irrefutable. Even by the Elders. Even if every Clan Elder disagreed.

"What will we do?" Another voice from behind them.

They turned to face the beginnings of their new clan. Their new nation.

Exchanged a glance.

Philomena stepped forward, head held high. "There is an army marching across the world that would destroy Equi'tox, and leave nothing but blood in its wake." Her gaze swept the small crowd before her, and Fanrell felt a swell of pride at the steel in it. "No longer will we hunker down in our clans. No longer will we divide up our lands and clash at the borders. If the clans are coming together, then we will *fight back together*."

She shook her fist in the air, and more than a few of the wanderers nodded their agreement.

Then she turned her gaze up to meet Fanrell's, her eyes swimming with emotion.

"It is time to join the world that is waiting for us."

53

THREADS OF CLOUD

Fae's leg was agony.

She'd overworked it the day before, and now she was paying the price. She perched on the edge of the bed, massaging the abused muscles when there was a knock at her door. She looked up and tried to wipe the desire to be left alone from her face.

"Come in."

The mouthwatering smell of a cooked breakfast was followed by Alexi as he ducked around the door, a tray crowded with overlapping dishes balanced between his hands. It was a miracle none had crashed to the floor already. He lowered the tray to the table before anything could topple from it. "Good morning, fair Fae." He flashed her a smile, bright white against his olive skin and dark stubble. "I have brought nourishment for your body. And once you have eaten" — he tapped his head — "we will work on your mind."

Fae, who'd been scanning the items on the tray, raised a questioning eyebrow.

Alexi cleared his throat, the light in his striking eyes dimming. "I have been injured in battle before... worse than you, Fae." His gaze skimmed her leg, her shoulder, before returning to her face. "And I know how effective *assvissi* is. For *physical* wounds." He hesitated.

"What do you mean, Alexi?" Fae's curiosity shaped itself into a frown.

The combat trainer shifted uncomfortably, then pulled out the desk chair to sit beside the bed, elbows braced on his thighs, the corded muscles of his arms bunching with the motion. His eyes lifted to meet hers. "I know you are healed. Yet you rest as if your wounds still pain you."

"They do!" Fae rubbed at her leg in emphasis, a hiss escaping her as she worked over a particularly large knot.

"From inactivity." Alexi clasped his hands before him. "Everything you experience — from pain to joy — is just signals. It is up to you how much it controls you, or if you control it. The body needs to move. To remember what it is for. Yours is *made* to move. To dance." She flinched at his choice of words, and he stopped. He stared at her hard, something in his gaze softening. He stood, gesturing to the tray of food. "Eat. Then meet me in the Aurora Gardens, on the western wall."

He stopped at the door and flashed a crooked smile over his shoulder. "Don't make me come back to find you."

The Aurora Gardens were designed with air currents in mind, low borders and gravel paths carving the grass into eddies and swirling lines. Somewhere near the centre, was a small circle of lawn, barely big enough for Fae to stride two paces across the grass without scuffing the gravel that spiralled in to meet it.

Alexi stood on the curve of a path of dried bark, and nodded his welcome. "Good." He waited for her to lean her walking stick up against one low-lying wall, then stepped close and clasped her shoulders. He smiled. "Remind your body what it is made for. We will spar tomorrow." Then he turned, and retreated into the labyrinthine garden.

"Wait!" Fae reached out a hand, and then dropped it to her side. "Where are you going?"

Alexi threw her a grin over his shoulder. "You do not need me for this, fair Fae. I just brought breakfast." He lengthened his strides, and disappeared behind a hedgerow. "See you tomorrow!"

And then she was alone.

The wind rustled through the plants nearby, and inside her, air stirred.

Fae's response was a knee-jerk smothering of the element, shoving it back into the depths of herself. Her heartbeat thumped loudly in her chest. She fisted her hands to still the trembling that settled there.

She was scared of her magic.

She'd lost control too many times. Hurt too many people.

Her knuckles pushed against her skin. It wouldn't happen again.

Fae breathed deep, drawing the clear, mountain air deep into her lungs, and straightened. Closed her eyes. And went looking for the threads of her aura.

Before she'd thrown herself into a war she obviously had no hope of winning on her own, Fae had hoped to take her nightmares back from Athanasius, the way he'd taken them from her in the first place. She'd half wondered if she was ready to do it, when she visited him in his apartment. And then she'd crumpled, and all thoughts of taking on more darkness had her shrinking from the task. She felt terrible for leaving him with it. Dirty. Selfish.

She began to weave the threads of her own aura into a cage. Slowly at first, and then with more confidence. She would at least spare the world any more pain of her doing. Her magic would not escape her again.

Perhaps now she would be able to face reclaiming her nightmares, safe in the knowledge that no one would come to any harm because she was too weak to control the elements while trapped in the darkest corners of her mind.

Manipulating her aura was like playing the harp with threads of cloud: unless she plucked at them just right, they parted beneath her fingers like wisps of smoke. They were fluid and intangible and yet she knitted the filaments together with a combination of skill, ragged will, and a dogged, determined, refusal to fail.

She lost track of how long she teased and coaxed those fibres, but when she was done, her element-aspects huddled clustered inside a gilded cage. Air flitted against the bars. Fire roared in protest. Earth sulked. She ran a hand over the threads of the prison she'd built, at once mournful and relieved. Then she tucked the cage in next to her heart, where the elements belonged. Where the only person they might hurt, was her.

Opening her eyes, she took a deep, shuddering breath, and let it out slow. Calmed herself.

No one else would be hurt because of her.

She allowed herself a tear of remorse. She'd spent a year mourning the loss of her powers. Only to find she'd been capable of more than she'd ever dreamed.

More than she could ever handle.

The tear trailed down her cheek, slowly cooling in the mountain air. Until finally, it dripped from her jaw, and disappeared into the grass.

Fae's chin wobbled as she took one final breath, and let it go.

She squared her feet, and moved into some warm-up stretches.

Alexi had been right of course — as soon as her muscles loosened up, the cramping, stabbing pains in her leg and shoulder eased.

She set her feet wide, and lunged slowly from side to side. Her eyebrows came up in surprise at how easy it was. Only that morning, her leg had hurt so much she'd hissed from the pain. She rolled her shoulder, bringing her arm around in small, then larger circles. It felt different, but then from what Arissa had told her of her injuries, that was to be expected.

Emboldened by the success of her stretching, she moved into some combat exercises: a combination of *Gestral* forms and techniques that Alexi had taught her.

"Fancy a partner?"

Fae spun to find Luca standing behind her, framed by the shrubbery. She hadn't seen him since they'd returned from Throldon. Since he'd flown them over Arland, deep into the Ice Fields with no one but the stars for company. True, she hadn't left her room since then either. But he could have come to her. She'd... needed him to. Something inside her shifted uneasily at the revelation.

She looked at him properly. His hair was messy, as if he'd run his hands through it too much, and dark half-moons hung under his eyes. Caution flitted like a shadow across his face. He gestured to her practice and clarified, "For sparring."

She turned her back on him, and reached over to pick up her walking stick. Now that he'd finally come, now that he was finally standing right there, his absence over the last few days burned like acid in her gut. Taking a stance, she proceeded to use her stick like a short staff. "Why are you here Luca?" *Why now?*

He hesitated as if surprised by her response.

"I wanted to check on you," he admitted.

"Why?" She spun, whipping the stick under her arm as she turned so that, for a moment, it pointed directly at his chest. She brought it back, thrusting it behind her while keeping her eyes on him, anger boiling in her chest. "Why do you care now? You haven't found it in yourself to come by before now."

A muscle in Luca's jaw bunched, the only sign of his discomfort. "I thought you might want some space to... to figure things out."

"And how did you *figure* I'd do that?" She jabbed the stick to the side and turned, flipped it back over her elbow and into the other hand. Her teeth gritted, and she felt sweat drip down her back. "How am I supposed to work through what happened — what *I* did?" She pivoted, coming around to face him again. "No one knows what happened in Throldon. No one else was there. But *you* were. You killed people too."

Luca's expression shuttered. "Those weren't the first I've killed to protect. And they won't be the last."

"But they were for me!" She whirled on him, breathing heavily, the stick raised in the air between them. Anger burned inside her but guilt was what corroded from within. Guilt was what was twisting her into knots: guilt and shame and fear and complete, all-consuming self-loathing. "I've never killed anyone before..." She swallowed the lump in her throat, shoved back the tears forming in her eyes. "I thought I could count on you at least. I've had no one to talk to about it. About how it feels like I'll never be clean again. About how I can't trust *myself*..." She thumped her chest with the flat of her hand, choking on the words. "Not only has this power scared the shit out of me, ripped chasms in the world, but now it's killed people. *I* killed people. Indiscriminately." She pushed away the image of that stain on the riverbanks of the Amedi. Of how far it had stretched. Tried not to think about how many people would have been caught in that blast. "And Taniq may never walk again, because even when I try to help—"

"Did you visit Taniq?"

"I didn't — I couldn't. I asked Irya to look in on him for me."

Luca's brows knitted. "She shouldn't have worried you with that."

Fae narrowed her eyes at him. "She's the only one who hasn't hidden truths from me in the name of 'not worrying me with it'."

A look of regret and pity flickered across Luca's face. Fae wrapped her fingers around the wood of her stick, her grip strong enough to break it if she set her mind to it. She looked at the white of her knuckles pressing against her skin, at the grass between them, anything to avoid seeing that look on his face.

Something fluttered in her chest. Fire. Slamming itself against the bars of the cage she'd built for it. A flare of pain heated beneath her ribs, but that's where it stayed.

Right where it belonged.

She loosed a slow breath.

"Are you alright?"

Fae risked a glance up at Luca's question. He watched her with the wariness of someone a step too close to a wild animal.

Her eyes flashed, the gold ring around the irises flaring bright.

"Don't worry, you won't see any more outbursts from me. I took care of it." She wondered at the strange sense of satisfaction she felt at seeing his brow furrow, at the worry now replacing the pity on his face.

She threw him a dark half-smile as she strode from the garden.

"Problem solved."

But as she walked away, the look on Luca's face suggested that it was anything but.

54

EVEN MOUNTAINS MOVE

Fae threw all her weight behind the punch.

Alexi grunted behind the pads he held up for her, but didn't move.

She punched again. And again.

They were in one of the smaller training rooms inside. The ceiling felt too low, the walls too close after weeks of training under the open sky.

But Fae hadn't wielded her elements for days now, so she supposed it shouldn't matter.

It seemed appropriate. She'd locked her element-aspects away, and now so was she, confined to this small space for her training while the damage to the arena — damage *she'd* caused — was assessed and made safe again.

Alexi had understood her need for distraction, for the kind of release that came from moving her body, had understood that she didn't have the words for what whirled around her head. Not yet.

And so, for the very same reason Luca had suggested she begin training with Alexi in the first place, she used it to clear her mind. To chase all the clamouring thoughts away, using her body until she was so exhausted she could do little more than collapse into bed at the end of the day.

And if there was an edge of worry in the looks he threw her way, she chose not to notice.

She drove her fist into the pad again.

"Break." Alexi stepped back, dropping the pads between them. He pulled them from his hands and threw them to one side. "Water." He walked to the side of the room where a bench had been set with a pitcher and stack of glasses.

Fae let her arms drop, swinging them by her sides before reaching out for the glass Alexi handed her, a wary look dancing around his eyes, as it did most days now.

But she couldn't stop too long, or the thoughts would start spiralling through her head again.

How the Aethyr had given her power to defeat a broken god.

How she'd never been meant to wield Source Magic.

How much hurt she'd caused already.

How easy it had been to kill.

She drained her glass and moved over to the small rack of weapons against one wall. She pulled a staff from the rack, spinning it in her hands as she took up position in the middle of the room again.

Alexi raised a brow. "It is important to rest, Fae."

She shook her head. "I don't need to rest." She'd done enough of that. Now she needed to move. To fight. To do *anything* but stop. She lifted the staff in a beckoning gesture, and shot him a half smirk. "What? You worried I'm going to knock you flying?"

She'd come close to doing it on a couple of occasions. He'd even grudgingly admitted that she was giving him a run for his money. There weren't many who committed as much time and energy to training as she did.

They didn't have as much to lose if they failed.

Alexi didn't rise to her taunt, instead pouring himself another helping of water with deliberate slowness, condensation beading on the surface of the glass.

Fae bounced on the balls of her feet and jabbed out with the staff to tap him on the ribs.

"Come on." She retreated back to her position. "Scared?" she jeered.

"Yes, Fae." He turned, his expression one of utter sincerity. Not the playful Alexi she was used to. "I am scared for you."

She stopped, her voice flat as she said, "You don't need to be scared of me anymore."

He shook his head. "Not scared *of* you, fair Fae." He stepped closer. "Scared *for* you."

"Why?"

"You train harder than anyone here. Your focus is razor-sharp. You are improving so fast I can barely keep up, and I've been doing this hundreds of years." His brows knitted. "But you are holding it all inside. You do not truly let go."

She frowned in confusion. "Holding what inside? What am I supposed to let go of?"

"The training is supposed to help release the trauma inside you. To help you work through the emotions." He reached out to jab her in the chest. "But you are holding it all here. You need to let go, or it will burn you." He cocked his head to one side, as if a thought had just occurred to him. "When was the last time you wielded your magic?"

"That's something I'd like to know too."

Fae turned to find Luca leaning in the doorway, a frown framing his usual inscrutable expression.

Planting her staff, she idly picked at a nail. "I don't see what that has to do with anything."

Both of them just watched her, worry clear on Alexi's face, something hard and assessing on Luca's. She shifted uncomfortably under their scrutiny.

Finally Luca said, "Come with me."

"I'm training."

His eyes flicked to Alexi, who nodded. "We're done for today."

Fae glared at his betrayal, but replaced her staff and strode from the room, back straight.

As soon as she left the Warrens, the chill northern air cooled the sweat on her skin, and she shivered. Luca held out her coat, retrieved from the corner of the training room. Snatching it from him, she shoved her arms through the sleeves and plunged her hands deep into the pockets.

She didn't quite know why she was angry at him. Other than his recent abandonment of her. She eyed him from under scowling brows, averting her gaze when he glanced towards her.

"This way."

He led her past the rubble of the arena wall, and into the tunnel that would take them out of La'sa.

The wind beyond the mountain walls of La'sa was unforgiving, and she shrugged further into her coat. When she'd first arrived out here in nothing but a nightdress, it had seemed a barren stretch of snow and ice with no signs of life for miles around. Now, wrapped in her shearling-lined coat, and with actual boots on her feet, she could appreciate the landscape with clear eyes.

To the west of the entrance, a stream flowed down the mountainside, the wind keeping its glittering surface free of snow. The frozen flow of water made ribbons of ice, melting just enough to glisten in the midday sun. Come night, it would freeze anew, and begin the tortuous process all over again tomorrow. It likely only fully thawed in the height of summer, but until then it was stuck in this purgatory, destined to relive each cycle over and over until the days were long enough to melt it all the way through.

A bit like La'sa, waiting for the world to be safe enough for Magi to emerge again.

On the other side of the river, snow-dusted evergreens rose up from the ground, pointing their powdered arrow-heads to the sky. Snow flurries drifted from their branches with every passing breeze.

It was quiet out here. Not silent, but the natural quiet of wind whispering past, shifting branches, the flutter of wings as birds settled and took flight among the trees, the crack of ice melting in the sun, the soft rush of snow blowing across the Ice Fields.

Fae tipped her head back, and closed her eyes. For the first time in a long time, her mind wasn't spinning with problems she couldn't solve.

For once, she felt... peaceful.

If she ignored the constant pain in her chest. The pressure of elements clamouring to be let out.

Nearby, Luca watched her, his midnight eyes glinting with purpose.

Listening to the sounds around her, Fae noticed the instant they stopped. Her eyes snapped open.

All around them, the world stood utterly still.

No wind rustled the trees, or blew the snow across the Ice Fields. The birds and the stream were silent. Unnaturally, eerily quiet.

She spun to face Luca. "What are you doing?" Air rattled the cage beside her heart.

He crossed his arms. "I could ask you the same."

"What do you mean? I'm not doing anything."

"Is that how you'd prefer it?"

She frowned. "What?"

Luca slid his hands into his pockets and stepped closer, his features uncharacteristically repentant. "I know I haven't been a willing ear, but you haven't talked to *anyone* since Throldon. And I know plenty of people have offered. Sheree. Arissa. Irya." Fae felt a pang of guilt. They had all tried talking to her. But she hadn't wanted them to know of the shadows that haunted her. Didn't want them to know what she'd done. Didn't want to see their faces change when they learned what kind of thing she was.

Luca saw all of it pass across her face, and did not balk. "You've kept it all locked inside you." His brow furrowed. "And don't think I hadn't noticed that you haven't wielded any Source Magic since Terrence's ill-conceived attempt last week." A flicker of anger edged his voice, and Fae had no doubt the High Magi had all had something to say about that particular disaster.

"It's not safe." Her eyes flared, and her voice cracked. "I'm not safe."

Luca ignored her. "Look around." He gestured to the stillness in the air, the trees standing sentry, the snow lying inert on the ground. "Does this seem natural to you?"

Fae shook her head. It felt anything but. At first glance, it was lovely. But the lack of movement was unsettling.

He nodded. "This is what you're doing."

Fae's eyes snapped back to him, but his were on the trees.

"At first, it looks calm. Maybe even peaceful. But over time..." A huge clump of snow lifted from the ground to their left and floated over to the trees. It halted above one of the larger ones, hovering in mid-air, shedding flakes like an isolated snowstorm. The air remained still. The tree remained still. Nothing moved but the falling snow, slowly burdening its branches.

A *crack* rent the air, and one of the larger branches, laden with more snow than was natural, tore free of the trunk, crashing to the ground, leaving a gaping hole in its wake.

Luca turned back to Fae. "Nothing is meant to be utterly still, Fae. Even the mountains move, in their own time." He released the air, and wind howled across the Ice Fields again, blowing the extra snow free of the trees, exposing the gap in the evergreen even more. Nearby branches rustled, and Fae spotted small critters scurrying in to investigate a new potential shelter. The stream of ice cracked in the gentle heat of the sun.

"There is movement in everything. Everything needs room to grow. To learn. To shift. To adapt. To change." He pointed to the tree. "If the tree does not move in the wind, does not bend when it is burdened, it will be buried. It will break." He stepped in front of her, leaning so close she could feel the warmth of his breath on her skin. "You are like the tree. Refusing to move, to bend. You need to acknowledge that your burdens are burying you. Let them go, or you are going to break."

Fae glanced over at the tree. At the dark gap in its side, the great wound where the branch had pulled free. She knew what Luca was saying made sense. But she was also *not* the tree. The tree wouldn't tear up the earth when it moved, when it bent.

But it would if it fell.

You will become the thing you fear to be. Athanasius's words, spoken in the dark, came back to her.

She swallowed, squeezing her eyes shut.

"I can't trust myself to let go." She hated the way her voice shook. "Every time I do, someone gets hurt."

Strong hands came up to cup her shoulders. "Trust *me*."

Fae opened her eyes, and saw a softness she'd only ever caught glimpses of before in his gaze.

Stillness settled around them again, and when she looked up, a wall of hardened air surrounded them. The wind continued to blow across the Ice Fields, knocking snow from the trees and lifting birds into the air, but at their feet, the snow lay still. Waiting.

Fae reached out, and brushed a hand against the shield.

"I'll keep you safe."

She glanced back, and the intensity of his gaze stole the breath from her. The sense of *other* that she sometimes got from him retreated, and all that was left was his earnest desire to help her. To... save her.

He'd been there for her when her nightmares took over and shook the earth. He'd walked through her fire when it threatened to consume her. And he'd flown thousands of miles to rescue her from bloodthirsty sorcerers.

So now, when he was offering to keep her safe?

She believed him.

She let go.

She released her hold on the cage nestled beside her heart, letting the threads dissipate back into her aura. The weight she had carried since locking a part of herself away lifted, and she felt it in her very bones as the elements slipped back into place under her skin, expanding to fill every cell of her body with coloured light.

She breathed for what felt like the first time in days, and with that first breath, came an outpouring of grief and regret and shame and guilt. As the first tear spilled onto her cheek, motion stirred at her feet.

Snowflakes drifted up from the ground, defying gravity as they answered her turmoil. The air in her lungs tore through her in ragged sobs, answered by the air around her. It caught in her hair as it whipped past, taking the snow with it until she was surrounded by a blizzard contained only by Luca's shield. She didn't feel the fire erupt from her hands, didn't notice when her guilt and shame turned to hate. Hate of what she had become.

She wished the power had broken her instead of the earth.

That she had died fighting Anson instead.

It would have been better if she had.

Palms against her cheeks, fingers in her hair, and her face was tilted upward to meet the embers in Luca's eyes as he crushed his lips to hers.

The feel of his skin against hers was like light poured over her shadows, chasing her self-doubt and loathing into the forge of her centre to be remade. Her mind emptied out, and all that was left was where his lips met hers, the scrape of his fingers at the nape of her neck, twining in her hair, and how there wasn't enough air...

The wind and snow dropped, fire searing through her veins in a heady rush.

Luca pulled back, his breathing ragged as he gripped her face between his hands.

"Don't you *ever*," he panted, "believe you'd be better off dead." He pressed his forehead to hers, and she found her chest rising and falling in sync with his. She hadn't realised she'd voiced her thoughts aloud. But Luca had always somehow known the darkest parts of her. Had always managed to flood them with light. "The existence of bad things in this world are not your fault. Anson, blood sorcerers — they are not your doing." He brushed his lips to her brow, and straightened, dropping his hands to her arms. "You took lives. But you saved thousands too. That you weigh those lives so heavily against your own, that you carry them with you, is a mark of your goodness."

Fae lifted her eyes, and found a pain in his that mirrored her own so acutely, it was like a dagger to the heart.

The pain of weighing lives. The pain of carrying them. The pain of being unable to save them. It was his pain too.

And in that moment she knew why he hadn't come to her after Throldon.

She opened her mouth to tell him she saw him — that she saw the guilt and regret that haunted him and she understood it all — when something caught her eye over his shoulder.

Luca followed the direction of her gaze. "I thought I got your attention better than that..." And then he saw it too. Raised a hand to shield his eyes. "What the—"

But Fae knew what it was. Just couldn't quite believe it.

Because flying towards them over the endless expanse of snow and ice, in varying sizes, were dragons.

55

FAMILY

The two halves of Fae's life collided in the Crystal Chamber of La'sa.

On one side, the High Magi sat in their usual seats, Luca shifting his armchair closer to hers. Irya joined them, sitting on his other side.

On the other side of the room, Ty stood with Kagos and Aiya, while Aren and Stef perched on the nearest empty chairs.

When they'd landed outside La'sa, their reunion had been somewhat... stilted. Her friends had fought at her side to win back Throldon over a year ago; she'd forged deep bonds with each of them. But these last few months had seen her vanish without a trace, reappearing without explanation to level a battlefield, only to retreat in the arms of a stranger.

Understandably, they eyed her with a mix of confusion and hurt.

Instead of facing the mess she'd made there, she focused her attention on the figure behind them.

"Jade." Fae recognised the dark-skinned girl from the southern camp. "You got out."

The girl nodded, her eyes surveying the unfamiliar faces. "Your escape was exactly the distraction I needed." She inclined her head towards Luca. "Thank you for the dramatic entrance."

"Pleasure." Luca's expression was guarded, but Fae swore she detected a glint in his eye.

Kallis leaned forward on his stool, forearms braced on his legs. "Clearly some introductions are lacking."

Luca shot him a look. "Kallis" — he indicated the Umbra-Incendus before sweeping his arm to take in the others — "Madja, Demilda, Terrence, and Irya." Each nodded as they were announced. "Over to you, dragon."

Kagos narrowed his eyes, but turned to indicate his companions in turn. "Elf Eldra Ty Dy'la, elf scouts Aren and Stef Longstem, and dragonrider Aiya Salaam." He folded his hands into his sleeves again. "You can call me Kagos." Because his full name was unpronounceable to anyone who wasn't dragonkind.

Kallis jerked his head to Jade. "And you?"

Fae caught her eye. "Jade was helping me escape before Luca interrupted." In the corner of her eye, Luca raised an incredulous eyebrow.

"And, pray tell" — Demilda swept her mass of black braids over one shoulder — "whose are the dragon younglings currently terrifying the stablehands?"

"They're mine." Jade's tone left no room for misinterpretation.

Terrence pinned her with shrewd eyes. "Seems there's a longer story there."

"But it's not the reason we came." Ty stepped forward. His storm-grey eyes were weighed down with dark circles. Fae had never seem him so... haggard. "The southern army marches here. You are all in danger."

A gasp went up among the High Magi. Irya's eyes closed, and a heartbeat later, a string of expletives issued from her lips.

Luca glanced her way. "How did we miss this?"

Irya's colourless eyes flashed open again. "You know, I really thought I could trust that the world wouldn't go to shit while we sorted out our own problems for once." She grimaced. "Clearly I was mistaken."

Madja's brows knitted together. "But they won't find us." Her eyes darted to Luca. "They can't."

Kallis's gaze flicked between Kagos and Jade, standing apart from the others. "How did *you* find us?"

Kagos spared Jade a glanced before answering. "We followed the scent of blood magic."

Kallis swore, then turned to Luca. "You weren't kidding then."

Luca shook his head. "I guessed the Thamib forces were being influenced by the blood sorcerers when I saw their camp. This confirms it."

Aren cleared his throat. "How?"

Irya was the one to answer this time. "That army *was* marching to claim more fertile territory for the Thamibian Empire. They're a desert empire — not much farming potential that far south." She jerked her head at Luca and Fae. "If they've diverted their entire army to follow these two, then their goal isn't land. It's power."

Jade nodded. "The Sorcerer Supreme was invading Throldon for its proximity to the Hearthstone Mountain range. He wanted a dragon. A fully grown dragon to replace mine: the more powerful, the better. He said he had people under his influence — I don't think the army generals are aware they're being manipulated." Her eyes slid to Fae. "Now he wants you."

Fae's eyes widened in alarm. "But how are they tracking me? They didn't get around to taking any blood. He said they had to... purify me first." She shuddered at the violation. Jade's eyes flared, as if she too knew what that meant.

"They're tracking your kills." Kagos answered bluntly, ignoring Fae's flinch. Luca closed a hand over hers. "I saw them collecting blood from the site of your battle."

"They're serious then," Demilda said.

Ty raised a brow. "Why do you say that?"

Demilda turned to him. "It's a lot harder to track someone from exogenous blood," she explained calmly.

"From *what* now?" Aren asked.

"Blood that hasn't come directly from the target."

Colour drained from Fae's face. "So now they're coming here." To a community of Magi that had managed to stay hidden and safe, away from the bloodshed of the world for centuries. She swallowed thickly. "Maybe I should have stayed."

Luca's hand gripped hers even tighter as Jade said, "Then they'd have an even more potent fuel for their dark magic." She waved a frustrated hand at Kagos and Aiya. "It's bad enough that *they're* here." She levelled a finger at Kagos. "*You're* exactly what they wanted to start with. Thank the gods the hatchling stayed behind at least."

Kagos huffed his indignation. "I could hardly leave you to deliver this news alone when you're under the influence of blood magic yourself."

"Wait—" Fae glanced at Jade. "You're — they have your blood?"

Jade's lips pressed into a line. "A small amount from me and each of my dragons. Distance helps to fight its pull." Her nostrils flared. "But I can still feel it, even here."

Terrence's eyes narrowed. "So what happens when they're at the gates?"

Jade met his glare. "I'll fight it then too."

Luca let out a long breath, releasing Fae's hand to run his fingers through his hair. "I thought all the blood sorcerers died out in the war. But it seems they simply found a way to conceal their presence, even from you, Irya."

"Thank goodness they chose to drag a stomping great army around with them for the purposes of allowing me to follow their movements then." The Echo smiled sweetly, twining her hair absently around one finger.

"Where did they even come from?" Fae wondered aloud.

"Just as magic is everywhere, so are the people who wield it," Demilda answered. "Sorcerers have been around as long as Magi. And spread just as far at one point. Most of them practiced magic peacefully. But there are always some who can never have enough power. Just like your old friends in the Unity, or the Survivors. Only these ones use the blood they spill to corrupt magic."

Luca continued, "Magi blood would be a particularly strong — not to mention perverse — power source for blood magic. Even back when sorcery was more commonplace, there weren't many who were willing to cross that line."

"I still can't quite get over the fact that there's such a thing as blood magic." Fae felt sick to her stomach thinking about it. Was that what made the dead rise to fight against her?

"Of course there is," Terrence grumbled. "If you can control an element by knowing its essence, why not control a living creature by using its blood? And by extension, why not use the lifeforce contained in that blood to boost one's own magic?" His frown carved deep furrows in his forehead. "Assuming you have no morals or ethics or common decency to speak of."

An uncomfortable silence fell over the group.

Aren's eyes darted between his companions and the High Magi. "So... any ideas?"

Irya arched an eyebrow. "You're the ones who flew all the way here to warn us about it. What was *your* plan?"

"We came for Fae." Ty's gaze slid to her now. "To help. To bring you home if you were in danger." His eyes passed around those assembled, narrowing slightly at Luca, before coming back to Fae again. The corner of his mouth lifted. "Although perhaps I underestimated you again on that front."

Fae shook her head in disbelief. She looked at each of her friends. "Why would you want to help me?"

Ty's face wrinkled with confusion. "What do you mean?"

She stared at him, fearing the truth, and yet unable to hide from it.

"Don't you hate me? For what I did?" She looked down at her hands, as if she could still see the blood coating them. "I'm dangerous. I... I killed..."

Kagos snorted. Actually *snorted*. "Shall we compare numbers?"

She started. "What?"

"Do you hate me, Spiritchild?"

Fae blinked. "No, I—"

"Do you think less of me for the lives I took defending Throldon a year ago? I assure you, they were not the first." His gaze of liquid obsidian bored into her as Fae recalled the battle in which he'd withheld his killing fire — risked his own life — until he'd had no choice but to wield it with deadly consequences for the Survivors that fought them.

She shook her head. "Of course not." He'd been magnificent, and the only reason she'd lost only one friend that day instead of five. More.

"War has always marched over the bodies of the innocent," Aiya said quietly. "You stood before it and saved hundreds, if not thousands of lives." Her grey eyes were wide with sincerity. "Everything you've ever done, every step you've taken has been in the name of saving lives. How could we possibly hate you for that?"

"If I'd been on the walls, I would have done exactly the same." Aren stood. And added, with a tilt of his head, "But with less fire. And significantly more arrows."

Beside him, Stef merely nodded his agreement.

Ty stepped forward. "We don't hate you. We love you." He spread his arms to indicate his companions. "You're our family. And family look out for each other. *That's* why we're here."

A lump found its way into Fae's throat and all she could do was nod her thanks, eyes blurring.

"Good." Kallis surged from his stool. "Now that we've established we're all fighting the same fight, shall we get down to the business of what we're going to do about the blood sorcerers tracking us down and the army they're bringing with them?" He looked over at the new arrivals. "What do you lot have to offer?"

As the conversation turned to planning and tactics, something new inside Fae stirred. Intangible, it wasn't one of her elements. But it lifted her heart, and she felt lighter than she had in days. Maybe even longer.

She turned to Luca, and found him already watching her, a look like awe ghosting his features.

"What?" she murmured.

Luca shook his head, and the look was gone.

Later, in her room, Fae pulled out the game Sheree had brought her.

The forgiveness — the acceptance — from her family had unlocked something inside her that she hadn't realised was locked. She breathed easier. Her mind cleared.

Her elements, instead of skulking inside her like scolded children, floated near the surface, ready to draw on at a whim. They'd retreated from her after Throlden. She'd been holding herself back from them too. Not out of fear of the elements themselves, but out of fear of what she would do with them. But the trust that Kagos and Ty and the others had in her let her believe that, maybe, she might trust herself.

And that inner trust, tentative though it was, gently prised away the stranglehold she'd had on her power.

Sliding open the small wooden box, Fae gathered up the elements and tipped them into their divots in the board: the sand to represent earth, the tiny vial of water, and the down feather for air. Finally, she lit the tinder with its flint.

The flickering light of the tiny flame reflected in the mirror to play shadows over the wall. Fae breathed deep, using Terrence's techniques to centre herself.

And then, she invited her elements out to play.

It was as easy as breathing. One by one, she lifted them to her fingers. First, fire twirled around her index finger, wove across the back of her hand to circle her wrist, and back again. Then air brought the feather to float over the tip of her middle finger, bobbing gently there, held by the softest of breaths. Water flowed from its divot to encircle her ring finger, and swept about it like a tiny, ever-flowing stream.

And then, with barely a thought, the sand lifted from the board.

Fae gasped as earth finally answered her, turning her hand over to watch as it snaked around her little finger in a delicate figure of eight.

At her slightest wish, the elements moved from her fingers to wrap around her wrist. They played across her skin, weaving about one another up and down the length of her forearm, and back to dance across her fingers.

Finally she bid them halt, and they did, each of her fingers holding an element at their tip.

She sensed dark within her, as it always would be, but for now it seemed content to watch from the shadows.

And there was that glimmer of something else...

As Fae played the earthly elements over her fingers once more, she felt that perhaps she might have a little faith in herself after all.

56

AN AGE FOR NEW BEGINNINGS

They had, at best, two weeks before the southern army reached them. Every day counted.

Finally free of her own self-imposed shackles, Fae threw herself back into training. She pulled rivers of water from the air with Madja's guidance, blew fiery infernos over a laughing Kallis, raised walls of hardened air around Luca, and built mountains with a stunned Terrence. She spent additional time with Kallis, learning how to weave dark like smoke, competing to see who could smother the other in shadows first.

Luca still hadn't shown her light, but she was still half afraid she would never find it. It felt as though there was no place for light inside her after all the terrible things the elements had done in her hands. She didn't deserve it.

Kagos had made himself very comfortable with the High Magi, exchanging ideas and stories about their respective hidden communities, and perusing the Archives to compare records. Apparently, the libraries at Alyla — the elven community adjacent to the Hearthstone mountains — had managed to retain records from the centuries prior to the Rains as well.

It occurred to Fae that, given the lifespan of an adult dragon, he might even have had friends in common with some of the Magi here.

In between her continued Eah'lara training, Irya had taken Aiya and

Jade under her wing, showing them around La'sa while Kagos deliberated the finer points of magic with the High Magi. If there was purpose to their discussions besides academic interest, Fae had yet to comprehend what it was.

Alexi drafted Aren and Stef into preparing defences outside La'sa. With the help of various Magi, they laid traps out in the snow to confuse, mislead, and hopefully distract the army long enough for the High Magi to find and deal with the blood sorcerers.

"What *is* the plan once the army gets here?" Fae sat back in her squashy armchair one evening, a week before the southern forces were expected. The Meeting House common room already had a fire lit to chase away the chill; the doors seldom closed for long before the next visitor came through. Opposite her sat Kallis, Ty, and Demilda, who had surprised her by spending most of her time constructing obstacles on the Ice Fields with the crews led by Alexi. The resulting tangle of magical wardings and physical traps had become affectionately known by its architects as "Pharro's Puzzle".

The High Magi swept her braids to one side before sinking back onto the couch, throwing her feet onto the pouffe before Kallis with a groan.

"We're hoping to draw out the sorcerers by, um, *diverting* the army's attention." A small smirk tugged at her lips, "They'll have to redraw the maps after this."

Kallis chuckled and shifted his feet aside for her. "Been doing a bit of landscaping have you?" His copper eyes sparkled with amusement. Ty shook his head at the exchange.

Fae cocked her head. "What?"

He smiled ruefully. "I've never felt so useless in my life," he admitted. "I'm a healer and leader of a people who've lived a peaceful existence for centuries. I thought Throldon was teaching me so much more but this..." He gestured to encompass the world beyond the room in which they sat. La'sa. The approaching army. Magic. "I want to help, but I'm out of my depth." He ran a hand through his golden hair, the ends grown long enough to brush the nape of his neck. "And I'm a long way from home."

"There's always a need for healers, friend." Kallis flicked his fingers toward the fire, making the flames flare.

Fae stood to add more logs to the fire. Kallis might make the flames jump higher, but that would also burn through the wood faster.

"Don't underestimate yourself," she said, somewhat unsettled to hear Ty of all people lacking confidence. "You've saved me from many a disastrous idea in the past. Perhaps it's your pragmatism and wisdom that we need."

Ty lifted a brow. "Pragmatism." He pointed to Kallis. "Fire and shadows." Demilda. "Water and air, right?" She nodded, and he swung his finger around to Fae. "And, what, a bit of everything? And you think my magical power is *pragmatism*?"

Kallis snorted a laugh, and Demilda kicked his feet off the pouffe. "Shut up," she breathed.

Fae rose, and stepped up to Ty's seat. Clasped his hand in hers. "Firstly, it's more than 'a bit' of everything." A laugh creased around his eyes. "You taught me to believe in myself when no one else did. You put me back together when I threw myself into danger. Without you, I would not be here several times over. And you managed all that without a sniff of magic." She gave him a lopsided smile. "Don't be so quick to dismiss yourself. For all we know, you may be the one that holds all this together."

Kallis snorted again. Demilda kicked him again. Hard.

"Shut *up*," she hissed.

Ty looked up at Fae, his eyes lined with silver. "Maybe it's *your* wisdom we all need to hear," he said, voice suddenly hoarse.

The door to the common room flew open to crash against the wall. Cold air blew in, the fire guttering in answer.

Luca stood on the threshold, eyes wild.

"They're here."

They ran up to a vantage point perched over the southern entrance tunnel. Madja and Terrence beat them to the stairs, and fanned out to either side, Madja jamming a bright wooly hat over her mane of untamed silver hair as she reached the top. Kagos stood looking over the Ice Fields in his same black silk robes, seemingly impervious to the cold, a dark statue against the crisp white backdrop. Aiya stood at his side bundled in her flying leathers, the deep funnel collar buttoned all the way up so that only her grey eyes were visible. The largest of Jade's dragons — the red — had joined her today, his bronze eyes swirling with something that looked a lot like distress. The dragon younglings had grown even in the short time they'd been in La'sa, and Alpha's body was now too big for the stables originally given over to him. He'd taken to perching atop the ridge line around the Core, and flying short sweeps across the town centre to stretch his wings.

To one side, Irya stood with Aren and Stef, her eyes closed while the elves squinted into the distance.

"I can't see anything." Aren folded his arms with a frown. The sun was beginning to set, skimming its orange glow across the snow.

"They're there." Jade shifted from foot to foot, her body practically thrumming with nervous tension. Kagos said nothing, simply glowering at the horizon.

Irya frowned, and her eyes opened. "They're there." She nodded to Jade. "Your sense of their magic is turning out to be quite useful."

Jade shook her head, visibly agitated. "It's horrible. The dragons sense it. Like a constant, ear-splitting shriek in their minds." She clasped her hands, wringing them until the whites of her knuckles stood out starkly against her brown skin. Stef sidled closer, looking as if he might comfort her, but stopped at a respectful distance. Alpha watched him with sharp eyes as Jade continued, "I don't feel it like they do, but I can feel their distress." Her eyes darted to Kagos, who remained stoically staring over the darkening Ice Fields.

On closer inspection, Fae saw the lines of strain bracketing his mouth. As if Kagos did indeed sense the unbearable shriek of nearby blood magic.

Stef fixed his polished-steel gaze to the horizon, as if he could see the forces massing there. "An army should not have been able to travel so fast," he observed.

"They used blood magic before to boost the speed and stamina of the troops." Jade rubbed the chill from her arms. "They were looking for dragons then." A shudder rippled through her. The Magi were a far more motivating prize.

"They won't be able to detect La'sa," Luca said, coming to stand beside Fae, subconsciously shielding her from what was to come. "It is warded, its protection linked to each of the High Magi." A look passed between Madja and Demilda, hovering behind him, too quick for Fae to interpret. "We are safe here."

Jade's amber eyes were bright against the snow. "They will break it." She fixed Luca with a look of utter despair. "The Brotherhood will stop at nothing for their power. It is all they know. And Kohl is obsessed beyond reason."

Luca stilled beside Fae, his whole body rigid as the colour drained from his face. "Kohl?"

Jade nodded. "You know him?"

Luca's eyes flickered. "I used to." His voice dropped to a breath on the wind, his gaze drifting to another place, another time.

"Well, he's the Sorcerer Supreme. The one who wants the dragons. And now you." Jade glanced pointedly at Fae. Fear suddenly erased any confidence that had carried her this far, and her face crumpled. "I shouldn't have come here." Her arms came up to grip her shoulders. "We shouldn't have come." Stef put his arm around her then, tucking her close as Alpha nuzzled into her other side, crooning softly.

Madja watched Luca, a sadness in her eyes as he wrestled with himself. Fae wondered how many of those in La'sa would be forced to face the demons of their past before this was through.

Terrence stepped forward.

"We'll meet them on the Fields." His eyes scanned the barren expanse of snow and ice between La'sa and the approaching army. "They won't need to go looking for La'sa if what they're looking for is right in front of them." He turned to face Jade. "How many will come?"

"I know of a dozen Brothers besides Kohl." Jade straightened from Stef's side. "And as many acolytes, although I don't think they'd be involved." Her lips pressed into a line. "The Brothers consider themselves elite. Everyone is beneath them, even their own followers."

"So we're looking at potentially thirteen blood sorcerers, who will definitely play dirty." Terrence turned to Luca. "How many have we got who've face blood sorcery before?"

Luca shook his head. "Not many. Blood magic was never a common path." His jaw tightened, and Fae wondered if Kohl had been on that path before, or if the intervening years had changed the man he used to know.

"I will face them with you." Kagos finally spoke, his voice strained.

Aiya's face was drawn, like she wanted to protest, but knew she couldn't.

"You can't." Jade's eyes widened. "You'd be serving them exactly what they want on a silver platter. You should get as far from here as possible."

But Kagos just shook his head. "You said yourself, they are no longer here for the likes of me." His gaze drifted to Alpha. "Dragonkind and Magi have been hidden away long enough. It is an age for new beginnings. It is time to make the world a safer place for both our peoples to return to."

A look passed between Aren, Stef, and Ty, and the silver-eyed scout stepped forward.

"Count us in. Can't have Kagos claiming all the glory."

Terrence made a sound in his throat. "No offence, but you've never encountered magic wielders before, let alone of this ilk."

Aren lifted a brow with a smirk. "No, but I'm a damn good shot."

"They are flesh and blood, aren't they?" Stef folded his arms.

"Just as much as the next man." Irya glared pointedly at Terrence. "How many times have I got to tell you lot that there is more to life than throwing magic around?" She raised a finger and tallied those present. "We have thirteen here, six with Source Magic. Alexi will mop the floor with you if you don't invite him to join in, and there are enough combat-capable Magi here to make a difference." The Echo planted her hands on her hips. "You've already laid the groundworks..." She waved a hand at the Ice Fields, peppered with tricks and traps, and rapidly fading into dusk. Magi-summoned mists thick enough to spread over hot toast, ice mazes and hidden crevasses deep enough to swallow an army's flank. The grin that worked its way across Irya's face was chilling in its menace. "Now all we need to do is make them regret ever leaving that southern dustbowl in the first place."

57

SEEK THE LIGHT

Despite Irya's galvanising words, there was still the small matter of the army the sorcerers were leading to La'sa's doorstep.

But for some reason, the Echo was a lot less worried about them.

"That army does not want to be here. It's not equipped for it, and I'd bet the troops have no idea why they're plowing through knee-deep snow when they were supposed to be conquering green, fertile lands for their empire." She led them through the rapidly emptying La'sa to the weapons store. It turned out the Archives were long prepared against the need to evacuate, with tunnels and caverns leading through its dark depths, and out. While most of the population headed into the northern quadrant, Fae followed Irya against the flow of people to the training rooms, Ty, Aren, and Stef on their heels. Jade had gone to gather her dragons, Kagos and Aiya with her. Luca and the others had gone to assemble more Magi to fight.

They reached the weapons store and Irya pushed the door open. "I'd put good coin on their generals turning tail and running right back home without the influence of blood magic."

"And what if the blood magic can't be removed?" Ty asked.

Irya waved a hand impatiently. "Too many ifs, elf-man. Let's deal with what we've got first, shall we?" She pulled a wicked knife from the rack and slotted it into a belt sheath already buckled around her waist. Then selected such an assortment of star-shaped blades that Fae wondered how on earth she wasn't cutting herself handling them, let alone how she meant to wield them in a fight. Irya, somehow sensing the attention she drew, winked. "Don't tell me you let my appearance deceive you?" With a deft flick of her wrist, she sent one of the stars spinning through the air. Quick as a blink, it stuck fast in a target pinned to the opposite wall.

Fae gaped. "How—?"

Irya's grin was cat-smug. "I'm better than I let on." She plucked an armoury's worth of assorted blades and secreted them about her person.

Across the room, Aren and Stef selected a bow and two quivers laden with arrows each.

"Fae." Ty turned from the rack. Across his upturned palms lay the twin swords Alexi had tried to give her before.

She reached out and took them from him.

The swords were heavy in her hands, but it was like *they* were weighing *her*; her worthiness to carry them. Her eyes followed the gleaming line of the blades. Once, she had danced with swords such as these. But then she was too lost in darkness to be the falling leaf, to honour the dance she had once loved.

She wasn't broken anymore.

"Thank you." Fae took one in each hand, and gave the blades an experimental slash. A little weightier than she was used to, a little straighter, but well-balanced, the wrap on the grips worn and comfortable. They sliced through the air like extensions of her arms. Tears pricked at the back of her eyes.

She had the strength to wield the swords now. She thought perhaps she always had, she'd just needed to find it again.

Ty hefted a bow and well-stocked quiver of his own.

"Let's go." Irya pulled her coat around her, concealing yet more blades in the process. She pulled her hair back and began braiding it close to her scalp as she stepped from the room.

The Warrens were quiet as they made their way back to the Core, and Fae realised how accustomed she'd become to the constant background murmur of La'sa going about its business. Torches flickered in their sconces, the blue of the ice darkened to black in the absence of daylight. The others were quiet around her, as if they too noticed just how still the town had fallen.

Just as they stepped out into the unnatural stillness of the night, a muttering sound caught at Fae's ears, echoing in the corridors behind her. She pulled up short.

In the dim glow of a side passage, a figure peeled away from the shadows, trailing one arm along the walls as if using it to guide him forward.

"Hello?" Fae squinted into the gloom. The muttering continued.

"Fae, what is it?" Irya came back to see what had caught her attention. Just as the figure stepped into the torchlight.

"Ath?" Fae reached out to steady the Dreamweaver as he stumbled towards her.

"Father what are you doing?" Irya's brow furrowed in alarm. "You're supposed to be heading to the Archives with the others!"

Athanasius shook off his daughter's hand and clutched at Fae's sleeves. "There are rumours. Voices in the ground. They speak to me. They scream in their dreams. There is darkness and fire and tearing and too many pieces to put back together again." His glazed eyes slid sideways, fixed on something that only he could see. "The ants don't see. They poke and they prod and they crawl all over but they can't stop it. The flower drinks the rain and cowers in the dark. But it needs the sun." His hands tightened painfully on Fae's arms as his eyes suddenly snapped back to her, the flicker of the torches giving his gaze a wild cast. "Seek the light or all is lost!"

"What does he mean?" Fae asked Irya without taking her eyes from Athanasius.

Irya shook her head. "I don't understand it. Does any of it sound familiar?"

Fae shook her head. "This isn't my nightmare." But something about what he'd said niggled in the back of her mind.

She closed her eyes. She knew what she had to do.

Irya's hand closed over her shoulder. "What are you doing?"

"I'm going to take back my nightmare. It's time." And she hoped one less nightmare might help the Dreamweaver make sense of what he was seeing.

Irya stepped in as close as her father's grip on Fae would allow. "I strongly disagree. Now is *not* the time to test this."

"I'm not testing anything." Fae opened her eyes to meet the unwavering hazel of Athanasius's gaze. He watched her intently, as if some lucid part of him was waiting for her to set him free. "Your father's going to help me, aren't you Ath?" The tension in his arms loosened the tiniest amount. His eyes fluttered closed on a sigh, anticipating his release. He'd been haunted by her demons long enough.

Fae closed her eyes again, and looked into Eah'lara.

The colours of the Spirit Realm were muted, like a cloudy day, the normally bright nebulae subdued. The threads of the Aethyr quivered. Spirit dust hung expectantly in the air.

Before her, Ath's aura pulsed, the whisper-fine fibres of his being flashing erratic warnings in his head.

Fae had constructed a cage from her own aura. She could do this too. She had to.

Show me. She directed her thoughts to him. His abilities were loosely based on those of an Echo. She hoped he could hear her.

Instead of replying, the cloud-like fibres of Ath's aura parted like curtains of spider-silk, baring himself to her.

Slowly, cautiously, Fae stepped into the Dreamweaver's mind.

Up close, navigating Ath's aura was like dancing through a forest of coloured streamers made of mist and cloud and shafts of starlight that twinkled as she passed. Lights passed along the streamers, carrying messages or thoughts or memories; a strange and extraordinary city of dreams. As she brushed past a ribbon of yellow mist, she had the distinct impression of sitting down to tea in Ath's apartments, calm and peaceful — home. Another length of cool blue cloud tasted of the Archives and hours of fruitful research. One beam of shimmering autumnal light felt exactly like Irya standing beside her, holding her hand.

It would be easy to get lost in the thoughts of someone like Ath, she thought. But she wasn't here to see a life through his eyes. She was here to bring him back to it.

Stepping through the ribbons and streamers and threads of his mind, Fae worked her way to the centre, where dreams lived.

She'd once asked Irya about it: why she could never sense anyone's dreams from looking at their auras. The Echo had explained that dreams were deeply subconscious — a part of the psyche only accessible when the conscious mind was at rest. When the visible aura quieted, that was when dreams shone.

So that is where Fae went. Right to the heart of Ath's subconscious.

And, deep inside his mind, in a cocoon woven of the most delicate threads, a tight knot of dark fibres twisted and contorted, shooting fearful sparks into the aura surrounding it. The bright city of dreams was shuttered around it, as if Ath's mind had closed itself off here, shut itself away.

Fae eased closer to the knot. It pulsed in recognition as she approached, a wave of terror and darkness reaching out towards her.

Once, it would have sent her cowering into a corner of herself.

But every fractured, broken piece of it belonged to her. Every darkness faced, every fear overcome.

No longer would she deny the pieces that made her whole.

She'd come to claim this last one.

Fae reached in. Careful not to disrupt Ath's aura, she scooped up her nightmare, and drew it from his mind.

With a shudder that felt like relief, the curtain that had opened for her slammed shut, shoving her from his mind in a rush.

Reeling from the sudden ejection, Fae glanced back at Ath's aura. The erratic signals flashing warnings across his mind abated, leaving a serene glow behind.

In her hands, the tangled knot of her fears and self-doubt began to unwind, the threads snaking up her arms to join with her aura as if they'd never been away.

Lifting one arm, she inspected the way they nestled in among the brighter threads — the darkness a part of her whole. Not a threat, not a weakness. A reminder of a battle won. An irreplaceable piece of what made her who she was. A scar on her soul.

She had overcome her fear. And become something better. Something stronger.

A feeling of completeness she hadn't known she was missing settled over her.

When she opened her eyes, Ath's clear gaze smiled back at her.

"That's my girl."

Relief swept through Fae on a wave that nearly took her feet out from under her. Ath gripped her shoulders and leant his brow against hers.

"What's going on?" Aren jogged back to join them. The gentle light of dawn was beginning to permeate the mountain. How long had she been in Ath's aura? "Alexi passed us. The sorcerers have reached the edge of the Puzzle. We need to go."

Fae went to follow him back to the gates, but Ath squeezed her shoulders. She turned back to find his eyes clear and earnest.

"The earth dreams of its pain, Fae. We are running out of time. If the beast wakes, the world as we know it will end."

"The beast—?" Fae glanced at Irya.

But Irya was staring at her father, her eyes wide with horror. "That's just a story," she whispered.

Ath shook his head. "All stories are truths, wrapped up in time, child. If we do not heal the being upon which we live, I do not know what will become of us."

A thundering *boom* rocked the mountain.

"Time to go!" Ty's voice called from the end of the corridor.

Fae stared at Ath. "I don't know what to do."

Ath smiled at her. "Have faith."

Another *boom*, closer this time.

"Let's go!" Aren tugged at her arm, and Fae was running, Irya close behind her.

Ath watched them go, until the blue glow of the mountain and the turns of the Warrens hid him from view.

58

BLOOD-RED ROBES

Out on the Ice Fields, poised before the gates of silver and steel, Magi and non-Magi of La'sa stood shoulder to shoulder with dragons, elves, and a human who was not quite human.

Grim-faced, they wore the expressions of a people prepared to die in this fight, knowing that behind them, hidden by the wards of the High Magi, was something worth fighting for.

Five-hundred-year-old children hid in the Archives along with their elderly, probably another five-hundred years older again. Centuries of history, knowledge, and lore was tucked into the dark stacks, as well as artefacts, discoveries, and sciences that the current living world couldn't even dream of.

They were fighting to preserve an entire civilisation. And perhaps even the salvation of the rest of the world.

That was if Fae could stop it from falling apart.

Or waking.

She was still reeling from Ath's words. If the earth was, in fact, a great celestial beast curled up to sleep among the stars, then what did that make her?

A plume of powdered snow exploded into the air a mile away, the flakes glittering as they fell back over the line of tan and metal that split the ground from the sky.

The army was getting closer.

Fae turned to Luca. His face was a pale shade of itself, his eyes hard, lips pressed into a grim line. Like the other High Magi, he wore no weapons, depending solely on his magic.

Fae's hands clenched into fists as she worried over what she might have to do to survive this battle.

How many she may have to kill.

"They've entered the maze then," Demilda remarked as another plume of snow erupted into the air. Her many braids were scraped back from her face into a bunch at the nape of her neck, her profile stark in their absence.

Terrence stood beside her, arms hanging at his sides, slightly bent, as if he was moments away from launching himself into the fray. Kallis's copper eyes glowed with the flames held within, waiting to be released. Madja's face was drawn with worry. She was the only one who looked as if this was the last place she wanted to be.

Around two dozen other Magi of varying abilities were arrayed outside the walls with them — some by their side, some invisible behind La'sa's barrier, a last line of defence. A handful of non-Magi were interspersed among them; like Alexi, they had not accepted the option of being left out of this fight. Rylan stood with the Magi outside the barrier. He exchanged a grim nod with Fae before returning his gaze to the horizon.

Irya stood on Fae's other side, her eyes closed as she watched from within Eah'lara.

As they watched, the army grew nearer, individual soldiers detaching from the mass of sand-coloured troops to work their way through the Puzzle. Bridges like those used to traverse the Amedi River were laid across ice crevasses. Soldiers marched over comrades sacrificed to spring the traps. The maze was simply blown apart with a combination of trebuchets and the war machines Fae had seen on the field against Throldon.

Then the army stopped advancing. There was movement in the ranks.

Alpha, perched on the ridge behind them, let out a piercing shriek.

Fae whirled. The dragon spread his wings wide, his long neck extended as he called out his warning. Below, crouched behind the Magi, the other dragons squawked in answer.

"What's that?" Aren asked, his eyes drifting to Jade.

Irya gasped, her brow furrowed. "No way..."

Fae gripped her arm, torn between her and Jade. "What? What is it?"

Jade frowned as she squinted up at Alpha. "Horse-men?"

In the distance, cries went up from the advancing army, and the sounds of their progress shifted from methodic destruction to the clamour of chaos. Shouting and screaming and the clash of weapons rang out over the snow. The ranks broke, the perfect linear formation turning to a roiling mass of confusion and panic. White powder flew up into the air, obscuring the army from view.

"What the hell is going on?" Kallis demanded.

"Irya," Luca murmured, watching her closed eyes.

The Echo broke out in a grin. "It's the centaurs! The bloody centaurs have engaged the army."

"What?!" A chorus of voices echoed.

Fae exchanged a glance with Ty. "Fanrell," she breathed. "He did it." He'd said he would seek help for them. He'd crossed the plains of Arland to honour his brother, and to request aid from his people. But the centaurs were notoriously insular. She'd never thought he would convince them, let alone make it in time.

"How did he know to come here though?" Stef asked with a frown.

"Let's not worry so much about the how and just be bloody glad they did!" Irya grinned as she opened her eyes and turned her white gaze to Luca. "So many of them, Luc," she said, wonder in her voice. "It's like a new Equi'tox."

"Are there enough?" Luca's brow was creased with concern despite Irya's enthusiasm. Something still worried him.

"There'll have to be."

Alexi stepped forward. "We must help them."

"We have to defend La'sa," Terrence said, keeping his eyes trained on the battle raging on the Ice Fields.

"They cannot find La'sa behind the barrier."

"They made it this far," Irya pointed out.

"Yes, but they were tracking me." Fae glanced from Kagos to Luca. "Weren't they?"

Kagos dipped his head, conceding her point.

"Where *are* the sorcerers?" Aren squinted into the distance.

Jade's fist clenched at her sides, her gaze fixed on the cloud of snow hanging in the air and the ghostly shapes clashing behind it. "They're coming." Above, Alpha bellowed a challenge, the remaining dragons taking up the call. The smaller black — Fearless — spread her wings and hissed her hatred to the sky.

Across the Ice Fields, a group of figures emerged from the white, their blood-red robes stark against the snow.

59

DARKNESS INSIDE

Fanrell aimed a kick to the head of the human poised to strike at Philomena's flank. The metal helmet did little to protect the man from his fury, and the soldier crumpled to the ground, his blood leaking out to stain the snow a marbled red.

Despite his protests, Philomena had insisted on charging into the fray along with the rest of them — a force of over a thousand young centaurs.

And since crashing into the army amassed on this empty expanse of ice and snow, they'd already proved themselves to be the superior force. Fanrell bared his teeth in pride.

Around him, the humans were routing into complete disarray. Some of them stood to fight, some ran in terror as the clans charged them down.

Before him, Philomena whirled as blood sprayed her side, blue eyes blazing. Her hair was scraped back into a rope that swung about her shoulders, the strawberry blonde flecked with red, matching the streaks of war paint daubed across her cheeks and down her sides. She jerked a nod at him, a silent question in her eyes. He nodded a wordless answer.

"'Meena!" A voice called out over the mêlée. Philomena swung around and caught the spear tossed her way by Helena, fighting nearby, her fiery hair catching the dawn light. They'd been snatching up weapons as they went, turning them on the soldiers who swarmed at their feet.

"It's not fair really is it?" Helena grinned, sweeping a southerner off his feet with a single powerful blow of her arm. "They're so puny!"

"But they are armed," Fanrell reminded her. "And they have the numbers. Do not get complacent!" They began pushing through a hastily assembled formation of tan-coloured soldiers, the three of them joined by Tomas, a male whose tribal tattoos merged almost seamlessly with the black of his lower body.

"Helena is right," he said as he covered Fanrell's left flank, Helena at Philomena's right. "These humans are still no match for us." He grabbed a sword mid-swing before it had a chance to land its blow, wrenching the weapon from the soldier wielding it while aiming a well-positioned kick to the ill-fated man's chest. He did not rise again. Tomas hefted the sword in his hand and threw it like a lance, skewering another southerner through the neck. "Where are we heading?"

The snow was causing visibility problems. Kicked up into the air with all the fighting, it hung there, glittering, preventing them from seeing beyond the battle itself.

Philomena looked for whatever had drawn the army here.

"The army was marching towards something further north," she said as they fought their way through the fray. She threw her spear at a southern woman about to hack at the exposed flank of a centaur. The soldier screamed as the spear pierced her shoulder, and the centaur kicked back, sending her flying.

Helena slashed indiscriminately with her purloined sword, dealing out injuries with haphazard accuracy. "So what? Do we care what they wanted? I thought we were just stopping them before they painted the clan lands red." She abandoned the sword with a grunt when it became wedged in a soldier's armour. "Although they don't seem to be worth the bother."

Fanrell grabbed another spear sticking up from a fallen soldier as they passed. Tomas had already found a replacement for his sword.

"If they achieve their goal here, the clan lands will be drowned in shadow." Philomena's eyes scanned ahead of them, desperately searching for a sign of something dangerous enough to cause such an outcome. "But I cannot see what it is, or what exactly they will do." She growled her frustration and pushed forward, the others picking up their pace to match hers.

When they finally made it to the northern edge of the army — what had been the front lines before their attention had been wrenched around to face the centaurs — they were faced with yet another inexplicable piece to Philomena's riddle.

"What the—" Helena voiced the thought going through all of their heads.

Ahead, walls erupted from the ice while deep crevasses cleaved the ground. Someone had gone to great lengths to defend a featureless stretch of the Ice Fields. Lethal pits were concealed beneath thin layers of ice, clouds of mist obscuring yet more traps hidden in the maze. But no sign of *what* they were meant to be defending.

"There!" Philomena pointed. A dozen figures made their way across the Fields, the obstacles simply melting before them. Their robes were a deep blood-red — all except one. One of the figures wore pure white. "That's him." The one from her vision. The one who harboured darkness inside.

And there to meet them, was another group, too far away for Fanrell to make out.

"Who are they?" Tomas raised an arm to shield pale eyes against the glare of the snow.

"I don't know." Philomena watched the two groups as they neared each other.

Helena glanced at her. "What do we do now?"

Philomena's brow furrowed, confusion and concern warring over her features.

"I don't know."

60

SPILLED BLOOD

Fae watched the sorcerers approach, instantly recognising the Sorcerer Supreme in his silver-edged-white. Kohl.

"We can handle them, can't we?" She looked around the High Magi. Her control of the Source Magic now was such that she barely had to think before the elements answered to her. If the High Magi could match her, surely they had the combined ability to hold off a dozen sorcerers.

Didn't they?

The dragons keened behind them, their distress palpable. Alpha launched himself from the ridge to land beside his siblings. Jade's features paled, sweat beading her brow.

They'd known the blood bond between her and the Sorcerer Supreme would prove a liability in battle, but they'd made the executive decision to have everyone bound by blood magic outside of the barrier. La'sa was hidden behind it, the mountain itself rendered invisible to outsiders. They didn't want Kohl to go looking any further than the Magi arrayed before him.

Irya gave Fae's hand a final squeeze, and Fae watched as she retreated to stand with the elves a few paces behind.

Kagos, Aiya, Aren, Stef, Ty, and Irya. And now Jade as well. Without magic to help, they were undoubtedly the bravest of her friends to stand and fight beside her. She turned back to face the sorcerers.

They would not get past her.

"Alexi," Luca murmured. "Take the others to assist the centaurs. If that army turns its attention back towards us, La'sa is lost. They'll overrun it before the wards have a chance to deflect them."

Alexi didn't hesitate. He rounded up the Magi and non-Magi who'd insisted on defending their home, and led them away, leaving the High Magi to face the sorcerers.

A few sorcerers' heads turned to watch them leave, but their focus was trained on Fae and Luca as they stepped forward. Madja and Kallis stood to their left, Demilda and Terrence to their right. The others stayed back, waiting.

Kohl stopped ten paces away, his Brothers spread out behind him. His bronze skin and black hair gleamed in the sun, the silver edging his robes catching the morning light. He looked like a god, come to survey his domain.

The dragons fell eerily silent, their bronze eyes whirling. Aiya and Stef closed ranks around Jade. Kagos glared at the sorcerers as if his obsidian gaze alone could wipe them from the Fields.

The Sorcerer Supreme surveyed the group before him, his soulless black eyes scanning each of them, weighing them and dismissing them in a single glance. His eyes lingered on Jade, even lifted to appreciate Alpha's impressive form looming over them. Finally, his gaze came to rest on Fae.

"I must thank you for leaving such carnage in your wake, my dear." He smiled, but it was cold, the kind of humour found in dark places. "We would never have been able to track you all the way here if you weren't so content to kill."

Fae stifled the urge to flinch at his words. The barb struck true, but she refused to show it. Beside her, Luca shifted so that his arm brushed hers — a silent reminder of his presence, and of his words uttered in the snow.

The move wasn't missed by the Sorcerer Supreme. His eyes snapped to the Magi.

"Luca Fialli." He sneered. His accent was strangely smooth. Nothing like Jade's rolling syllables. "You haven't changed a bit. I thought you dead. *Friend*." The last word dripped with such venom it was a miracle Luca still stood.

"Kohl Reksus," he replied flatly. "I could say the same for you." He eyed the sorcerer. "I thought you died with the rest of the Brotherhood. Clearly, I was mistaken."

Kohl's lip curled, hatred radiating from every inch of him. "It seems we were both misinformed."

Tension crackled in the air between them.

Luca's jaw tensed. "What happened to you?"

Kohl laughed, and it was cold and hollow. "What happened to *me?*" He stared at Luca like he was joking. "I survived, friend. The dragons wiped out my people without a second thought and I was left with *nothing*." He spat the words, as if they burned him. "I rose from the ashes of the old Brotherhood — from the spilled blood of *my people* — and became unbreakable." The beatific smile that spread over his lips chilled Fae to the core: it was triumph coloured with an unsettling edge of madness. He cocked his head to one side and considered Luca, as if appraising a new set of robes. "What's your excuse?"

Luca stilled, and the grin on Kohl's face spread even wider. "Do they even know?"

"We know everything Luca's done for us," Demilda said, her musical voice turned hard as steel.

"Do you now?" Kohl regarded her, hawk-like. His black eyes flicked back to Luca. "I thought you were above such practices, friend."

Beside Fae, Luca was barely breathing.

"What's he talking about?" she whispered.

Kohl straightened, raising his voice to call over them. "I'm sure my dear Jade would be interested to hear the saviours she was so quick to run to are just as capable of using her dragons as I am." He levelled his gaze on Luca again. "You know you could join me. Finally bring both branches of magic together. We'd be unstoppable."

Luca shook his head. "You've become corrupted by your power, Kohl. Blood magic? It is taboo for a reason. Look at what it has done to you. What happened to the man I knew? The boy from the Wolds?"

At his words, Kohl's face twisted into an animalistic snarl irreconcilable with the calm demeanour of a moment before.

"I would not be so quick to deal out your judgements Luca." He bared his teeth. "Do you really think I can't smell it on you?"

"Luca," Fae breathed. What was he talking about?

Luca's gaze flickered.

"Ah." Kohl glanced between them, a wicked glint in his eye. "Not everyone then."

"Please." Luca's lips hardly moved, the tension around his eyes the only sign of his panic. Fae turned back to the sorcerer.

Kohl smiled. "While our dear friend Luca here admonishes me for harnessing forbidden magics, what he neglects to mention is how his blood, too, is bound." He let out a laugh. "You reek of blood, Luca. Did you really think I wouldn't notice?" Triumph lit his eyes. "So we're really not so different after all. From the Wolds, to the War, to opposite ends of the earth — how both those boys fell." His mouth curled into a mocking sneer.

Fae's eyes darted to Luca's, to see the truth of Kohl's words etched on his face.

"Luca..."

"I did what I had to, to protect what's left of my people," Luca said, and Fae noticed how careful he was with his words. How careful he was not to reveal La'sa, hidden in the wards behind them. "What you've done is only for yourself." Kohl simply smirked.

Fae stared between them, then at the other High Magi. None of them seemed surprised by this revelation. So they'd all known? They'd all sat there and told her how abhorrent blood magic was, when they'd known Luca was using it all along. The sting of betrayal arced through her.

"What did you do?" she hissed at him.

Luca's jaw clenched. "Our protection was built with mine and Kallis's magic. Light and dark, like I told you." His gaze flicked to his fellow High Magi before returning to hold hers. "But it is bound to all five of us. In blood." His voice dropped so low she almost missed his next words. "To protect everyone else."

Fae's eyes widened as comprehension dawned on her. The High Magi had bound their lives to the protection of La'sa. They'd used blood magic, the most perverse magic, for the purest purpose.

And if they died defending La'sa, their lives would add to the tally Luca carried with him every day. La'sa would fall. The toll... Fae swallowed the lump in her throat. Blinked back the burn of tears.

"Come, Luca." Kohl stepped forward, his arms held out as if he intended to embrace him. "Let us not fight. Join us instead. We have all of us been relegated to the shadows of the world for too long. Let us remind the mundane of why they ought to fear us."

"That is exactly the kind of thinking that had so many of us hunted like animals. Sold into service. Killed." Luca shook his head. "No, Kohl. This ends now."

Kohl sneered at his words. "Perhaps for you. *I* will endure." At some unspoken signal, the twelve sorcerers behind him snapped out their wrists, and red sparks leapt from their fingertips like scarlet claws. "Hand over your pet" — Kohl jerked his chin at Fae — "and perhaps I'll let you live."

Fire danced in Fae's veins, and to either side of her, she felt the elements answer to the High Magi as they drew upon them.

Luca's eyes blazed. "No."

Kohl gave no further warning. With a shriek of fury, he lifted one arm over his head, his hand crackling with crimson sparks.

Time slowed as Fae watched. The sparks in Kohl's hand solidified into a javelin of blood-red lightning. His arm twisted to grip the weapon and drew back, readying to throw.

She blinked, and the javelin was hurtling straight for Luca.

The lightning sparked and twisted as it flew through the air, undecided on its final form. It hissed and spat, careening across the space between them, drawn to Luca as if by some force other than Kohl's aim, destined to end a life, to spill blood in some sort of morbid symmetry, and all Fae could do was watch as death flashed towards him.

The lightning hit solid air inches from Luca's face, dispersing across a hardened barrier in a harmless shower of sparks.

Relief swept through Fae before red sparks crashed against more shields of colour around her, and all hell broke loose.

Kallis threw a cloak of dark towards the sorcerers while Madja hurled ice spears at them through the murk. Demilda held a shield of hardened air around herself and Terrence while he pulled the ground out from beneath the sorcerers, dropping them into a pit in the ice.

Luca drew fire, wreathing his arms in his element to throw flames straight at Kohl.

But they were outnumbered on magic wielders. Two of Kohl's Brothers flanked him, while the other ten were spread out between the remaining High Magi.

The sound of crumbling mountains shook the ice behind Fae, and wind buffeted her as the sound of huge, leathery wings lifted into the air. Kagos and Aiya had taken to the skies.

Kagos roared his outrage, and swooped down to pluck one of the Brothers from the ground, the shadow of his black wings chasing across the ice beneath him. Red sparks flashed as the sorcerer attempted to fight back before he was torn into two, his torso landing in the snow several feet from his legs.

Kohl watched with an air of mild interest. Then he pulled back one sleeve.

A glimmer of gold glinted briefly at his wrist before he covered it with his hand, red sparks charging the air between his palms.

Jade screamed. Fae spun in time to see her crumple to the ground, cradling her head, her face twisted in agony. Her dragons shrieked in answer, their bronze eyes whirling with fury and pain. Their wings jerked out to the sides, like puppets pulled by invisible strings. Alpha's head whipped back and forth as he tried in vain to shake free of a call he could not ignore.

As one, the dragons lifted into the air, their movements unnatural and forced, and flew straight for Kagos.

Kagos pulled out of a dive towards a second sorcerer when Envy threw herself into his path, clawing and shrieking as her purple wings caught on his dorsal ridge. Aiya yelled out from atop his back as the rest of Jade's flight swarmed them. Kagos beat his enormous wings, the resulting downdraft whipping up yet more snow from the ground as he banked, drawing the dragons away from the sorcerers.

"No... No no no," Jade moaned, her hands braced on either side of her head, eyes screwed shut. "Fight back. Fight back," she muttered. Stef crouched beside her, powerless to do anything to help. To either side of them, Ty and Aren had taken up their bows, and were firing at the sorcerers, who deflected their shots with swirling shields of sparks. Aren's silver eyes narrowed, assessing every move of his opponent, searching for the opening. Ty drew back arrow after arrow, the muscles of his arms bunching as he moved smoothly from one shot to the next, brow knitted in concentration. Irya stood, eyes closed, surveying the carnage from Eah'lara. Her arm whipped out, and a star-shaped blade sank into the flesh of a sorcerer, distracting them long enough for Demilda to score a hit. The Echo reached into her coat, and another blade flew across the field. A bolt of scarlet lightening arced towards her, and she leapt, eyes still closed, spinning smoothly in the air to dodge the attack while throwing another star.

Fae turned back to the sorcerers. Seconds had passed. And yet already everyone was locked in a battle to the death.

All because of her.

Across the field, her eyes found the empty black of Kohl's gaze. He smiled an invitation.

Inside, her elements clamoured to come out. Answering a need in her to make everything right.

To save everyone caught up by this sorcerer's greed.

To repair the earth that gave her the power to fight him.

Fire wreathed her arms.

Beside her, Luca switched to air.

And without a word exchanged, they threw their elements forward, the fire and air combining to hurl an inferno at Kohl that even a Sorcerer Supreme could not withstand.

61

BATTLE OF GODS

Fanrell watched as Kagos took to the sky.

He hadn't expected the dragon to be here — had he followed the army? He wondered who else had come north, and what had drawn them here.

A group of humans peeled away from those fighting the robed figures. They ran across the Ice Fields towards the ongoing battle between army and centaurs, casting worried glances behind them as they went.

The humans reached them just as an inferno roared across the ice.

Helena swore, and Fanrell shoved Philomena behind him, throwing an arm up to shield his eyes. The fire had come seemingly from nowhere, and blazed bright enough to blind.

One of the human males, olive-skinned and wearing a sleeveless leather jerkin over bared arms, turned to watch as flames met scarlet sparks over the ice. Even in the light of day, the orange-red glow gilded his face.

"Shit," the human murmured. He waved the others past him. "Go, go. The army cannot be allowed to reach La'sa." Thirty or so humans threw themselves into the fray, as distinctive from the soldiers as the sun from the moon, their cold-weather garb easily distinguishable from the tan uniforms of the southerners. A handful of them drew weapons as they went, the rest of them drawing ice and fire from thin air, felling enemies with a simple wave of their arms. One of the humans, a young male with copper hair and green eyes, stopped to watch the battle for a moment before he, too, joined his people fighting the army. As he went, Fanrell spotted flames dancing across his palms.

Fanrell would have stared, except that a battle of gods appeared to be unfolding across the ice from where he stood. Flames flared bright and hot, the ice beneath gleaming where it melted. The air shimmered between the two sides, like a mirage. Smoky shadows enveloped the robed humans, only to be blown apart from within by a shower of crimson sparks. Red lighting lurched across the space between them, intercepted by a wall of rock and ice erupting from the ground. In the skies above, Kagos tangled with several smaller dragons, dodging and banking as if to avoid harming them.

Fanrell glanced sideways to the human who stood beside them. "Who are they?"

The human blinked up at him, as if he hadn't noticed the presence of four centaurs standing at the edge of one battle, watching another. His eyes were a mix of blue and green and earthy brown. His stubbled jaw clenched as he turned back to the terrifying display of powers over the ice.

"They are the High Magi of La'sa, fighting blood sorcerers who would bleed any being of power dry to fuel their unnatural spells."

Fanrell watched as another volley of sparks was met with fire. He had no problem imagining which side was which. Philomena had already told him the one in white was black inside.

Tomas jerked his chin at the magic wielders. "Who will win?"

Lines bracketed the human's mouth, his body as taut as a bowstring, eyes fixed on the battle.

"Pray that it is not the sorcerers."

62

SOMETHING LIKE HOPE

Fae threw up a wall of air. Luca hurled a vortex of fire at Kohl.

The Brother to his right deflected it with a a spiral of red runes that flared on impact, spitting sparks.

The Brother to his left was already tracing a fiery shape in the air with both hands. The instant it was complete, he slammed his palms into the centre, and a rod of scarlet lightning shot from each point, arcing towards them at breakneck speed. Fae drew a sheet of water from the air to absorb the projectiles, the lethal charge dissipating in a blinding flash before being pulled to the ground.

Above, flashes of colour caught the sun as Kagos fended off Jade's dragons. Blood so dark it was almost black dripped onto the snow below, and Fae didn't know if it belonged to him or one of the others. With a flick of her fingers, she incinerated it before the sorcerers thought to use it.

They were horribly outnumbered. Kallis and Madja were holding out against the five sorcerers facing them, but Demilda was flagging beside Terrence, and her opponents were pushing their advantage.

The *twang* of bowstrings punctuated arrows and blades shooting past from behind, pulling at least some of the sorcerers' attention, but it wasn't enough.

And then a bolt of red lightning went wide.

And struck the hidden mountain behind them.

Luca flinched.

Demilda cried out.

Terrence stumbled, the earth he wielded falling to the ground.

Kohl's eyes went wide, and a triumphant grin spread over his face.

Fae whirled.

Magic rippled like a shimmering curtain hanging in the air, the scarlet of the sorcerers' blood magic staining the barrier to allow glimpses of the silver-and-steel gates of La'sa.

And the hidden Magi arrayed before it.

"What's this?" The hunger in Kohl's eyes was terrifying. He turned to watch the Magi fighting alongside the centaurs across the ice, flashes of Source Magic marking them among the throng. "You're not protecting *them*." He turned back to the revealed barrier. "You're protecting *that*." His tongue darted out to wet his lips. He glanced at each of the High Magi in turn, nostrils flaring as if he could smell their fear. "What are you hiding, I wonder?" He cocked his head, eyeing the rippling magics. "Target the barrier."

The sorcerers turned their efforts to the magic around La'sa.

The effect was immediate.

Demilda stumbled to her knees, her face a mask of pain. Terrence gritted his teeth and continued to throw rock and ice, but his movements were laboured, and the sorcerers deflected them easily. Kallis's shadows flickered, and he loosed fire, sending it across the ice like oil to lick at the sorcerers' robes while their attention was on the barrier. Madja planted her feet and pulled ice spears from the ground, scattering them out wide to take on as many of the sorcerers as she could reach.

Fae tried to shield them all, but it wasn't the High Magi that needed protecting. She glanced behind her. She couldn't hold a barrier around a mountain. She turned back and threw out fire with Kallis, the flames catching on the robes of two sorcerers. They stumbled away, batting and stamping on the flaming cloth, while another launched a spray of scarlet blades back at them.

Fae shielded in time, but Kallis was too slow, his focus split in half. Sparks exploded from his side and shoulder, and he staggered back with a grimace, blood soaking his shirt. Fae went to run to him when a hand landed on her shoulder.

"Don't." Luca looked back at her, his gaze set with grim

determination... and something else. He stared into her eyes, as if searching for something. Something like hope.

That look... it sent a chill into her heart.

A crackle filled the air, and he threw up a shield, his gaze not breaking from hers. Sparks scattered with a hiss. He leaned in. "Hold this line." He stepped back again, and a blade of light appeared in his hand. In a single motion he drew it across his palm. Blood welled in the cut, dripping down onto the snow.

"Luca, what—?" Fae stared at him as he began mumbling words under his breath, teeth gritted, bracing himself.

His eyes met hers again.

"Do not let them pass you." He slammed his palm to the ground.

The air rippled with power as it burst from him, waves of magic surging out, knocking everyone off their feet.

Everyone but the High Magi, who stood firm.

Madja panted as if she'd just run ten laps of La'sa. She glared at Luca. "What did you do?"

Luca slowly rose to his feet. His eyes were wild, his face flushed. He had the look of someone staring down death. "I gave you a chance."

Across the ice, the sorcerers scrambled to their feet. Kohl stood, an amused smile playing across his lips.

"Nice trick, Luca, but it's only a matter of time. You can't hold out against all of us." He hefted another crimson javelin, and hurled it at the barrier, his Brothers following his lead.

The High Magi braced for the onslaught.

But it was Luca alone who fell, whose legs collapsed beneath him, dropping him to his knees. The other High Magi stood unaffected.

Terrence stared at him. "You idiot."

Luca trembled as the sorcerers threw everything they had at the barrier. At him. "Only if it doesn't work," he forced out through gritted teeth.

He'd severed their bonds to La'sa. To give them a chance to fight back.

He'd taken it all on himself.

Fae's chest tightened. He was doing what he hadn't been able to do five hundred years ago. Taking all of the fire, so the others could live.

"You think that'll work?" Kohl called out. "You can't possibly think you're strong enough to withstand me and my Brothers alone?" He laughed, and it was cold and mocking. "What arrogance, even from you, Luca! You'll die, and then so will the rest of your brethren. And I'll still bind your little pet to me. And there will be nothing in the world powerful enough to take what's mine again."

Demilda sent a ball of wind at him, knocking him back and obscuring his next words. Madja pulled ice spears to erupt in jagged spikes from the ground, forcing the Brothers to leap back or be impaled. One was too slow and cried out as ice tore up the length of his arm. Kallis threw out a wall of fire that split into ribbons of flame reaching out to wrap around necks and limbs. Terrence went back to basics, digging great hunks of stone from beneath the ice and lobbing them at the sorcerers' heads. It was as if they'd been unleashed. Irya, Ty, Aren, and Stef added their shots to the mêlée, taking advantage of, and adding to the distractions.

Four sorcerers fell, but the rest were still pummelling the barrier with their magic, and Luca bore the brunt of the impact through the blood bond. His arms braced on the ice, shaking as he held himself up, refusing to concede the final distance to the ground. His face contorted in agony, sweat dripping from his brow, and Fae heard the sounds of his pain leak out past gritted teeth as the barrier was struck again, and again.

Seeing victory within his grasp, Kohl began targeting Luca directly. Fae threw her elements in his path, alternating with the others to protect him. She held up a shield of hardened air while Madja threw ice daggers at Kohl. Terrence summoned a wall of solid rock while Fae lashed out with her fire whip. She was forced to draw water to catch a hail of crimson sparks, while Demilda pulled air away from the sorcerers, slowing their attacks for an instant. Ty and Aren and Stef peppered the Brothers with arrows, but they were fast running out of ammunition. Irya was slowing too, carefully choosing each target before surrendering another blade. In between attacks she called out warnings to the others, her view of the Spirit Realm giving her one advantage the sorcerers didn't have.

Luca roared as the barrage of magic continued to batter the shield around La'sa.

Then, one of Terrence's boulders caught the sorcerer closest to Kohl in the temple. The Brother crumpled to the ground like paper. Kohl's eyes went wide with fury as he tallied his remaining Brothers. Only half remained standing.

With a snarl that wasn't quite human, Kohl brought his hands up again, and ruby-beaded gold glinted at both wrists.

He has two *bracelets?* Jade had only warned them about one.

He floated his hands one over the other, palms turned inwards, level with the bracelets, and scarlet lightning flashed between them.

His eyes found Fae's, and his feral grin was tinged with more than a hint of madness. "I'm surprised you believe death will stop us." The motionless figure of the sorcerer at his feet twitched. "You forget that I control life itself."

Around him, the lifeless forms of his fallen Brothers lurched to their feet, their movements awkward and stilted. The torso of Kagos's first victim dragged himself over the snow, eyes stained with blood.

Horror curled through Fae, wrapping gnarled fingers around her throat. It was just like on the battlefield, except now it was the sorcerers themselves risen from the dead to fight again.

An arrow whipped past her, quickly followed by a second, pinning the torso's arms to the ground.

Ty stepped up beside her, a third arrow nocked and trained on the next undead sorcerer.

"You're not alone, Fae." He loosed the shot. It struck the walking corpse in the leg, and it stumbled. Aren appeared beside Ty, his silver eyes flashing as he worked on immobilising sorcerers that had no business walking again. A knife flew past Fae's other shoulder, and Irya was beside her too. Behind them, Stef defended Jade, still fighting against her own blood bond.

Ty nocked a new arrow, and released it with enough force to throw another undead off its feet. "You work on the magic. We'll keep these ones occupied." Because no matter how many arrows were lodged in the corpses, they just rose again, and kept coming.

She had to take out Kohl.

Fae called air, and the delicate, flitting form inside her swelled until its wings were wide and fierce. With a single beat, she drew a storm from the sky, and hurled it at the Sorcerer Supreme, hoping to interrupt his casting.

As soon as he stumbled, she pulled earth from beneath the ice, her element-aspect trumpeting its distaste of the creatures trespassing here as it rose up to encase Kohl in a prison of earth and stone.

When his Brothers ran to free him, she called water from the ice, and pushed a waist-high wave across the ground, snatching their feet out from under them and sending them sprawling.

Fire roared through her veins as she finally flung spears of flame into the tomb she'd built for the Sorcerer Supreme. This was one life that would not weigh on her.

Everything went quiet, the only sounds those of the battle that continued between the centaurs and the army across the ice.

The undead sorcerers were still. The dragons hovered in place. Jade gasped as if she'd been drowning this whole time, and was only now able to breathe.

Luca lifted his head, chest heaving.

The remaining Brothers slowly pushed to their feet, soaked through. One began tracing symbols in the air, his red sparks guttering when matching spears of ice and fire appeared before his face.

Kallis grinned at him through the pain of his injuries. "I wouldn't." Madja's blue gaze was unforgiving beside him.

As one, they watched the prison of earth on the ice. Silent and still.

"Did we do it?" Fae barely believed it.

Then Jade cried out.

63

BENIGN MALICE

The pain was too much.

Jade couldn't think straight.

Her mind was not her own. Her body wasn't.

The dragons keened inside her head, their pain magnifying hers.

Kohl's grip on her was crushing. She was drowning in blood, broken beneath his will as it pressed down on her with the weight of a mountain. And the threads that she clung to like a lifeline thrummed with such pain until she wasn't sure where she existed inside it anymore.

And then, the pain stopped.

She gasped, the relief a new kind of pain in itself.

The ice was still.

Above, Alpha and the others hovered around Kagos, wounds leaking from all over his body. Wounds that he'd taken to avoid harming her family.

She sent up her silent thanks to the old dragon for sparing them.

"Did we do it?" Fae breathed in front of her.

And then fresh agony crashed over Jade.

She was vaguely aware of crying out, but the world disappeared behind a haze of red and a wave of nothing but pain.

She knew if she could only get hold of a blade, that the pain would stop.

What?

Desperate for it to end, she lunged for Stef.

He staggered back, but she grabbed the knife at his hip.

Fae. She was the reason this was all happening. If she could get even a drop of her blood on the blade... not to kill — they needed her alive — just enough... Kohl could make this all stop.

NO! These weren't her thoughts.

But Kohl's laugh echoed through her head, and she was already running at Fae, knife in hand.

Fae spun in time to see Jade lunge for the knife at Stef's hip, her face twisted in anguish, her motions awkward and stilted.

Stef, taken completely unawares by her sudden flurry of motion, was too stunned to react.

And then, tears cutting down her cheeks, Jade launched herself at Fae.

Everything happened too fast.

Jade's eyes were filled with guilt and shame and pain.

The blade in her hand glinted with benign malice, merely a tool to be directed.

Stef lurched for Jade's arm.

Luca shouted something.

Jade's blade was coming for Fae.

She was fighting every step of the way. At the last minute, she wrenched the blade up...

Then Fae was shoved roughly to the side. She stumbled. And turned.

Ty stood before Jade, his hand on her shoulder, her hand on his chest, as if they meant to dance in the snow.

Except for the wide-eyed horror on her face.

And the blood dripping onto the snow between them.

The earth prison exploded outward in a shower of crackling red lighting and sparks.

But all Fae could see was Stef's dagger protruding from Ty's chest.

64

KNIFE EDGE

Time slowed to a crawl.

Jade fell back as if burned. Her hands came up to cover her mouth until she realised they were slick with blood.

Fae dived for Ty as he crumpled to the ground.

Aren's eyes went wide, his lips stretched into a shout as he aimed an arrow at Kohl.

The Sorcerer Supreme batted it away with a wave of his hand as he emerged from his prison, the stone crumbling behind him.

A jagged bolt of red lightning struck Madja in the back.

Terrence hauled up a wall of earth between them and the sorcerers.

Kohl tore it down in an instant, advancing on them, his remaining Brothers on his heels.

But Fae's attention was fixed on the dagger in Ty's chest. His shirt was soaked almost black with blood, the stain running red out onto the snow. She clutched at him, all her healer's intuition leaking from her as his eyes began to lose focus. Should she remove the dagger? Should she put pressure on the wound? There was *so* much blood.

Ty gasped for breath. "Fae, I—" Then he just stopped.

Fae stared at his eyes, their familiar storm-grey gazing vacantly at the sky.

A space hollowed out inside of her.

And thunder rumbled within it.

Her mind went blank, her understanding of the world turned on its head.

Every moment drew out, like the pause between the breath and the scream.

Every sound was muted. Every sight, sharp as shattered glass.

She blinked. In the time it took her eyes to open again, Ty was still...

She glanced up at Jade, her hands red with blood, her eyes wide with horror.

But Jade wasn't the one who'd wielded the knife. Not really.

Fae blinked again.

Calm as the sky before a storm, she passed a hand over Ty's face, gently closing his eyes. Tenderly tucked his yellow-gold hair behind one ear. She leaned forward to press her forehead to his, a touch they'd exchanged a hundred times before.

Before.

Before Ty died.

The earth pitched under her feet.

Fae stood. Turned.

The sorcerers were advancing, the High Magi sporting their fair share of injuries. Demilda's dark skin had leeched of its rich colour, Madja lay prone on the ice, unmoving. Kallis was fighting back, heavily favouring his wounded side. Terrence was working to intercept as many of the shots destined for the barrier around La'sa as he could, but Luca still cried out as a few found their mark.

There was too much for her mind to process. People she cared about were hurting. People she cared about were dying.

People she cared about were gone.

There wasn't enough room in her heart for the pain she felt. For the loss, and the hate, and the hurt.

She felt empty. She felt as if she might explode.

Fae's eyes found Kohl, and the gold around her irises flared bright.

The earth thundered, as if some giant approached.

The sky darkened.

The wind chilled until ice crystals hung suspended in the air between them.

And then Fae erupted.

Fire licked over her skin so hot it burned, but she was beyond caring.
Air spiralled through her hair.

Water hardened into needles of ice that hovered at her waist.

And the earth itself rolled at her feet in response to her grief.

Kohl's eyes lit up, his lips stretched into a mad grin, as if he'd been presented with his prize.

Someone called her name, but it came from another place, far away from where her grief and rage held her.

Kohl's lips moved, and his sorcerers advanced on her, stances wide as the earth bucked beneath them. The undead Brothers stumbled towards her with empty, blood-filled eyes.

Dark joined her fire and both lashed out in tongues of black and orange to wrap tendrils around the sorcerers, choking and burning before tossing them aside, where the corpses simply rose again. Water coalesced around their heads, drowning them where they stood. She threw ice needles and stone spears at Kohl in an unceasing hail of death. The Sorcerer Supreme laughed at her display of power, blocking her attacks with circles of scarlet sparks. Batting them away with swords of crimson lightning.

Despite the death she rained down on the sorcerers, the elements tugged at her hold, eager for more. To be released to their fullest extent. To rage, to destroy.

But somewhere in the deepest recesses of her mind, the words of the Dreamweaver whispered.

You will become the very thing you fear to be.

The earth shuddered, and she felt it in her bones. In her soul.

She pulled the elements close to her, and they swirled around her body like a storm in a marble.

The sorcerers continued to advance on her, but she feared what would happen if she unleashed herself on them. How many others would be caught up in her power.

She balanced on a knife-edge. Control on one side. Utter destruction on the other.

Luca called out to her, the sound reaching her through a waterfall.

Through the whirling mix of elements, she watched as Kohl raised a wrist to his mouth, and bit down on the bracelet he wore there.

Red glistened on his lips.

A flurry of motion off to the side caught her attention as one of Jade's dragons — the black — plummeted from the sky.

"No!" Jade screamed as Fearless swooped down to take up the dagger Kohl held aloft, and then beat her ebony wings towards the maelstrom of power that surrounded Fae.

He still hadn't given up on obtaining Fae's blood. He was truly insane.

Stop! she cried down her bond, but it was slick with blood.

Jade stood frozen as Fearless took the blade and dived towards Fae.

Above, Alpha bellowed his rage and fear, but the blood bond held him in place too.

Kagos glanced between them, and comprehension lit his obsidian eyes. He folded his wings and dropped from the sky, angling to intercept the smaller dragon. But not fast enough.

Fearless collided with the elements crashing around Fae, her wings crumpling, the force of the impact throwing her back across the ice. Towards Jade.

Jade grabbed for the blade as Fearless lurched to her feet. But the dragon struggled against her, caught in the grip of Kohl's control. She reared to pull away, and the dagger sliced a bright line across Jade's face. The effect was instant.

Fearless shrieked in horror. Her talons spasmed open and the dagger fell from her grip as she rushed to Jade's side.

Jade shrank away, blood dripping down her cheek.

But something had changed.

The oily sheen of the blood bond fell away from the threads within her.

Beside her, Fearless keened anxiously, butting her wedge-shaped head against her face, her bronze eyes clear.

With a sudden flurry of leathery wings, the rest of her flight landed around her, and Jade's mind was flooded with love and concern as each of her dragons came forward to check her over for themselves.

I'm okay, she assured them, tense with the fear that Kohl could wrench them away at any second.

But their movements were their own. The bonds within her hummed with nothing but love.

They'd broken the hold of the blood bond. Somehow. She touched a hand to her cheek and it came away wet with her blood. Was that why the Brotherhood had always been so careful about bleeding her?

She looked back at Kohl. White hot fury simmered in his gaze.

Alpha stepped in front of her, wings spread to shield her from the Sorcerer Supreme's wrath. As if on command, the others surrounded her, a living shield.

He will not harm you again. Alpha's rumble echoed in her head. The threads of the rest of the flight thrummed in agreement.

No, she agreed. Whatever came next, they would fly far, *far* away from wherever the Brotherhood ended up.

Through the flurry of wings around her, she watched as Kohl turned his fury back to Fae.

But he'll kill everyone else.

Kohl's face was twisted with rage when he turned back to Fae.

Without warning, he lashed out.

At Luca.

"*No.*"

Fae threw her arms out wide, and her elements were unleashed.

Fire roared and leapt across the ice. Earth rumbled deep within her, the ground underfoot trembling in agreement. Water rushed through her veins. Air whipped up the snow, screaming its cold fury. Dark whispered promises of death in the shadows.

Kohl brought his hands together and then flung them out towards her.

A crackling net of crimson lighting swept across the ice.

A wave of her fire rolled out to meet it.

They clashed in an explosion that shook the ground, hot air billowing from the collision. Flames flared out wide, red arcing through the air around like crackling, fiery wings.

Fae pulled stone from under the ice and hurled it through the fire. The flames parted around the spears, enough for her to see red sparks shatter the stone from within. Scarlet lightning leapt across the space between them, a blood-red whip that snaked towards her neck. She drew water from the snow to deflect it to the ground, but in the split second she was distracted, Kohl threw another crimson net towards her. It lowered over her, a dome of lightning sparking closer and closer.

But her elements were no longer so easily cowed. Water and wind burst from her, the force of it seen and heard for miles, the lightning flung in skittering sparks that lit up the sky.

Enough. This was not a god she fought, just a man who thought to make himself one. She had fought worse before.

And she was stronger now.

A storm darkened the skies, and wind swirled up around Fae, ferocious gusts twining about her arms as she held them outstretched. Her feet parted company with the ground as she lifted into the air.

Kohl raised his arms above him, wreathed in lightning. He threw a red bolt at Fae but it caught in the turbulence around her and ricocheted into the skies again, missing Kagos by mere feet.

At her silent command, the wind whipped furiously around the Sorcerer Supreme, condensing until he was caught in his own personal storm. His robes snapped around his ankles. A blizzard blew up around him, nearly hiding him from view. Half his attention turned towards attacking the elements directly, until he could no longer throw his lightning for fear of it being caught in the maelstrom with him.

The elements led the assault now. Fae barely had to think of what came next. A thought, and thick snow peeled up from the ground to envelope Kohl in a life-size snow globe. One more, and fire licked at his feet. The snow melted to reveal the Sorcerer Supreme caught in a giant bubble of water, holding back a closing hollow within with flickering shapes of blood-sparks.

The gold around Fae's eyes flashed, and the storm above lit up in response.

White lightning arced down from the sky.

Kohl's eyes went wide as the lighting scattered through the water around him.

Fae clenched her fists and watched as the water pressed in around the Sorcerer Supreme.

Despite his efforts, there was no escape. The water lapped at his pristine robes. He threw more blood magic to push back the water at his feet, and it soaked into the ends of his hair. He shrank from the water at his head, and his arms were enveloped. He pushed back with his hands, and the water came up to his knees. Finally, his magic spluttered and failed. And the Sorcerer Supreme was engulfed.

Without his perverse power sparking around him, Kohl appeared almost harmless, his hair and robes floating innocently in the water. Fae watched, wondering if she could simply wait, and watch him drown. Then she noticed the ribbons of blood drifting from each wrist; markers of what he had wrought.

No, such an ending was not fitting for this human horror.

The bubble burst, vomiting Kohl onto the ice, soaked to the skin. He looked up to where Fae hovered above him, her unforgiving gaze pure gold. For the first time, his eyes rounded with fear.

His lips formed a silent *no*.

Lightning coursed down from the sky.

Not a single bolt missed.

One, two, three jagged blades of lightning struck the Sorcerer Supreme, lighting him up from within. His back bowed so violently it might have cracked. His lips stretched impossibly wide, his teeth clenched tight. A ragged sound that was nothing human issued from him.

Kohl's form glowed a sickly red as the lightning poured through him, as if all the blood he wielded had tainted him to the very end. Steam hissed from his robes. His arms spasmed. His eyes rolled back in his head.

As quick as it had started, the lightning stopped. The Sorcerer Supreme crumbled to the ground, his charred corpse smoking gently.

A deathly quiet fell over the Ice Fields. By now, the battle between the southern army and the centaurs had come to a stunned halt as every member watched the confrontation between the Brotherhood and the Magi unfold.

The wind blew oblivious across the ice.

It was over.

Fae drifted slowly back down to the earth.

As soon as her feet touched the ground, she staggered.

"Fae!" Luca lurched towards her, his body still not quite obeying him.

Fae threw out a hand as her knees folded beneath her.

"Don't!" He stumbled to a halt at the tone in her voice. "Don't come any closer!" Her elements weren't finished yet.

Far below, in the heart of the earth, something was unfurling, awakening.

The ground bucked, throwing everyone from their feet. The dragons squawked their protest. Demilda crawled over to Madja's prone form. The remaining sorcerers glanced about with wild eyes.

The earth heaved again, and it was like nothing she'd ever felt before. This was no mere tremor. This was as if the earth was trying to shake itself apart. Pressure building, needing release.

And as the elements within her clamoured to be let out, Fae felt the earth tremble through her.

Pain and confusion radiated up towards her, like a great beast waking too early from its winter slumber. She felt it in her bones, in her blood. It vibrated through her every cell. And her elements trembled too.

And then control was wrested from her once more.

The pressure from below burst forth, the elements forced from her again.

And the pain of the earth screamed through her.

65

OF THE STARS THEMSELVES

The whole world shook.

Luca fell back as a column of fire speared up from Fae. The flames hit the cloud cover, spilling their orange-red glow across the sky.

"Fae!" He scrambled to his feet, every inch of him screaming in agony. He'd taken the brunt of the attack on La'sa himself, and his body was close to giving out on him entirely. His vision swam, sliding in and out of focus. The ground pitched beneath his feet — but was that him, or Fae? Something tickled the side of his face, and when he lifted a hand to it, it came away sticky with blood.

The wind picked up again, pulling snow and debris into a vortex that spiralled around Fae. Lightning crackled through the air. The earth pitched and rolled like waves on a choppy sea.

A deafening *pop* rang out across the ice as the ground split, fissures spider-webbing outwards from Fae. Great sections of earth dropped out from beneath them, tumbling into the cracks. The remaining sorcerers huddled together, their eyes darting from one crack to another, until the ground beneath them simply fell away, and the earth swallowed them whole.

A sinkhole opened up nearby, the ice tumbling down into the bowels of the earth. It started small, but the edges crept outwards, rushing towards where the elf brothers stood with Jade.

They scrambled back, but Jade lost her footing as she ushered her dragons away from the fall. The ground tumbled away beneath her, and she tipped into the gaping maw of the sinkhole.

Just as she slid towards certain death, Aren gripped her wrist and hauled her out of harm's way. As they backed away from the rapidly-expanding chasm, another piece of ice crumbled into the opening, and Stef plummeted out of sight.

Jade screamed, and before anyone could act, a silver streak shot past her, Delita diving into the breach.

The rest of the dragons crowded around the edge of the sinkhole, ignoring the slowly unravelling world around them, their bronze eyes whirling as they awaited the fate of their sister.

An eternity passed before Delita's delicate silver wings crested the hole, straining to lift Stef to safety.

As Aren hauled his brother back to solid ground, and Jade threw her arms around the neck of her dragon, Luca turned his attention back to the explosion that was Fae.

"Luca!" Irya sprinted across the snow towards him.

He grasped at a fragile hope. "Can you reach her?" If Irya could reach Fae's aura, she might be able to knock her unconscious. It was an extremely risky move. Only the Dreamweaver was gifted enough to manipulate auras that skilfully. But he wasn't here.

He'd discussed this possibility with Irya before the battle. She'd been ready to intervene if events spiralled beyond their ability to control. They had both hoped not to need her.

But she shook her head as she approached. "I can't get past that." She gestured to the elemental storm crashing around Fae.

Luca nodded. He'd suspected as much.

He pressed his lips together as the earth splintered again.

There was only one thing for it.

As the earth shuddered again, he turned his body into the storm.

Fae was lost in pain.

She was coming apart at the seams. She was being undone. Unmade.

She might have been screaming, but the agony searing through her veins made it impossible to tell.

The earth's pain radiated through her bones, and somewhere in the depths of it she was aware of her own connection to it. Like a tree, she was rooted in the earth itself. She was an extension of it. The world was coming apart, and so was she.

Somewhere inside her, she grieved for Ty. For the love they'd had, and the loss of a friend.

Somewhere inside, she was horrified by what she'd done to Kohl.

Somewhere inside, she was glad.

Maybe it was time for an end.

Her power had gone unchecked for too long, and the line cleaving her from the infinite well of Source Magic had finally burned away.

She was a tap with no faucet. A river without a dam. She was no ant to crawl upon the back of a great celestial being — she was *part* of that being, since the moment the Aethyr planted their seed within her mother's womb. And there was no limit to the power that flowed through her.

She was a child of spirits, and a child of the earth. And what were they, if not children of the stars themselves?

The world fell away from her. If the wind whipped past her face, she did not hear it. If flames licked at her skin, she did not see them. If the earth lay solid beneath her feet, she did not feel it.

She had been here only once before, when the Aethyr had merged their powers with hers. She had been lost in it then too.

But this time, the earth's pain bellowed through her.

Her skin split as the power poured through her.

Beneath the earth's roaring, something else tapped at her awareness. A mouse in a den of lions.

Someone grabbed her hand with rough, calloused fingers.

"Fae!" Luca stood before her, battered and bleeding, as if he'd fought through a storm to be by her side.

Fae blinked past her pain. Ice and snow and rocks and earth flew through the air around her. Beneath her feet, the ground was blackened with char, and she saw with distant curiosity that she was wreathed in flame, the inferno arrowing up to pierce the sky. She lifted her other hand, and saw glowing fissures spread across her palm, echoed on the ground beneath.

Luca gripped her shoulder. Her gaze drifted back to him. Blood leaked from his ear, scratches decorated the side of his face like lacework. His wide midnight eyes rippled with fear as they darted over her, but the fear was not for his own safety.

"You can stop this!" Luca yelled over the roar of flames that he tried valiantly to shield against. Even through his shield, she could smell his skin burning.

The earth bucked beneath them, and his grip on her arms tightened. "Fae!"

Fae felt as if she were miles away, while she stood in the heart of the storm. "I don't know how to." Her voice was so fragile, she wondered how he would hear it. The ground heaved like the back of a great beast rising from sleep. Fae's jaw clenched. Great fissures snaked out from her, whole sections of the Ice Fields fallen into gaping chasms. As if in answer, a white hot pain spiked through her. The skin split down her neck. She cried out.

This was it. She had failed. And now the world was being unmade.

Strong hands shook her, jolting her back to the face before her.

"Fae." Luca's gaze pierced through to her very soul.

She shook her head. "It's too late."

"While there is breath in our bodies and light in the world, it is never too late." He released his grip on her to hold his burnt hands between them. A soft glow shone from his cupped palms. "There is still light." He looked up at her. "And I know it is in you too." As he said the words, something inside her flickered in recognition. "It's not over yet."

She stared at the light he was offering her. "I don't know how to," she repeated. A tear slid down her cheek. He was asking the impossible. Inside her, there lived only darkness. Not the dark that Kallis had taught her to wield, playful and secretive. No, this was the cold black of her soul. The kind that swallowed her whole. The kind she'd never escape.

She wished it would end, so she could rest.

But so many were relying on her. She was their only hope, and yet she had none of her own.

She choked back a sob. The earth shuddered in response, and a line splintered down her chest, splitting the skin there too.

Luca's face twisted as she cried out her pain. "Let me help."

Those three words undid her.

Tears streamed down her cheeks. Her face screwed up with the effort it took her to part the flames enough to let him in, to hold them at bay enough for him to stand beside her unburned. The pressure eased as he reinforced her shield with his own, and then he took her face in his hands, as if he had all the time in the world. There was a softness in his gaze that she'd never seen before.

"It might not feel like it right now," he said, "but you are strong. You are a good person. And you are more than enough." He leaned his head against her brow. "And I have loved you since the moment you asked me to stay." Fae stared up at him, and the naked emotion in his eyes took her breath away. Where she had always sensed something *other* in his gaze, now she saw only him, full of love and light. And it was all directed at her.

A warm glow bathed his face, coming from the palms he had pressed to her cheeks. The flickering feeling inside her turned like a flower towards his light, and began to grow.

He drew her up to him, and brushed his lips against hers. "I love you, Fae."

If his first words undid her, those ones remade her.

The light brightened, and the feeling inside her swelled.

"I love you." His kiss deepened as she kissed him back, the light in his hands almost blinding.

Finally, she understood what the feeling that grew inside her was. What blossomed in answer to Luca's love.

She whispered against his lips, "I love you too."

The smile that broke across his face was dazzling, the light pouring from Fae's skin reflected in his eyes. He pulled her to him, one hand in her hair, the other around her waist as he crushed his lips to hers once more.

Light bloomed wherever he touched her: her lips, her face, her back, her hips.

And within Fae, light answered. It swelled inside her, filling her up, her head dizzy with it.

The storm vanished from view, the fire faded from memory, the earth stilled beneath her feet. The cracks in her skin inched closed as Luca's light poured over her.

And as his light healed her, her light rushed forth.

Light broke through the storm to flood the Ice Fields.

Light cascaded into the earth, illuminating the chasms that threatened to swallow them whole.

And as the final tear in her skin sealed shut, light burst from Fae's chest to bathe the sky.

Fae's awareness broke into a thousand pieces, following the light on its path.

The maelstrom around her dropped, the inferno receded, and her light shone out across the Ice Fields like a beacon.

Nearby, her friends stood stunned on the ice before La'sa, squinting in the glare of her incandescence.

Across the snow, the two armies had stopped to watch. Alexi stood beside four centaurs, his arm raised to shield his face.

Beneath her, the earth calmed. The light soothed over fissures and rifts like a balm, and where it touched, roots and vines sprang from the ground to pull the chasms together.

Fae's light took on a will of its own, sweeping into the darkest depths of the earth, to its beating heart. There, it softened to a warm glow that reminded her of Arolynos — peaceful, tranquil, calm. The kind of light that might coax a smile from a dark day.

And, in her very bones, Fae felt the earth quiet.

For an instant she had the impression of an immense presence regarding her. Weighing her.

The great celestial beast grumbled at the momentary disruption from its sleep. Finally pacified, it lay back down to rest.

The rifts in the earth began to slam shut, and Fae's awareness sprang back into her. She lurched upright with a gasp as if all the air in the world still weren't enough.

She gripped Luca's arms as she reeled back into herself, head spinning.

Blackness waited in the wings of her mind.

She was spent. There was nothing left to give.

The last thing she noted before unconsciousness enveloped her, was that Luca was falling too.

66

DIRT IN THE RAIN

A great beast faces her.

The shape of it is flat and wide, like the rays that roam the ocean waves, smooth wings tapering out from its body to a rounded edge. Set in a broad face, eyes like pools of black watch her.

Mountains rise from atop its back. Waterfalls cascade down rocky sides. Plains and forests divided by snaking rivers. Deserts shored by boundless oceans spilling over vast wings as they undulate in space.

Mesmerised, she lifts a hand to brush its face. Fingers meet starlight. It plays like liquid night over her skin. And when she draws her hand back, it is painted with star-flecked night too.

Quiet sunlight filtered through Fae's eyelids as she woke. She blinked her eyes open, and the room eased into focus.

She was in the Healing House, the crisp linens under her fingers bright white, the windows open to the gardens. Someone had cleaned her up, and dressed her in soft cotton pyjamas.

Above her, the flaming outline of a small lion cub played with a hummingbird of petals and leaves borne aloft on a breeze. A palm-sized dolphin watched them over the edge of the jug on the windowsill, its shape held together by water alone. At the foot of the bed, what looked like a stone elephant the size of a small puppy lay curled up on the sheets.

"They've been doing that since you stabilised." Fae turned her head, wincing at the motion. Kallis reclined in a chair in the corner of the room, a dark, nebulous form curled up like a cat on his shoulder. "This one prefers company, oddly enough." He reached up to tickle the shadow, and she could have sworn it shivered in appreciation.

Fae pulled herself up to sit against the headboard. She felt as if she'd gone twenty rounds against Alexi. She reached for the water glass beside her bed. "How long—?"

"It's been a week." The small glimmer of humour in Kallis's coppery gaze guttered. "You burnt yourself out. We didn't know if you'd wake at all." His jaw tightened. Fae didn't think she'd ever seen him so distressed. He forced a smile onto his face and stood. "But you're awake now. Madja will be beside herself. She's been driving us mad worrying about you."

Fae frowned. "Where's Luca?"

He came and sat on the edge of the bed, careful not to disturb the sleeping elephant. Up close, she could see his normally glossy hair was rough and unkempt, the blue-black strands knotted in places.

"He's recovering too. He hasn't woken yet."

"But—" He'd pulled her fracturing pieces together. So that she could heal the earth.

Kallis's smile was thin. "He bore the defence of La'sa on his own so that we could fight back. That took a toll. Try not to hold it against him." He patted her hand.

As he spoke, the battle came back to her in flashes. The army. The sorcerers. The dragons. Crimson sparks shaped into arrows and shields. Elements thrown into the fray. Fire. Water. Earth. Air. Dark. Blood on a man's lips. Blood on the snow.

Blood on the snow.

She closed her eyes against the sting of remembered grief. The companion forms of her elements snuffed out around her.

"Ty." Tears spilled down her cheeks. He'd died protecting her. And there was nothing she could do to change it. A gaping hollow in her chest stole the breath from her lungs.

Kallis simply held her hand and sat with her as she cried.

· · ·

When Fae's tears finally dried up, Kallis helped her across the hall, to the room where Luca recovered.

He wore the same plain cotton sleepwear she was dressed in. She sank into the armchair by his bed, and reached over to smooth the hair from his face. He looked so peaceful, the unfathomable look he normally wore smoothed over in sleep.

"Kallis, have you seen where I put my— Fae!" Madja stood in the doorway. A pile of linens tumbled from her arms as she flew at Fae to envelop her in a bear-like hug. "Thank the gods you're alright! You had us worried sick! What were you thinking, burning yourself out like that? You could have gotten yourself killed!"

"I'm sure that was her intention all along," Kallis muttered dryly.

"I'm sorry, Madja." Fae patted her back breathlessly, her neck craned at an awkward angle, face buried in a tangle of silver hair. "I'll try not to do it again."

"Don't make promises you can't keep, dear." Madja released her, her eyes gleaming with tears. She let out a sigh, and like the tide receding from the shore, the tension melted from her body. She cracked a smile. "I am so glad to see you awake, Fae. It seemed so unfair for everyone else to have healed, only for you to be left abed."

"What do you mean everyone else healed?" Fae glanced between her and Kallis.

"Your light," Kallis explained. "It flooded through La'sa, and everyone's injuries just... disappeared. Everyone." He gestured to Madja. "I was sure Madja wasn't going to walk away from that battle. But when your light receded, she rose again as if nothing had happened." He waved at himself. "My wounds washed away like dirt in the rain. Even the patients sheltering in the Archives are healed." He gave Fae a pointed look. "You and Luca are the only ones in here."

Fae's throat closed up. If only she'd figured it out sooner, Ty might have lived.

As if sensing the direction of her thoughts, Madja clasped her hand between hers. "You saved everyone who could be saved." She smiled sadly. "And you shouldn't have had to." She cupped a hand against Fae's cheek. "You remind me so much of my daughter. Always thinking the world was hers to put to right."

Something pinged in the depths of Fae's memory. "Sasha."

Kallis mumbled something about being somewhere else, and ducked from the room.

Madja nodded. "She was conscripted into the War of the Races. She wasn't ready for it, but she wasn't given a choice." She shook her head, dashing a tear from her eye. "When you arrived here, so unfamiliar with your Source Magic, and yet forced into the position to wield it..." She took a minute to compose herself before smiling back at Fae. "You have the same spirit that she did."

"What happened to her?"

"She died trying to wield more than she could handle." Madja's lips pressed into a thin line. "She should never have been there in the first place."

"Her magic killed her?" Fae glanced at Luca's prone form, a new fear rising up in her.

Madja's expression darkened. "The ignorance and greed of people who don't understand us is what killed her. Like those imbecile sorcerers trying to control Jade's dragons. We're lucky they didn't kill them." She straightened in her seat, and brushed some imaginary lint from her blouse. "What's past is past. We don't stand for our own to be treated that way anymore." She stood to lay the back of her hand against Luca's brow. "He'll come through. It was love and stubbornness that made him push himself too hard." A small smile played at the corner of her mouth. "But perhaps we needed a little of that, huh?"

"*I* needed it." Fae's eyes followed the rise and fall of Luca's chest, her voice barely more than a whisper as she recalled the way the light in her had answered to him.

Madja stayed for a while, straightening the linens, fussing and tidying things that didn't need tidying before she left Fae to watch over Luca alone.

Fae woke again with a horrible crick in her neck. She'd fallen asleep in the chair.

She sat up and eased her head from side to side, wincing as a sharp ache lanced from the back of her head down to her shoulder. She kneaded the protesting muscles in the curve of her neck, dropping her head to get at the worst of the knots.

The sheets rustled on the bed.

"Hey."

She jerked upright, neck spasming in objection.

Luca's eyes were open, his head turned towards her, a smile tugging at his lips.

"Hey," she breathed.

She stared at him, words skittering out of reach. After hearing Kallis and Madja's concerns, the relief of seeing him awake overwhelmed her until she couldn't breathe.

He stared at her, a twinkle in his eye.

"Are you alright?" he said eventually.

The laugh that escaped her was half-hysterical. "I suppose so." She glanced pointedly at the bed. "How are *you* feeling?"

He adopted a thoughtful expression, and the sheets shifted at the foot of the bed as he wriggled his toes. He lifted his hands and wriggled his fingers too. He turned back to her. "I appear to be unharmed. A miracle, all things considered."

Fae sobered. "If you hadn't been there..."

"But I was." Luca took her hand and drew her onto the bed, pulling back the covers to tuck her in beside him. Fae rested her head on the pillow, warm from Luca's body heat. Their eyes met as he settled back down alongside her, his deep indigo seeing into her very soul.

"I was there. And you were there. And you did it." He draped an arm over her waist, his hand pressing into the small of her back. He closed his eyes. "Now shh. Not all of us can bounce back after burnout like you, apparently." He tugged her closer, tucking her head under his chin. They'd never embraced like this before. They'd never held each other close. And yet, it felt like the most natural place in the world for her to be. All the tension melted from her. She was reminded of how he'd watched over her when the nightmares plagued her sleep. He made her feel... safe.

"I can hear you thinking," he murmured over her hair. He brought a hand up to smooth over the strands his breath disturbed. "Sleep. It'll all be here when you wake."

Tangled in his arms, Fae fell into her first truly restful sleep since leaving Arolynos.

67

PEACE

When Fae woke next, it was morning again.

She gently disentangled herself from Luca's arms and slipped from the bed, smiling when he grumbled in protest at her absence. She padded back to her own room in search of clothes, and found her usual leggings and jumper folded neatly on the bed. A note rested on top of the bundle:

Welcome back.
Come and find me when you've finished canoodling.
- Irya -

Fae couldn't help the laugh that escaped her at the dryness of Irya's note. She could just picture her friend's eye-roll punctuating the words. She pulled on the leggings and tugged the jumper on over her pyjama shirt.

The day was clear and crisp when she stepped out into La'sa, the sky a rich cerulean blue, the sun warming the bite from the air. Light sparkled off new windows, and the streets smelled of fresh sawdust. Everywhere, repairs were being made, clean, new-built cabins sitting beside old, weathered chalets. The trees that had fallen during the most recent quakes had been sectioned and piled up by the Meeting House, the debris cleared and swept away.

It felt like a new town.

Fae's eyes were drawn to the collapsed wall of the arena, gaping like a wound in the southern quadrant. Men and woman moved over the rubble like ants in a line, carrying it away to be piled up neatly elsewhere.

Before the thought had even finished forming in her mind, Fae's feet were moving along a path so familiar, she could likely walk it in her sleep.

Standing in the ruins of the arena, Fae wondered why she hadn't thought to do this earlier. Then she spotted a figure she hadn't expected to see, directing the various helpers.

"Taniq!" Her voice came out hoarser than she'd expected from lack of use, and she had to try twice more before her friend turned around.

"Fae!" He came over, his steps strong and even. Fae stared at the legs that should have had a long journey to recovery. "You're walking," she said.

A shy grin split his face. He ducked his head, absently running a hand through black hair in desperate need of a trim. "Yeah. After that light flooded La'sa, it was like I was never hurt. I just got up and walked." He shot her a bashful glance, his eyes flicking up to meet hers. "I'm told I have you to thank you for that."

Fae shook her head, her eyes darting to the mountain of rubble that Taniq had been all but buried beneath. "It was my fault you were hurt in the first place."

He smiled ruefully. "How many times have we got to tell you our own horror stories of learning to manage the elements?" His caramel skin flushed red as he added, "It's not your fault. And I wanted to help."

"I'm still sorry."

Taniq waved a hand between them, his cheeks turning impossibly more red. "I don't blame you for what happened. But if it'll make you feel better, I forgive you."

Fae nodded. "Thank you." She caught his eye and jerked her chin at the collapsed wall. "Do you think you could clear everyone from the rubble? There's something else I need to make right."

Taniq hesitated only a moment, then raised an eyebrow. "Really?"

A smile tugged at her lips. "Really."

A fresh grin spread over his face. "Absolutely! This, I want to see." He turned and began issuing commands so at odds with the reserved person Fae knew.

In no time at all, the workers filed away from the rubble, retreating to a safe distance. She noticed a few centaurs numbered among them. Before long, Magi and non-Magi alike had lined up on the far side of the arena. No one left. All of them wanted to see what came next.

She felt their eyes on her as she shook her hands out, rolled her neck. She closed her eyes and took a deep, calming breath.

She reached inside herself, and found earth eager to rise to the challenge.

Ready? Fae asked her once-reticent element-aspect, but also, herself.

Earth trumpeted a joyful response within her, and the image of that tiny stone elephant curled up on the bed rose to mind, growing into a giant of a being, ready to move mountains.

Fae's eyes opened, and they flashed gold in the sun.

The stones that had laid inert since that abortive attempt at wielding earth began to rise. A few at first, and then more, until every single piece of the collapsed wall floated in the gap, ready to be put back in its rightful place.

A collective gasp went up from her audience, and joy swelled in Fae's chest. She was doing it!

She turned to Taniq, her grin so wide it hurt her cheeks. "Where shall I put these?"

A few delighted laughs rose up from the crowd as Taniq gaped, his grey eyes round with amazement. A fellow Theras nudged his shoulder, and he shook himself, blinking back to the present.

"Right, Therasae!" He waved the Magi forward. "Guide each block into place. You know what to do!" He sidled back up to Fae. "Can you hold them up while we work?" The look in his eyes was both amazed and worried. For her.

Earth trumpeted its indignation within her, and she couldn't help her answering laugh. "I'll hold it up as long as you need."

Taniq flashed her a grin. "Alright then!" And he ran forward to help.

With Fae holding the stone, the Therasae had the energy to direct the blocks into the right positions before signalling for her to release them in place. As the day wore on, the wall began to take shape again.

Around lunch, a wry voice sounded behind her.

"I said come and find *me*, not come and find more work to do."

Keeping half her awareness on holding the stones in place, Fae looked over her shoulder to see Irya standing with arms folded, her foot tapping impatiently on the shale. She came to stand beside her so Fae could return her attention back to the task at hand. The autumnal shades of her hair glinted like rubies and gold in the sun.

"I haven't seen Eah'lara this calm in a long time." The Echo kept her blind gaze forward, but Fae knew she was seeing more than the arena with those eyes.

Something unknotted in Fae's chest at the words. She hadn't looked in on the Spirit Realm since waking, afraid of what she would see after her loss of control on the battlefield. "That's good."

Irya arched one eyebrow. "You could say that." The corner of her mouth twitched before she schooled her expression back into nonchalance. "You should take a break."

"I'm not tired."

Irya nodded towards the workers. "No, but they are."

Fae looked again at the Therasae directing stone blocks twice the size of a man in places. Now that Irya had pointed it out, she saw signs of fatigue among them. She hadn't noticed it before; everyone had been buoyed by her presence and help, the effect masking their need to rest.

She waved Taniq over, and he jogged towards them, wiping sweat from his brow.

"I'm going to take a break," she said, not giving him the opportunity to insist that he could go on, as she knew he would. "Where shall I stack the rest of it for now?"

Taniq's smile shifted to a look of horrified guilt. "Oh, gods! Of course! You're only just recovering! I'm so sorry I should have asked sooner! Yes put them down, um..." He scanned the arena. "Along the eastern wall. Let me just clear everyone away." And before she could reassure him, he was jogging away again to do just that.

Irya shook beside her, poorly concealing her mirth.

"This is your fault," Fae grumbled to her. Irya slapped a hand over her mouth, the creases around her eyes deepening as silent laughter bubbled from her.

Once the stone had been safely deposited, Irya dragged Fae from the arena, leaving the Therasae sprawled out on the sun-warmed floor, talking and laughing at how quickly the morning's work had gone. A few waved and wished her well as she passed. A few gave her a smile and shook her hand.

"Don't start letting that go to your head now, or I'll have to take you down a peg again," Irya muttered as she pulled her away from the last of the well-wishers and into the blue glow of the Warrens.

They were accosted many more times before they finally reached the Meeting House at the centre of La'sa. But instead of going inside, Irya led Fae down a winding path around the side of the building, emerging into the kitchen gardens. A selection of chairs had been brought out to take advantage of the warmer weather, and a gathering of both new and familiar faces lounged in the sun.

Kallis was talking with Alexi and a centaur with a pure black coat, his pale torso covered in black tribal tattoos that blended seamlessly into his dark lower body. He had light, severe eyes, but he seemed comfortable enough in his present company. Terrence was deep in conversation with Aren and Fanrell, the latter having arrived with a veritable army of his people. A smile pulled at Fae's lips at the memory of their last conversation in Throldon. They'd both doubted the centaurs would rally to defend anyone other than themselves, and yet, here they were. His amber eyes met hers as she approached, and he nodded briefly, so many words conveyed in a single gesture. She smiled, and nodded back.

Beside Fanrell, two female centaurs talked to Madja and Demilda. One had delicate features with chestnut pinto colouring to her lower body, bright blue eyes and long, strawberry-blonde waves. The other stood a head taller than her companion, with fiery red hair and rich roan colouring. She looked as if she could take on an army on her own. Kagos stood imperious as always to one side, while Aiya, Stef, and Jade spoke in lowered tones. Jade's dragons were absent, but a cry from above had Fae glancing up to see two of them wheeling above the Core, their colourful wings spread wide as they rode the warmer air.

"I hear you're putting me to shame already." Fae turned to find Luca entering the garden from another side path, Arissa at his side. "You couldn't just rest, could you?" A smile pulled at his lips, and Fae was struck by how much younger he looked when he wasn't trying so hard to be inscrutable. As if carrying the weight of an entire population had been ageing him, despite the magic that surrounded La'sa.

A thought crashed into her with the force of an army several thousand strong.

"The barrier!" She turned to the High Magi. Luca had taken the burden of holding up the barrier on his own. When he'd fallen with her, had it fallen too?

Demilda raised a hand to calm her. She'd threaded her black braids with new beads, and they clinked softly as she moved. "One of the many things we mean to discuss, Fae. Peace."

"And now that we're all awake" — Kallis shot Luca a pointed look, though the glance was tinged with relief — "we can do just that."

Arissa helped Luca to an empty seat, and then turned to leave. But as she passed Fae, she stopped to fling her arms around her friend.

"I knew you could do it," she mumbled into Fae's hair. Before Fae could hug her back, she straightened, smoothing her skirts. "Good to have you back, Fae." She shot her a wink, and Fae could have sworn she saw a glint of tears in her eyes before she bustled past.

68

FOR THE FIRST TIME

I t took a while for introductions to be made, and everyone wanted to welcome Fae and Luca back. Then Irya told them all what Fae had been doing with her first few hours after spending a week unconscious, and she was bombarded anew with questions about how she felt and comments on her recovery.

No one knew the depths of Fae's reserves. Fae quietly suspected there were none, and that she channelled the limitless power of the earth itself through her veins. But she wasn't ready to share that just yet.

Eventually, they all settled down to discuss what was going to happen next.

Fae's first question was, "What about the army?" The thousands of southern soldiers that had marched the length of the continent to lay siege to a hidden community.

Alexi laughed, the sound deep and bright. "After your display, they laid down their weapons. I believe they intend to march back home." He rubbed a hand through the short crop of his hair. "I don't blame them. Even living with Magi, I have never seen anything of the like." The admiration was clear in his voice.

Fanrell added, "My people have rounded up their weapons. They watch them now. They will not try anything offensive before they leave."

"Not to mention they barely have enough sorcerers left to launch more than a glorified tea party now." Kallis's smirk was pure feline pride.

"But how do we know those few won't try anything?" Demilda's concern was mirrored by a few others.

"I took care of them." Madja crossed her arms, her tone flat and cold.

Kagos glanced at her, his eyes gleaming with curiosity. "What did you do?"

She shrugged, her silver mane shifting. "I gave them a taste of their own medicine."

There was a pause. Then Terrence spoke, his voice low with disapproval. "Madja."

"If we can bind ourselves to protect our own people, I don't see what's wrong with binding those monsters to protect the world from them." She glared at him, daring him to argue.

Kagos nodded, his lips curving in approval. "Clever."

"You used blood magic." Fae looked between the High Magi.

"It was justified," Madja said.

"It's forbidden magic for a reason, Madja!" Terrence's face darkened.

"And utterly justified." Luca spoke up for the first time. The others turned to him. "Blood magic is forbidden. Because it tends towards acts of evil." He looked to Madja. "You bound their magic against others?" She nodded. "Did you include conditions?"

"Of course I did, I'm not a monster!" Madja puffed out her chest indignantly. "They can go about their lives freely, but they cannot use blood magic to take the power or control of another living thing." Which, as far as Fae understood blood magic, effectively neutralised it. She glanced at Jade, who nodded her approval.

"There are others back in Pharro," she reminded them.

"Let their Brothers serve as a warning to them." Demilda flicked her braids over her shoulder, her dark skin gleaming in the sun. "We can deal with them just as easily."

"May I remind you that this was hardly easy?" Terrence grumbled.

"It's not like we can march ourselves down past the Thamib Desert to take care of it," Luca answered. "I suggest we let that unfold how it will."

"We will lead them and their army south." Fanrell spoke up. "We would introduce our people to the world." He exchanged a glance with Philomena, the smaller female beside him. They'd told the story of the

Ateth Legarrh and how the spirits had guided so many to wander from the clan lands. But Philomena was their Oracle, and Saw more than any other. "The centaurs have held to their traditions of isolation for too many generations." Fanrell gestured to his compatriots. "We, and the others that joined us, are destined to find our own way. And we would begin that by making friends of La'sa."

"I think I speak for all of us when I say we would be honoured to count you as friends." Alexi looked around the High Magi, waiting for any objections, but none were forthcoming. Fae hadn't realised he had the authority to make such decisions, but as each High Magi nodded their agreement, she couldn't see why he wouldn't. He'd defended La'sa for five-hundred years, same as the rest of them. His lack of magic did not invalidate his ability to speak for his people. She found that the idea warmed her.

"Throldon would welcome you," Fae said, knowing that her mother and Hal would love to see more centaurs in the city. And Ipgar and Remi would benefit from the presence of more of their own people. "But I'm not sure if a human city will be comfortable for so many of you." Centaurs preferred the open skies, and there were few places in Throldon that adequately accommodated that need.

"We are wanderers." Helena, the fiery female shifted her great hooves, tail swishing behind her, ever restless. "We would be honoured to visit these places, but we would not stay over long."

Philomena glanced up at Fanrell before adding, "We have been restricted to a small corner of the world, when we are meant to run. Perhaps some of us will settle, form their own clans. But for now, we roam." She smiled, and the look Fanrell returned to her was filled with such love, Fae felt as though she was intruding on a private moment.

Aren cleared his throat. "We'll go with you." He shifted uncomfortably in his seat, and his eyes took a sorrowful cast. "We must return Ty to our people. Sheha will wish to see him before his ashes carry him on the wind."

A lump formed in Fae's throat. "I'll come too." She wouldn't leave her sister to grieve alone. And she had some goodbyes to say. "But I will return here." She glanced to her left, to where Luca watched her. "I belong here."

"Well I'm glad you figured that out because otherwise I'd have to hunt you down and haunt your dreams." Irya shot her a wry smile.

"That's just mean." But Fae smiled back. She looked around. Little more than a year ago, her family had consisted of only a handful of elves. But since then, with their strength and support, she'd found her mother, and added members of every race of the world to that family. And now...

Luca's hand found hers as her throat closed up, tears burning behind her eyes. He weaved his fingers between hers, squeezing her grip. She nodded, not trusting herself to speak, and shot him a watery smile.

Kagos straightened where he stood, having forgone a chair in favour of looming ominously at the edge of the circle. "We will, of course, take you back." He inclined his head to Aren and Stef. Then turned to Jade. "Then we return to Hearthstone."

Jade brought a hand to her chest. "Me? Why would I go with you?"

He pushed his arms further into his sleeves. "Hearthstone is the home of dragons. Your flight needs to be among their own kind."

"I won't force them to go anywhere." She folded her arms, the amber in her eyes flashing as she glowered at him.

"Nor will we." Kagos fixed her with his own obsidian gaze. "The fact remains that they have a lot to learn about being dragons. Rather than creatures of a cage." He glanced abruptly at Aiya, a sign that she'd interrupted him mind-to-mind. A small line creased his brow. She tipped her head pointedly to one side.

He sighed. "We will return to Hearthstone. You are" — his tone was strained, as if he struggled to speak with such courtesy — "*welcome* to join us. If you feel that would be... *appropriate* for you and your flight."

Jade shot Aiya a grateful smile. She inclined her head to Kagos. "I would be glad to consider it."

Kagos gave a curt nod of his head. And if he had more to say on the subject, he kept it to himself. Fae smothered the laugh that bubbled in her chest.

"What of your barrier?" Aiya spoke aloud for the first time, turning to the Magi. Her flying coat was folded over the back of her chair, and she'd rolled up the sleeves of her linen shirt, baring her creamy brown skin to the sun. She fingered her braid where it hung over her shoulder. Her cheeks flushed when she noticed Irya's eyes on her. "Shouldn't you think about putting it back in place?"

It was the question Fae had wanted answering too. But as she looked around at the ones qualified to answer it, none seemed willing to voice an opinion on the matter.

Finally, Luca cleared his throat. "I think we'll leave it awhile."

Fae gaped at him. Her eyes darted around the others, looking for someone to challenge him. The barrier had kept the Magi safe for half a millennium. And just when an army had marched almost to the gates, they wanted to leave La'sa more vulnerable than it had ever been?

But the High Magi seemed unconcerned by the proposal. Terrence clasped his hands before him, twiddling his thumbs. Demilda inspected her nails. Madja exchanged a quiet smile with Kallis. Alexi outright grinned.

Irya was the first to break the awkward silence. "Well thank the spirits for that. About time I had the chance to get old and wrinkly." She lifted her chin, turning this way and that. "I think I've got what it takes to age gracefully, what do you think?"

"I think you're beautiful." Aiya clamped a hand over her mouth as soon as the words came out, her skin flushing an impossible shade of scarlet. Kagos raised a dark brow in her direction.

Irya stared at her before mumbling something that sounded like "Thanks," her gaze dropping to her lap. It was the first time Fae had seen her friend *bashful*.

Jade snorted, drawing the attention to her. "What?" She looked around as if she couldn't believe she was the only one in on the joke. "You haven't been following these two around La'sa for the past two weeks. It's about time one of them said something."

Noticing Aiya squirm under the scrutiny, Fae decided to redirect the conversation again.

"What will happen to everyone in La'sa without the barrier?"

Luca shrugged. "That's up to them. It's always been up to them. Some will stay, some may leave to find somewhere new. But we'll begin ageing again, and see out the rest of our natural lives like the rest of the world. The Magi are done with hiding."

"And what is 'the rest of your natural life'?" Elven lives were measured in centuries. Humans lived only a few decades. Dwarves, somewhere in between. With their mixed heritages, was there any way of even guessing how long a Magi might live?

But the corner of his lips kicked up. "The Source restores us as we wield it, but it's been a few centuries since any of our kind were able to live peacefully to the end of their days." He shrugged again, his smile broadening. "In all honesty, I don't know."

Fae frowned. "You seem strangely happy about that."

Luca laughed, and the sound was so wild and infectious, Fae found herself smiling along with him.

"For the first time in over five hundred years, I don't know what tomorrow will bring." His eyes sparkled with unrestrained joy as he leaned forward and took both of her hands in his own. "And I can't wait to see it."

EPILOGUE

HEALING

It was winter in La'sa.

Snow piled up thick against cabin windows. Children who hadn't been children for centuries laughed as they chased each other around the gardens with snowballs held high, primed and ready for launching. Young Mizulae erected ice barriers to hide behind, while Incendi melted frozen projectiles before they could hit.

Fae chuckled as a particularly enterprising young Aurora sent her snowballs on twisting air currents to catch her opponent in the back of the head.

"Clever." She turned at the familiar voice behind her. Luca leant against the back door of the Meeting House, a smile tugging at his lips.

"They've had a few hundred years of practice."

Luca tipped his head to one side. "True." He lowered himself to sit beside her on the step. They watched the children play.

So much had changed. And yet so much remained the same. She leaned her head on his shoulder.

The southern armies had returned to the nations across the desert... and a delegation had returned, arriving in Throldon with a strange message from the Eminence of Pharro. An apology, a renouncing of any practitioners of blood magic, and an attempt at repairing relations between the two nations. It seemed the Eminence had been the one most under the Sorcerer Supreme's influence, and had developed an unsurprising hatred of magic. Which could prove problematic for the Magi.

That had prompted quite the discussion for the Council of the Races.

Fae's lips quirked up at the memory. Her mother and Hal had their hands full with that one.

She sighed. She missed her mother. And Sheha. Her sister had returned to Arolynos to spread Ty's ashes, and to mourn. Fae saddened to think of her alone, but she knew she would be well cared for, and perhaps the peace of Arolynos would be a balm to her at this time.

Jade had decided to journey to Hearthstone in the end, and had flown back with Kagos, Aiya, and Max. Irya checked in on them more often than anyone else, and Fae wondered when the Echo would finally make good on her threats to visit.

Now that the world seemed to have settled into a sort of rhythm, it felt like the opportune moment for the people of La'sa to finally begin spreading their wings. There would always be people who feared the unknown, feared *them*, but that was no longer reason enough to hide.

She'd heard talk about places to visit, descendants to track down, things to see after so many years hidden behind one mountain. But it was a hard habit to break — La'sa was safe. It was known. It would take a while for them to trust that they could survive what the world had to throw at them.

If the messages from Hearthstone were anything to go by, Fae thought that maybe Irya might even be the first of them to leave.

Luca cleared his throat. "Annie gave birth to a baby girl this morning."

Fae whipped around to stare at him. The Magi with the cherry-red hair who worked in the Archives had been the first to fall pregnant after the barrier fell. She and her partner had been ecstatic at the news, but the wider implications of her pregnancy were anticipated by the entire community.

Fae had grown accustomed to the children in La'sa all being several centuries old. Annie's daughter would be the first of a whole new generation of Magi.

She grinned. "That's..." Amazing. Incredible. More. Words didn't do justice to what this meant to the people of La'sa. That they could finally move past the age of hiding, past the fear of the world beyond this mountain. That they could finally grow as a people. That they could celebrate something as simple as birthdays again.

Light flickered inside her, butterfly-soft. The element of healing, and of love.

Fae looked to the sky, joy filling her heart, and let it shine.

ACKNOWLEDGMENTS

When I finished writing Spiritchild, my intention was for that to be the end of Fae's journey. One, nice, self-contained story. All wrapped up in one volume.

But the longer I sat with it, and the longer I worked on its publication, the more I realised that there was more to Fae than one book. And I guess, by extension, more than one book in me. So I hope you'll forgive me this sequel.

Writing one book took a small army. Writing the second took an emotional support network without which I would still be sat frozen in front of my keyboard.

Huge thanks as always to Sara Starbuck: editor, cheerleader, the one who makes me believe I really can do this, and the one who constantly makes me strive to be a better writer with every book. Thank you so so much for your insight and encouragement.

To Lena Yang, for your eternal patience in bringing Earthchild to life, in bringing all the little details together to create something so beautiful. I am forever grateful to have your art grace the cover of my book. Thank you.

To Bella, for being the best advocate of my books an author could hope for.

To Liv, for all the voice messages in response to my "could you take a look at..." texts.

To Sophie, for taking the time to read and love Fae as much as I do.

The Bruce and Helen, for helping me figure out if my medical assumptions are in any way plausible.

To all the people at Clay's — Belle, Abbie, Bex, and Kei — for bringing my books to actual life. Publishing can be a scary journey sometimes, but nothing is ever too much and you make the printing part look easy!

To my Fantasy Fellowship family. Ironically, words cannot adequately describe how much help you've been to me (believe me I've tried but this section is supposed to be short and I've already agreed my page count). Just know that you're all awesome. Keep doing what you do.

To Sarah, Shannon, Els, Amy, Jay, Amy, Louise, Sarah, Erin, and James for Spiritchild's beautiful book tour. I am so grateful to know you all.

Huge thanks to my parents for their support and encouragement, for believing in me even when I don't believe in myself, and for showing off my book to anyone who'll listen.

Thanks to my boys for reminding me that the goal is to build a library, one book at a time.

And finally to Jonny, for being the first reader of all my words, for pushing me to do the things, reminding me to dream big, and giving me a leg up so I can reach for the sky.